About the Authors

Susan Stephen  eeting her husband o ta. In true Mills & l came engaged on Fri Susan enjoys entertai re. To relax she reads, and when she's had enough of relaxing, she throws herself off mountains on skis or gallops through the countryside singing loudly.

Some people know practically from birth that they're going to be writers. **Catherine Spencer** wasn't one of them. Her first idea was to be a nun, which was clearly never going to work! A series of other choices followed. She considered becoming a veterinarian (but lacked the emotional stamina to deal with sick and injured animals), a hairdresser (until she overheated a curling iron and singed about five inches of hair off the top of her best friend's head the day before her first date), or a nurse (but that meant emptying bedpans. Eee-yew!). As a last resort, she became a high school English teacher, and loved it. What's an English teacher's area of expertise? Well, novels, among other things, and moody, brooding, unforgettable heroes: Heathcliff, Edward Fairfax Rochester, Romeo, Rhett Butler. They all pointed her in the same direction: breaking the rules every chance she got, and creating her own moody, brooding, unforgettable heroes. And where do they belong? In Mills & Boon novels, of course, which is where she happily resides now.

After spending three years as a die-hard New Yorker, **Kate Hewitt** now lives in a small village in the English Lake District with her husband, their five children and a golden retriever. In addition to writing intensely emotional stories, she loves reading, baking and playing chess with her son—she has yet to win against him, but she continues to try. Learn more about Kate at kate-hewitt.com

The Greek Mavericks

COLLECTION

July 2019

August 2019

September 2019

October 2019

November 2019

December 2019

Greek Mavericks: The Greek's Unforgettable Secret

SUSAN STEPHENS

CATHERINE SPENCER

KATE HEWITT

MILLS & BOON

THE SECRET
KEPT FROM
THE GREEK

SUSAN STEPHENS

PROLOGUE

Eleven years previously...

LIZZIE WAS ON FIRE. He watched her brown eyes blaze bullets at him from the well of the court. She was just eighteen, with flowing red hair and—controversially at this most subdued of gatherings—black leather trousers, a skimpy top, tattoos and a pierced lip. He would have had to be unconscious not to want the force of nature that was Lizzie Montgomery

That didn't change the facts. This was a court of law, and he, Damon Gavros, was part of the team from Gavros Inc—an international shipping company registered in Greece—attending court in London. He was there to support his father, who was appearing as the chief prosecution witness in the case of Gavros Inc. versus Charles Montgomery, fraudster.

It was a shock seeing Lizzie again in court—though to say he regretted sleeping with her last night wouldn't be true. Even had he known who she was then, the fire between them would almost certainly have led them down the same road and to hell with the consequences.

They'd met for the first time the previous evening, when Lizzie, obviously distressed, had been refused a drink at the bar where he'd been sitting quietly in a corner, thinking about bringing to justice the man who had tried to defraud his father out of millions. Seeing a woman distraught, yet refusing to go home, and a barman on the point of ejecting her, he'd intervened. Taking Lizzie back to his place, he'd plied her with coffee and they'd got talking.

Lizzie was her name, she'd told him. He'd had no idea she was Charles Montgomery's daughter. She was hot, funny, and almost too happy to laugh at herself. She was looking forward to college. He was just about to leave college. One thing had led to another, and now it was too late to repair the mistake even had he wanted to.

Just how much of a mistake he was about to discover as Lizzie's father was taken down to the cells and he found Lizzie waiting for him outside the court. Her language was colourful. The slap came out of nowhere. He supposed he deserved it.

Touching his cheek, he held her blazing stare. She was half his size, but when Lizzie was roused she was a firebrand—as he had discovered last night in bed.

Uncaring of the crowd gathering around them in the expectation of a scene, she balled her fists and raged at him. 'You *bastard*! How could you have sex with me last night knowing *this* was going to happen?'

'Calm yourself, Lizzie.' He waved the Gavros legal team away. 'You're making a spectacle of yourself.'

'Calm myself?' she exclaimed bitterly. 'Thanks to you, my father's a convicted criminal!'

Charles Montgomery would always be innocent in Lizzie's eyes. As far as she was concerned the rest of the world—and most especially the man she'd clung to, panting out her lust the previous night—could go hang.

'And don't look at me like that,' she blazed. 'You don't frighten me,'

'I should hope not,' he agreed.

'Don't!' she warned, deflecting him when he reached out to comfort her.

In his peripheral vision he could see the Gavros security men politely but firmly ushering the spectators away, and now the head of his father's legal team was approaching. He waved him back too. Lizzie was due *some* consideration. Her voice was shaking with shock. The judge had wanted Lizzie's father to be an example to others who might think of following his lead, and had handed down a prison sentence lengthy enough to shock everyone in court.

'Your father hurt a lot of people, Lizzie. It wasn't just my family that suffered—'

'Stop it! *Stop it!*' she screamed, covering her ears with her hands. 'All you care about is money!'

'I have a family to protect,' he argued quietly. 'And not just my family but all those people who work for our company. Don't *they* deserve justice too?'

'And you're such a *saint*!' she yelled before swinging away.

Guilt speared him as her shoulders heaved with silent sobs. Would he have acted differently last night if he'd known this would happen? However hard he tried, he could not regret having sex with Lizzie. His only thought now was to comfort her, to shield her from curious eyes, but Lizzie Montgomery was in no mood to be consoled.

'I *hate* you!' she yelled as her friends came over to lead her away.

The words sounded torn from her soul. 'Well, I don't hate *you*,' he called after her.

Lizzie wasn't to blame for her father's actions, and however misplaced her loyalty might be he could understand it. He felt the same about *his* father, who had spent a lifetime building the business Charles Montgomery had almost destroyed.

Damon's father had always been keenly aware of the families who depended on him—a responsibility that would pass to Damon one day. He looked forward to following in the great man's footsteps. Lizzie didn't know it yet, but she was another of her father's victims. His best guess was that by the time her avaricious stepmother had finished with her Lizzie would be out on the street.

'I'd like to help you,' he offered.

'*Help* me?' Lizzie derided. 'Not this side of hell freezing over! Go back to your wealthy friends and your comfortable life, rich boy!'

Several more ripe epithets followed as Lizzie's friends tried to lead her away.

He would miss Lizzie. Who wouldn't? Even in just one night he'd seen that she was a wildcat with a heart of gold.

'My father's innocent! *Innocent!*' she yelled back at him with every ounce of strength she possessed.

'Your father's been found guilty on all counts,' he countered mildly, 'and by the highest court in this land.'

Breaking free of her friends, Lizzie spun round to face him. 'Because of you and your kind!' she raged, in a tone that was closer to an agonised howl than it was to speech. 'I'll never forgive you for this! Do you hear me? *Never!*'

He smiled faintly as he turned away. 'Never say never, Lizzie.'

CHAPTER ONE

'DAMON GAVROS! LONG TIME, no see!'

Damon Gavros! Lizzie felt weak. Surely there had to be more than one Damon Gavros in London? She could hardly breathe as Stavros, her excitable boss, burst into the busy restaurant kitchen where Lizzie was ploughing her way through a mountain of dirty dishes at the sink. No. There was no mistake. She didn't have to turn around to know it was *the* Damon Gavros when she could feel Damon in every fibre of her being. Was it really eleven years since they had last seen each other?

Steadying herself against the sink, Lizzie braced herself for an encounter she had never expected to happen—least of all here in the safety of her workplace.

Images of Damon started flashing behind her eyes. Impossibly compelling and dangerously intuitive, Damon Gavros was the only man to have made an impact on Lizzie so powerful that she had never forgotten him—never *could* forget him. And for more reasons than the fact that Damon was the most charismatic man she'd ever met.

'Welcome! Welcome!' Stavros was calling out on a steadily mounting wave of hysteria. 'Damon! *Please!* Come in to the kitchen! Follow me! I want to introduce you to everyone...'

Lizzie remained rooted to the spot. Head down, with her

fists planted in the warm suds, she drew a deep, shuddering breath as a spurt of the old anger flashed through her. Standing outside that courtroom in London eleven years ago, she had never felt more alone in her life, and she had cursed Damon Gavros to hell and back for being part of the root cause of that upheaval.

Now she could see that Damon and his father had done a *good* thing, and that the fault had rested squarely with Lizzie's father, who had defrauded so many people out of their life savings. At the time she had been too confused and angry and upset to see that. It had only been when she had returned home and her stepmother had thrown her out of the house that Lizzie had finally accepted that her father was a crook and her stepmother was a heartless, greedy woman.

And Damon...?

She'd never forgotten Damon.

But where had he been for the past eleven years?

He certainly hadn't been part of Lizzie's life. Not that she held him responsible for anything except his absence. In fact she thanked him for making her life infinitely richer. She wondered what he would think of her now. She'd been such a rebel then, and now she was conventional to a fault. Would that make him suspicious?

Her body trembled with awareness as he drew closer. She hadn't felt this affected by a man in eleven long years. She'd sworn off sex after Damon—and not just because no man could compare with him.

Damon and Stavros were growing closer to the dishwashing section of the busy kitchen, and the warmth between the two men reminded Lizzie of the warmth between Damon and his father after the trial. How she'd envied them their closeness. To have someone to confide in had seemed such an impossible dream. Looking back, she could see now that the court case had done her a favour. She had learned to stand on her own feet and now, though she didn't have much, she earned her living honestly and she was free.

'Lizzie!' Stavros's voice was full of happy anticipation as he called out her name across the banks of stainless steel counters. 'May I present a very good friend of mine, recently returned from his travels…? Damon Gavros!'

She turned reluctantly.

There were a few seconds of absolute silence, and then Damon said, 'I believe we know each other.'

Damon's voice slicked through Lizzie's veins like the slide of warm cream. It was so familiar she felt as if they'd never been apart.

'That's right,' she agreed, trembling inside as she made sure to give Stavros a reassuring smile.

'I'll leave you two together,' Stavros said tactfully, practically rubbing his hands with glee at the thought that he had finally managed to play Cupid.

'It's been a long time, Damon.'

'Indeed it has,' he agreed, scrutinising her with matching interest.

She felt vulnerable. She was hardly kitted out in her armour of choice for this reunion, in rubber overshoes, with an unflattering overall over her old clothes and an elasticated protective hat covering her wilful red curls, and her face was no doubt red and sweaty from the steam of the kitchen.

And I don't know you, she thought as she stared into a ridiculously handsome face that had only improved with age. Apart from the information in press reports about his public persona, she didn't know who Damon Gavros had become. And if he was back in London for good she had to find out.

Incredible eyes. Seductive eyes. Laughing eyes...
Dangerous eyes. They saw too much.

Damon's impact on her senses was as devastating as it had ever been—which was the only warning Lizzie needed that she should take care. From the flash of black diamonds on his crisp white cuffs to the faintly amused stare that could obliterate her sensible mind at a stroke, Damon Gavros, with his power and money, was the most terrible threat to everything Lizzie held dear.

And still her wilful body clamoured for his attention while her sensible mind screamed caution. Damon was overwhelmingly charismatic, as well as physically imposing, but it was the power of his mind that dominated everything—and that frightened her.

'Success suits you,' she said, carelessly speaking her thoughts out loud.

He gave a slight nod of acknowledgement to this, but made no reply. That was probably the best he could do, after finding her here in the kitchen.

Business pundits spoke of Damon's unparalleled success, and his monumental wealth since taking over his father's company. When their articles weren't referring to him as the world's most eligible bachelor, they were dubbing him the benevolent billionaire, because of his charitable interests. She doubted he'd feel charitably disposed towards *her* if he discovered how she'd lived for the past eleven years.

Tamping down her alarm, Lizzie accepted that they'd both changed. She was more savvy, and better able to handle Damon.

'Why don't we get out of here?' he suggested.

'I beg your pardon?' She looked at him in surprise, thinking she must have misheard him.

'I'm not keen on holding our reunion here, are you?'

His stare seared through her, and for a moment she didn't know what to say. The thought of going anywhere with Damon Gavros was alarming.

Damon could understand Lizzie's surprise at seeing him. Seeing her had been a shock for him too—especially finding her so changed. He was keen to know what had been happening to Lizzie over the past eleven years, and why on earth she was working here.

'I'm sure Stavros can spare you for an hour or so,' he insisted.

Confident that Lizzie would follow him, he was already halfway to the door.

'I can't,' she said flatly, bringing him to a halt. 'As you can see…' She spread her hands wide in the ugly rubber gloves when he turned around. 'I'm working.'

It had never occurred to him that she might say no. 'Stavros?' he queried, turning his attention to her boss, who was hovering at the back of the kitchen.

'Of course,' Stavros insisted with enthusiasm. 'Lizzie deserves a break. She can join you at your table. My chefs will prepare a feast—'

'I'd rather not,' Lizzie interrupted.

Damon had caught a glimpse of shabby jeans and a faded top beneath Lizzie's overall and could understand her reservations. Stavros's restaurant was seriously high-end, but now they'd met again he was determined to find out everything about her, and bury the hatchet so many years after her father's trial.

'We don't have to eat here—somewhere casual?' he suggested. 'Another time, Stavros,' he was quick to add, with a reassuring smile for his hovering host. 'I'd like the chance to fill in the past eleven years, wouldn't you?' he said, turning to Lizzie.

She gave a nervous laugh. This was so unlike the Lizzie he'd known that he felt instantly suspicious. 'Unless your eleven years includes a husband or a fiancé?'

'No,' she said, lifting her chin to regard him steadily. 'It doesn't.'

'Then, do you have a coat?'

'Yes, but—'

'An hour or so of your time?' He shrugged. 'What harm can that do?'

Stavros intervened before she could reply. 'How can you refuse?' Stavros asked Lizzie, with a warm smile and an expansive gesture so typical of the genial restaurateur. 'I'll get someone to take over your work. Go now,' he chivvied, 'Lizzie never takes time off,' he confided to Damon. 'Half an hour for old times' sake?' he urged Lizzie, doing Damon's work for him.

Short of being rude to both of them, there was only one thing Lizzie could do.

'I'll get my coat,' she said.

She went to the staff bathroom and sluiced her face in cold water. Staring at herself in the mirror above the sink, she wondered where eleven years had gone. Did it matter? Damon Gavros was back. She had to handle it.

At least Stavros was delighted. He was always trying to fix her up with a man. *Billionaire and pot-washer?* Even Stavros couldn't make *that* one fly, though Damon seemed happy enough. That had better not have been a smile of *triumph* on his lips. Lips that had kissed her into oblivion, Lizzie remembered, trying not to think back to the most significant night of her life.

Her heart jumped when she walked out of the restroom to find Damon relaxed back against the wall. Had he always been so hot?

Yes, she thought, smiling politely as he insisted on helping her with her coat.

To his credit, his expression didn't falter, though her coat, with its plucked threads and plastic buttons, and a collar that had already been bald when she'd bought it in the thrift shop, was miles too big for her. She'd just needed something warm, while Damon's coat had probably been custom-made. It was a soft alpaca overcoat, in a blue so dark it was almost black.

With a cashmere scarf slung casually around his neck, he looked like the master of the sexual universe. He had to be thinking, *What the hell has happened to Lizzie Montgomery?*

Life. Life had happened to Lizzie Montgomery, Lizzie reflected as Damon held the door. And life changed people. For the better, she could only hope, in both their cases.

'I'm driving myself tonight,' Damon explained as he stopped by the passenger door of a fabulous brand-new black Bentley with a personalised number plate: DG1.

'Of course you are,' she teased in a pale imitation of her old self. 'Chauffeur's night off?' she suggested.

Damon chose not to answer as he opened the passenger door. The scent of money and leather assailed her the moment she sank into, rather than perched on, the most incredibly comfortable pale cream kidskin seat.

'This is lovely,' she observed, looking around as Damon slid in beside her.

She didn't want him to think she was so downtrodden and disadvantaged that she was overwhelmed by his obvious wealth. She'd been bold when they'd first met, and now, in spite of how she must appear to Damon, she had everything she could possibly need. He might have made millions, and she might be poor, but there were more ways than one to feel a deep sense of satisfaction with life and she'd got that.

When Damon started the engine it purred—in contrast to the jangling conflict inside Lizzie. Pulling smoothly away from the kerb, he joined the sluggish London evening traffic. This was how the rich travelled, she concluded. They didn't bounce along, crushed on every side in an over-full rush hour bus. They glided in their opulent private space, enjoying classical music playing softly in the background.

'Do you enjoy your job?'

The blunt question jolted Lizzie back to the unlikely reality of being cocooned inside the most luxurious vehicle in London with the world's most eligible bachelor.

'Yes,' she confirmed, lifting her chin. 'I have great friends at the restaurant—especially Stavros. I'm exactly where I want to be, working alongside genuine people who care for me as I care for them.'

Damon seemed taken aback for a moment, and then he said, 'Hungry?'

She was—and for more than food, she realised as Damon flashed a glance her way. She hadn't felt like this in eleven years, but he only had to look at her for her to remember how it had felt to be in his arms. Which was a complete waste of good thinking time, she accepted, drawing her shabby coat closer around her trembling body.

'Surprising even myself, I'm hungry too,' he admitted.

'You can take me back.'

'Now, why would I do that?'

She stared down in shock as his hand covered hers. He'd better not be feeling sorry for her.

He drew the Bentley to a halt on the Embankment running alongside the river Thames. By the time she had released her seat belt he was opening her door. It was such a romantic view it took her attention for a moment.

'Burger or hot dog?' he said.

She almost laughed. Perhaps it was just as well he'd shaken her away from the romantic sight of the Palace of Westminster and stately Big Ben. It wouldn't do to lose focus around Damon. 'Hot dog, please.'

'Ketchup and mustard?'

'Why not be lavish?' she said.

He gave her a look and turned away, allowing her to take in the powerful spread of his shoulders as he started chatting easily to the guy behind the food stand not far from where they had parked. Damon had always got on well with everyone—but how would he handle what she had to tell him?

Not yet, she decided. She would have to know this older, shrewder Damon better before she could tell him everything. She had to know what made him tick and how he lived his life.

As he handed the hot dog over their fingers touched and a quiver of awareness ran through her. It seemed that however hard she tried to remain detached, so she could think straight, her body insisted on going its own way. And her body wanted Damon as much as it ever had.

'Thinking back?' he said, reading her mind.

Thinking back to when she had been an eighteen-year-old virgin with nothing certain in her future except that it would change? Yes—unfortunately. 'I'm thinking maybe I have too much sauce?' she suggested.

'You *always* had too much sauce,' Damon observed.

She decided to ignore the jibe. Damon was standing under a street lamp, leaning back against it, and the spotlight suited him. He was so dark and swarthy—so compelling in every way. The shadowed light only enhanced his sculpted features.

'I didn't realise how hungry I was,' she said, biting down hard on the delicious snack in an attempt to distract herself from Damon's brazen physicality. And, truthfully, it was a treat to have someone other than Stavros buy her a meal and to care a damn if she enjoyed it.

'Where did you disappear to after the trial?' he asked with a frown.

'Where did I "disappear to"?' she repeated thoughtfully.

Good question. Not to a loving home—that was for sure.

'Who'll support me now?' That had been Lizzie's stepmother's first question when Lizzie had returned home to find her suitcases waiting in the hall.

She should have known what was happening, but she had rushed up to her bedroom, thinking to bury her grief in her pillows, only to find her bedroom had been cleared. She had wasted a few precious minutes railing against fate before pulling herself together and accepting that this was her life now, and she'd better get on with it.

On her way out of the house she'd found her stepmother in her father's study, going through the drawers of his desk. 'I guess we'll both have to work,' Lizzie had said.

Her stepmother's expression had twisted into something ugly. 'I don't *work*,' she'd said haughtily. 'And if you think you can persuade me to let you stay, you're wasting your time. You're one expense I can't afford.'

That had been the last time they'd seen each other, and it had taken Lizzie's stepmother less than a week to replace Lizzie's father with a richer man.

She decided on a heavily edited version for Damon. 'It wasn't all bad,' she said, thinking back. 'The shock of finding myself homeless was good for me. I had to stand on my own two feet, and I found I enjoyed doing it.'

'Sacrificing your dreams?' He frowned.

'Sometimes dreams have to wait,' Lizzie said frankly. She'd done more than survive. She'd thrived, and had proved herself capable of far more than she'd imagined.

'You've got ketchup on your chin—'

She sucked in a fast breath as he wiped it off. His touch was still electric.

'Next time I'll take you out for a proper meal—'

'Next time?' she queried. 'So you're back for good?' Her heart drummed a tattoo as she thought about all the implications of that.

He chose not to answer her question. 'Stavros says you work too hard. You have to take a break sometime,' he insisted.

What else had Stavros told him? she wondered. She had so much to lose. Damon had been absent from her life for a long time, but he was still a core part of her existence. He didn't know it yet, but he could rip her world apart on a whim.

'Soda or water?' he asked.

'Water, please.' Her throat was tight and dry.

As Damon turned to speak to the vendor she thought back to her first deception on their night together, when she'd been a virgin pretending not to be, embarking on a romantic adventure with a handsome Greek—or so she'd thought. Her life had been in chaos at the time. She hadn't been thinking straight. Hated by her stepmother, she'd been desperate for her father to notice her.

She'd failed.

She'd almost failed with Damon too. Clinging to him, begging him to take her so she could forget her wretched home life, she had exclaimed with shock as he'd taken her, and he'd pulled back. It had taken all her feminine wiles to persuade him to continue.

Of course she was on the pill, she'd insisted.

He'd used protection anyway.

Belt and braces? she'd teased him.

Damon had proved to be a master of seduction, a master of pleasure, and they'd made love all night. But there had been chances to talk too, and it had been then that they had discovered a closeness that neither of them had expected. Surprising both of them, she was sure, they had enjoyed each other's company.

'Let's walk.'

She glanced up as Damon took the top off her bottle of water. 'I'd like that.'

A walk promised a welcome break from the past. She could take in the majesty of London instead…that was if she could stop looking at Damon.

Life and responsibility had cut harsh lines into his brow and around his mouth, but those only made him seem more human. Harsh, yet humorous, ruthless, yet empathetic, Damon was an exceptional man.

'When I'm in London I walk a lot,' he revealed, glancing down, his eyes too dark to read. 'Sometimes it's good to be alone with your thoughts, don't you think?'

'That depends who you are and what you're thinking, I suppose,' she said, remembering how quickly their whispered confidences in bed had turned to mistrust the following day in court. It would take more than walking together to clear the air between them, she suspected.

At the time the press reports—coming on top of everything else that had been happening at home—had destroyed Lizzie's confidence. She'd lost her self-belief, as well as her confidence in her own judgement. She'd lost her trust in everyone—and in herself most of all. But then she'd realised that with no one to pick her up she'd better get on with it, and so she'd rebuilt her life along very different lines, far away from privilege and trickery.

A pawnbroker had given Lizzie her first break, taking what few scraps had remained of her mother's jewellery in exchange for enough money to pay her first week's rent. She remembered begging him not to sell her mother's wedding ring. 'There's nothing exceptional about it,' she'd protested when he'd informed her that he wasn't a charitable institution. 'You must have dozens like it—'

'Not with three seed pearls set in the centre of the band,' he'd said as he'd studied the ring with his eyeglass.

'I'll clean your shop for nothing,' she'd offered in desperation. 'I'll pay you back with interest, I promise...'

But life had caught up with her, making the necessity of keeping a roof over her head more important than her mother's wedding ring, so it would have to wait. Maybe one day...

'Something wrong?' Damon asked as she bit her lip and grimaced.

'Nothing. Why?' she gazed up at him evenly.

'You made a sound like an angry kitten.'

She made no comment. Being compared to a kitten would not have been her choice. She felt as if the past few years had required her to be a tigress.

'Enough?' he said, when she shivered.

'I'd better get back,' she agreed.

The Bentley sat waiting for them, gleaming black and opulent. It was attracting admiring glances from passers-by, and now they were attracting interest too, as they approached it. The elegant vehicle was a fabulous representation of privilege, and Lizzie thought it the most visible proof of the yawning gulf between them. She couldn't imagine what people must be thinking about the suave billionaire and the shabby kitchen worker getting into a car like that.

Did there ever come a point when a cork stopped bobbing to the surface? she wondered as Damon opened the passenger door and saw her safely settled in?

No. She hadn't come this far to give up now.

'Home?' he asked.

So he could see where she lived?

'Back to the restaurant, please.' She tried not to look at him. 'There are things I need to pick up.'

She didn't want him visiting her home. She couldn't risk it. This had been pleasant, but there was more to life than Damon's riches and his personal success. What Lizzie was protecting was infinitely more precious, and she had no intention of risking everything she cared about by acting carelessly now.

Damon had the power to steal everything away from her.

She wouldn't let him. It was as simple as that. Whatever it took, that wasn't going to happen.

He started the engine and the Bentley purred obediently.

'Your mother was Greek, wasn't she?' he asked conversationally as he pulled onto the road.

'Yes, she was.'

'I suppose that accounts for your unusual colouring. I never thought about it before, but with your Celtic red hair and those chocolate-brown eyes and long black lashes your colouring is quite unusual...'

'I suppose it is,' Lizzie agreed, realising that she had never thought about it either, beyond the fact that when things had been at their bleakest she had sought refuge in the warm, home-loving Greek community in London, where there was always someone who knew someone, she reflected wryly. But wasn't life like that? Paths crossed, then separated, and then crossed again.

'I think we should see each other again.'

She stared at Damon in amazement, feeling a little defensive. 'Should we? Why?' Her heart thundered as she waited for his reply.

He shrugged. 'I promised you a proper meal?'

'I won't hold you to that.' But they would *have* to see each other again, she accepted. That was inevitable now.

'We'll make a date before I leave tonight,' he said, glancing across at her.

Would they? Could she risk spending an entire evening with Damon? Could she risk becoming relaxed with him and yet not telling him about anything of significance that had happened in her life over the past eleven years? Could she risk her feelings for him only to lose him again—and for good this time?

She had never shrunk from a challenge yet, Lizzie concluded as Damon slowed the Bentley outside the restaurant, whether that challenge had been battling the demand for clean plates when Stavros's industrial-sized dishwashers decided to pack up in the middle of service—or having a second meeting with the man who didn't know he was the father of her ten-year-old child.

CHAPTER TWO

No one—not even the tall, imposing figure towering over her as he opened the car door and stood back—would ever come between Lizzie and her daughter.

Thea had never asked about her father. In fact Thea had shrugged off all mention of a father, which Lizzie had come to think was for the best when it had proved impossible to get in touch with Damon.

Lizzie's experience with her *own* father was hardly encouraging. She had never got past the fact that he'd rejected her. Lizzie's mother had been an heiress, and had had an obvious use, but once her mother was dead and the money was spent Lizzie's father had lost interest in her.

Lizzie had been too young to understand at the time, but she still remembered her wonderful mother being sad and wanting Lizzie to have a better and more exciting life. Maybe that had fuelled Lizzie's night of rebellion with Damon. It was very easy to mistake lust for love at eighteen—as it was to take a late, loving parent's suggestion and bend it to suit her own, hormonal eighteen-year-old's will.

'Goodnight, Damon, and thank you—'

'Not so fast,' he said, catching hold of her arm. 'We haven't made that date yet.'

'Do you really want to?'

'Do you need to consult your diary?' he countered.

'I do have other things to do,' she pointed out.

'But nothing important, I'm sure…?'

Damon's black stare bored into her. She had to think of something fast—and that something didn't include blurting out that they had a child together, here on a busy London street.

'Why don't you come back to the restaurant some time?' *And give me time to think and plan how best to tell Thea about this.* 'I'm usually there each night, and we can fix something up.'

'No kidding?' he murmured.

Letting her go, he pulled back.

She watched Damon drive away in his Bentley until the limousine had turned the corner and was out of sight. The logic she'd used at eighteen for keeping her pregnancy to herself felt more like a selfish cop-out now. Yes, she'd been facing huge upheaval in her life—and, yes, it had been a fight to survive, with her character largely unformed and her reaction to crises untested—but maybe she could have done something differently, or better.

But when Thea had been born Lizzie had wanted to protect her from the hurt Lizzie had felt when *her* father had rejected her. She didn't know that it wouldn't happen to Thea. Why would Damon want a child?

As the years had passed and her conscience had pricked she'd tried to get in touch with him, but his people had kept her away. And then, in another unexpected turn, Thea had proved to be musically gifted—a talent Lizzie believed Thea had inherited from *her* mother. Lizzie's mother had used to say she had music flowing through her veins instead of blood. And once Thea's musical life had taken off, Lizzie had been completely wrapped up in that. Thea had

recently won a music scholarship to a prestigious school
in London, where she was a boarder.

Didn't Damon deserve to know all this?

'Back already?' Stavros exclaimed with obvious disappointment. 'You don't look happy, Lizzie-*itsa*. What's
wrong?'

'I had a lovely time,' she insisted, determined to wipe
the concern from Stavros's face. 'And I've come back to
help you to clear up for the night.'

'You shouldn't have come back. You deserve a little
happiness,' Stavros complained with a theatrical gesture.

Did she? She was guilty of failing to contact Damon,
because keeping him in the dark had allowed Lizzie to
carry on her life with Thea without the interference of a
very powerful and wealthy man. She would be lying if she
said she didn't feel threatened now.

She would have to tell him about Thea, Lizzie realised
as she set to and got to work, but she would choose the
time.

Which would mean seeing him again!

Anxiety washed over her in hot and cold waves. There
was a more important thing to do first—and that was to
prepare Thea for the fact that her father was back.

Lizzie Montgomery! He couldn't believe he'd found her
again.

Was it a coincidence?

Opening the front door to his penthouse apartment,
located on the top floor of one of the most iconic land-
marks in London, he accepted that he'd just visited one of
the most popular Greek restaurants in London, and with
the way the grapevine worked, someone had always been
bound to know Lizzie.

Coincidence or not, being close to the woman he hadn't

been able to get out of his mind for more than ten years had been the most extraordinary experience. Seeing Lizzie again had reminded him of a night that hadn't been just about sex—though the sex had been more than memorable.

Pouring a Scotch, he strolled to the window and stared out across the London skyline. The shallow society beauties he normally wheeled out for public events bored him. Where sex was concerned, they couldn't keep up. He was a hard, driven, solitary man, whose life revolved around his work.

And he hadn't been back in London five minutes before the first thing he did was to search out all things Greek.

Maybe to find Lizzie?

Okay, so he had. What of it?

He remembered Lizzie mentioning her love of her mother's country, its culture and its cuisine, that night. She'd love to visit Greece one day, she'd told him when they had been lying side by side in bed, sated, with their limbs entwined.

He *would* see her again. It was inevitable. Eleven years couldn't simply be dismissed over a hot dog with ketchup and mustard. Especially when his intuition told him that Lizzie was holding back more than she was telling him. He wanted to know why she was washing pots when she'd had such big dreams. What was holding her back?

He'd succeeded by working as his father had—alongside men and women who were his friends. Granted, he'd had every advantage. His father was a good man, while Lizzie's father had been a swindler and a cheat who had sucked his victims dry, but that still didn't explain why Lizzie was working in a restaurant, washing dishes.

Would she thank him for interfering in her life?

Did he care?

He took a deep swallow of Scotch and tried to imagine her life after the trial. However she'd played it, it couldn't have been easy for her when he'd walked into Stavros's kitchen to find her at the sink. He *would* buy her that meal. He owed her that much, and he wanted to know more about her.

'Can I get you a drink, sir?' the waiter behind the bar at Stavros's restaurant asked him the next evening, when he returned to the restaurant.

'I'm not staying,' he explained. 'Could you please tell Ms Montgomery that there's somebody waiting to see her at the bar?'

'Of course, sir.'

As the waiter hurried away he cast his mind back to that other night. He couldn't remember talking to anyone as he'd talked to Lizzie that night. She'd trusted him, he remembered with a stab of guilt. He had never expected to find the happiness his parents had enjoyed for forty years, but that night he'd thought he could find some temporary distraction with Lizzie—until the shock of discovering who she was at the trial.

No one had ever stood up to him as she had. He admired her for that.

He glanced towards the kitchen, wondering what was keeping her. His body tightened on the thought that she was only yards away. Pushing back from the bar, he stood up. He couldn't wait any longer for her to come to him.

'No.' Lizzie held up her hand as soon as she caught sight of him. 'You can't just walk in. You've got to warn me first.'

'With a fanfare?' he suggested with a look.

'You can't walk into my place of work, looking like a…a Hell's Angel,' she exclaimed with frustration as her glance roved slowly over him, 'and demand that I leave with you right away.'

He lips pressed down and he shrugged. 'You won't need your overall.'

She huffed and gazed skywards. 'Thanks for the charming invitation—but, no.'

Undaunted, he pressed on dryly. 'It's a great night for a bike ride.'

'Then go and enjoy it,' she suggested.

'You don't mean that.'

She raised a brow.

'If Lizzie wants time off she can have it,' Stavros announced, appearing like a genie out of a bottle from the pantry. 'No one works harder than Lizzie-*itsa*. I keep telling her she should get out more—treat herself to some new clothes, and a hairdo while she's at it—'

'There's nothing wrong with Lizzie,' he said, maintaining eye contact with her.

'Of course not,' Stavros placated. 'It's just that she puts everyone else first.'

'As do you, my old friend,' he said, feeling guilty that he'd shut Stavros out. 'Shall we go?' he added to Lizzie, who was still staring at him mutinously.

She had never looked more beautiful. Her shapeless apron and clumpy overshoes tried to strip away her femininity but failed utterly in his eyes. Even with those bright red curls, made frizzy by the heat in the kitchen, peeping out from under the ugly cap, she was beautiful.

The loose ends from eleven years ago had never been in more need of tying up.

'So you couldn't stay away?' she challenged.

The way she stared him directly in the eyes made his senses roar. 'That's right,' he agreed.

'You're *do* know you're in the way? This is a busy professional kitchen—'

'Then leave with me and the congestion will clear.' He angled his chin to smile into her eyes.

'You're impossible!' she complained.

'I'll see you outside,' he told her.

'In your dreams,' she flashed.

He had *great* dreams.

He caught a glimpse of Lizzie's eyes darkening as he left the kitchen. If she only knew how he wanted to drag her away from that sink and lower her, naked, into a warm, foaming bath, where he would wash her, pleasure her and make love to her until she couldn't stand up, she might not be reaching for her coat now.

How had he stayed away for eleven years? Yes, he'd been working tirelessly to rebuild the damage done to his father's business, so his parents could retire in comfort, but he'd taken himself away to the furthest reaches of the world in an attempt to lose himself to everything familiar. And there, in the seemingly endless miles of the desert, he had found himself, and a purpose, which was to help those who had not been as lucky as he had. Why had he needed to get away, and to do this? Was it penance for the shame felt at the way he'd treated Lizzie—the way he'd turned his back on her after the trial?

'Don't keep me waiting,' he warned her. He was eager to pick up the threads he'd left loose for the past eleven years and weave them into a pattern he could understand.

Damon was waiting for her outside on a bike. Whatever next? It was a monster of a thing—big and black, purring rhythmically beneath him. In the deep dark shadows of the night, sitting astride the throbbing motorbike, Damon

Gavros was quite simply the hottest thing on two hard-muscled legs.

He handed her a helmet and helped her put it on. She tried not to react when his fingertips brushed her skin, sending tidal waves of sensation streaking through her.

'Just a short ride,' she warned—a warning for herself more than him. 'Is there an approved way of mounting this thing?'

Damon laughed as he secured his helmet, lowering the black visor so she could no longer see his eyes. 'You have to climb on behind me and put your arms around my waist.'

There was every reason not to do so.

'You'll have to relax,' he said when she tried to keep her distance. 'And hold on.'

She might have yelped when the bike surged forward. She wasn't sure. She was too distracted by Damon…by *holding* Damon. The power of the bike throbbing between her legs didn't help.

Damon judged the traffic expertly, and soon they were moving smoothly through the night. Of all places, he took her to a funfair. She supposed it was neutral ground, where there wasn't much option but to relax. There was certainly plenty of noise and colour, and dazzling flashing lights.

Dismounting from the bike, she removed the helmet, then glanced at Damon's outstretched hand. 'Maybe this isn't such a good idea,' she said, pulling back.

'This is an *excellent* idea,' he insisted.

She remembered, then, that Damon's easy charm was as much a part of his nature as the steely side that had played its part in condemning her father to a lifetime in jail—a punishment that had almost certainly led to his early death.

Maybe it seemed odd that she was mourning her father's passing, but however he had treated Lizzie she still thought him weak rather than bad. He certainly hadn't stood a chance against the Gavros team.

'Lizzie?'

Damon's voice brought her plummeting back from an uncomfortable past to an incredible present.

And the future...?

She preferred not to think about that. Not yet. She would. Of course she would. But not while Damon's shrewd eyes were searching hers. She would choose the time, and she would choose the place, and it wasn't now.

He bought tickets for the big wheel. As she climbed into the small cabin and the door closed on the two of them, trapping Lizzie inside with her memories and with Damon, it was hardly reassuring to discover that her body instantly responded to his heat and his strength, reminding her with painful attention to detail of how it had felt to be naked in his arms.

'You've turned pale. It's not too high for you, is it?'

'I'm certainly out of my comfort zone,' she admitted, thinking about Thea, and how Damon was likely to respond when he found out they had a daughter together. 'It's a long way down...' she mused quietly.

'You look exhausted,' he observed.

'It's hard work in a professional kitchen, and I've got more than one job.' He could easily find that out. Better she tell him than that he started sleuthing. She needed the money to pay the rent, and to cover all the extras at Thea's school.

'Don't you ever take time off?' he pressed.

'Hardly ever,' she admitted. And what time she had, she spent with Thea.

'And you live alone?'

The big wheel was a mistake. She couldn't get away from Damon's questions. To answer him meant telling him that she lived on her own most of the time—even in the school holidays—and Thea was often away, playing with the orchestra. Lizzie tried to go with her when she could, which meant finding a job in a bar, or as waiting staff to pay her way.

Their next trip was to Greece.

'Lizzie?'

'Yes. I live alone,' she said, quickly pulling herself together.

'It must have been a long road back for you?'

It was hard to concentrate. All she could think about now was Thea's upcoming trip to Greece.

"Lizzie?' I said it must have been a long road back for you?'

'I like my work,' she said distractedly.

'But it's repetitive,' Damon pointed out, 'and with no personal reward—'

'Apart from earning my living and keeping my pride intact, do you mean?'

'I didn't mean to offend you. I'm just curious.'

And now she was all heated up. How dared Damon stride back into her life and start judging her?

Wouldn't Thea be happier with a father who could give her so much more than she could?

No. She would not, Lizzie thought fiercely. 'Let's get one thing straight,' she said on the wave of that thought. 'I don't need your pity.'

'And you won't get it,' Damon assured her with matching force.

CHAPTER THREE

BUT IT WASN'T long before Damon was questioning her again. 'So what happened to your dream of attending that art college in Switzerland?' he pressed as their cabin sank steadily towards the ground

'I had lots of dreams when I was eighteen.'

Unfortunately they hadn't tallied with her stepmother's plans for Lizzie, and as those dreams would have been paid for by her father, using other people's money—mostly Damon's family's—Lizzie realised now they had been meaningless.

'I owe you an apology.'

'For showing loyalty to your father?'

Damon read her so easily, Lizzie thought as his powerful shoulders lifted in a shrug.

'You don't owe me a thing,' he insisted.

Their stares met and held for a potent few seconds, but all that did was allow Lizzie time to consider the big truth she wasn't telling Damon. She couldn't tell him yet. Not until she was sure of him—or as sure as she could be.

'We were discussing your dreams?' he prompted.

'*You* were,' she argued, with a spark of her old dry humour. 'Life's a series of compromises, don't you think? If you can't adjust, you flounder.'

'And you've had to do a lot of adjusting?' Damon guessed.

She remained silent.

'I can't imagine you floundering,' he admitted. 'Even at eighteen you had a good head on your—'

'Reckless shoulders?' Lizzie supplied. 'I had too much emotion in play back then.'

'And not enough now?'

His suggestion silenced her. Damon's searching glance was disturbing in all sorts of ways. She couldn't regret her rebellion eleven years ago, or her search for one night of love—which was probably the best way to describe the most memorable night of her life. How could she regret anything, when making love with Damon had created Thea?

'Penny for them?'

The smile that could heat her from the inside out was back, tugging at the corner of his mouth. 'You wouldn't want to know.'

'Try me,' he pressed.

Confide her concerns in him? Tell him how much of a struggle it was to keep the boat afloat, or that when Thea needed something for school Lizzie couldn't always guarantee she'd come through? This was the man who had walked out of her life without a backward glance—as her father had. This was the man she had been unable to reach again and again. She had to remember that—always. She couldn't face that coldness again. She had more pride than to do so. And more love for Thea than to allow her precious daughter to live through something similar.

And there was another way of looking at it. Damon might not *want* to know. What respectable billionaire would want to hear that he had a child with the daughter of a convicted felon? Would Damon believe Thea *was* his child? The shame of her father's crime had tainted Lizzie. Sometimes she believed she would never throw it off. That same shame taunted her now, with the thought that even if Damon were prepared to accept that Thea was his daughter he might not entrust her to Lizzie's care?

Whatever the consequences, her course was clear. She must first tell Thea, and then Damon.

'We're down,' he said, startling her.

'Yes…right…' she said, glancing around to see the cabin had settled on its stand. 'What a relief.'

'Vertigo can be devastating, can't it?' Damon commented, but his look was shrewd and it stripped her lie bare.

They didn't stay at the funfair. By mutual silent consent, they headed back to the bike.

'Where did you live when you left home after the court case?' Damon asked as the noise of the fair began to fade into the background.

'On a park bench,' Lizzie said bluntly, thinking back.

'I'm being serious,' Damon insisted.

'And so am I,' she admitted. 'I spent the first night on a park bench—well, most of it…until it started raining.'

'And then?' His face had tightened into a grim mask.

Lizzie thought back to her first and thankfully her only terrifying, freezing night as a homeless person. She had quickly figured out that she must find a place to live fast or, quite simply, her appearance and the fact that she couldn't wash properly would make respectable people turn her away. With no money, that had meant finding a job—*any* job.

'I got a job the next morning,' she remembered. 'As a cleaner. I was good at that. I'd had plenty of experience,' she said dryly. 'My stepmother was too mean to pay anyone to do her cleaning, but she had me and she was very particular. It stood me in good stead,' she admitted.

'I can imagine.'

Could he imagine the woman who had insisted Lizzie must clean the floors on her hands and knees, rather than with a mop, and take a toothbrush to the corners of the room? Could he imagine that same woman making Lizzie do it all over again, after her stepmother had thoughtlessly trampled on the floor in her muddy boots?

'Actually, the cleaning jobs I managed to get were easy after my work at home,' she reflected.

'And where do you live now?'

'Haven't you asked Stavros?'

Damon dipped his chin to stare into her eyes. 'That's not fair.'

'You're right,' she agreed as they drew to a halt in front of the bike. 'Stavros has been nothing but kind to me.'

'Whereas I haven't?'

'You've only just come back to London. It remains to be seen,' she said bluntly.

'What makes you think I'd want to investigate your life?'

'Nothing,' she said quickly—too quickly. 'I have a small bedsit, if you're interested.'

'I *am*,' Damon insisted as he picked up her helmet.

'I know that look,' she said.

He frowned. 'What look?'

'The look that says, *She grew up like a princess and her fall has been swift and hard*. I can't tell you how many times I've seen that same look over the years. But you should know that I've never been happier than I am now.'

That was the truth, Lizzie reflected, calming down. She had a daughter who loved her, and jobs that paid the rent. And, yes, it was tough sometimes, but she had never once fallen into debt.

'Okay?' she challenged Damon as he handed over her helmet. 'Are we done with the third degree now?'

'We're done,' he conceded.

'I think we should talk about *you* for a change—'

'No,' he said flatly, startling her into silence with the force of his response. 'I'm a very private man.'

'Then perhaps you should understand how I feel.'

Damon regarded her coolly. 'Aren't you going to get on the bike?'

'Shall I salute first?'

He gave her a look that might make some people blink, but it only made Lizzie more determined to stand up to him.

This had definitely been an interesting encounter, Lizzie concluded as they roared back to the city. Neither of them was exactly soft or malleable. She had a daughter to protect, which gave her mama tiger claws as well as an iron will, while Damon was the hardest man she knew by some margin. For all his outward charm, which he could turn on when it suited him, Damon Gavros was rock through and through.

He drew to a halt outside the restaurant. 'Drink?' he suggested as she removed her helmet.

'I don't think so, but thank you—it's been an interesting evening.'

'One drink,' he insisted, getting off the bike.

In spite of her reservations, she had to admit that it was a pleasant change to be *this* side of the tastefully lit bar. Stavros had peeped around the kitchen door and had then retired with a broad smile on his face. That in itself was worth the sacrifice of sitting with Damon. All the drinks were on the house, the barman insisted, but Damon still paid.

'So,' he said, glancing at her over his bottle of beer. 'Tell me more about your stepmother, Cinderella.'

'Less of that,' she warned. 'There's nothing needy about *me*.'

Damon's lips pressed down, almost as if he agreed. 'So…she sounds like a fascinating character?' he pressed.

'Luminous,' Lizzie said dryly.

She would credit her stepmother with one thing: she'd helped Lizzie to face reality fast. Before her stepmother had arrived on the scene Lizzie would have been the first to admit she'd been spoiled. She might have reached adulthood with no concept of responsibility if she hadn't been thrown out of the house, had her faith in her father destroyed, her dreams crushed, *and* discovered she was pregnant—all in one and the same month. That would have been enough to wake the dead. And she certainly wasn't spoiled now. Her life was devoted to Thea.

'I don't want to talk about me. It's your turn,' she said.

'Maybe it's time for me to go,' Damon countered.

'Please yourself.' Burying her face in her glass of water, she sucked on the straw, refusing to say any more about a time when life had seemed to stretch ahead of her in an endless stream of promise—promise that had turned out to be fantasy.

Her father had appeared to have money to burn when she was young. Now she knew it had been other people's money he was burning—Gavros money, mostly. Nothing made him happier than lavishing money on his darling daughter, her father had told her as they'd planned one treat after another.

He'd been showing off to her stepmother, she realised now; hoping to catch another big fish like Lizzie's mother, the heiress. The joke of it was, the woman he'd chosen to bring home as his second wife had been a chancer like him, captivated by his apparent wealth.

Thinking her father was lonely, Lizzie had welcomed her stepmother to begin with. She had wanted nothing more than to see her father happy again. It hadn't taken long to find out how wrong she could be.

'You told me that night that you loved to paint,' Damon reminded her. 'Another dream down?' he suggested.

'I don't have time to dream now.'

'That sounds dull.'

So dull he stood up to go.

'I'll take you home,' he offered.

'No need,' Lizzie insisted quickly. 'Stavros arranges a cab for staff when we stay late.'

Damon nodded his head. 'Okay. Another time.'

Or maybe not. She wasn't sure she could live through this tension again. Wanting someone and knowing they were out of reach for ever was a torture she could well do without.

'You must enjoy heading up the family business,' she observed, for the sake of maintaining polite chit-chat as she walked him to the door. 'The press refers to you as a billionaire—'

'I hope I'm more than that.'

She could have cut off her tongue. The way Damon was staring at her made her wonder if he thought she was a mercenary chip off her father's swindling old block. There was a lot more to him than money and sexual charisma— she knew that—but everything was in such a muddle in her head she couldn't get the words out straight.

The newspapers often referred to Damon Gavros as 'educated muscle', with the recommendation that no one should even *dream* of crossing him—which was a great thought to say goodnight on.

His phone rang and he turned away to answer, putting a hand up, indicating two minutes as they stood outside the door.

'Business call,' he explained succinctly when he cut the line. 'So, I guess I'll see you again sometime...'

After all her prevaricating about seeing him at all, she now felt rocked to her foundations as Damon mounted the Harley and roared away. She *had* to see him again. She *must*. She stared after him as he disappeared into the night. That was Damon. A massive presence when he was around, and then gone so quickly it was as if he had never been there at all.

She did well to rely on no one but herself, Lizzie thought as she turned back to the restaurant.

But could there be a more mesmeric sight than Damon Gavros astride a Harley?

Damon Gavros naked...?

CHAPTER FOUR

LIZZIE, LIZZIE, LIZZIE... What are you hiding?

As he opened the door to his Thames-side penthouse flat Damon was still brooding. It had been shock enough to see Lizzie Montgomery again. To discover he could still read her as he had eleven years ago was even more unsettling—because he knew there was something she wasn't telling him.

He'd called in at the apartment to pick up his overnight bag. It was his father's seventieth birthday in a couple of weeks and his PA had called to remind him that Damon's go-ahead was still required for number of arrangements. They included a rather special youth orchestra from London that had been booked to play at his father's birthday party.

Too many loose ends had been generated by his absence abroad, Damon reflected as the driver took his bag. Lizzie had briefly derailed his plans, but they were back on track now. He'd like to see her again, but she'd have to fly out to the island. He'd fix it with Stavros, and his PA would make the arrangements.

That was how simple things were for him. He saw no reason for them to change.

As usual, Lizzie could hardly get a word in. She was meeting Thea for their daily snatched chat over brunch in a café just across the road from the music college, and today Thea was particularly excited.

'The new Gavros building is right next door to the music conservatoire,' Thea was enthusing. 'You should *see* it. Everything's been changed around and made super deluxe since that boring insurance company owned it.'

And the Gavros building was as dangerously close to the music conservatoire as it could possibly be Lizzie realised as she called for the bill. She hated it that the tension generated by the Gavros name was threatening to distract her from this precious time with Thea, but she had to find out more.

'You've been inside the Gavros building?' Her heart hammered nineteen to the dozen as she waited for Thea's answer.

'Of course!' Thea enthused, sucking gloopy milk from her fingers. 'We had to audition for the man—'

Lizzie's heart dived into her throat. 'What man? Was he tall and dark?'

'No. Short, fat and bald,' Thea said—to Lizzie's relief. 'He said he worked for the Gavros family. We're playing at a birthday party in Greece, on an island owned by the Gavros family.'

The Gavros family?

Thea glanced up as Lizzie inhaled sharply. Lizzie quickly distracted Thea with talk of new clothes. 'You'll need a sunhat, a swimming costume, and perhaps a couple of sundresses—What?' She laughed as Thea mimed thrusting her fingers down her throat whilst gargling theatrically.

'Sundresses are for old ladies,' Thea insisted. 'And *you* need new clothes more than me,' she added with engaging honesty. She frowned. 'You *are* coming to Greece to hear us play, aren't you?'

'Of course I am,' Lizzie confirmed, her stomach clenching with alarm as she thought about it. 'I haven't missed a concert yet, have I?'

'Good.' Thea relaxed.

Lizzie's concerns about the Gavros family would have to be put to one side. She'd take *any* job to pay her way. Practical considerations—like where the money for her airfare would come from—were secondary to Lizzie's determination that she would do whatever it took to support Thea.

'Do you know whose birthday party it is?' she asked casually as they went up to the counter to pay the bill.

'Some old gentleman, I think,' Thea said vaguely, clearly not too interested.

It didn't *have* to be Damon's father. *Thea's grandfather.*

Lizzie's stomach clenched tight. Sucking in a breath, she jumped straight in. 'You know we never talk about your father—'

'Because we don't need to,' Thea cut across her, frowning. 'And I don't *want* to,' she added stubbornly. 'Why do I need a father when I've got you?'

'It might be nice to—'

'Ha!' Thea exclaimed dismissively. 'We don't even know where he is. He's probably on the other side of the planet.'

'What if I *did* know?'

'But you don't,' Thea insisted. 'And if you talked to my friends at school about parents at war you wouldn't be so keen to look for him either.'

'Not *all* marriages are like that.'

'Just most of them,' Thea said confidently. 'And we're happy, aren't we? Why would you want anything to change?'

'But what if things *did* change?' Lizzie tried gently.

'I'd change them back again.'

Thea sounded as confident as Lizzie had once been.

And now their precious time together was up, Lizzie realised. She had to go to work and Thea had to go to school.

'We'll talk again,' she promised.

'In Greece,' Thea reminded her.

'In Greece,' Lizzie confirmed as she raised her umbrella to shelter them both.

Organising his father's party was a welcome change from Damon's usual work. He was enjoying it far more than he'd expected to. The high spirits of the volunteers was heartening. Everyone wanted to do their bit for the man who had done so much for them. Damon's father was universally loved. He'd brought prosperity to the island, and now he'd retired and passed the baton on, Damon was determined to do the same for those who had remained loyal to his father.

They would do more events like this, he decided. Mixing with good people had reminded him that not everyone was a fraudster or a gold-digger.

As he'd learned during the course of his meteoric rise, massive wealth brought vultures flocking, and they came in all shapes and sizes. Which was the only reminder he needed that what he'd seen in Lizzie eleven years ago had been the possibility for something more. He looked forward to his plans where Lizzie was concerned coming to fruition. And Stavros had proved a staunch ally.

The setting for his father's concert couldn't be bettered, he concluded as he walked across the sugar sand beach. An open-air stage had been erected on the playing fields behind the school where the youth orchestra were staying. The orchestra was already here and rehearsing and, like everyone else within earshot, he'd been entranced by their music.

One particular young livewire, with black bubbly curls and mischievous eyes, had just played the most extraor-

dinary solo. She was the young violin prodigy everyone
was talking about. She wasn't self-conscious or inflated
by her success, as she might have been. She just loved her
music—as Thea had told him.

He smiled as he remembered her explaining, 'Thea's a
Greek name. I'm a bit Greek.'

He'd laughed. 'I'm a bit Greek too,' he'd told her.

'No. You're *all* Greek,' she'd argued, staring up at him
intently. 'I can tell that from the colour of your eyes.'

'Is that such a bad thing?'

'No. It's a very *good* thing,' she'd assured him. 'My
mother's half-Greek, and my grandmother was all-Greek.
I'm a bit Greek because I choose to be. You should meet
my mother,' she'd added, squinting against the sun as she
studied his face.

'Should I?' Another matchmaker, he'd thought, groaning inwardly.

But this matchmaker was different, he thought, remembering Thea's dramatically mournful expression as she'd
explained, 'My mother's young, and very beautiful, and
she's all alone.'

'Tragic,' he'd agreed, playing along. 'But I'm sure that
if she's anything like you she won't be alone for long.'

After which he'd thought he should extricate himself as
diplomatically as possible. Thea might have the makings
of a great matchmaker, but he wasn't looking for a match.

Stavros had saved Lizzie. His cousin had a beach restaurant on the island owned by the Gavros family, and
his cousin just happened to be desperate for more staff…
according to Stavros.

Another coincidence? Or not?

Lizzie had known she couldn't afford to be picky when
Stavros had adopted a dreamy expression as he'd described

the island of his birth, adding, 'You haven't heard from Damon, I suppose?'

'No,' Lizzie had admitted, thinking it better to break it to him that, sooner rather than later, that Cupid had failed. 'And I don't expect to.'

So here she was, standing outside Cousin Iannis's restaurant, on what looked and sounded like a party night. She was feeling optimistic. How could she not, when Thea had called to say she had settled in and everything was going really well, and she'd made a lot of new friends on the island?

It was hard not to fall in love with the island, Lizzie thought as she stared up at the star-peppered sky. It was warm even this late at night, and the candles glowing inside the restaurant gave everything such a welcoming glow. Traditional music was playing, and the scent of delicious food made her hungry.

Iannis had picked her up at the airport, and now he ushered her inside and directed her towards the kitchen.

'We're in training for the big birthday party next week,' he explained above the din of crashing plates and shouts of, *'Oopa!'*

Iannis was the double of his cousin Stavros, and Lizzie doubted either man needed an excuse to hold a party. They were both kindness personified. Stavros had insisted on paying for her flight, saying he owed her holiday money, and now there was this—the warmest of welcomes.

'No work tonight!' Iannis insisted as she glanced at the row of servers' aprons hanging on pegs in the lobby outside the kitchen. 'You've only just arrived, so tonight you're my guest at the party. Your apartment is just up those stairs by the entrance door—' he indicated where '—and your luggage is already on its way up to your room.'

'You're too kind.'

'No. *You're* too kind,' Iannis argued. 'Stavros has told me all about you—and he has insisted that I mustn't work you too hard. No buts,' he warned. 'Your time here is to be a holiday. It's all arranged.'

Flinging the door to the kitchen wide, he ushered Lizzie in to meet his staff.

She froze on the threshold. 'Damon?'

What was he doing here?

Leaning back against the wall, looking as hot as sin, Damon raised a brow and smiled faintly as she walked in.

'Are you stalking me?' she challenged lightly.

'Surely it's the other way around?' he countered in his low, husky drawl.

She was instantly tense, thinking of Thea just a few miles down the road.

'Lizzie?' Damon pressed.

He was instantly suspicious. 'Damon,' she replied coolly.

Lifting her chin, she met his stare steadily. Pulses of heat rushed through her. He was so unbelievably good-looking, and she needed thinking time. She should have known he would be on the island—after all, his family owned it—but somehow she'd just blanked the possibility from her mind.

'Is something distracting you?' he asked.

Oh, so much! 'The sight of such delicious food,' she lied.

He looked at her as if he didn't believe a word of it. 'It certainly is a distraction.'

'I didn't expect to see you,' she admitted.

He raised a brow, and his eyes burned with amusement as his gaze roved openly over the outline of her body beneath her jeans and simple top. She would have said something, but with Iannis looking on with interest she knew that wouldn't be wise. She hated to disappoint her matchmakers, and she wouldn't be rude in front of them, but neither Iannis nor Stavros knew her history with Damon. And nor would they, if *she* had anything to do with it.

'Damon has been working all day to make things special for my staff,' Iannis explained. 'We are catering the big birthday party next week.'

That was all she needed to know. Why else would Damon be here if it weren't for the fact that it was his father's birthday they were talking about?

'He wanted my people to have a night off,' Iannis was explaining proudly.

Lizzie quickly pulled herself together. 'That's very good of him,' she agreed.

'And as soon as you've settled in you must come down to the party,' Iannis insisted. 'That's right, isn't it, Damon?' he pressed.

'Most definitely,' Damon confirmed, with a look at Lizzie that sucked the breath clean out of her lungs.

'Eat—drink—dance—make love!' Iannis exclaimed helpfully, with a wide smile. 'That's all that's allowed tonight.'

So long as they weren't all compulsory, Lizzie thought, while Damon's wicked smile reached his eyes and stayed there.

'Oh, and there are some gifts waiting for you on the bed upstairs,' Iannis added.

'Gifts for *me*?' Lizzie glanced at Damon.

'They're nothing to do with me,' he said.

So gifts from whom? Lizzie wondered.

'I'll see you downstairs as soon as you've had chance to freshen up,' Damon called after her as she left the kitchen.

She turned at the door. 'I'm not sure I'll be coming down again.'

'Of course you will.'

He said this in a way that made her run up the stairs as if the hounds of hell were after her.

Closing the door on her apartment, she closed her eyes and sucked in a deep, steadying breath. Damon only had to look at her for lust to surge through her veins, and that was dangerous. She was a very different person now from the girl she'd been at eighteen. She had far more sense, Lizzie told herself firmly as she switched on the light and looked around.

The first thing she saw were the 'gifts' laid out on the bed. She knew immediately who they were from, and rushed across the room to pick the dresses up and hold them to her face. Then she reached for her phone.

'Sundresses for the old lady!' she said, laughing happily as Thea came on the line.

Thea giggled. 'Do you like them?'

'I love them—but you shouldn't be spending your money on me.'

'I bought them at the market on our first day here. As soon as I saw them I knew I had to buy them for you. I fell in love with the sunny yellow one right away, and the blue's so pretty.'

'I love them both,' Lizzie admitted. She would never have wasted her scant funds on buying anything so frivolous for herself.

'Do they fit?' Thea demanded.

'They're perfect.' Hugging the dresses close, she battled to contain her emotions.

'Be sure to wear one of them for the concert.'

'I will,' Lizzie promised. 'I'll see you tomorrow. I can't wait to hear you play.'

'Playing the violin isn't *everything*,' Thea informed Lizzie, stalling her thoughts in a way that had never happened before.

'What do you mean?' Lizzie asked, wondering if she'd said or done something to discourage Thea.

'Just that. Love's far more important than anything else,' Thea explained loftily. 'Love is all I care about now. I'm in a romantic phase.'

'I see…' Lizzie said faintly.

She didn't see at all. Instead she wondered if she'd ruined two people's lives now.

She had to stop this, Lizzie accepted. She was always feeling guilty about something, and she had done so since her father's trial. As soon as she had discovered how many innocent people he'd harmed, and thought about the many expensive gifts he'd bought for her over the years, she had been plagued with guilt until it had become part of her psyche.

'Gotta go,' Thea said, startling Lizzie back into the moment. 'I'll send you a text!'

'Bye, sweetheart…'

She was the luckiest woman on earth, Lizzie thought, smiling as she stared at the small screen filled with kisses. She was so lucky to have Thea in her life, and she would never take that joy for granted.

The joy in which Damon should be sharing?

CHAPTER FIVE

GUILT HAD SNUFFED out Lizzie's happiness. She hated deception above all things. It was too strong a reminder of her father's betrayal. But the rules still applied. She *had* to tell Thea before Damon. And she couldn't just blurt it out down the phone. Thea had to be warned first…prepared. It would have to be done with the utmost sensitivity, and it was hard to find enough time to do that with a child who was always rehearsing.

Clinging to practicalities—as she always did when she couldn't see her way ahead clearly—Lizzie explored her small apartment. It was such a luxury to have all this space after the confines of her tiny bedsit back in London. The walls were simply whitewashed, and the floor was polished wood. There was a small kitchen at one end, with a fridge thoughtfully stocked with essentials, and a balcony where she could eat breakfast overlooking the sea. The bed looked big and felt comfy, and it had a lovely sky-blue throw at the foot that matched the rug on the floor… All the colours of Greece.

So, had she finished procrastinating? Was she going to freshen up now and go downstairs to see Damon?

Of course she was. Soon…

She spotted a local bus timetable amongst some magazines. She'd need those times for when she went to the school tomorrow to hear Thea play…

Glancing at her watch, she knew she couldn't put it off any longer. So, heading to the bathroom, she stripped off and took a shower. Turning her face up to the refreshing spray, she hugged herself and thought of Damon… Damon holding her… Damon kissing her… Damon making love to her—

She had to forget about it!

Forget Damon making love to her when he was in the same building, downstairs?

And another thing—if she didn't tell him about Thea soon he'd find out for himself.

Thea first and then Damon.

It seemed a long time ago since she'd discovered she was pregnant with Thea, and now every second seemed to be flying past, Lizzie thought as she towelled down.

On an impulse, she chose to wear one of the sundresses Thea had bought. She smiled when she put it on and felt better immediately. There was a lot of truth behind Thea's statement. Love was all that mattered. Sometimes Lizzie wished she could see life as clearly as a child. One thing was certain. She had to right this wrong.

Putting it off over the years had a lot to do with the heartache she'd felt when her father had rejected her. Add to that her fear of losing Thea, and Lizzie would be the first to admit that she was just plain scared. She had always met problems head-on before, but the problems had never carried such a risk before.

Where *was* she? He shot another impatient look towards the stairs. His work was done. The second shift of people in his team had just arrived to take over the work in the kitchen. He was determined that Iannis and his staff would have a wonderful evening to thank them for all the work to come. He and his team had made sure of it. There was no reason for him to stick around.

No reason except Lizzie.

'Leaving so soon?'

His stare flashed up. Lizzie's comment had surprised him. She was calling to him from the top of the stairs.

He rested his fist on the wall. 'And if I am...?'

She shrugged. Her face was in shadow, so he couldn't see her expression. 'If you want to go—go. I won't hold you to your promise'

As she came slowly down the stairs her wildflower scent assaulted his senses. Her hair was still a little damp, and was hanging in tight curls, and her face was make-up-free. She was wearing a pretty sundress that exposed her pale, fragile skin and clung lovingly to the outline of her breasts. She had teamed this with simple sandals.

The punch to his senses was extraordinary. She eclipsed all the society beauties he'd dated put together. His body responded accordingly, and it took all his willpower to rein it in.

He'd wasted a lot of time dating women who made no demands on him and barely scratched the surface of his interest. Lizzie was different. She'd always been different. She was the one woman who intrigued him, who made him want to know more.

'Are we going to stand here in the passage?' she asked him as people squeezed past.

'After you,' he invited.

He watched her walk ahead of him, small and proud, pale and sexy, with her striking red hair bouncing freely around her shoulders like a shimmering cloak of fire. The desire to grab a hank of that hair in his fist, so he could kiss her neck and see if that tiny tattoo of a tiger cub was still there, was overwhelming.

His libido badly needed a break, he concluded as they joined the couples dancing between the tables.

The next moment she had turned to face him and her arms were wrapped around him.

'What?' he murmured, staring down.

'Are we going to dance, or are we just going to stand here?'

He'd forgotten nothing.

'I'm glad you didn't leave,' she admitted as he took her hand in his.

She held his stare levelly, as if she wanted to say something but couldn't quite put it into words. There was something driving her to be with him, to stay with him, but if it wasn't sex what could it be?

'I think we'd better dance,' he agreed. The urge to feel her pressed up against him was irresistible.

'If you're brave enough.' She laughed.

'I've never flinched from a pair of sandals in my life.'

She looked at him and almost smiled openly, frankly, as she had eleven years ago, but she looked away as they began to move. She didn't need to hold his stare for them both to know that the contact between them was electric.

They were just relaxing into the rhythm when a band of partygoers crashed into the restaurant from the beach, performing a no-holds-barred version of the Conga.

Letting go of him, Lizzie pressed back against the wall to let the line of whooping dancers through. They stared at each other when they could as the seemingly endless line of bodies passed between them. Lizzie shrugged as it went on and on. He smiled ruefully. The wait seemed interminable, but finally the last of the revellers went by and, reaching out, he linked their fingers.

No other woman came close to making him feel this way, he thought as he slowly drew her towards him, and when every part of them was touching as they danced he knew he'd missed her even more than he could say.

She only had to hold Damon's hand and feel his other hand settle in the small of her back for nuclear explosions to be set off inside her. How could she have forgotten how good it felt to be this close to him? If only life weren't so complicated, she thought as he greeted old friends with warmth and good humour.

She had to get real, Lizzie accepted. Life *was* that complicated. Damon was a billionaire. She was nothing and no one. She could either enjoy this interlude for what it was, or invite trouble back into her life.

It was all very well, coming up with these good reasons for remaining detached, but when Damon drew her close and his hands became seductive spells she started trembling with awareness. She hated herself for being so weak, but she couldn't do anything about it. He *had* to feel how she responded to him—he must.

He did, Lizzie realised as her pulse went off the scale. The dark humour in Damon's eyes was all the proof she needed.

And then the band slowed the tempo and the music grew seductive. The melody wrapped a cord around her heart and pulled it tight. Music could always strip her emotions bare. She might not be a musician, like her mother or like Thea, but she responded as they did, and the plangent tune was currently ripping chunks out of her heart.

As if he sensed this, Damon tightened his arms around her, and in spite of all her sensible reservations she went to him as willingly as a boat slipping into its mooring. Her body burned with heat as he linked their fingers, bringing them to rest on his chest where she could feel his heart beating.

This was as close as two people could be without making love. Her body was floating in an erotic net. She was made of sensation. Her worries dwindled as reality faded away. She had often daydreamed of being reunited with Damon, but this was so much better than her dreams.

If she closed her eyes the years melted away and she could think herself back into his bedroom, where whispers and touches had been magic spells and the smallest shift of Damon's fingers had delivered messages only she had been able to read. She wanted that back. She wanted to recapture the trust they'd shared for that one night. But would Damon ever trust her again when he learned about Thea? And could she blame him?

'Tense again?' he said. 'What's wrong now?'

When Damon stared into her eyes it was impossible to lie to him. 'You,' she said. 'It's time I went to bed. It's been a long day. Thanks for the dance.'

He caught hold of her hand. 'You can't leave it like that.'

'I just did. The mood is wrong. Too many people.'

'Sounds serious,' he said.

'It will keep.' *She hoped.* As her secret had been kept for eleven years, she had to believe it would keep a little longer.

She had already danced with Damon far longer than she'd had intended. But the band worked against her, segueing into another tune, allowing Damon to bring her close again.

Allowing? How hard did she fight him?

How could someone so much bigger than she was hold her close and prove they fitted together perfectly? Just for a few moments she allowed herself to close her eyes and rest her cheek against his chest. It felt so good. His thigh brushed against her intimately—*by accident*, she told herself firmly. She was so on edge she was ready to believe anything.

He'd been tender and gentle on that night, as well as hot as hell and sexy, and sometimes she longed for that tenderness and intimacy of thought as much as the sexual act. She wanted that too, of course. She was a normal, healthy woman, and it was impossible to be this close to Damon without thinking about sex.

That night had drawn them closer than either might have expected. He'd confided his hopes for the future, his love for his family, and his desire one day to have a family of his own. She'd told him about the holidays she remembered having as a child, when her mother had been alive. Summers had seemed to last for ever then, and Lizzie's life had been full of warmth and a love she'd thought would go on for ever.

And then had come the hollow black part. She hadn't burdened him with that. And then the greatest gift of all—Thea. Motherhood. Responsibility. Love. She'd embraced all three with gratitude, but if life had taught her one thing it was never to take anything for granted.

'If I didn't know you better I'd say you had a guilty conscience,' Damon commented when she shifted restlessly in his arms.

'No guilt,' she said.

'Not even a tiny bit?"

She chose not to answer that. Of *course* there was guilt. There was more than one parent in Thea's life. How much *more* guilty could she feel?

Damon had often wondered if that first scorching spark between them would stand the test of time, and here was his answer. Sensation ruled him when Lizzie was in his arms. No other woman could come close to making him feel the way she did. His body was a raging conflagration of lust.

But what he liked best about her was her honesty. When other women would tell him what they thought he wanted to hear, Lizzie told him the truth, uncaring of the consequences. The temptation to kiss her—to kiss every part of her—was overwhelming, but once he started he wouldn't stop, and this was neither the right place nor the right time.

'Maybe you *should* go to bed now,' he agreed. Releasing her, he stood back. 'Alone,' he murmured when she stared up at him.

How had she allowed things to go this far? Lizzie wondered. At this moment in time she would have followed Damon to Hades and back. The thought of parting from him and going upstairs to bed held no appeal at all, yet just a few minutes ago she had known it was the only sensible thing to do.

Iannis intervened, moving between them and insisting on shepherding them to his table.

'The night isn't over yet,' he declared. 'Eat! Drink! I have reserved two places at my table—'

How could they let him down?

'Stavros would never forgive me if I allowed his favourite couple to miss out on the best part of the party—my food,' Iannis explained proudly.

Lizzie thought Damon very restrained in not mentioning that it was *his* people who'd cooked tonight. More importantly, they weren't a couple, as both Stavros and Iannis seemed to think. There was only Damon Gavros, billionaire, and Lizzie Montgomery, single mother with a child to protect.

* * *

'And now we dance the *kalamatianos*!' Iannis announced when the most delicious feast had been consumed.

He made a signal and a chord rang out. All his guests wanted to join in the famous national dance, and there was a group exodus from the tables.

'As my honoured guest, you shall have the honour of leading the dance,' he told Lizzie, handing her the traditional white handkerchief to hold aloft.

Her mother had taught her the steps of the dance when Lizzie was a child. They had often danced it together, with her mother humming the tune and Lizzie waving a little handkerchief over her head.

'If you'd rather not...?' Damon murmured.

'Try and stop me,' Lizzie said, standing up.

The distinctive twang of the bouzouki was like a rallying call. The rhythm, starting slowly and building up, made each Greek heart swell with longing. Waving the white handkerchief, Lizzie was the Pied Piper, drawing her flock to the area in front of the restaurant where the beach met the land beyond.

'I'd kick off your sandals,' Damon advised.

He was doing the same, she noticed. How ridiculous to find his feet sexy. She had to stop this *now*. One more dance and then she was definitely going to bed.

It was as if a lightning bolt zapped through her when Damon seized one end of the white handkerchief, effectively joining them by a shred of cloth. Lizzie tightened her grip as Damon's heat seemed to invade the fabric, scorching her fingers, travelling on from there to her heart—

Really?

She was tired. Her mind was inventing things. They were dancing and that was all. But it wasn't just dancing, and it wasn't just music, it was memories wrapped up in a tune: a little girl dancing with her mother, holding her hand and believing that life would stay the same for ever.

'Lizzie…?' Damon murmured with concern.

Her eyes had filled with tears, she realised, dashing them away. 'Why do you have to notice *everything*?' she demanded impatiently.

The music suddenly picked up pace, forcing all the dancers to watch their feet rather than chat to their companions. Arms stretched out and resting on each other's shoulders, their cries of *'Oopa!'* grew louder, and as the dancing grew wilder several couples collapsed on the ground, laughing. But the band didn't stop.

Soon it was Lizzie's turn to grow dizzy, but as she stumbled Damon's lightning reflexes saved her. 'I'm going to show you the island tomorrow,' he said as he steadied her on her feet.

She glanced at him in surprise. 'You can spare the time?'

He'd never looked more dangerous, she thought, and he was waiting. Decisions had to be made. Common sense told her to stay away from him, but getting to know him all over again took precedence.

'I'd have to ask Iannis.'

'*Would* you?' he flashed.

They both knew Iannis was only too keen to keep his part of the bargain with his cousin, and give Lizzie as much free time as possible.

'Maybe a couple of hours?' she said.

'Good. That's settled.'

'But I'd have to be back by two,' she said, remembering Thea's concert in the afternoon.

'That's no problem for me,' Damon assured her.

'Then, thank you. What time in the morning?'

'Eight. And bring a picnic.'

'Don't you have flunkies to do that for you?'

'They're away with my butler at the moment.'

Damon smiled, a flash of strong white teeth against his swarthy skin. She couldn't match it. Things were moving too fast.

She tried telling herself that if he could be as relaxed as this when he learned about Thea things would be okay, but she knew it wouldn't be that simple.

CHAPTER SIX

SHE HAD TRIED to get hold of Thea the next day, before she set off with Damon, but Thea had been having breakfast before an early rehearsal for the afternoon concert. And now Lizzie was out of touch, clinging to a handrail on board Damon's powerboat as they crashed through breakers as high as houses on the open sea.

He was full of surprises. The value of his air, sea, and land craft alone would fund a small country, with change to spare. He was standing at the helm, controlling the massive craft with one hand, as casually if its immense power was just another extension of his magic.

He looked more like a marauding brigand than a respectable billionaire, with his swarthy skin and unshaven face, she thought, taking in the ripped and faded shorts, his bare feet and faded top.

'Have you never been on a powerboat before?' he asked as she lurched towards him.

'The closest I've come to this is the cross-Channel ferry.'

'Then it's time to widen your horizons.'

She murmured in reply. She'd tried that once before, and now she preferred to limit her horizons to Thea.

'So, where are we going?' she asked. 'No—don't turn to look at me!' she yelped as Damon swung round. 'Shouldn't you be concentrating on where you're going?'

He laughed. 'I know *exactly* where I'm going.'

Yes. That was what she was afraid of, and she only wished she felt half so confident as Damon looked.

Having rebuilt her life, Lizzie controlled it within certain boundaries, but those boundaries seemed to be disappearing fast. Telling Thea about Damon and then explaining to Damon that he had a daughter had seemed so straightforward in the planning, but time was rushing past and she seemed no further on.

'Is this our destination?' she asked as he slowed the powerboat. It was beautiful. She stared around with interest at the picturesque bay.

'It's called Cove Krýstallo,' Damon explained. 'Or Crystal Cove. This area has always been a favourite of mine on the island, and now I've built a house here.'

And not just a house but the most magnificent dwelling Lizzie had ever seen, she thought as he eased back on the throttle. The mansion was built of blush-pink stone. Low built, to blend in with its surroundings, it was elegant and vast. It could be called a beach house, she supposed, because of its seafront position, but it was a beach house fit for a billionaire.

She was so far out of the customary modest rut that she shared with Thea, it was becoming ridiculous.

'We'll be back for two. I haven't forgotten,' Damon said as she frowned and shook her head with incredulity.

'Thanks.' She supposed she should be grateful that he couldn't read her mind.

As he turned away to lower the anchor she took stock. Apart from her anxiety at being introduced to yet another example of Damon's incredible wealth, the consequences of being alone with him in this secluded bay were finally coming home to her. It didn't help when a rogue wave crashed against the hull and she lost her balance, cannoning into him. As he steadied her his touch woke memories better forgotten.

She pulled away self-consciously and was glad when he made a joke of it.

'Lost your sea legs?' he suggested, staring at her with amusement.

'I don't think I ever had any.'

She could still feel his touch, where his hand had lingered on her shoulder, and feel the heat created when he had stared into her eyes.

There was no point in aching for something she could never have back, Lizzie told herself firmly. And why would she *want* it back? The last time she'd had sex with Damon he'd enjoyed it, and then had cut loose and disappeared. Only Thea had made that night more than worthwhile.

Thea had made Lizzie's life incalculably richer, while Damon had played no part in her life aside from that one night. And she wasn't eighteen now, twisting her mother's dying wish for Lizzie to have a better and more adventurous life into an excuse to have sex with Damon here in his private cove.

'Race you to shore?' he suggested, straightening up after checking the anchor was safely attached to the seabed.

'Do you need a head start?' she suggested, straight-faced. It wasn't too far to shore, and she was confident of her abilities in the water.

He laughed, and the ache of longing inside her increased.

'I'll give you a ten-minute head start,' he offered, with the same deadpan expression.

'You'll be sorry,' she warned with a laugh.

She was wearing a bikini beneath her shorts and top, and quickly stripped off.

Damon's look scorched over her. Ignoring how that made her feel, she climbed onto the rail, telling herself that if ever there had been a need for the refreshing shock of chilly water, this was it.

She caught a glimpse of Damon's half-smile as he watched her dive in. She also saw the power in his thighs and in his shoulders and back, and the taut outline of his buttocks beneath his faded denim shorts.

The next thing she knew she was shrieking with excitement as she surfaced. The all-embracing chill of the ocean after the balmy warmth on deck was just the reboot she needed. Kicking off strongly, she headed for the shore, with no thought in her head other than to get there before him.

She trod water to look back, only to see him closing in fast. She set off again, with the excitement of the chase driving her now. She was a strong swimmer, and competitive, but even with the waterproof pack containing their picnic to hamper him Damon was slicing through the water like an arrow. He soon passed her, and only slowed when he'd reached the shallows, where he stood and turned to watch her power in.

'Not bad,' he commented. 'But I'll carry you the rest of the way.'

'You will *not*,' she protested and, finding her feet, stood up.

She shrieked in complaint as Damon ignored her and swung her into his arms.

'Put me down,' she said, pummelling him as she struggled to break free. It was like beating her fists against rock.

'If I put you down you'll cut your feet on the shells,' he said.

'And you've got hooves?' she shot back.

He laughed.

She'd forgotten how strong he was. Fighting him only

brought her into more intimate contact with him. But still she couldn't give up. 'I'm not a baby, Damon. Put me down—'

'And I'm not a nursemaid to waste my time bandaging your feet.'

Thwarted, she went as stiff as a board and tried her best not to relax against him. It wasn't so easy to forget the last time Damon had carried her like this—which had been out of his shower and back to bed on the morning of her father's trial. They'd made love again, and then he'd told her he had an appointment to keep.

She'd thought nothing of it at the time...until she'd seen him in the courtroom. If she'd learned one thing from that experience, it was that Damon could be ruthless.

He put her down on the cool, damp, close-knit moss above the shoreline. Dropping the waterproof pack on the ground, he helped her to set out their picnic.

When that was done, she sat back and leaned on her elbows with her face turned to the sky.

'Penny for them?' he asked as she sighed.

'I was just thinking that it's very beautiful here,' she said, inhaling deeply as a cover for the fact that her thoughts, having travelled back to that night and that morning, and all the mixed emotions that had filled her eleven years ago, were refusing to settle down again.

'It *is* very beautiful,' he agreed, coming to sit at her side. 'Lucky for you Iannis could put you up,' he commented. 'What made you think of coming to this island in the first place?'

Lizzie's eyes flashed open. She was instantly on high alert. 'Stavros suggested it,' she said quickly. 'I'm very lucky to have such good friends.'

'You are,' he agreed. 'And it appears that fate is determined to throw us together.'

She huffed out a short laugh as Damon glanced at her. She couldn't read his expression, but she knew enough to be wary. 'Bad luck for both of us, I guess.'

'If you say so,' he murmured. Knocking the top off a bottle of beer, he brought it to his lips. 'Whatever made you come here, you should take the chance to relax while you can. What have you got to lose?'

Everything, Lizzie thought as Damon drank deep.

Putting the beer down, he rested his chin on his knee and studied her face. 'I'm glad you got rid of the lip ring.'

She touched her lip, feeling faintly affronted. 'That was a long time ago.'

'You've changed a lot,' he agreed.

'Eleven years.' She shrugged. 'What did you expect?'

Damon's lips pressed down, but he didn't answer.

'Why didn't you like my lip ring?' she asked, frowning.

'Because it got in the way when I kissed you.'

'That isn't…' Heat ripped through her when Damon leaned in.

'Isn't what?' he said. 'Fair?'

'Sensible,' she said as he curved her a smile.

'Sensible?' he mocked, sitting back. 'Is that what you are now?'

'No one stays eighteen for ever, Damon.'

'No,' he agreed. 'But whatever age you are you can still live and feel and dare.'

'Oh, I *dare*,' Lizzie assured him, angling her chin to stare him in the eyes. 'I just don't want to be hurt again.'

'Hurt?' He frowned. 'Do you expect me to hurt you?'

'I just know I won't give you the chance.'

'It was *you* who stormed off,' he pointed out.

She couldn't deny it. She had, Lizzie remembered.

'Are you going storm off now?' he asked.

'As I said, I'm not eighteen.'

'No. You're much improved.'

The smile behind his eyes had just become dangerous. Being this close to him was dangerous enough, without that hard mouth teasing her with a faint smile. Her sensible mind said, *Leave now, move away, make him take you back to the restaurant.* But it was hard to be sensible when she wanted him so much.

She'd only have to move by the smallest degree for their lips to touch, and for Damon's arms to close around her.

And then she did, and they did, and she was lost.

She was back.

The rush of triumph inside him was like nothing he'd ever known—not for eleven years, at least. She was everything he remembered and more, and she came to him as if their years apart had disappeared. She pressed against him, responding fiercely as he kissed her. She was strong and sure, and every bit his match.

Their tongues tangled as she clung to him, and when he eased her legs apart with his thigh she arced her body against his in the hunt for more contact. Cupping her buttocks with one hand, he unlaced the strings of her bikini with the other as they traded kisses hungrily.

Glancing down nearly wrecked his control. He was painfully and hugely erect, while Lizzie was as sensitive as he remembered. He only had to stroke her lightly to hear her purr. He parted her lips and found the tiny bud. He teased and then pulled away, then teased some more as she clung to him, gasping out her pleasure.

'Beneath me now,' he instructed softly.

There was no need to ask. Lizzie was way ahead of him.

'Slowly,' he advised as she bucked towards him.

'Why?' Her eyes challenged him.

'Because it's been a long time.'

She raised an amused brow. 'Like I don't remember?'

Neither of them could forget, it seemed. The memory of taking her, of sinking deep into Lizzie's tight, moist heat, was seared on his brain for all time. Maximum control was essential as he prepared to rediscover the woman he had enjoyed like no other.

He stroked and kissed and took his time. Lizzie was all hunger and need, and he had to slow her down. Teasing her, he cupped her between the legs, denying her the contact she wanted.

He smiled as he watched her eyes darken. 'I've got you now,' he whispered.

'You think?' she whispered back.

'Shall we put it to the test?' he suggested, still teasing her with kisses.

'This is your island, and this is your beach, so I guess you can do anything you like,' she said, seeming pleased at this idea.

'Do you want me to?'

'What do you *think* I want you to do?'

He smiled as she moved restlessly beneath him.

Hearing foil rip, she lifted her hips, and she was so aroused that at his first intimate touch she was reaching greedily for release.

This was the Lizzie he remembered from eleven years ago. This was the woman with whom he'd made love on every surface in his apartment—including pressed up against the floor-to-ceiling windows, where anyone who'd wanted to could have seen.

'You're right,' he agreed. 'We—*you*,' he amended as he pinned her wrists above her head '—can do anything you want to do while you're here.'

'Including to you?' she said. 'Can I use you for my pleasure?'

'I don't see why not.' He grinned. 'But that would be for *my* pleasure too.' Pressing her knees back, he moved between them. 'Hold them for me.'

'Like this? So I'm exposed…?'

She sounded so excited.

He told her yes.

She did as he asked, and now her brown eyes were almost black, with just a rim of sepia around her pupils. She was right on the edge.

'Don't tease me,' she warned.

'Pleasure delayed is pleasure intensified,' he taunted softly.

'None of that rubbish now,' she warned him.

Taking hold of his arms, she arranged herself to her liking and shuddered out a soft cry when he gave her just the tip.

'What?' he murmured, sinking deeper.

'You…this…'

He rocked his hips forward and gave her a little more. He pulled out completely before sinking even deeper into her tight, warm grip. The pleasure was intense. It took everything he'd got to hold back so she could get used to the invasion. She was throbbing around him, insistently drawing him on. He only had to move the smallest fraction for her to wail and let go.

Helpless in the grip of violent release, she bucked frantically back and forth, while he held her in place, making sure that she benefited from every last pulse of pleasure.

'Worth the wait?' he murmured when she quietened.

She was still groaning rhythmically against his mouth as the pleasure pulses, having faded, continued. He started to move again and she immediately responded, moving with him, needing more.

Making love to Lizzie was instantly familiar all over

again. He knew exactly what she needed, and it gave him the greatest pleasure to give it to her. The only change he noted was that her appetite had grown.

It was a long time later when he hauled her to her feet and they ran to cool down in the sea. He swung her into his arms both times, to avoid the shells, and when he carried her back to shore and they dressed she reminded him that they had to get back.

'An appointment?' he confirmed. 'I remember. Sadly no time for the house today.'

'Another time?' she said.

'Why not?' he agreed.

As they linked fingers to walk along the sand, to a soundtrack of rolling surf and seabirds calling, he wondered if he'd ever felt closer to anyone. Trust was a great thing, and he was glad he'd got Lizzie's back.

He was proud of her—not for that reason, but for the way she'd fought back after the trial. She'd barely spoken of it, but he knew she must have had a rough time. The spirit he remembered so well from eleven years back must have carried her through, and it was no wonder that Iannis and Stavros liked her so much, and Stavros had wanted her to come to the island.

Rediscovering her Greek heritage would be good for Lizzie. There was nothing like a return to the homeland for restoring confidence and faith in the future.

'Your new house is very beautiful,' she said, glancing over her shoulder. You must be very proud of it?'

'I am,' he admitted, 'especially as I had the pleasure of helping to build it.'

'That must have been great,' she agreed.

He was pleased that she understood the pleasure he'd found in working with his hands. 'It was,' he confirmed.

He glanced back too. Looking at his new place through

Lizzie's eyes gave him the same thrill that he'd felt when he'd first sat back to study his design on paper. He'd planned for the house to be in complete harmony with its surroundings, and he believed he'd succeeded.

'It's fabulous,' Lizzie confirmed as they both paused to admire it.

'I did have some help,' he admitted dryly. But he felt the pleasure that only a man who'd selected each piece of stone from the quarry could feel. 'Without the craftsmen I employed it would never have been built. I worked as their lowly assistant.'

'That must have been a bit different for you,' she said, 'but from the look on your face I guess you enjoyed it?'

'More than you know,' he agreed.

'Well, it was well worth the effort. You've created something really beautiful.'

'*You're* beautiful,' he said, swinging her into his arms. 'And one day I will bring you back here.'

Would he? Lizzie wondered. Would Damon want her within a hundred miles of him when he found out the truth about Thea?

'Beautiful' didn't begin to describe his new home. It was a dream home. It was the type of home Lizzie wished she could give to Thea.

And Thea's father owned it.

Her mouth dried when she compared Damon's glorious beachside mansion to the one room she shared with Thea in London when Thea was home from school. How could she deny Thea this incredible lifestyle? Thea could have half a dozen music studios and no one would ever complain about the noise.

'You could paint here,' Damon said.

She swung around to stare at him in confusion for a

moment. Her head was so full of Thea, as it always was, that she couldn't switch track to herself.

'You used to love painting,' Damon prompted. 'I remember you telling me.'

'I did,' she agreed. Incredibly, on that night eleven years ago, they had grown close enough to discuss lots of things, including pastimes and hopes and dreams. 'You told me that work was *your* hobby,' she remembered.

'Correct,' Damon confirmed. 'And it still is.'

'I didn't have a clue what you meant by saying that back then,' she admitted. 'I'd only just left school and had no idea that the world could be so tough.'

And the rest, she thought.

And now you do? Damon's look said.

She didn't deserve the compassion in his eyes. Damon had been forced to become even more work-obsessed after the trial, thanks to the damage done to his family's business by her father. Damon had righted all those wrongs, but maybe life would have turned out differently for him if there'd been no fraud, no trial, and they had never met.

CHAPTER SEVEN

DAMON SEEMED DETERMINED to reassure her. 'It's good to have you back,' he commented as they walked on.

And good to have *you* back, Lizzie thought, though she knew better than to expect it to be for ever.

She lowered her gaze so Damon wouldn't be able to see how she felt about him.

'I was worried I'd lost you again,' he admitted. 'I'd keep seeing flashes of the old Lizzie, but then she'd slip away.'

There was a good reason for that, Lizzie thought, hanging back. 'You can't recapture time, or make it stand still, Damon.'

'But I can care that you were hurt,' he argued firmly. 'And I can care that I was partly responsible for causing that hurt. I can care that your father abandoned you, and your stepmother kicked you in the teeth when you had no one left to defend you—'

'I didn't need anyone to defend me. I was fine on my own—better, probably. I think we look at success differently, and I'm actually *pleased* with the way things have turned out.'

'How *can* you be?' he said frowning.

Thea was always front and foremost in her mind, and that left her nothing to complain about. 'When I once had such big dreams, do you mean? I see things differently now. I don't owe any money. I've got a roof over my head and enough food to eat.' And, more importantly, a daughter she adored, and Thea didn't go without anything if Lizzie could help it. 'You don't need to feel sorry for me,' she said with absolute certainty.

'I don't feel sorry for you. I *admire* you,' Damon insisted.

'Well, that sounds a little bit patronising.'

He seemed surprised. 'I apologise if you think that, because it's the last thing I intended. I *do* admire you, and I think it's great that you—'

'Survived?' she supplied edgily.

'I think you've done more than that, haven't you?' he argued. 'I was going to say that you've got great friends, and a life you enjoy, so nothing else should matter.'

'I'm glad you see it that way.' She was determined to move on to safer ground—which meant switching the spotlight to Damon. 'And *you've* done very well for yourself too,' she said dryly. 'Understatement,' she added with a grin.

His lips pressed down as he shrugged. 'I had a strong family behind me all the way. And I took over an existing business with an excellent reputation.'

That Lizzie's father had almost destroyed.

'Stop,' he warned, reading her. 'No one, least of all me, blames you for your father's crimes. The only thing that *does* puzzle me,' he admitted, 'is that you always had what it took to get ahead, but for some reason it hasn't worked out for you as well as I expected. Obviously I'm curious to know why.'

She brushed his remark aside with a casual gesture, though everything inside her had tightened in a knot. 'I wouldn't waste your time investigating me.'

He huffed a laugh, but she didn't kid herself that this

was over. Damon's interest in her life over the past eleven years had been well and truly stirred, and he wouldn't let go now. Nothing would satisfy him but a full explanation.

'In case you hadn't noticed,' he said in excuse, 'you interest me. No one had ever taken me on as you did outside that courtroom. You were only just eighteen and, apart from your fair-weather friends, you were on your own. I was older, surrounded by family and a legal team, but *nothing* stopped you. There's nothing wrong with asserting your rights and showing loyalty to your family—that's something I really get. You were right to stand your ground—and right to rage at me. I *was* a bastard.'

'You admit it?' Amusement cut through her anxiety for a few moments. 'Maybe there's hope for you yet.'

She should have known that Damon would take advantage of this lighter mood. He jumped straight on it.

'So, are you going to tell me what happened to the promises you made to yourself about developing your painting and your cooking, and all those other dreams?'

'What is it they say about promises?' she countered. 'Aren't they like pie crusts, made to be broken?'

Damon's gaze sharpened on her face. 'If there's one thing I won't believe it's that you gave up your dreams easily. There must be something big you're not telling me.'

'There is,' she agreed. 'It's called life.'

He looked at her sceptically.

'Life moves on, Damon, and we have to move with it.'

Eleven years of fighting, with her only goal being to make a good life for Thea. Her goal remained the same today, and it didn't allow for dreams.

'That's enough,' he declared, swinging her into his arms. 'I won't send you back with a frown on your face.

She laughed. It was such a relief to escape the dangerous topic.

Damon carried her across the shells to the sea so they could swim back to the boat. She exhaled raggedly when he set her down at the water's edge and his hands skimmed her breasts. She stared into his eyes, wondering if it was wrong to feel this happy, and if she'd be made to pay. If happiness was an indulgence she didn't deserve she was going to be in debt for the rest of her life, because she was drowning in the stuff.

She sucked in a breath as Damon's hands touched her breasts. 'Your breasts are fuller than I remember. And your nipples are a deeper, rosier pink—'

Pregnancy, she thought, immediately tensing. She was right not to count on happiness lasting. It hadn't even made it back to the boat.

'I'm older,' she dismissed with a shrug.

He huffed a laugh. '*So* old,' he agreed dryly, adding, 'You never could take a compliment, could you, Lizzie?'

As Damon stared into her eyes, as if searching for the truth he knew she was hiding, she grew increasingly anxious. 'What time is it?' she asked, worrying about Thea, worrying about Damon, worrying about everything...

'Time enough,' he soothed, running his fingertips down her cheek to her lips. 'We'll be back before two. We can see the house another time. I blame you for being so irresistible.'

As he took Lizzie's face between his hands he felt her tremble. His fingers ploughed into her hair, his thumbs caressed her jawbone just below her ears, but she couldn't be soothed and when he kissed her he felt tears on her face.

He blamed himself. He'd been so busy driving forward after the trial, trying to make everything right again for his father, that he hadn't spared a thought for Lizzie, and now he could only imagine what she'd been through.

'I'm sorry,' he whispered as her shoulders shook beneath his hands. 'This is my fault. The way I treated you was—'

'No. Please don't say that,' she argued fiercely. 'You're a *good* man, Damon. If your father hadn't spoken up mine would have destroyed even more people. I didn't want to see his faults then, but I can see them now.'

'We should get back,' he murmured.

'Yes,' she said, staring into his eyes.

Damon's kisses were drugging reminders of a time she would never forget. His body pressed against hers was a reminder her of how safe she felt in his arms. Fate was cruel—acting as if they were meant to be together, meant to have had Thea, meant to meet again in Stavros's restaurant and here on the island. Fate was taunting them, she suspected.

Damon pulled away first and glanced out to sea at the powerboat in a silent signal that their idyll was over. They both had to return to their lives and to reality, and to all the problems that lay ahead of them.

Lifting her chin, she said, 'I'm ready if you are.'

The first thing she did when they were back on the powerboat was check the clock, to make sure she would be in good time to catch the local bus to Thea's concert. She felt embarrassed when Damon caught her looking, and wondered if he thought she was trying to hurry the time away.

'Thank you,' she said softly.

He made a sound of acknowledgement, but there was plenty to do as he prepared the powerboat for leaving, and no more time for conversation. Not that there was anything left to say—not before she'd spoken to Thea.

He was frustrated by Lizzie's reluctance to admit that there was something troubling her. She trusted him enough to have sex with him, but not enough to allow him to help her. What could be *that* bad?

After eleven years he would have been more surprised if they *didn't* have things to tell each other, but if it was another man, and that was why she couldn't say anything, then she was no better than her father. He refused to believe that of her.

He should have asked her straight out—would have done if they had devoted more time to talking and less time to sex. He might expect the Greek community to close around her, but why hadn't Stavros said something? Why hadn't Iannis? Didn't *they* trust him either?

He respected their silence—he was forced to admit that. He just hated being in the dark, and apart from hearing third-hand while he was in the desert that Lizzie's father had died in prison, and that her stepmother was living with another man, he knew next to nothing about those eleven years where Lizzie was concerned.

They had an uneventful journey back to the other side of the island. They disembarked, exchanged the usual pleasantries, and then he drove her to the door of the restaurant. But everything had changed; she was tense now.

'Thank you,' she exclaimed with relief. 'You said you had somewhere to be too? I hope I haven't made you late?'

He shrugged. 'A visit to my parents' home to discuss the last-minute arrangements for my father's party can be delayed as long as it needs to be.'

She glanced at him with concern. 'You're sure?'

'Don't be late. Go,' he insisted.

'I can't thank you enough,' she said, turning to give him one last rabbit-in-the-headlights smile.

He ground his jaw at the knowledge that whatever had brought bold and feisty Lizzie back to him it had now, for reasons unknown, taken her away again.

He kept the engine purring in neutral long enough to see her disappear inside the restaurant, and then his phone rang just as he was about to drive away.

'No problem,' he told his father, who had asked if Damon would mind delaying their meeting.

'You can go and listen to the orchestra instead of me, and give me a report,' his father suggested.

'I'd love to,' he said dryly.

Maybe music could 'soothe a savage breast', he reflected, thinking about Lizzie and the secret she found so hard to share with him.

CHAPTER EIGHT

IANNIS HAD PROMISED Lizzie that she could set her watch by the local bus. And so it proved to be. She got off the bus outside the school grounds where Thea was due to play that afternoon with ample time to spare.

She took a moment to smooth her lovely yellow dress and her hair. Her old lady dress, Lizzie thought, smiling as she remembered what Thea had said. It was a beautiful dress, made all the more lovely by the thought behind it. It had been a long time since Lizzie had worn anything but jeans and a top, or a server's uniform, and she wanted Thea to know how much the gift of a dress meant to her.

The school was set in a picturesque valley between lush, vine-covered hills. It thrilled Lizzie to think that Thea's talent had brought her to such a beautiful place. Set like a jewel in an aquamarine sea, the island boasted shady olive groves and sparkling rivers and, though it was hot today, there was a covered awning to keep both audience and performers cool.

Nothing had been overlooked. Refreshments had been set out on trestle tables, and it promised to be a wonderful afternoon. Excitement gripped Lizzie as she anticipated another performance. This one was more of a rehearsal, and that, together with knowing that Damon was visiting his parents allowed her to relax and enjoy the fact that Thea

Floros—as Thea was known now, having taken Lizzie's mother's name—would be the star soloist today.

Lizzie glowed with pride as she joined the line of parents waiting to take their seats. When at last the gates to the school opened and everyone filed in Lizzie only wished she were taller, so she could be the first to catch sight of Thea. For now she had to be content with shuffling along at a snail's pace, walled in by a platoon of parents, but then people finally started sitting down and she could see the children.

'Eísai entáxei. Megáli chaméni efkairía?'

'Are you all right?' someone translated for Lizzie as she swayed.

She caught hold of a nearby chair for support.

'It must be the heat,' she excused. 'I don't see this much sun in London, but thank you for your concern.'

The kindness of strangers couldn't help her now. How could Thea be talking to *Damon*? He wasn't supposed to be here. He was supposed to be visiting his parents. And Thea wasn't just *chatting* to him, as a child might talk politely to a stranger who had expressed an interest in her music, she was laughing with him as if they were old friends.

Two dark heads with the same thick, wavy black hair. Two sets of laughing brown eyes. Two tanned faces with features so similar, so strong, and both so beautiful.

Thea had said something that had made Damon shove his hands into the back pockets of his jeans, throw his head back and laugh. Lizzie felt the chill of exclusion. What could they be saying to each other? How much did Damon know?

Worse! How much did *Thea* know?

She had never seen Damon looking so relaxed, or Thea so happy. Theirs was such an unexpected rapport it frightened her. It had always been just the two of them before.

Thea and Lizzie… Lizzie and Thea. But now the likeness between father and daughter was startling.

Seeing them together for the first time was the most unnerving experience of Lizzie's life. It wasn't just that Damon's full-blooded Greek genes had prevailed over Lizzie's part-Greek, part-Celtic mix, but the fact was that anyone could see that Damon and Thea were father and daughter. Could Damon see it too? Could Thea?

She stood motionless, watching, numb with shock. It was too late to do anything properly now. The moment had come and gone, and watching Thea and Damon together stirred new fears. How quickly Lizzie's father had lost interest in her, once his life had changed. She'd been determined to protect Thea from that. But now she wondered if she'd been over-protective. Had she got everything wrong?

Both Damon and Thea had cause to hate her. And she'd done that all on her own. Damon's first thought would be to protect Thea. Could she blame him for that? How could she, when Lizzie had kept Thea from her father? Would Thea be angry? Would Thea reject Lizzie in favour of the man who could give her so much more? And would it be right for Lizzie to stand in Thea's way if that was what Thea wanted?

She had to remain calm, Lizzie concluded. She could not go to pieces now. She'd been strong for eleven years, and if ever there was a time to be strong it was now. She couldn't move at the moment anyway. There were people blocking her way. All she could do was stand and watch Thea and Damon, wondering if she could have done something differently or better.

Shame. That was what she felt most. She should have found a way to tell them both the truth long before now.

And then, as if Lizzie and Thea were joined by some magical cord, Thea looked up and saw her.

Calling out, 'Mama! Mama!' at the top of her voice, she came running full pelt towards Lizzie.

'Mama!' Thea gasped when she reached Lizzie's side. 'You *must* come and meet my new friend, Damon Gavros! Okay—you stay there,' she said when Lizzie remained unresponsive. 'Save him a seat and I'll make sure he sits next to you. I've lined him up for a date with you later. I told him how beautiful you are—'

Racing away again, Thea retraced her steps and rejoined her friends in the orchestra.

Could a heart break and shatter into pieces? When Lizzie saw Damon's face she felt sure it could.

'Come with me,' Damon said when he reached her side.

He spoke quietly, but in a tone so hostile that everyone around them turned to stare.

'I can't—the concert's about to begin.' Lizzie glanced at the stage where Thea was sitting.

Thea was her anchor. She couldn't move.

'You can and you *will* come with me,' Damon assured her. 'The children don't play their pieces until after the speeches of welcome, and what I have to say to you won't take long.'

She couldn't make a scene—not here, of all places. Thea was sneaking glances at Lizzie to see how her matchmaking was working out. The last thing Lizzie wanted was to give Thea anything to worry about just before her concert began.

'Okay,' she agreed.

Smiling and waving at Thea, she indicated how long she'd be with five fingers held up.

Thea's smile was so broad and her eyes were so bright with hope that Lizzie knew she'd never felt so ashamed in her life as she walked away with Damon. There was disappointing your child, and then there was completely betraying her.

Damon ushered her ahead of him inside the school, where they would have some privacy. It was cool after the heat of the sun, and deserted. Their footsteps echoed on the tiled floor as he led the way into a classroom.

Closing the door, he leaned back against it, trapping them inside the empty room. 'When were you going to tell me?'

When Thea knew, of course.

She raised her chin to confront a man she barely recognised. Damon had pitched his voice low, but it was harsh with shock and anger. She stood about six feet away, with nothing to hang on to except her determination to try and do the right thing.

'I planned to tell you as soon as I had explained to Thea that you were back in our lives.' And then another horrible thought struck her. 'Have you told Thea?'

'Do you think I'm *mad*?' Damon's eyes flared with rage. 'How could you think I'd do something like that?'

'Because I don't know you—' That was true. She didn't know the man he had become. 'It's been a long time, Damon.'

'A *very* long time,' he agreed in a voice turned to ice.

Remembering Thea's happy face the moment she'd spotted Lizzie, waiting to take her seat, Lizzie knew she was overreacting in this instance, and that neither Damon nor Thea had made any connection between them until Thea had run up to Lizzie. Then Damon must have known.

'And in all that *very long time* you couldn't find the right moment to tell me that we had a child?'

He was incredulous. And furious. But she was armed too. 'It wasn't all about *you*, Damon.'

'Or you,' he fired back. 'Was a child so unimportant you just forgot to mention it?'

'Thea—not *a child*. And there is *nothing* more important to me than Thea.'

'How about giving me a chance to feel the same?' he suggested cuttingly.

Damon was incandescent with fury, but she hadn't expressed her feelings for almost eleven years. She hadn't had that luxury. She'd been too busy being a mother and keeping food on the table, a roof over their heads.

'I had a lot going on,' she said, battling to rein herself in. 'When I did try to contact you, your people blocked me, and I didn't have the resources to keep on trying to call. And even if I had…' She shrugged angrily. 'What would you have done?'

His jaw ground tensely. 'I wouldn't have been as insensitive as *you*.'

'Insensitive?' Lizzie clenched her fists. 'This from the man who turned his back on me after the court case, in spite having slept with me the night before? No doubt you'd washed your hands of everything to do with my family by that time. You'd got your victory, so everything else—including me—was done and dusted.'

'I moved on—as you did,' Damon countered coldly.

'I moved on because I had to. I didn't have a home to go to. You walked away without a backward glance.' Her shoulders lifted tensely. 'You didn't care what happened to me after the court case.'

'You weren't my responsibility,' Damon said coldly, and with a good deal of truth.

'Correct,' Lizzie agreed. 'But you can be quick to help those you want to, can't you Damon? You just couldn't see beyond bedding me, and you certainly didn't *care* about me, did you? So don't you dare come back now and start accusing me of handling things badly. We both made mistakes—'

'You can't turn this around on me.'

'Why not?' Lizzie challenged. '*You* walked away.'

'There was nothing to walk away *from*.'

With a shake of her head, she laughed angrily. 'Exactly. All I am to you—all I ever was—is a one-night stand.'

'And you had so much going on in your life that letting me know you were expecting my child came well down the list.'

'You just don't get it, do you?' Lizzie exclaimed. 'I didn't have your resources. I was thrown out of my childhood home with just the clothes I stood up in. I didn't have any money. I certainly didn't have a phone. I didn't know where my next meal was coming from, let alone whether I could manage to put a roof over my head. And at that stage, Damon, you were the *last* person I'd have thought of calling. Why would I, when you'd made no attempt to find me?

'I had no one to rely on but myself—and don't think for one moment that I'm complaining, because it was a good thing. Being alone taught me self-reliance and helped me to be a better mother for Thea. It made me strong and determined, and I learned that if I took one step at a time I could survive—I could put a roof over my head and I could care for my baby. Those were the only things that mattered to me—not you, nor me. Beyond keeping healthy for Thea's sake, the only thing I cared about—still care about and always will care about—is Thea.'

'You should have come to me,' he ground out.

'Should I?' she demanded. 'If I could have found you, do you mean? After I'd repeatedly contacted your people and been turned away I made one attempt to appeal to my stepmother, one woman to another. I told her I was pregnant and begged her to help me find you. She laughed in my face and told me never to return. She couldn't have a slut damaging her reputation, she said. Yes, it was a slap in the face,' Lizzie agreed, 'but it pulled me together fast and I managed very well without her—and without you too. It didn't take me long to learn that I was better on my own.'

'You didn't give me the chance,' Damon said with a shake of his head. 'You didn't give me the chance to know my child. And, yes, I was away for a lot of the time, but since I came back I've taken you out twice, and yet you never hinted that we had a daughter together. Do you have an explanation for that?'

'Yes, I do. Thea had to know first. I was protecting *her*. And if you can't see that then you're not fit to call yourself her father. *That's* the difference between you and me,' she added. 'You have all the power and money in the world, and I have nothing, but when it comes to Thea you won't get past me.'

'I wouldn't be so sure. I have rights,' he said.

'You have *no* rights,' Lizzie argued, feeling calmer.

'*I*... I have no rights?'

Damon almost laughed—as well he might. A man who could command anything that money could buy, would find it difficult, if not impossible, to conceive that there was something on this earth he couldn't have.

Lizzie felt as if ice had invaded her veins, but nothing would stop her when she was in defence of her child, and Damon had to hear this. 'You have no rights because there's no father listed on Thea's birth certificate.'

'A DNA test would soon establish my rights as Thea's father,' he said confidently.

'*If* I allowed such a test to take place.' Lizzie lifted her chin. 'The fact that your name doesn't appear on Thea's birth certificate means that you have no legal rights over Thea unless I allow you to.'

'I'll fight you every way I can,' Damon threatened, frowning.

'Again?' Lizzie said quietly. 'Before you deploy your legal team, you should know this. Thea doesn't want to know her father. She never has. She asked me to stop talking about him because we were all right as we were, and she didn't want some mystery man entering her life.'

'She might change her mind if she knew it was me.'

Damon's voice was so cold it chilled her.

A burst of applause drew their attention to the window. The conductor was mounting the stage.

'I have to go.' She turned for the door. Damon remained where he was. She hesitated with her hand on the door handle. Squeezing her eyes tightly shut, she drew in a breath and then turned back to face him. 'You should hear her play. You'll regret it if you don't.'

She walked out of the room and didn't stop until she was outside the school. She felt as if she were suffocating, and gulped in air. There was no one behind her…no sound…no footsteps…no Damon.

He was incapable of feeling anything—numb, existing on autopilot. He was breathing, maybe. He stood in the silence of an empty room until the first swell of music from the youth orchestra prompted him to act.

Lizzie was easy to spot, with her shining red hair in a sea of ebony locks. There was only one empty seat left in the entire audience and that was next to her. He could have stood at the back, or at the side, but that might have looked odd to Thea.

Lizzie didn't acknowledge him as he sat down. He didn't acknowledge her. They might have been two strangers. Two strangers with a daughter between them.

He had a daughter.

He kept on repeating the phrase over and over in his head, as if it would finally make some sense to him.

The young musical sensation Thea Floros was his daughter... Floros was Lizzie's mother's maiden name.

The pieces clicked into place one after the other as he sat immobile in a state of shock. Another part of his brain was agitatedly wondering how to make up for eleven years. He had a child, and that changed everything.

The little violinist he'd got on with so well with was his daughter. And Thea was her name. He had a daughter named Thea...

Repeating this was both surprising and wonderful, and he kept on repeating it as the orchestra played.

'Damon?'

He heard Lizzie murmur something to him, but he couldn't answer. He didn't want to answer her. He didn't want to speak to her. He wasn't ready to share the way he felt right now with anyone—especially Lizzie. He couldn't have put his thoughts into words, anyway, and not just because the concert had started and even a cough would be inappropriate. They couldn't discuss something as monumental as this in public.

Where could they discuss it?

There was no approved course of action. All his experience had left him completely unprepared for this. He was encased in ice, preserved and separate, untouchable, unreachable—as Lizzie had complained he was all those years ago.

He registered without emotion that this strange state of non-feeling stillness must be the calm before the storm. When he blew he would take everything with him.

And then Thea stood up.

At first he stared at her, as if she were an automaton in a museum, safe behind glass, and he was a visitor show-

ing a passing interest in one of the exhibits. If he felt anything it was curiosity—that he could look at his daughter
and not know what to feel.

But then she lifted her bow and started to play.

CHAPTER NINE

MUSIC COULD TOUCH HIM. It always had been able to touch him. Thanks to his father's passion, music had always played a huge part in his home-life when he'd been growing up. Music could unlock him, and now Thea had freed emotions inside him that he hadn't even known were there.

They must have been locked away for years as he drove forward with the business, allowing nothing to distract him. At the time he'd thought emotion a selfish indulgence and it had become a habit, he supposed. His focus had been all on working as hard as he could so his father could retire. It was only now, as Thea wove magic with her violin, that he realised how empty his life had become.

His daughter was filling it—filling him—with emotion, until it threatened to overflow. The melody she was playing so skilfully was uncomplicated, but it tugged at his heart and forced a response from him. Eleven years he'd missed of this child's life. Eleven years. Feeling her kick in the womb, seeing her born and holding her in his arms for the first time, celebrating her first birthday and the elation of watching as she took her first steps—all gone. Hearing her first words and encouraging her to stride out bravely on her first day at school—

'Damon? *Damon...?*'

Someone was shaking his shoulder, he realised, coming to fast. Feeling tears on his cheeks, he swiped them away.

His aide dipped down to speak to him. 'I'm sorry to break in on your private time,' the man whispered, 'but we have an emergency at one of the plants—a fire. It's contained now, but we could do with your steer on to how to handle the aftermath.'

'I'm with you,' he said, getting up. His workers were another family to him, and almost as close as his own. Whatever they needed, he was there.

Thea was family. Thea was his family.

His stare met Thea's as he rose from his seat. It was a magical split-second. Fate had dictated that she finish her solo just as he stood. Everyone was standing to applaud. He had hoped she wouldn't notice him leaving. He might have known she would know immediately. She was his daughter, after all.

She smiled at him—a smile that lit his world. It was innocent and happy and he smiled back, held his daughter's open, trusting gaze, while the woman at his side—Lizzie—tugged at his arm repeatedly.

He pulled away sharply. Her hand was an unwanted intrusion on his naked skin. Raising his hands to applaud Thea, he ignored his aide's edginess and obvious desire to go. He could spare these few seconds to let Thea understand and see how deeply he had appreciated her performance.

For each second he held eye contact with Thea he could feel Lizzie's distress. Her tugs were becoming more insistent, and her voice, though it seemed to come from a long way away, was obviously distraught. But he couldn't be distracted. His attention was centred on his daughter—as if in these few seconds he was making up for eleven years of separation.

'Damon—'

'I'm coming,' he snapped at his aide.

With one last long look at Thea, he moved into the aisle and strode away.

Lizzie sat in her seat motionless long after the other audience members had left. People moved past her. She barely registered them. She felt cloaked in doom, and it was a doom of her own making. Of all the ways for Damon to find about Thea, this had to be the worst. How must it have felt for him to be sitting next to his daughter's mother, only to discover that the woman he had made love to was apparently as untrustworthy as her scumbag father?

She had felt Damon quite literally shrink away from her. And she'd seen the look he'd given Thea. It had been the leader of the wolf pack acknowledging his cub. If the thought of a blood relationship between Damon and Thea hadn't struck anyone else yet, it soon would. The ease between them, coupled with their incredible likeness, signalled their bond like a flashing beacon.

Thea was a bright child. How long would it take *her* to work it out?

Having never heard Thea express the need for a father, Lizzie began to wonder if that had been to save her feelings. They had been a team of two for ever, and now they were three—though not a team, and without any explanation from Lizzie.

She found herself flinching when Thea came running down the aisle, swinging her violin case as if she didn't have a care in the world.

And why should she?

But everything was about to change for Thea. Remembering how that had felt for herself when she was eighteen—almost twice Thea's age, with twice Thea's experience of life—Lizzie shrank a little more inside.

'Mama!' Thea exclaimed. 'Did you enjoy the concert?' Thea was hopping from foot to foot, still fired up on adrenalin, when she reached Lizzie's side. 'Did you notice that note I got wrong?'

'I only noticed that you played beautifully,' Lizzie said honestly, on a throat so tight she could hardly breathe.

'I played for *you*,' Thea announced, throwing her arms around her mother to hug her tight.

This was the wake-up call she needed, Lizzie realised. She *wasn't* a useless mother. She was just a mother and she'd always done her best. She was a hostage for life, and she welcomed that knowledge. She'd no doubt get things wrong again in the future, but she'd always strive to put them right. She would never stop trying when it came to Thea.

'I can't wait to hear you play again,' she said warmly when a few of Thea's friends gathered round. 'I think you're amazing—all of you.'

Lizzie's heart melted when Thea turned a beaming smile on her friends, as if to say, *This is my mother and she really gets us.*

'Love you, darling!' Lizzie called out as Thea raced away with her friends.

Glancing across the playing fields, Lizzie could see Thea and her group of friends gathering up a feast from the buffet, to carry off and eat beneath the shade of the olive trees. Sensing Lizzie was still staring at her, Thea turned and gestured vigorously that Lizzie must join them.

Lizzie drew a deep breath and told herself firmly that whatever happened next she could deal with it. She had dealt with things for eleven years now, and would continue to do so. She would do anything to protect Thea.

And Damon? What about him?

She'd lost him before she'd had chance to know him. He could never be part of her life now—though he would surely be part of Thea's. That would be up to Thea, Lizzie determined as she hurried across the parched playing field to join the children.

'There he goes!' Thea yelled, pointing to the sky as Lizzie approached.

Shading her eyes, Lizzie stared up as the rhythmical thwack of a helicopter's rotor blades passed overhead. Damon would be flying off to wherever he was needed most, she guessed.

Guilt flooded her again. She'd worked so hard to get things right for Thea, and now she'd fallen at this, the last hurdle. She might never get the chance to speak to Damon again except through lawyers, and she had always planned to bring Thea and Damon together carefully, sensitively— anywhere *but* in a courtroom.

She shuddered at the thought. There was no excuse, although her reasons for not telling Damon sooner were complex and mostly rooted in the past. Believing he'd de- serted her too, so soon after her father's rejection, she'd vowed never to love again, never to risk her heart again— and she had kept that vow until Thea was born, when she had discovered a love so deep it had almost drowned her.

Her father's rejection, coming at such a vulnerable and hormonal time in Lizzie's life, had left her with an over- whelming desire to protect Thea from that same pain.

Looking back, she saw that the world her father had as- pired to was shallow, and based on what people had in the bank rather than what they were really worth, and that in turn had left her with a lifelong suspicion of wealth. She knew deep down that Damon was a different kind of rich, and that he'd not only worked hard for everything he'd got but had done good with that money. But the glamorous world he inhabited still troubled her. She would never belong in a world like that—though in time Thea might, Lizzie allowed.

'Okay…' Thea looked up expectantly at her mother.

'Okay, what?' Lizzie asked lightly, pinning a smile to her face.

'Do. You. Like. Him?' Thea asked, testing her facial muscles to their limit. 'Damon Gavros,' she explained impatiently. 'I saw him sitting next to you. We *all* did,' Thea added, grinning as she gazed around at her friends.

So now she had an audience. Lizzie's stomach sank. She shrugged and smiled through it. 'Of course I like him. What's not to like?'

'Well, that's good,' Thea said. 'Because he's on his way over—'

'What?' Lizzie's world tilted as she swung around in panic.

Damon was not supposed to be here. He'd just flown away in his helicopter.

'We're all thrilled you like him,' Thea said, her voice penetrating Lizzie's fog of incomprehension, 'because we need ice cream and we're hoping he'll buy some.'

If only life were that simple, Lizzie thought. She almost laughed. Impending hysteria, she guessed. It took a child to point out the obvious. There was ice cream, and there was a man with enough money to buy each of them a serving. Damon was no more complex or disturbing than that as far as Thea was concerned.

And long may it remain that way, Lizzie thought.

'Why don't you stay here with your friends while I go and see what he says to your suggestion?' she offered.

'Not *he*—Damon,' Thea insisted. 'You have to use his name if you stand a hope of getting close to him.'

'Right…' Lizzie pressed her lips together in a thin smile.

She had no chance of getting close to Damon, but now wasn't the time to disillusion Thea. There was no more time to waste. She had to head him off before he reached them and Thea sensed that something was wrong.

'Damon—Damon Gavros!' Thea called after her. 'He has the same name as this island. You can't forget it.'

She would *never* forget it, since it was gouged on her heart, Lizzie thought as she called back to Thea, 'Back soon. Sit tight and I'll see what I can do.'

'Not too soon!' Thea yelled after her. 'We've got stuff to do…so you've got the whole evening with *Damon*. See you tomorrow!'

As the children's giggles rose behind her Lizzie knew she had to make things right before they got a lot worse. She had to reach a compromise with Damon if they weren't going to end up fighting each other through every court in the land. Though how she was supposed to fight Damon Gavros and his legal team, she had no idea.

Not yet, Lizzie thought, firming her jaw, but when it came to Thea she'd fight to the death.

He was feeling icy calm as he strode across the field towards Lizzie. Business could do that for him. He could always see the way ahead where his work was concerned. It cleared his head when other areas of his life were complicated. He had given precise instructions to his aide so the fallout after the fire would be dealt with. Everyone would receive the care and compensation they deserved. He wouldn't stint. He never did where family was concerned.

And now for Lizzie, who was coming to meet him, diverting him away from the group of children—which was just as well. When they were a few feet apart he jerked his head to suggest she follow him. He noticed Thea was watching, and smiled for her benefit.

The multinational conglomerate he controlled with such ease was nothing compared to the complexities of human relationships, he decided. *This* was the minefield, right here. He felt no animosity towards Lizzie. He felt nothing. But his mind was made up. The direction they would take from here was clear. Lizzie might have procrastinated for eleven years, but making fast decisions based on the evidence in front of him had always been his forte.

He led the way to his helicopter and noticed the moment when realisation struck Lizzie. Damon had two helicopters. In fact he had a fleet of helicopters. He never knew when he or one of his executives would need to move fast. He had never needed to move faster than he did now.

He opened the passenger door and made sure Lizzie was settled before helping her to fasten her harness and explaining how her headphones worked. There was no tension or anger in his voice. There was nothing. Lizzie's face paled, as if she found his manner more chilling than if he'd raged at her.

The short flight brought them above his beach house. It was here that the future would be spelled out.

A kaleidoscope of images flashed through Lizzie's panicked mind as the helicopter hovered over Damon's spectacular beach house—or mansion, as Lizzie thought of it. The contrast of the simple home she'd made for Thea with this, and with all Damon's other homes across the world, was painfully stark.

She could get a sense of perspective through the clear floor of the helicopter beneath her feet... The carefully cultivated gardens, the Olympic-size swimming pool and the tennis courts beyond. There was even a putting green.

Ivory sand fringed the bright blue ocean in front of the house, and she could see Damon's cutting-edge powerboat rolling gently on the lazy waves.

Compare that to a grimy London street and a front door that opened on to someone else's hallway and it was no wonder her heart was beating in double time.

And it wasn't just Damon's possessions or his way of life that she found so threatening, but his super-keen intelligence and innate skill. Damon might say he'd had advantages, and he had, but he'd taken them, and transformed his father's business into a stratospheric success. Some people took a bus to work, while others—like Damon—handled a helicopter with the same ease as a compact car, she mused as the sleek craft settled seamlessly on its skids.

What would Damon make of their daughter's obsession with thrift shops? Lizzie wondered as Damon came around to help her out. Would he understand that Thea needed to express her quirky side with things she couldn't find on the High Street? Or would he think that Lizzie's lack of financial resources had condemned Thea to wearing second-hand clothes? Would he understand *anything* about Thea?

Was it wrong and selfish of Lizzie to think, *Thea is my baby*? Was it wrong to look down at Damon's capable hands as he freed her harness and refuse to acknowledge that this man had played an equal part in the creation of their child?

Thea is the child I carried in my belly, and then on my hip, and always, always in my heart, Lizzie thought as Damon walked ahead of her.

But he could offer Thea so much more than she could. Thea had to confine her violin practice to one hour a day in London when she was at home, or they would have to find somewhere else to live. That was what the owners of the house had told Lizzie. How many music studios could Thea have in a house like this?

Sparkling white granite chippings crunched beneath their feet as they walked up the elegant path towards the front door. Everywhere she looked was something amazing…the vast planting arrangements at each side of the door, the banks of flowers below the windows, all immaculately groomed.

Damon could easily afford to buy any priceless violin Thea set her heart on, Lizzie thought as he inserted a code into the panel at the side of the door and it swung open. *She* had to work three jobs just to pay for the extra sheet music Thea needed for school.

By the time the door opened she had worked herself up into a real state. Damon had all the power in the world. She had none. He had a legal team at his beck and call. She didn't even have enough money to call a lawyer in England from Greece.

Was she about to lose Thea?

No! Lizzie thought fiercely. Not while she had breath in her body.

She walked into the vaulted hallway and stared around numbly. Whatever she had expected Damon's new house to be like, this was so much *more*. The space, the light, the air, the simple luxury surrounding her… It was all extremely tasteful, with décor in a palette of soft neutral shades. And it was empty—as if waiting for someone to move in and imbue it with life.

This was not the way he had imagined it would be when he brought Lizzie into his new home for the first time. They had only looked at it from the beach before, because— ironically—they'd had to get back for Thea's concert. Fresh from making love to Lizzie, he'd had the crazy notion of sweeping her into his arms and carrying her across the threshold. And then they'd make love on every surface in the house.

Not this time.

He led the way into a lavishly equipped but as yet unoccupied study. The room was spectacular. A wall of glass faced the electric blue bay, and the desk was a long, plain piece of wood, its only ornament a computer. The surface of the desk was as smooth as glass. He'd planned, prepped and planed it himself, finishing it with beeswax.

As Lizzie ran her fingertips over the surface he remembered the pleasure he'd had making it, the simple joy of working with his hands. Creating things like the desk allowed him to escape the rattle of business for a while and just *be*. Simplicity in all things always gave him pleasure. Honesty did the same.

He drew a breath and turned to face Lizzie.

'Damon, I—'

He silenced her with a raised hand. 'Please. Sit down.'

'I'd rather stand, if you don't mind.'

The tension in Lizzie's voice was like a taut band on the point of snapping. He felt no pity. Beyond knowing that if she broke down it would delay things and get them nowhere, he felt no empathy at all. He positioned himself with his back to the window while Lizzie remained by the door. He saw a flicker of fear in her eyes, but then it was gone. She was determined to stand up to him. But he held all the cards and she held none—they both knew that.

Although he hadn't forgotten Lizzie's determination to refuse him equal rights, and the fact that he wasn't even mentioned on Thea's birth certificate...

On reflection, it seemed that perhaps Lizzie held the trump card.

Her arms were ramrod-straight against her sides, her

fists clenched so tight her knuckles were like polished ivory. The blood had drained from her cheeks and her eyes were huge in the ashen wasteland of her face. He had experienced emotion briefly, when Thea had played the violin, but whatever his daughter had unlocked was gone now. It was for Thea alone. He dealt with all problems the same way—by being incisive and emotion-free—and he would do that now.

'You don't know her,' Lizzie told him quietly, as if anticipating what he might say. 'Thea doesn't know you. You can't just walk into her life and claim her, Damon.'

'You don't know *what* I can do.'

Her lips had turned white. She knew the power he wielded.

Her brow pleated. 'Are you trying to intimidate me?'

'Never,' he stated factually. 'I am simply trying to reclaim what's mine.'

'And what then?' she asked him tensely.

'That's what I have to find out. I have to find a solution.'

'*We* have to find a solution,' Lizzie argued quietly.

'You've lost your chance,' he said frankly. 'It's my turn now. I think you should sit down. We have to put our personal differences aside and consider what's best for Thea.'

'Thea is all I ever think about,' Lizzie assured him, with a blaze of passion in her eyes.

'I haven't been given that chance,' he pointed out with supreme restraint.

The disappointment he felt in Lizzie was acute. She was as shallow as the rest of them. Self-interest ruled her. She might never have told him that they had a daughter together if he hadn't walked into that restaurant in London. She would have kept Thea to herself.

Pain stabbed him when he thought about the years that had been lost. He had to turn away for a few moments and pour them both a glass of iced water to give him something else to focus on while his rage subsided.

'Why aren't you angry?' Lizzie demanded.

He almost laughed.

'Are you incapable of feelings?'

'Declara!'

He'd spilled the water on his desk. *Incapable of feelings?* This entire situation had rocked the foundations of his life.

Snatching up a cloth, he mopped up the spill before turning to face her. 'Perhaps *you* can afford to be emotional, but I can't. How would it look in business if I railed at my competitors and made every decision on a wave of passion?'

'This isn't a *business* decision,' she fired back. 'This is our daughter. *Thea.*'

'I'm glad you've finally remembered,' he countered with scorn.

'So this is just another exercise in winning for you?' Lizzie suggested.

'Far from it.'

She had no idea of the turmoil inside him. He'd only ever known happy, uncomplicated love—love without boundaries, the type of love that a parent gave to a child, the style of unconditional love that his parents had given to him. It was love without demands, love that would sacrifice everything, and he hadn't been given the chance to experience that same love with Thea.

The love he felt for Thea already was incalculable. It was as if eleven years had been compacted into a single day of knowing and loving his child. His head was reeling with love. Eleven years of Thea's existence had been lost, never to be reclaimed. From the night of her conception to the night before her birth, when she'd been nothing more than a tiny light waiting to take a tilt at life, and on to this moment, here in his study, where he was talking about Thea to her mother.

All of those precious moments were lost. Everything that had been Thea before now had gone, never to be reclaimed.

CHAPTER TEN

HIS LOST TIME with Thea had lodged in his heart, where it was lashing around, demanding an explanation. Lizzie thought that because he was acting so contained he felt nothing, when for the first time in his life he didn't know if he could trust himself to handle this meeting as well as he must. He only knew that for Thea's sake he had to.

In order to bring himself to talk to Lizzie at all, he had listed the *good* things she had done. Thea had turned out well. Raising her as a single mother with no family couldn't have been easy for Lizzie. Eleven years ago she had been just eighteen and pregnant, with no home, no money, no family—no one at all to rely on but herself. She hadn't just *cared* for Thea, she loved Thea without boundaries, in the same way that he'd been loved as a child, and Lizzie had raised Thea without the good fortune his parents had enjoyed.

He couldn't claim any credit for Thea beyond her existence. She was all Lizzie's work. That was why he'd found Lizzie washing pots in London. It all made sense now. She'd kept nothing for herself and had put all her dreams on indefinite hold for Thea.

But Thea was *his* daughter too, and he had been denied every moment of her existence—even the knowledge of it—up to now. So, although he could rationalise the situation and give Lizzie some credit, things could not go on as they were.

'I won't let you take her, Damon.'

He stared at Lizzie. He'd seen flashes of her vulnerability, but it would be a mistake to think her vulnerable now. His mother had always told him that there was no stronger opponent a man could face than a mother fighting for her child.

'No court would allow any man to walk into a child's life and take her from the mother who has loved her from the instant she first felt her stir in the womb—who has loved her unreservedly ever since—unless that man could prove both that he was the father of the child and that the mother was unfit to care for her. And no one—not even you—can prove a lie, Damon.'

'I'm not just any man,' he argued tensely. 'I'm a father. *Thea's* father.'

'I will fight you every step of the way,' she warned him. 'I'll fight your money, your power, and your legal team too. Do you *really* think you can defeat a mother in defence of her child? Even *you* don't have the weapons for that, Damon.'

His feelings were rising. He felt fury that she would deny him Thea even now—and yet he knew acceptance, however reluctant, that his own mother would have said the same.

He wasn't as callous as Lizzie thought him. She had been in his thoughts too. She'd never left them, really. In the desert, when he'd been working with his team, she had intruded on his thoughts at night, and in the day he'd kept her in mind to ease some of the horrors he'd seen. But she'd kept the most important thing on earth from him, and he could never forgive her for that.

She had cheated him out of Thea, as her father had

cheated his father. How could he ever trust her again after that?

'You'll have to—' He'd been about to say, *consult a lawyer*, when Lizzie leapt ahead of him—but in the wrong direction.

'I don't have to do anything you tell me to,' she assured him. 'It's up to you to launch your case—try to destroy me as you destroyed my father.'

'Lizzie...' he modulated his tone. 'We've been over this ground several times. We both know that what happened in court that day was for the best.'

'What *I* know is that my father was weak and you were strong. Is that what you plan to do now? Crush me?'

Grinding his jaw, he refused to be drawn, but Lizzie had the bit between her teeth.

'Get this straight,' she blazed at him. 'Thea stays with *me*. We choose a time to tell her that you're her father, and we do that together. Above all we try to be civilised about this.'

'And then Thea makes her choice,' he said mildly, employing all the reason he used in business. 'Thea isn't a baby. She's a highly intelligent girl with a mind of her own. There isn't a judge alive who wouldn't want to hear what she has to say.'

Lizzie's heart lurched. Closing her eyes briefly, she reeled through a new scene in court. Penniless mother. Billionaire father. What would the judge make of that?

It was a matter of trust, she concluded. It boiled down to her belief in the strength of the love that she and Thea shared. It was just the thought of that love being put to the test in front of strangers that made her feel terrible for Thea. Why should a ten-year-old child have to go through that? This was never what she'd wanted.

'We'll see,' was all she could reply.

When it came down to it, love was all about trust, Lizzie reflected. Yes, love could be hurt and doubt, but it was also hope. She'd lost all hope of love with Damon, but Thea's future was still untarnished—and it would remain that way if Lizzie had anything to do with it.

'Tell me one thing,' she said. 'Did you never once feel guilty for walking away after casually destroying my life?'

'You left with your friends, as I remember it.'

And her life *had* badly needed shaking up. She accepted that.

'What happened to those friends?' Damon probed.

'When the money ran out, so did they,' she admitted frankly. 'Fair-weather friends, as you yourself called them. I made a clean start. I was lucky enough to make more friends—real friends—who couldn't have cared less if I could afford to wear this label or that, or if my father gave the most lavish parties. Though in fairness to those old friends,' she admitted, 'their parents wouldn't allow them to see me. First there was the shame of my father's imprisonment, and then the fear that I might want a loan to see me through, and finally, to cap it all, I was pregnant, with no sign of a husband or partner.'

'So, not really your friends at all, then?' Damon said.

'No,' Lizzie agreed. 'I know the difference now. Being pregnant with Thea gave me a very clear focus on life. Motherhood changed me for good. I grew up overnight. I had to, to make a go of things for Thea. I even found that I wasn't so stupid after all.' She shrugged wryly. 'Being a mother was actually something I was good at.'

He couldn't deny that. 'But you should have contacted me.'

'I did! I told you that I was blocked by your people.'

'You should have kept trying until you reached me. I

would have helped you if I'd known. I would have definitely wanted to be part of Thea's life.'

'*Would* you? Can you be so sure of how you would have reacted back then? You were a lot younger too, Damon, and you've had a long way to travel to reach this point. Domesticity would have hindered your progress. It might even have stopped you setting out.'

'Domesticity?' he queried with a frown.

'Just a figure of speech,' Lizzie said coolly. 'Perhaps it's all worked out for the best. One day I might show you the stack of unopened letters I sent to your office. They were all marked "Returned to sender". I wrote to you as soon as I was settled,' she explained, in answer to his unspoken question. 'I *did* think about you and the part you should be playing in our lives. And not just because of your money, Damon. I was never interested in that.'

'What part are you talking about, then? A full part?'

'That would have had to be decided then—just as it has to be decided now. I can only tell you that your personnel team deserves a collective medal for protecting your privacy.'

He could believe that. He was never readily available to anyone outside his immediate family. Those who didn't have him on speed dial—which was most of the world— had to jump through many hoops before they could even reach the assistant to his assistant PA. Reaching his PA was next to impossible.

'I *did* want you to know about Thea,' Lizzie insisted quietly, 'but I didn't want anything else from you—not in a material sense.'

She turned away from him and gazed off into the middle distance. He guessed she was reliving all the exultation, fear and hope of an expectant mother. She'd had no one to share those moments with…no family, no parents, no one at all. And then, when Thea had arrived, she must have been like a ray of sunshine, bringing happiness into every life she touched, just as she'd touched his already.

'Where *were* you?' Lizzie demanded angrily, perhaps taking his smile as he thought about Thea for scorn. 'Where were you when I was being examined by the midwife and not knowing what to expect? Where were you when they were taking scans of Thea and I was scared half to death, thinking they might find something wrong with her because I couldn't always afford the best food or to eat healthily? Where you were you when I was in labour and frightened? Where were you when your daughter was born? Where were you when they took blood from her heel and she cried with pain? *Where were you when I needed you?*'

As Lizzie's voice tightened into a wordless scream he didn't think about the past, the present or the future. He didn't think about the rights and wrongs of the situation at all. He just grabbed her close and held her tightly to him as tears streamed down her face. And then he kissed her, and kept on kissing her, while she shuddered and then remembered to fight him—punching and shouting as she vented her frustration, until her passion veered onto a different track and she clung to him like a drowning man to a raft.

'Hey, stop…stop…' he insisted, kissing her face, her eyes, her lips, her brow. 'Calm down, Lizzie—'

'Calm down?' she demanded, rallying enough to pull back. 'Can't you see what I stand to lose, you stupid man? *Everything!*'

Beautiful, tempestuous Lizzie. *This* was the woman who had bewitched him eleven years ago. He'd calmed her then, but could he calm her now? Even *he* didn't know. He'd never seen a human being so distraught.

Sweeping her into his arms, he carried her into one of

the bedrooms and kept on kissing her as he shouldered the door closed behind them. He kissed her as he carried her to the bed, and she made no attempt to move away when he put her down. She made no attempt to move at all beyond covering her eyes with her forearm as he kicked off his shoes.

Stretching out his length against her, he drew her into his arms with the intention of soothing her—but Lizzie was way ahead of him. Fingers flying over the buttons down the front of her dress, she whipped it over her head. When he attempted to take it from her she defended the cheap sundress like a lioness. Folding the soft yellow material neatly, she leaned across the bed to place it on a chair.

'No, Lizzie…no.'

He'd planned to take things slowly, but the moment he turned to face her she sprang into his arms and, lacing her fingers through his hair, wrapped her legs around him, kissing him as if they were facing the end of the world.

He considered himself a just man, but he wasn't a saint, and primal need soon overcame his finer feelings. Doubt, rage and resentment forgotten, he ripped off his clothes, only knowing that he'd missed her. *Theos!* How much!

Her hunger to blank everything out was all Lizzie could think about—that and claiming her mate, maybe for the last time. There was no chance for foreplay, or for teasing advances. Delaying tactics of any type were barred. She needed oblivion *now*.

She exclaimed in triumph as Damon threw her on her back. Planting his fists either side of her head, he loomed over her—big, powerful, majestic and ultra-efficient when it came to mind-blanking.

Drawing her knees back, she locked her legs around his waist. She knew exactly what she was inviting, and she exulted in the shock of his possession as Damon plunged deep. She lost control immediately. She didn't spare a thought for whether she should or not. There was no finesse, no manners at all.

Shrieking and bucking, she grabbed at him, driving him on with her fingers pressed mercilessly into the steel of his buttocks. She was determined to catch every last throb of pleasure, and when sensation robbed her of thought she exclaimed gratefully and noisily in time to each crashing wave.

'More!' she gasped as she dragged in some much-needed air.

She was laughing with excitement as Damon dragged her to the edge of the bed. Arranging her to his liking, with her hips balanced precariously on the edge, he pressed her legs back and stood between them.

'You like it deep? You like it firm?' he suggested, with the faintest of smiles on his mouth.

'What do *you* think?' she challenged.

Lifting her legs onto his shoulders, he rewarded her with a fierce, fast rhythm that had her plunging over the edge almost at once.

'Greedy,' he growled, sounding pleased.

Bringing her into his arms, he carried her across the room to the wall of windows. 'Is *this* what you want?' he said as he pushed her naked body against the glass. 'Now the whole world can see the butterflies you've got tattooed on your backside.'

Dipping at the knees, he thrust deep and relentlessly, until she came apart in his arms, wailing and shrieking.

When she gasped, 'Too good…' he demanded to know if she had any more tattoos that required his attention.

'Why don't you take a look?' she suggested.

She'd been starved for too long, Lizzie realised, as

Damon continued to move deep inside her and she continued to bask in oblivion, where sensation ruled—*or was that to hide?—*

Again? Really? Was *again* even possible?

It was, she discovered, wailing as she fell.

This time it was so intense, and lasted so long, she might even have lost consciousness for a few moments. When she came round it was to find Damon still moving steadily and deeply, his big, slightly roughened hands locked firmly as he kept her in position for each firm thrust.

'Don't do anything,' he commanded in a low, husky tone. 'Don't move at all. Relax every muscle and let me do all the work.'

She did as he asked and was rewarded with pleasure. Clearly seeing it in her eyes, Damon smiled fiercely against her mouth, and as he kissed her he rotated his hips, keeping them tightly locked together, and she fell again.

'What about you?' she asked when she was finally able to speak.

Pulling out completely, Damon thrust deeply again, with a groan of satisfaction, and a few firm, fast strokes later he brought them both over the edge.

'Bed?' Lizzie suggested as he cupped her face in his hands.

'Lightweight,' Damon whispered against her mouth.

'You're insatiable.'

'And you seem pleased about that,' he commented.

'I am,' she admitted.

'You're the same,' he insisted. 'You just don't know it yet.'

'Then why don't you prove it to me?'

Swinging her into his arms, he carried her across the room and into his bathroom, which was the most opulent haven of luxury she'd ever seen. Black marble covered the walls and floor, and there was elegant furniture. High-end products in industrial-sized crystal jars were just begging to be used. And there were mirrors everywhere.

The sight of herself in Damon's arms, both of them naked and intimately entwined, was the most arousing thing that Lizzie had ever seen.

'That insatiable thing…' Damon murmured as he steadied her on the warm marble floor.

'What about it?' Lifting her chin, she blazed a challenge into his eyes.

'It's time I proved it to you…'

CHAPTER ELEVEN

THIS WAS NOT like Lizzie's shower in London. No chance of a lukewarm dribble trickling out of a rusty showerhead. Damon's shower was a powerful blast of water at the perfect temperature, and it was instantly warm.

'Billionaire's perks?' Lizzie suggested as she turned her face towards the refreshing stream.

Taking the exclusive shower gel out of her hands, Damon washed her all over with long and increasingly intimate strokes. And then he trained the showerhead where she was most sensitive, skilfully massaging her with tiny, tantalising blunt-edged needles that took her arousal to new heights.

'Hands flat against the wall,' he instructed.

How could her body be so sensitive? The warm water had made her nerve-endings super-responsive, Lizzie supposed as Damon trained the water over her back and her buttocks.

Resting her head against the wall, she groaned with pleasure as he nudged her legs apart to direct the pounding water so skilfully she found yet another way to lose control. He caught her as her legs buckled beneath her, but even that wasn't enough for him. Resting her leg high on his thigh, he thrust into her, working steadily to bring her to the edge again.

'I can't…' she protested, shaking her head, certain this was true.

'Yes, you can,' he insisted softly—and he proved it beyond doubt.

After the shower he swaddled her in warm, fluffy towels and carried her back to bed. 'Sleep now,' he said.

'Sleep?' she complained softly, staring into his eyes.

'I have work to do,' Damon told her, pulling away.

And then, just like eleven years before, he was gone.

How had she ever managed to sleep? Lizzie wondered as she woke to find sunlight blazing into the room. *Damon's bedroom*. She turned over in bed. The other side was empty. The pillow was smooth. She'd slept through the night. But where was Damon?

As the events of the previous night came flooding back she sat up and realised that she'd had her first untroubled night's sleep without nightmares in ages. There had been no ghoulish return to a hushed courtroom full of haunted faces. She must have been totally exhausted to sleep like that. Having glutted herself on Damon, that was hardly a surprise. But now she sat up to listen she thought the house was empty.

She was just a temporary visitor who had outstayed her welcome, Lizzie thought, feeling awkward as she swung herself out of the bed. They were supposed to be telling Thea today—that was what they'd decided in the dark hours of the night. Had Damon gone on ahead of her?

No! Thea must hear it from her mother, Lizzie thought as she rushed to take a shower.

As she stood beneath the water that had felt so soothing only hours before her mind filled with terrifying images. They included Damon taking Thea away on his powerboat, or in his helicopter, or his jet—how would she ever find them again when he had homes all over the world? She'd made a very poor job of finding Damon over the past eleven years, so he would easily stay ahead of her now.

Grabbing a towel, she closed her eyes and accepted that her fears had no base in reality. All she had to do was get herself back to the restaurant somehow, so she could change her clothes, and then call Thea to arrange to meet her at the school, where Lizzie would explain everything.

Plan made, she prepared for the most vital explanation of her life.

Thea came powering towards Lizzie through the gates of the island's school. Throwing herself into her mother's arms, she exclaimed, 'You're wearing the *blue* dress today!' Thea's smile was sunny, but her sharp gaze missed nothing. 'You never wear dresses unless it's for a special occasion.'

Lizzie cheeks burned red with guilt beneath Thea's scrutiny. 'I put the dress on for *you*. I went back to the restaurant specially—'

'You went *back*? From where?' Thea queried, fully in sleuth mode now. 'Where were you *before* the restaurant?'

'None of your business.'

Lizzie laughed. In spite of her tension, Thea's suspicious expression could always crack her up.

Thea narrowed her eyes. 'You were with *him*, weren't you?'

If only life was as simple as making a choice between a blue dress and a yellow dress, Lizzie thought, feeling a flutter of nerves now the moment had come to tell Thea the truth about her father.

'I love both dresses equally. You've got excellent taste.'

'That's not the question I asked you. What I want to know is, how did you get on with Damon?'

'Thea!' Lizzie tried and failed to be stern. 'As far as I can tell, he's a very nice man.'

'A *"very nice man"*?' Thea pulled a face.

'He's a good man,' Lizzie conceded carefully. She had to begin somewhere, but she could hardly pretend that she and Damon were bosom buddies right now.

'And…?' Thea pressed. 'Will you see him again soon?'

'I think it will be hard to avoid him on the island,' Lizzie said, speaking her thoughts out loud. 'But we should see him together next time—'

'No!' Thea cut in with disapproval. 'How is your romance going to flourish with *me* there? You have to see him on your own.'

'I thought you liked him?'

'I do—but only if he makes you happy.'

'He enjoyed hearing you play,' Lizzie said, to break the sudden tension.

'He can come to a concert and hear the entire orchestra play,' Thea dismissed, clearly eager to move on the subject at the top of her agenda. 'It's *you* I'm worried about, not him.'

Lizzie's sinking feeling increased. 'We really need to talk about this.'

'Why?' Thea demanded.

'Because—'

Lizzie could see that Thea wasn't interested. Thea might be a musical prodigy, but she could be as difficult as any other ten-year-old child, and right now Thea's ears were closed to reason.

Lizzie still had to try. 'Because there's something I should have told you a long time ago. Why don't we sit in the shade and chat as we wait for the bus?'

Thea shrugged, but she plopped down on the bench next to Lizzie.

'So…you like Damon?' Lizzie began cautiously.

'A lot,' Thea said with a frown. 'We hit it off right away. But you already know that, so what's this about?'

Would Thea hate her when she told her? Would the reasons for her not telling her sooner about Damon matter, or would Thea believe that Lizzie had kept Damon away from her on purpose?

This wasn't about *her*, Lizzie concluded, or how *she* felt about the situation. This was about Thea and Damon, and Thea deserved to hear the truth.

'I'm glad you like Damon, because there's something I need to tell you about him—'

'He's asked you to marry him?' Thea exclaimed, leaping up from the bench.

'Not exactly,' Lizzie confessed. 'What I've got to tell you goes a lot further back than this trip to Greece.'

'Is he my father?'

Lizzie was stunned speechless. *'What?'* She felt as if she'd been punched.

'Well? Is he?' Thea demanded. 'Is Damon Gavros my father? Yes or no?'

'I wanted to break it to you gently—'

'There's only one way you can break news like this,' Thea insisted, 'and that's with a brass band. *Yes!*' she exulted, punching the air. 'I *knew* it!'

Lizzie put a steadying hand on Thea's arm, and for once wished someone would do the same for her. 'We're still all right, aren't we? I mean, you and me…the two of us?'

'Of course we are,' Thea confirmed impatiently. 'We'll carry on exactly as before. Won't we…?'

Lizzie would have walked over hot coals to take the look of uncertainty from Thea's face. 'Of course we will,' she said fiercely. 'No one's going to interfere in our lives.'

'Good,' Thea said. Her slender shoulders lifted in a

shrug. 'He's never been around before, so why would he want to interfere now?'

'He *will* want to have some part in your life, Thea. He's your father, and you can't blame him for not being around when he's only just found out about you.'

'That doesn't give him any *rights* over me,' Thea said stubbornly. 'Believe me,' she said with agonising certainty, 'I'm quite an expert on this. Most of the kids at school have parents who are divorced, or about to be divorced—I listen to everything they say about it.'

'But I'm not married to Damon.'

'What difference does that make?' Thea demanded.

'I wanted to tell him as soon as I knew that I was pregnant with you, but I couldn't—'

'I don't care,' Thea declared, hugging Lizzie fiercely. 'I only care about *you*. I don't need anyone else,' she blurted on the brink of tears, instantly on her mother's side. 'We've done all right together, haven't we?'

'Of course we have.' Thea needed reassurance far more than she did, Lizzie thought as she dropped kisses on the top of Thea's head. 'And we'll continue to do all right, you and me.'

'Well, then…' Thea said, pulling back and looking up. '*Why* does he have to be part of my life?'

Holding Thea so she could look into her daughter's eyes, Lizzie said quietly, 'You've got nothing to worry about—*nothing*—do you hear me?'

'I hear you,' Thea said with absolute confidence.

This was not at all the way Lizzie had imagined things would turn out. Knowing Thea liked Damon, she had imagined Thea would be thrilled to learn Damon was her father. She had seemed thrilled, to begin with, but now Thea appeared to be more threatened than pleased by the news.

The important thing was that Thea understood that nothing would change between Thea and Lizzie because of these new circumstances.

'Why don't we meet him?' Lizzie suggested. 'You don't have to worry because I'll be there. You can get to know him slowly—in your own time. We both can, and then we'll take it from there. The one thing I promise is that you will *never* have to do anything you don't want to do.'

'Does that mean I can stay with you?' Thea blurted, her cheeks red and shiny with bottled-up emotion.

'Of *course* you can!' Lizzie drew Thea close.

'Because some of the girls at school never get to see their other parent, and I don't want that. I don't want to be away from you. I *love* you!' she exclaimed.

When Thea threw her arms around Lizzie, to give her the tightest hug ever, the dam finally broke and Lizzie cried.

He was waiting for Lizzie's call. *Take as much time as you need,* he'd told her. He'd step in when Thea was ready to meet him, and then Lizzie and he would have a discussion as to how to proceed from there.

He was confident all the problems could be ironed out. All that mattered to him, and to Lizzie too, was Thea's happiness. He *did* have one irritation to handle, and that was the media who were sniffing around. His people had contacted him to warn him.

Rumours always followed him. He was one of the richest unmarried men in the world, so he supposed media interest was inevitable. He'd told his team to downplay it.

'If you do, they will,' he'd said.

'I doubt it, when Ms Montgomery has a dark-haired child who happens to be the spitting image of you *and* happens to be the child prodigy playing at your father's birthday party,' the head of his legal department had informed him.

'What if she *does* look like me?'

He mapped Thea's face in his mind. He couldn't believe he hadn't spotted the similarities between them before. He and Thea were obviously related, and that was a fact the press could hardly be expected to miss.

'There's bound to be speculation,' his lawyer advised. 'You'd do well to put the rumours to bed before they get out of control.'

'It's no one else's business,' Damon said coldly. 'I'm entitled to a private life and I intend to keep it that way: *private.*'

'You can't allow emotion to blind you to what might be going on here, Damon.'

'What are you suggesting?'

'Just that there are gold-diggers everywhere,' his lawyer continued doggedly.

'Are you referring to Ms Montgomery?'

'She *is* her father's daughter,' his lawyer said smoothly.

Damon bunched his fists. He knew the lawyer was only doing his job, and Damon had never wanted yes-men around him to boost his ego. The lawyer couldn't be faulted for braving his displeasure by giving him the plain truth.

'I'll give your advice some thought,' he conceded. 'In the meantime I expect you to keep the press off both Ms Montgomery's and her daughter's backs.'

'And yours,' his lawyer said.

'And mine,' Damon agreed wearily. If he didn't give the man one concession, who knew where the lawyer's enthusiasm for his job might lead?

CHAPTER TWELVE

SHE MUSTN'T HOPE for too much, Lizzie thought. This was just the first meeting between the three of them since Damon and Thea had learned the truth. Touch wood, it all seemed to be going well. Damon had invited them to his beach house, and Thea's eyes had rounded like golf balls as she'd stared around, but…

Why did there always have to be a but?

Because maybe she hadn't gone about this the right way. Perhaps she should have given Damon and Thea a chance to get to know each other before telling them that they were father and daughter.

Was there a right way to do this?

And then there were the practical points that they hadn't ironed out yet, Lizzie thought as Damon showed them around his glorious mansion. There were priceless rugs underfoot and striking works of art on the walls. The furniture was sleek and modern, and the house was kitted out with every luxury item imaginable—including an elegant grand piano in the hall beneath the sweeping marble staircase.

And still it echoed.

This was luxury on an unprecedented scale, but it told Lizzie nothing about Damon. There were no personal items, no photographs, no trophies, no memorabilia at all.

And every footfall and whispered word between them travelled aimlessly around the vaulted space. It made Lizzie nostalgic for her cosy bedsit, where she had cuddled up on many a night with Thea.

This mansion was a sumptuous new build, waiting to have a family's personality imprinted upon it. And, even supposing things could be ironed out between Lizzie and Damon, how were they going to manage this? From being two separate units, could they become one?

What would be lost along the way? Lizzie thought as they walked from a cinema room to an indoor gym and a swimming pool complex, and on again to a full-scale library. Her independence? Lizzie wondered with a frisson of alarm. Or Thea's carefree take on life? Either way, she couldn't relax into the tour of this fabulous house and pretend she belonged there.

Thea had to be worried about the future too. She wasn't easily impressed—except maybe by a thrift shop find, or some priceless violin she'd seen in an auction house catalogue—and she had never lusted after riches. She had everything she needed, she would often tell Lizzie, but now Lizzie was beginning to wonder if Thea said it just to reassure her.

She would soon find out.

Lizzie's trust fund was heavily depleted, she accepted. Her father and stepmother had seen to that. The only time Lizzie felt secure was when *she* was in control. She might not have much, but what she had she'd earned, and she was confident she could make a safe and loving home for Thea.

Watching Thea and Damon together, the two of them so seemingly relaxed, made Lizzie edgy. She knew Thea well enough to know when Thea was being polite, rather than genuinely enthusiastic, and she suspected that was the case now, but she couldn't be sure until Thea expressed an opinion.

All she wanted was for Thea to be happy, but was this the way? Lizzie wondered as Thea reached out a hand, as if needing her mother's support. She crossed the room quickly to take hold of Thea's hand, sensing a need for reassurance beneath Thea's outwardly happy front.

Thea wasn't satisfied with holding hands, and threw herself into a hug, as if she needed to feel the security of her mother wrapped around her. 'Stay with me,' she insisted in a fierce whisper. 'You're part of this too.'

Was she? Lizzie wondered. Or was three a crowd?

He saw the concern on Lizzie's face and knew she was holding her feelings in, not wanting to influence Thea. They were both keen to keep this first meeting between the three of them as relaxed as possible.

How was it going so far?

Not so well, judging by Thea's white face.

'I'll leave you both to take a look around the house on your own,' he said. 'Take your time.'

'You're leaving us?' Thea said suspiciously.

There was an undercurrent behind those words that told him in no uncertain terms that it would take a lot more than one day to make up for eleven missing years.

'I'll take you back to the school when you're ready,' he reassured her. 'You two need some time alone to get used to the idea of having me in your life.'

'Do we *have* to?' he heard Thea ask Lizzie as he walked away.

Well, *that* was an unrivalled success, Lizzie thought cynically as Damon drove them back. If anything, things were tenser now than they had been before.

'Don't forget the party tomorrow,' Thea reminded Lizzie as Damon pulled up outside Thea's school.

'Party?' Lizzie exclaimed, and then she remembered. There was so much going on she could barely keep up.

'Tomorrow afternoon at the old gentleman's house.' Thea glanced at Damon. 'My...grandfather?' Thea frowned as she tested a word that could mean very little to her yet.

'That's right,' Damon confirmed. 'And my father can't wait to meet you.'

Things were moving fast, Lizzie reflected. Too fast, maybe, and none of it was easy for Thea.

'I'll be there,' she promised Thea.

She'd have to juggle her work schedule, as in spite of Iannis insisting she must take a holiday Lizzie had said that she'd help out with some of the last-minute preparations for the party.

Seeing Lizzie's concern, Damon stepped in. 'I spoke to Iannis on your behalf, so you can leave the restaurant early. I hope you don't mind?'

Before she could answer Thea piped up tensely, 'Are you going to organise *everything* in my mother's life now?'

'Thea!' Lizzie exclaimed, though she had to concede that Thea had a point.

'Thea's right,' Damon admitted, saving himself at the eleventh hour. 'I should have consulted you first, and I apologise. It's just that music is my father's joy, and he's very excited about tomorrow and the chance to meet you both.'

Thea wasn't taking things nearly as well as Lizzie had hoped. She would need a lot of reassurance going forward. And time. They both needed more time to get their heads around this new order.

'You don't have to work while you're here,' Damon told

Lizzie, meaning to be helpful, no doubt, but only succeeding in garnering more black looks from Thea.

Thea wasn't shy in expressing her feelings on the subject. 'My mother *likes* to work. She tells me so all the time.'

Lizzie didn't comment on that, but she did voice her concerns. 'If I don't work, how can I support us both?'

Damon's expression was his answer. *He* would provide for them. But that didn't suit Lizzie.

Meanwhile Thea's head was snapping from side to side, like a spectator at a tennis match, with an expression on her face that clearly said, *See? I told you what parents were like*—which was the last thing Lizzie had wanted.

When Thea had climbed out of the SUV outside the school, Lizzie took off her seat belt. 'I'll get out here too,' she told Damon. 'Thanks for the lift. I'll catch the bus back to the restaurant.'

It would be a relief to leave the tension in the enclosed cabin of the SUV behind, but that was only a minor reason for her taking this decision. She wanted to reassure Thea, and that was more important than anything. She also wanted to tell Damon that this wouldn't work if he insisted on acting without listening.

But her priority was Thea, whose sigh of relief when Damon drove away was almost as deep as Lizzie's.

The party at the grand old mansion was in full swing by the time Lizzie and Thea arrived. Lizzie had managed to reassure Thea a little by this point, and they both found it impossible not to smile when they were welcomed to the Gavros family home with the warmest of greetings by the man they now knew was Thea's grandfather.

The man her father had defrauded, Lizzie remembered, incredulous that *anyone* could have a heart big enough to put the past in the past and give them such a warm welcome.

The large, impressive house was not what Lizzie had expected either. Far from being a stuffy museum, it was a cluttered home, slightly shabby, with dogs running around and cats commanding all the best chairs.

'Thea!' Thea's grandfather grasped her hands. 'I've heard so much about you. Welcome to our home,' he said, shaking Thea's hand formally—to give him chance to study Thea's face without being too obvious about it, Lizzie thought. '*Your* home too now,' he advised Thea gently.

As Lizzie watched on she felt a pang as Damon's father continued to look at Thea as if he were drinking in every last detail, thirsty for knowledge of his granddaughter. Lizzie's fears that Thea would remain tense, maybe even a little surly, quickly disappeared. They had both been re-assured by the old gentleman's warmth and his genuine manner. Thea had completely relaxed, and was returning his smile.

'I'm very pleased to be here,' Thea said politely, study-ing her grandfather with matching interest.

'Welcome home,' he declared, turning to Lizzie.

'Thank you.'

Lizzie was floored by the welcome. Damon's father had so many reasons to hate everything about her fam-ily, and yet he was greeting them with such warmth. Her emotions surged, regret and wistfulness competing as she thought back to another time, when her mother had been alive and they had lived in a loving and slightly chaotic home just like this.

'I hardly dare to shake your hand, young lady,' Thea's grandfather was confiding in Thea. 'In case I damage it!' he explained, which made them both laugh.

Infected by their *joie de vivre*, Lizzie relaxed enough to laugh too, while Thea insisted, 'My hand's made of tougher stuff than that.'

'And is your mother made of the same *tough stuff*?' Thea's grandfather asked, turning his wise gaze on Lizzie.

'My mother's the best mother in the world—*and* the most beautiful!'

'Thea—' Lizzie protested. Her cheeks fired red. 'We mustn't hog all of Kirio Gavros's time. He does have other guests.'

'But none as important as you,' Damon's father assured Lizzie. 'Your daughter speaks with passion. You're a very lucky woman. Please,' he added, gesturing towards an open door through which they could see the garden, 'enjoy the sunshine and the music. There's an ice cream cart, Thea—and it looks as if your friends are here to escort you,' he exclaimed as a group from the youth orchestra crowded round.

'You're very generous. Thank you,' Lizzie said warmly, turning to go.

'No. *You* are generous,' Thea's grandfather argued softly. 'You didn't need to come here. You didn't need to allow Thea to come here. So I thank you from the bottom of my heart.'

Hearing the break in his voice, Lizzie turned. 'Thank you for inviting us.' It still didn't seem enough after what her father had put him through, and impulsively she went back to kiss Damon's father on both cheeks.

'Don't be a stranger, Lizzie,' he whispered. 'The past is the past. Remember that always, and never let the past hold you back.'

When she finally broke away she had tears in her eyes. 'Thea—what do you say?' she called out, needing a few moments to rein in her emotions.

'Thank you!' Thea called back to her grandfather with a happy wave, before her friends dragged her away.

'Go and enjoy yourself,' Damon's father insisted, chivvying Lizzie across the hall with great warmth.

She had a lot to think about by the time she left the cool of the hall for the heat of the blazing sun.

'Over here, Mama—here, beneath the trees.'

Shading her eyes, Lizzie saw that with unerring good sense Thea and her friends had set up camp beneath the generous canopy of a jacaranda tree.

An elderly lady was introducing herself to the children as Lizzie approached. Was this humorous, twinkly sparrow of a woman Damon's mother? Lizzie wondered. Somehow she'd expected to find a tall, elegant, possibly fearsome lady, rather than this instantly likeable person.

She missed her own mother so badly for a moment she had to pause to let her emotions subside before she could walk up and introduce herself.

Damon's mother took her hand in both of hers. 'Welcome, Lizzie,' she said, smiling. She scanned Lizzie's face and her smile widened. 'We're so very pleased to have you here.'

This was said with such warmth that Lizzie's eyes brimmed a second time.

'Anything the two of you want,' Damon's mother added, glancing at Thea, 'please know that you only have to ask.'

'Thank you.'

This was so much more than Lizzie had hoped for. And the sincerity of Damon's parents said a lot about Damon. No wonder he'd worked so hard to put things right for them, to ensure that their retirement was worry-free. They all had a lot of lost time to make up for, but for the first time Lizzie wanted to believe that it might be possible.

'I'm glad you came.'

Damon's voice was deep and husky, and Lizzie tingled all over to hear him so close behind her. His mother had moved closer to the children to talk to them, leaving the two of them alone.

'Shall we?' he asked, leading Lizzie away from the happy tableau of Thea and her grandmother and Thea's friends.

Her body heated beneath his dark gaze. His sensuality was overpowering. She was spellbound by his sexual charisma, Lizzie concluded, and she badly needed not to be if she was to think clearly.

Damon halted at the side of a swimming pool, beneath the shade of an awning, where they could talk discreetly.

'Your parents couldn't have been more welcoming. You're a very lucky man.'

'They worked hard to make me what I am,' he countered dryly. 'And I didn't make it easy for them.'

She was sure he had not.

'This is a wonderful occasion…'

Lizzie's mouth dried as she gazed around. She felt threatened by this very different, very privileged lifestyle. Even her father, at the height of his showing off, had never lived in a property remotely comparable to this majestic home.

Bunting fluttered from the huge white marquee set in the centre of a flawless emerald-green lawn, while the surrounding garden was like a park full of colour, with ponds and streams and majestic fountains flowing. Behind this the grand old house watched over the proceedings with the elegance of centuries emblazoned on its grey stone. Lizzie wouldn't blame Thea if she was tempted to throw aside their bedsit for the chance to live somewhere like this.

'Everything needs careful handling,' Damon said, as if reading her mind.

She turned to look at him. 'Of course it does.' She followed his gaze to where Thea was chatting happily with his parents, both of whom had now joined the group of children.

'Shall we?' Damon suggested again, angling his chin towards the house.

She almost didn't want to leave. It was as if she feared losing her place in Thea's affections, was worried that she might be pushed out to make room for a new family and a new life.

'Now?' he prompted.

Why could neither of them be honest about their feelings? Lizzie wondered. The sexual tension between her and Damon was as fierce as ever, and they never seemed to have any problem expressing that, but where emotions were concerned they were both equally skilled at hiding them.

It was a lot to take in, Lizzie reasoned, but decided to break the ice first.

'I wish your parents hadn't been left out of the loop for so long,' she admitted as Damon held open the door into the main house for her.

'They do too,' he said frankly. 'But what can't be changed must be accepted and dealt with. The main thing is that they're both overjoyed to discover they have a granddaughter at this stage of their lives. Thea's happiness is all they care about. They have no resentment. In fact, far from it. They're grateful to you. They can't thank you enough. They know you've had a difficult life, and they also know I didn't make it any easier for you. They certainly don't pity you,' he added, anticipating her possible reaction. 'If anything, they admire you more than they can say. Come in,' he added, beckoning her into the house when she hesitated on the threshold.

She looked around with interest as Damon led the way through a hallway packed with a selection of boots and gardening tools to open the door on to a comfortably ramshackle sitting room. Everything she looked at wore the patina of age with grace. There were chunks out of chair legs where dogs had chewed, and threaded curtains where cats had climbed, and in spite of everything going on in their lives Lizzie felt wistful, knowing Damon had grown up in a *real* family home—which was exactly what she'd always dreamed of for Thea.

'You've never been frightened of change before, Lizzie.'

'Is that how it looks to you?' She laughed softly. 'I *am* afraid of change,' she admitted. 'I just hide it well.'

'And now I'm in your life you know there's more change coming?'

She shivered involuntarily. That sounded like a threat. 'There's change, and then there's your billionaire lifestyle,' she admitted. 'It might take Thea and me a long time to get used to that.'

'I think you'd both adapt pretty quickly.'

'We might not *want* to,' Lizzie pointed out. 'Thea still has to get used to the idea of having a father in her life and I'll resent losing my independence. I know you have a lot,' she said, with magnificent understatement, 'but you can't *buy* Thea or me. Nor can you direct a child to love or even accept you. That will take time, and even then there are no guarantees. I'm sorry.' She really was. 'You'll just have to wait and see.'

'That's not my way,' Damon assured her.

'Then you might want to rethink *your way*,' Lizzie countered, as mildly as she could. 'Thea is a young person with an independent mind—as I think you've seen for yourself.'

'And what about you, Lizzie?'

'The same goes for me—though my primary concern is Thea, and any decision I make will be based on that.'

'It's not my intention to steal Thea from you,' Damon was quick to add.

Then why even mention it? Lizzie thought.

CHAPTER THIRTEEN

THEY MADE ARRANGEMENTS for more meetings between the three of them, and then Lizzie left Damon so she could go and find Thea. The rest of the afternoon passed happily, if a little tensely, at least for Lizzie, but without incident. She stayed for the first part of the concert in the evening, but as Thea wasn't playing in the second half Lizzie returned to the restaurant and took the opportunity, while it was closed, to perform a stock-take and do a deep clean.

It was a relief to work with her hands and take her mind off everything else. Even with the wonderful Gavros grandparents, the warmest of welcomes, and Damon's obvious intention to make things right for Thea, Lizzie couldn't shake a feeling of uneasiness.

Maybe it was his mention of not stealing Thea from her. Why had that thought even entered his mind? The future was so hard to visualise, and that was what worried her more than anything.

Work saved her. It always had. She could feel her pulse steadying even as she mopped the floor. Work was the rock she had always clung to. It was the reassurance she needed to know that she would always be able to support Thea and herself.

'No wonder my cousin loves you,' Iannis commented when he returned from the party to find his kitchen in tip-top condition and a list neatly drawn up ready for his visit to the wholesalers the next day. '*Everyone* loves you, Lizzie.'

'So long as *you* do,' she teased Iannis, and then tensed at the sound of a powerful engine drawing closer.

'Uh-oh,' Iannis murmured. 'I'd better make myself scarce.'

'Please don't—'

Too late. Iannis had already disappeared into the pantry.

Lizzie glanced outside to confirm her suspicions. Damon, driving a stylish black Aston Martin DB9, had just opened the driver's door and climbed out. How was she supposed to stop every atom in her being yearning for him? Maybe she'd never get that under control. It wasn't fair for anyone to look so quite so stunning this late at night.

She smoothed her hair self-consciously, knowing that she certainly didn't look her best, and that even her best could never compete with Damon's darkly glittering glamour. He looked incredible, wearing nothing more than a pair of snug-fitting jeans and a slate-blue linen shirt with the sleeves rolled back.

'Why are you here?' She lowered her arms, realising that she was hugging herself defensively as he jogged up the steps. His arrival had charged the air with electricity, changing the mood—her mood, specifically. Damon changed everything.

'Hello to you too,' he remarked dryly. 'Why am I here? To take you on a moonlit drive.'

Lizzie shook her head. 'I don't think so. It's far too late.'

'I don't know what kind of carriages you're used to, Cinderella, but I can assure you mine is in no danger of turning into a pumpkin at midnight.'

'Less of the Cinderella, please. I'm all out of glass slippers.' He was close enough for her to feel his heat warming her, and to smell the faint scent of his exclusive cologne.

'We need to talk,' Damon insisted.

'I agree,' she said. 'But why now?'

'Why not now?' Damon argued. 'We can't keep putting this off. Neither of us wants Thea to be confused, and she will be if we don't get things straightened out between us.'

Thea was the magic word. He must know it would work. She could see the change in his eyes when she made her decision. 'I'd need to go and get changed first.'

'Okay.' Damon shrugged. 'You do that and I'll wait.'

'I'll be as quick as I can.'

And only because it involved Thea, Lizzie thought as she raced upstairs to change out of her work clothes, with her heart hammering off the scale.

He drew the car to a halt on top of the cliff overlooking the bay, where there was no sound other than the cicadas chittering and the ocean breathing rhythmically below. Lizzie was freshly showered. He could still smell the shower gel she'd used. She'd changed into casual jeans and a top, but she was still strung out.

'You need to relax,' he told her.

'How can I, when everything I care about is under threat?'

'Not from me.'

She didn't say anything, but her silence was a response in itself.

'So, what do you want to discuss?' she said at last. 'Because I think I need to see a lawyer before we decide to do anything.'

'Does it have to be so formal between us?'

She turned to stare at him steadily. 'Yes. I think it does.'

'Would it upset you to know that my asking you out to-night isn't *all* about custody and visitation rights?'

She stared at him blankly. 'I don't understand.'

'I needed to see you,' Damon said bluntly, 'and not to talk—not tonight.'

'You've got me here on false pretences,' Lizzie protested, clearly not impressed. 'We can talk, or you can take me back. Please,' she added as a tense afterthought.

'You have to have a life too.'

'You're my counsellor now?' She didn't wait for him to answer. 'For your information, I already have a life.'

'*Do* you? Do you allow yourself to?'

She laughed that off. 'I have the life I want.'

He let that pass, and reassured her by explaining that he wanted to get to know Thea slowly, and always with Lizzie around to help break any possible tension between them.

'I know this is going to take time. And I know you think I'm impatient, which I am, but this is something different. I do understand that.'

'For which I'm very grateful,' she said.

He smiled at her spikiness. It reminded him of the old Lizzie, full of fire and defiance. He knew that Lizzie was still in there somewhere. It was just that this Lizzie had devoted her life to Thea at the expense of her own.

'I want the two of you to come back to Greece and spend more time here. So you can both get used to the idea of having more options,' he explained.

That was as far as he thought it wise to take it while Lizzie was so tense and insistent upon seeing everything as a threat.

'Yes,' she agreed, and this time she didn't look away, but held his gaze steadily.

A different type of tension had been building between them while they'd been talking. Being enclosed in the confines of the car had something to do with it, and that tension would need an outlet soon.

'What?' he prompted, sensing that something else was troubling Lizzie.

'Your life will remain largely unchanged,' she pointed out, 'while ours will be massively changed.'

'You don't think my life will change? Of *course* my life will change. How could it ever be the same again? And your life will be better—and easier,' he insisted.

'I won't take your money!' she exclaimed. 'You seem to think that money is the answer to everything, but it can't even come close.'

'I have a daughter to think about now,' he argued firmly. 'Where are you going?' he asked as Lizzie fumbled with the door handle.

'Don't!' she warned when he leaned across to stop her. 'I need to get out and have some space to think.'

'On a cliff-edge?' he cautioned.

She had to get out of the car—she couldn't think straight with Damon so close and her whole being yearning for him. It could only lead to disaster if she stayed. How *could* she trust Damon? How could she trust *anyone*?

Part of her wanted to go back to the enclosed world she'd built with Thea, while the other part of her knew that that wouldn't be fair to Thea, or even healthy for Lizzie. First and foremost she had to calm down. She'd never been a coward. She'd always faced things head-on.

She turned to face Damon. They were still touching. His hand was resting on hers as he tried to stop her getting out of the car, and his body was pressed tightly against her. Fighting him was never going to be a good idea. They didn't have to do much to light the fuse between them, and there was far too much at stake now. Combine that with the passion Lizzie had been bottling up inside for eleven years, and this was a recipe for disaster.

'Have you ever made out in a car?' Damon asked, smiling faintly at her.

'No. And I've no intention of ever doing so,' she assured him, pulling back.

'Really?' Damon murmured, sounding not in the least bit dismayed 'Sometimes I find a release of tension helps to clear the mind.'

'I bet you do,' she agreed dryly, straightening her clothes.

She'd barely done that when Damon adjusted her seat in a way that made it instantly flat, and she shrieked with surprise.

'Well, it's definitely possible,' he observed, frowning as if he didn't *know* that throwing that lever would result in landing Lizzie on her back.

'I'll just have to take your word for it,' she said tensely, starting to struggle up.

'You can do more than that...'

As she was about to discover.

'Brute,' she whispered shakily as Damon dropped kisses on her neck. 'This is so totally unfair.'

'I suppose it is,' he agreed, working magic with his hands.

When Damon's mouth closed on hers and his tongue plundered all the dark, hidden places, she felt the response spread throughout her body like wildfire. Moving into the footwell on his knees in front of her, he nudged her legs apart and continued with the teasing.

'I think you like this,' he observed as his hands worked lightly, skilfully and steadily.

'You on your knees in front of me? What's not to like?' she somehow managed to gasp out.

He laughed, and she closed her eyes so she could only feel and listen to the sounds of pleasure.

He swiftly disposed of her jeans and underwear and, lifting her legs, rested them on the wide spread of his shoulders, giving her just enough time to grab hanks of his hair before plunging deep.

The sensation was incredible. There might be very little room for manoeuvre, with Damon's powerful frame taking up all the space, but he didn't need it to prove how proficient he could be even in the confines of the car.

'*Theos!* I've missed you,' he growled.

'It hasn't been that long—'

'Too long,' he argued fiercely.

She wasn't going to argue as he continued to move in the way she loved. Damon was a master of pleasure, and he knew her body far too well. He brought her to the edge in moments, and he kept her hovering until he commanded, 'Don't hold on.'

She needed no encouragement, and fell instantly, noisily and gratefully. Each pleasure wave stunned her, and she gorged herself on that pleasure. It was only when they both surfaced, with the moon acting as a spotlight, that they could see how far the car had moved forward.

'I'm really glad you didn't park on the edge,' Lizzie commented with relief.

Damon laughed, and then they were both laughing, still entwined in each other's arms.

If only life could be this simple and go on like this for ever, Lizzie thought.

'Could it be that you're starting to trust me?' Damon asked, and she levelled a long, considering look on his face.

Trust was such a big issue for Lizzie, and she didn't answer right away. Then, 'Yes, I am,' she said at last.

Drawing her into his arms, Damon held her and kissed her. 'Don't ever lose the faith again.'

'I won't,' she promised, snuggling close.

She only wished the little niggle of doubt inside her would go away.

'I *know* we'll move forward from here,' Damon said confidently.

'Not over the edge of the cliff, I hope?'

He pulled back to smile down at her and she smiled contentedly.

'I'm being serious,' Damon insisted. 'I hope you're not suggesting that I don't play fair?'

'Well, *do* you?' It was Lizzie's turn to lift her head and stare at Damon.

'I play to win,' he said.

CHAPTER FOURTEEN

NOTHING WAS EVER completely straightforward, Lizzie thought as she climbed into Damon's SUV outside the restaurant the next morning. Still intensely aware of him, thanks to a night that had left her wanting more, they were now on their way to the school to pick up Thea—just as regular parents picked up their children.

They had planned a return to the beach house to try and make a better go of things than they had last time. Thea would have a home in Greece as well as in England, Damon had told Lizzie before he'd dropped her off last night at the restaurant, and a music studio all her own. That had really chimed with Lizzie. Yes, she might have everything to lose—including her heart, to Damon—but she couldn't keep an opportunity like that out of Thea's reach.

'Good night's sleep?' he asked dryly as they turned onto the main road.

'Yes. You?' she asked in an innocent tone, knowing she hadn't slept a wink.

She'd told Damon to drop her off at the restaurant the previous night, but he'd wanted to take her back to the beach house, where they would be able to make love in comfort. She had shied away from that level of involvement. To wake up beside Damon and find herself wanting things she couldn't have wouldn't help anyone, and she needed to keep a clear head if she was to try and work out how to keep things running smoothly for Thea in their utterly changed lives.

Thea was waiting for them outside the school, and everything seemed to be going well to begin with. Thea was excited at the thought of going to the beach, and Damon was buzzing too.

'I've got a gift for you,' he told Thea, the moment they walked through the door of his beachside mansion.

'For *me*?' Thea said excitedly as Damon led the way into the house.

She was still a child, Lizzie thought, feeling more than ever protective. Thea loved presents, and Lizzie couldn't afford nearly enough of them.

Damon took them into the room that Lizzie had already planned in her fantasy world would be Thea's music studio. There was the grand piano, in one corner, and a new addition…a violin case…was resting on the piano stool.

'It's for you,' Damon explained when Thea remained hovering uncertainly by the door. 'The violin's for *you*, Thea. Call it an early Christmas present.'

'It's only June,' Thea said in a small voice.

That short comment was the only warning Lizzie needed that things weren't all right with Thea. She knew her daughter's moods.

Thea proved her right by being uncharacteristically subdued as she walked across the room. Reaching out one small hand, she tentatively trailed her fingertips across the violin case.

'Well? Aren't you going to open it?' Lizzie asked, glancing anxiously at Damon, who had also tensed, she noticed.

Thea didn't say anything. She snapped the catches, lifted the lid—and stood back.

'Is something wrong?' Damon asked.

Thea was pale when she turned around, and instead of saying any of the things they might have expected, asked simply, 'Is everything going to change now?'

'No, of course not!' Rushing to Thea's side, Lizzie gave her a hug.

'What do you mean, Thea?' Damon asked quietly.

They looked at each other over Thea's head.

Breaking free of Lizzie, Thea explained, 'I know this is a very valuable instrument, and I know I should be grateful. It's a very thoughtful gift…and I thank you,' she added in a small voice. 'But it's far too good for me—especially when I don't even know if I'll still be playing the violin when I grow up.'

This hammer-blow struck at Lizzie's heart. It took all she'd got not to show how shocked she was by Thea's remark. She couldn't believe she'd never sensed this doubt in Thea before, and felt immediately guilty. Had she urged Thea down the wrong path? She couldn't put her hand on her heart and be sure of anything.

Even Damon seemed lost for words for once, and Thea hadn't finished yet.

'My mother worked very hard to buy me my first full-sized violin,' she explained patiently to Damon, with all the seriousness a ten-year-old could muster. 'She worked long hours and put small payments down until she'd paid enough for me to take the violin home. We'd seen the violin I wanted in a pawnshop window, and my mother begged the owner of the shop not to sell it to anyone else,' she explained. 'And there's something else… Can I tell him?'

'No,' Lizzie said, flashing a warning glance at Thea.

'Tell me what?' Damon prompted.

'Nothing,' Lizzie said quickly.

'You speak for your daughter now?'

For an instant Thea looked as if she'd like to kill Damon and, pleased as she was at the way her daughter had leapt to her defence, Lizzie knew this was hardly helpful when it came to bringing the three of them closer.

'Thea, please…' she cautioned gently, but Thea refused to be stopped.

'My mother had to sell things at the pawnshop,' Thea said bluntly, with an angry frown on her face as she remembered. 'Special things she really cared about. She did that so she could buy me all the extras I needed at school and pay for my violin. Why would I want another instrument when mine was bought with so much love?'

A long silence followed.

'Maybe when you're older?' Lizzie suggested in the awkward break.

'No,' Thea argued. 'If I play the violin at all, no other violin could ever mean as much to me. The only reason I play so well is because *you* bought my instrument for me. I might not even *want* to be a professional musician when I'm older. I might want to be an airline pilot, or an engineer—or maybe a comedian?' Thea raised her chin as she considered this last option.

'You can be anything you want to be,' Lizzie agreed.

Damon's face remained expressionless throughout, and Lizzie almost felt sorry for him. Once again it came down to the fact that not everything could be bought with money and a gap of eleven years could not be easily filled. That was something they both had to come to terms with.

'You're right, Thea,' Damon conceded. 'I should have asked what you wanted before I bought the violin.'

'No—it's good. It's lovely,' Thea said quickly, obviously eager to make amends.

She wasn't a cruel child. Thea was sensitive, which showed in her music, and she knew when someone was hurt. Lizzie had never been prouder of Thea than she was right now.

'Can you return it to the shop and get your money back?' Thea suggested with concern.

'I'm sure I can,' Damon said confidently.

They were all on a steep learning curve, and no doubt they'd all make more mistakes, Lizzie thought as Thea turned to her. 'You're not upset that I might not want to be a professional violinist, are you?' she asked, staring into Lizzie's eyes with concern.

'It's your life,' Lizzie said gently. 'You have to follow your star.'

'I knew you'd understand!' Thea exclaimed, relaxing into a happy smile at once. 'And you *will* get your mother's wedding ring back one day, I promise. *I'll* get it back for you— Oops.' She glanced at Damon, and then at Lizzie. 'I shouldn't have said that, should I?'

Lizzie reassured Thea with a smile. This was exactly what she'd dreaded—that Thea would end up like Lizzie, feeling guilty all the time. So what if her secret was out? Thea hadn't meant any harm by it. And it was the truth. There had never been enough money for Lizzie to buy back her mother's ring.

She wanted Damon to know that she appreciated his gesture—that she understood that he was trying to make up for all the lost years by wrapping every birthday and Christmas present he'd missed into one fabulous gift. He'd done a really great thing, and for all the right reasons, but because he didn't know Thea his gesture had fallen flat.

A week later Damon watched Lizzie and Thea's plane take off into the mid-afternoon sky on its way to London. He'd worked hard in the intervening days to make up for his gaffe with the violin, and his reward had been seeing

Thea gradually return to the ease they'd shared before they'd known they were father and daughter.

He understood Thea's stout defence of her mother, and could only admire her for it. As Lizzie had said, it would take time to reassure Thea that things would be better now, not worse. And he was prepared to wait for as long as it took. For the first time in his life he couldn't afford to be impatient. Thea was too important for him to get this wrong.

It was only when he turned to go to his car that he realised how alone he felt now they'd gone. Had he always felt this way? The answer was an unequivocal no. He'd never known what he was missing before today.

He stood by the car, gazing up at the sky until the jet carrying Lizzie and Thea away became a silver dot before disappearing. He and Lizzie had made certain decisions, which included taking things slowly, but those decisions, so carefully made, didn't feel right to him now.

Climbing into the car, he released the handbrake and pulled away from the kerb.

Would Lizzie ever return to Greece?

He was so busy scrutinising the sky in the direction Lizzie's jet had taken that he almost drove into a ditch. He adjusted his steering fast.

Maybe it was time to adjust his life and his thinking too.

Thea had buried herself in a book for the duration of the flight home, giving Lizzie plenty of time to think. Everything had been almost perfect during their last few days on the island, she mused. If there *was* a problem it was Lizzie, with her courage for others and caution for herself. She had never used to be like that, but she had to keep everything safe and steady for Thea.

Was Damon right in saying she should have a life too?

Did Thea deserve a mother who could never pull back and see what was under her nose? *Was* she smothering Thea? Was that why Thea had said what she'd said about not necessarily following a career as a musician when she was older?

On the other hand Damon had got things right these past few days. His family had been more involved with Thea, and the more Lizzie had got to know them, the more she'd come to believe that having them in their lives could only be a good thing for Thea.

Now there was just the problem of Lizzie and Damon, and where *they* went from here...if they went anywhere.

There were grey clouds over London as the plane came in to land. The aircraft hit turbulence and juddered suddenly and Lizzie gasped and gripped the armrest.

'What's wrong?' Thea asked.

'Nothing. Everything's perfect.'

So why did she have to try so hard to convince herself that this was true? Couldn't she do as Damon asked and trust him for once?

Lizzie couldn't even put a name to the doubt inside her, except to say that it refused to go away. It was a relief when the plane broke through the clouds and they landed safely.

Lizzie kissed Thea goodbye at the gates of the school boarding house where Thea stayed during term time. Thea was popular, which made parting easier, though it was never easy for Lizzie on the bus ride home. She always felt sad when she left Thea at school—and especially now, when she knew that Thea wasn't wholly committed to a future as a professional musician.

Some fairly big decisions would have to be made soon. If Thea *did* decide to become a day pupil Lizzie would be the happiest mother alive. The complications it would throw up would just have to be worked through, like everything else. Flexi-working, Lizzie thought as she put the key in the door. That was the answer.

She'd just have to hope she could earn enough money working part-time and still be available when Thea needed her. She'd always found a solution in the past, so there was no reason to suppose that she couldn't do so again.

The house that encompassed her bedsit was empty… echoing and empty. The owners were obviously away.

Shaking off the feeling of loneliness, Lizzie picked up her mail and wheeled her suitcase into her room. A coffee first, and then she'd look at the important things.

There was a lot of mail to throw away first—flyers, menus from the local take-away restaurants—and then one very official-looking envelope, with the name of a legal firm that shot fear into her heart stamped in confident black letters across the top.

Coffee would have to wait, she decided as she turned the envelope over in her hands. The last time she'd heard the name of this law firm had been eleven years ago, in court.

Might as well get it over with…

She didn't even pause to shrug off her jacket. She just ripped the thick velum envelope open and took out the letter. She unfolded it and started to read.

For once she was glad of the small room and the bed immediately behind her as she sank down, trembling.

Was this what Damon meant by trust? Trust was as ephemeral as a puff of smoke. Trust was a state of mind for fools and romantics. And she had proved to be both, Lizzie concluded as she read the letter again.

Acting on behalf of Damon Gavros, the lawyer was asking—no, *demanding*—that a DNA test to establish Thea's genetic link to Damon must be undertaken at a clinic of his choice at the earliest opportunity.

*You will appreciate that my client is an extremely
wealthy man who must take sensible precautions. A
legal paternity test can settle matters such as child
support, child custody, visitation dispute, and in-
heritance issues, and will satisfy immigration requirements.*

*A strict chain of custody under the supervision of
this firm will ensure that samples taken remain in
compliance with all legal requirements—*

There was a lot more legalese, but she'd read enough.
It wasn't so much the request made by Damon's legal rep-
resentatives, but the fact that she'd been with Damon only
a few hours before the letter had arrived and he hadn't
thought to mention it.

Holding the letter, she sat on the bed with her head
bowed, thinking. It had never once occurred to her that
Damon would doubt Thea's parentage. She'd been a virgin when they'd met—which he knew—and she hadn't
slept with anyone else—which he also knew. Thea was
Damon's child. There wasn't the smallest doubt about it.
And yet he still wanted proof?

*Maybe he thought the apple hadn't fallen far from the
tree.*

Lizzie blazed inwardly as she thought about that. She
took after her mother—as Thea did—not her weak and
imprudent father.

The main thing now was to protect Thea at all costs.
She must remain calm. She wouldn't allow the test to happen. She had that power at least.

Even as she thought about it Lizzie felt her spirits
reviving. Thea would *not* be made to think there was
something wrong with her. And as for this lawyer suggesting that a man as rich as Croesus must take *sensible*

precautions—perhaps Damon should have thought of that when they'd made love.

Yes, she'd been willing enough, and, yes, he'd used protection. But there had been a lot of sex that night, and maybe Damon hadn't been as meticulous as he'd thought. She took responsibility too, and now it was up to her to protect Thea from every possible hurt.

But what angered Lizzie most was the way this had been done. What would have been so hard about Damon telling her to her face that he wanted a DNA test?

Her offer to give him time to integrate into Thea's life was a joke now. She'd had no idea that love came with a price tag attached. It seemed to her that Damon was only interested in protecting his precious bank balance. And how would Thea feel, having started to build a tentative relationship with her father only to be told that he needed proof that he was her father?

If new love was a tender green shoot, Damon had just trampled it. Thea would be heartbroken if she ever learned about this. Lizzie had never forgotten the feelings of abandonment she had suffered as a child, and was determined that Thea would *never* suffer anything similar.

It all boiled down to one simple question: was Damon Gavros fit to be Thea's father?

Going on this evidence? *No.* He was *not.* Either Damon wanted to build a relationship with Thea or he didn't, and no amount of test results could change that.

The twenty-four hours before he'd been able to file a flight plan to London had left him in a state of advanced impatience and frustration. He headed straight for the Greek restaurant when he arrived in the city, where he found Stavros in the kitchen. There was no sign of Lizzie, and his welcome from Stavros was unusually cool.

'She's at home,' Stavros told him, in what Damon could only describe as a hostile tone. 'Recovering,' Stavros added significantly.

'Is she ill?' Alarm iced him.

'Heartsick,' Stavros said, staring pointedly at the door.

He took the hint. 'Okay, I get it. I'm going. Her address…?'

'If Lizzie had wanted you to know where she lives she would have given you her address,' Stavros informed him with a cold stare.

'I need that address *now*,' he insisted. 'And her mobile number, in case she's not there.'

'Can't your *lawyer* supply those?'

'My lawyer?' Damon frowned. 'What's my lawyer got to do with this?'

The way Stavros shrugged sent an icy finger of suspicion tracking down Damon's spine. The head lawyer on his legal team had a notoriously itchy trigger finger, and remembering the warning he'd given Damon set alarm bells ringing.

'Lizzie's address and number *now*,' he urged, in a tone that even the loyal Stavros couldn't ignore. 'Please,' he added, consciously softening his tone as the restaurateur stared at him belligerently.

Finding Lizzie was too important to risk on a point of pride. He had only realised what he'd lost when she'd left the island. They'd started to build something that in these very early stages might all too easily be destroyed. He had to stop that happening *now*—not some time in the future. There had been too much delay on both parts.

'If you care anything at all for Lizzie and Thea, please help me,' he begged. When Stavros blinked with surprise at his obvious distress, he added, 'I *have* to see her now.'

Rather reluctantly Stavros jotted something down on a scrap of paper. When he handed it over Damon was reminded that he took too much for granted. He shouldn't have to ask for Lizzie's address. He should *know* her address. If he cared anything for Lizzie and Thea he should have every detail concerning them locked down.

He had lived a charmed life up to now, Damon concluded as he thanked Stavros and stowed the precious piece of paper in his pocket.

He left the restaurant at speed and leapt into his car. Tapping Lizzie's address into the sat nav, he sped away. The head of his legal team had always acted in Damon's best interests before—as seen through his legal eyes— and in fairness Damon expected him to take the initiative at his level, rather than always wait for instruction. But there were some things that should be out of his lawyer's control—and this was one of them. If he didn't make things right straight away Damon would be a man who had learned too late how much he had to lose.

He headed towards the suburbs at speed. An adored only son, he had entered the world on a cloud of privilege, and that sense of entitlement had continued on into his adult life. He saw. He seized. He conquered and his empire grew.

He'd always been able to see the path ahead clearly— until Lizzie had come into his life and changed the rules. Lizzie had changed everything, and he couldn't even be sure if she would agree to see him now.

Only one thing was certain in his immediate future, and that was that it was going to be the fight of his life.

CHAPTER FIFTEEN

DAMON? HOW COULD *Damon* possibly be parked outside her door?

For a moment Lizzie couldn't catch her breath, she was so shocked. *Damon had followed her to London!* She hadn't even had a chance to collect her thoughts properly after receiving his lawyer's letter yesterday—other than to call a family solicitor and make an appointment.

She froze behind the shutters of her room as she checked out the sleek black car parked outside the front door. The windows were tinted, so she couldn't see the driver, but she knew who it was. There was only one man who changed his car as often as his shirt, and always for a newer, sleeker model.

Better to have this out with him now, she concluded as she glanced at the letter, still lying on the table by the phone where she'd left it. Stavros had given her some time off, allowing her the chance to think her way through this nightmare. He'd winkled the truth out of her when he'd heard the tension in her voice.

Stavros had been furious too. He couldn't believe it of Damon, he'd said, adding that any lawyer sent by Damon Gavros would have to come through *him* first.

From being a wily matchmaker, Stavros had turned on a sixpence into Lizzie's staunchest defender. He'd wanted to send his wife over right away, to comfort her, but Lizzie had said she could handle things on her own. And she *would*, Lizzie determined.

She drew a deep, steadying breath before opening the front door. This wasn't the first hurdle she'd faced by any means, but perhaps it was the highest.

'Lizzie?' Damon called out. 'I know you're in there. Please open the door.'

She took a few shaking breaths and then swung the door wide. No way did she want Damon thinking that she was hiding from him.

Resolutions were one thing, but seeing Damon again was another. At least he was prepared for the vagaries of the London weather, she registered, taking in his heavy jacket and tough, workmanlike boots. Damon would look hot in a monk's robes, and in a thick sweater and jeans he looked as darkly, wickedly stunning as usual—while *she* felt exhausted and hurt, and above all furiously angry.

Her body should recoil from him after what he'd done, but nothing had changed where that was concerned. Her heart still raced and her breathing still quickened at the sight of him. Worse. Her body yearned as if it had no sense—but this time there was anger in the mix.

'Yes?' she demanded crisply. 'What do you want?'

'*Theos,* Lizzie!' he exclaimed. 'Thank God you're home.' He raked his hair in a familiar gesture. 'Let me in. We need to talk—'

'More talking?' she said, still barring his way.

'We have to talk when our daughter's involved,' he insisted.

Damon was a picture of power and dominance standing on the damp London street, while *she* had prepared for nothing and was wearing a faded old top, pyjama bottoms, and a pair of furry slippers on her feet. Her face was scrubbed clean of make-up and her hair was scraped back. Not her armour of choice, but she'd take it.

'*Our* daughter?' she queried. 'Are you sure about that?'

Damon's frown deepened. 'Of course I'm sure. Can I come in now?'

She stood back, and tensed as he brushed past her. She'd forgotten how big he was. This entire London house would fit into the hallway of his beachside mansion. She hesitated before opening the door to her bedsit, hardly able to imagine that they'd both fit inside.

She didn't waste time on pleasantries—especially as Damon didn't look around with interest, as she might have expected, but focused solely on her face. Going to the table, she picked up the letter and fanned it in front of him.

Lifting her chin to stare him in the eyes, she demanded, 'Did you authorise this?'

Damon's expression blackened as he recognised the name on the top of the letterhead. 'Of course not. What is it?'

'You don't know?'

'No, I don't,' he insisted. 'When did it arrive?'

'It was waiting for me when I got home.'

'May I?'

For the first time since she'd known him, she saw that Damon was badly thrown. She could hear it in his voice and see it in the deepness of the furrows between his eyes.

She handed him the letter and he read it quickly.

'Lizzie.' His eyes flicked up to meet her angry stare. 'I didn't ask for this.'

'So this firm of lawyers *doesn't* act for you?'

'You know it does. It must have been a terrible shock for you to recognise the name from your father's trial. I'm sure that's something you won't easily forgot.'

'Compassion? From you?' She huffed a laugh.

Could she believe him? Lizzie wondered. She wanted to, but sometimes it seemed that her whole life had been spent battling the disappointment of being let down.

'I felt sick to the stomach when I saw that letter.'

'This letter—this request for a DNA test,' he said, with what she was sure was genuine disgust, 'has *nothing* to do with me. Believe me, Lizzie. It's a matter of trust. You have to believe me.'

'I don't have to do anything.'

'You said you trusted me on the island,' Damon said steadily. 'Do you trust me now?'

She wanted to—so badly—but the past always stood in her way. 'I don't know what to think,' she confessed.

It didn't help that Damon's blistering glamour carried all the sultry heat of a Greek afternoon, which lent an aura of unreality to everything that was happening in the familiar surroundings of her small, cosy home. He could light up the damp London street without any help from the lamps outside, but could she trust him?

She really didn't know, Lizzie realised.

She felt as if she were being squeezed between Damon's lawyers, Damon's money, Damon, and an opulent lifestyle that was utterly alien to her. It was next to impossible to extract any judgement from that.

'I didn't send this,' he repeated softly, staring her in the eyes. 'I didn't ask for this letter to be drafted, let alone mailed to you. Your word is enough for me, Lizzie.'

Her word was enough for him? Trust was the most valuable currency of all in Lizzie's life, so why was she still holding back?

Because she had to make decisions for Thea too, Lizzie realised. This wasn't about her. It never had been. And she didn't know if she would ever feel confident enough to invite Damon in to their exclusive club of two.

'Will you be staying long?' she asked formally, feeling awkward, feeling edgy, feeling uncertain, when certainty was what she *had* to feel where everything to do with Thea was concerned.

'Apparently not,' Damon said dryly, putting the letter back on the table.

'I meant in London.'

'That depends,' he said.

She wouldn't give him the satisfaction of asking upon what it depended. She was in no mood to soften. This was her turf, her home, her sanctuary, and his lawyer's letter had breached that security.

'So, how did this happen?'

Damon shrugged. 'My legal team is over-keen.'

'That's not good enough.'

Not now the past had swooped over her like an ugly black cloak, blotting out the facts in front of her and re-placing them with horrors from another day.

'What does it matter if you authorised this letter or not? Your legal team work for *you*, in your name, as they worked that day to destroy my father. Do I want to hang around to see if any more letters like this arrive? Do I want to subject Thea to the risk of finding one some day? If you love Thea, as you say you do, I suggest you take this letter and shove it up your lawyer's backside, where it belongs—'

But she couldn't wait for that, and so she shredded it instead and let the pieces drop through her fingers like a shower of toxic confetti.

He was tempted to applaud, but guessed that wouldn't go down well. Lizzie was never more magnificent than when she was defending their child. If he had the whole world to choose from he couldn't find a better woman than this. He only wondered that it had taken him so long to realise Lizzie's true worth. He guessed that while he was a speed freak in business, and had everything down to a well-oiled art where that was concerned, he was a little less adept when it came to handling emotions and human relationships.

'You don't get to tell me what to do here. This is *my* turf,' Lizzie was telling him.

He had the satisfaction of hearing the pieces of the lawyer's letter crunch beneath his boots as he moved towards her. He would have liked to grind them through the floorboards and consign them to hell.

'I quite agree,' he told her.

There was a silence, and then she said, 'You do?'

'Yes.' He shrugged. 'You're right. That letter should never have been sent, but *I'm* ultimately responsible for it. My legal team thought they were protecting me. I know,' he said as her eyes lit. 'I hardly need protecting. But you do. And Thea does too. And I should be first in line to do that.'

Lizzie eyes betrayed all the uncertainty inside her, while *he* was stripped down to his most vulnerable, with everything to lose.

He'd fought off emotion all his life, wanting to fight for, and protect his parents. He'd fight now, if he had to.

'I won't let Thea suffer because of my naiveté,' Lizzie said, obviously still tense and worried, 'so if there's a copy of that letter in a vault somewhere, or on a computer, I want it destroyed.'

'It will be,' he promised. 'Thea will never know about the letter unless you tell her.'

'Well, obviously I won't.'

'You're not to blame for any of this, Lizzie. You never were.'

Damon's will was vibrating in the room like a tangible thing, tempting her to believe him.

'So you don't think I'm a liar, like my father?'

'Of course I don't. Would I be here if I did?'

She'd needed to hear that, but she still had to shake her head to try and dislodge the memories. The faces of her father's victims were always with her, reminding her that she should be punished too. She had enjoyed her last birthday party at home before the trial, as the privileged daughter of a supposedly wealthy man. She had adored her dress and everything else about that night—without realising that she'd been drinking and eating and dancing at the expense of so many vulnerable victims.

If only she could have that time over again—time to make things right and stop her father. If only she'd known—

'Lizzie, you have to stop this,' Damon insisted quietly. 'I understand what you're going through, but you can't change the past, and nor can you go on blaming yourself for what your father did.'

Easy for him to say, but guilt was eating her alive. Did he know that?

'And I suppose I can't blame myself for my father's death?' she suggested. 'But I still do.'

'What are you talking about?'

'They offered me counselling before I went to visit him in jail for the first time. I knew within five minutes that the person counselling me had no idea. Beyond offering me a box of tissues, a few murmured platitudes, and telling me that it would be "good for me to talk", she had nothing to offer—while I still had to get my head around the basics, like finding somewhere to live and putting food on the table. I didn't have time to waste emoting. All I could think of was getting out of that office so I could get on with the rest of my life.'

'And did you?' Damon angled his chin to stare at her.

'Yes. That day in court changed me. My father's death

changed me even more. It was a wake-up call and a turn-ing point for me. It told me in stark language that it was time to grow up.'

'You did have a lot of changes to get used to.'

'You think?' She found a small wry smile. 'I had to get used to the world I believed in turning out to be a fantasy. Having my only living relative in prison and losing my friends didn't help...' Her voice tailed away.

'I don't see how that makes you responsible for your father's death,' Damon prompted.

'I was angry with him and I was homeless,' Lizzie re-membered. 'By the time I had scraped together enough money for my first visit to the jail I got there and they said he was dead. He'd hanged himself.'

The feelings she'd suffered on that terrible day, swept over her now. They were weaker, of course. Time was kind like that. But the sense of abandonment had never truly left her. Like the grief at having any chance of making things right between Lizzie and her father stolen away, the shock of his death, and the realisation that time lost could never be recaptured, had changed her forever.

'*Theos*, Lizzie! You found out like that?'

'Exactly like that. It was kept out of the newspapers. The publicity wouldn't be good for the jail, they said. I'm over it now—of course I am,' she insisted. 'But after his death I went from feeling the weight of everyone's disap-proval to suffering their pity—which was almost worse. A lot of people turned away, and I can't blame them. It was as if Dad and me had both been infected with the same disease. I just wish I could have done something more to help him. Hence the ongoing guilt, I suppose.'

'You were very young.'

'Old enough to have a child.'

'Your father chose your stepmother in preference to

you,' Damon insisted. 'He wanted you in court because he thought you might be useful to him. That isn't love, Lizzie, that's taking advantage of someone's good nature—yours, in this instance.'

She felt naked and vulnerable, having bared her soul, and she went on the defensive immediately. 'You're very supportive, Damon. Will you give me the same level of support when I fight you for Thea?'

'I hope it doesn't come to that, but you can't keep our daughter from me.'

'You sound very sure.'

'I am. Because—'

'You have another team of lawyers?' Lizzie guessed.

'No,' Damon said carefully. 'I am sure it won't come to that. Because Thea has asked to see me.'

'Thea has— I'm sorry.' Lizzie paled. 'What did you say?'

'Thea has asked to see me now and again,' Damon explained. 'And that's what we've agreed on.'

'*You've* agreed this? Without consulting me?'

'Yes, Thea and I talked it over. We'll meet now and then…at least to begin with…and then, over time, we'll see more of each other, depending on how things go.'

'I can't get my head around this,' Lizzie said tensely. 'You've spoken to Thea without telling me?'

'She rang me. I could hardly refuse to speak to my own daughter.'

'Thea *rang* you?' Lizzie repeated foolishly. She felt as if the ground was shaking beneath her feet and every certainty she'd ever had was slipping away from her. 'You told me I could trust you…'

'You can,' Damon insisted.

'So you go behind my back and talk to my daughter—'

'*Our* daughter,' he interrupted. 'I gave Thea my number in case she ever needed it.'

'Why would she need it?' Lizzie challenged.

'I'm her father,' Damon said quietly. 'Who else would she call?'

'Me! She'd call *me*,' Lizzie insisted furiously. 'How could you do this? I'll never trust you again as long as I live. Get out. Get out now! *Get out!*'

She broke several nails flinging the door open.

In one breath Damon had denounced the letter and accepted Thea as his daughter, and then in that self-same breath he had admitted that he was speaking to Thea behind Lizzie's back on a semi-regular basis.

To say she felt unnervingly threatened would be massively understating the case. She was on the outside looking in at a relationship that was obviously developing between Damon and Thea without her involvement. How had it come to this? Had Thea already made her choice as to where and with whom she wanted to live?

She had to tell herself not to be so ridiculous. Thea was an intelligent girl. They loved each other. Love like theirs couldn't be threatened or stolen away by anyone.

And when Damon strode out of the house without a backward glance, leaving Lizzie with no idea if she'd ever see him again, she wondered if maybe that was a *good* thing.

CHAPTER SIXTEEN

HE CALLED HER from the car. He had been sitting right around the corner from Lizzie's bedsit for almost an hour before he called. Her tiny room was not the right forum for big emotions to run wild.

He smiled faintly as he waited for her to pick up, imagining the answer he might get when she did. This passionate creature was the Lizzie he remembered, and while one part of him wanted nothing more than to reassure her that she had nothing to worry about another part of him was glad to have her back.

'Hello?' She sounded suspicious.

'Hey…'

'What do you want, Damon?' She sounded hostile.

'To fill in a few gaps for you.'

'You think that will help?' she demanded sceptically.

'It can't do any more harm.'

There was a long pause, and then she asked, 'Where are you?'

'Not far away.'

Silence.

'If it helps with all that guilt you're carrying around,' he said, deciding to be blunt, 'you should know that all your father's victims got their money back.'

'How could they?' she demanded. 'My father didn't

have any funds left when he died. My stepmother saw to that.'

'The Gavros Foundation took care of it.'

'I should have known,' she murmured.

He waited.

'So I'm in your debt now?'

'You're in no one's debt,' he assured her. 'You were a victim as much as anyone else in that courtroom. I should have found a way to tell you what my family intended to do, but I was always too busy thinking about rebuilding the business.'

'That doesn't make me feel any less guilty,' she assured him. 'You shouldn't have *had* to rebuild your family business. You wouldn't have had to do that if my father hadn't defrauded yours.'

'Lizzie, if you're guilty I'm guilty too. I didn't spare a thought for the fallout of that day, beyond the financial implications for Gavros Inc. I seem to remember we'd had a good year, so it was no problem for the foundation to grant funds to the victims. Knowing they'd got their money back gave me a good feeling. But I didn't spare a thought for the emotional consequences. You're right. I was all about money then—ruthless and uncaring. I thought my duty was done, and that was enough.'

'And now?'

'And now I understand how incredibly courageous you've been.'

'Please,' she said wearily.

'I'm not patronising you. You were down on the floor and fate kept on kicking you. I only wish I'd been there to pick you up.'

'I didn't need anyone to pick me up,' she countered fast. 'I picked myself up. And about time too.'

'And now I need your agreement to move forward—the three of us together,' he explained.

'You didn't need my agreement to speak to Thea,' she pointed out with justifiable fire. 'So what's changed, Damon?'

'*I* have,' he admitted.

There was a long silence, and then she said, 'Where are you? And I want a GPS fix this time.'

He wondered if he'd ever felt so happy as he swung himself out of the car.

They met halfway down the street. Lizzie was in her slippers, with a coat thrown over her pyjamas.

'Can we start over?' Damon asked her as the rain started to pelt down.

'We'd better get back,' she said, pulling her coat over her head.

They ran for it, but by the time they got back to the house she was soaked.

And drained.

Exercising emotions was every bit as exhausting as a hard day's training at the gym, Lizzie had discovered, and after eleven years of holding things in that amounted to a *lot* of fatigue. The faintest of smiles on Damon's mouth was enough to bring her strength flooding back, but for how long? she wondered.

'You'd better come in,' she said. 'We'll talk in my room.'

'So you trust me now?' he said, leaning back against the door.

'Do I have an option?'

'No. And I've got a better idea than discussing this in your room. Come back to the island with me and we'll talk there. Not tonight. Sleep tonight, and tomorrow I'll come and get you.'

She was just figuring out the pros and cons of this when Damon seized the initiative. 'Where's your sense of adventure, Lizzie? All I've ever wanted is the best for you and Thea. And if you can't believe that believe this—'

Her world exploded into vivid colour as Damon drove his mouth down on hers. It was rain after a drought, a rock in a shifting sea of doubt and guilt. She wanted him—wanted this—tongues tangling and stroking in an arousing reminder of the act she longed for while she clung to him and he growled with pleasure as she pressed her body hungrily against his.

Eleven years of caution and protecting Thea with everything she'd got made it hard to give in to her own selfish pleasure, but with Damon's physical heat surrounding her, and her body begging her to relent, she was at least prepared to hear him out.

'What are you going to do?' she asked tensely when he released her.

'Heal you,' he said.

Damon left Lizzie in a tantalising state of extreme arousal after giving her instructions to pack. He'd seemed in a hurry to get somewhere, and she'd warned him that she wasn't very good at taking instructions. But she wasn't very good at feeling sorry for herself either. What good did it do?

When Damon's car had roared off and it was quiet again she felt lonely, standing on her own in the middle of an empty room in an empty house, and then she decided that she could sit down and cry or get on with things. She chose action.

First things first. She was hungry. An army fought on its stomach, and the Italian restaurant down the road was always bright and welcoming. She could walk there once she'd changed into some dry clothes. Right now pizza and a glass of rough red wine sounded like heaven.

Lizzie was carrying serious wounds from the past, and he couldn't be one hundred per cent sure of her unless he did something epic to reassure her that he really *had* turned a corner and was determined to see things through.

He was like a bear with a sore head as he drove away from her bedsit. The fact that his lawyer had acted without his authority still inflamed him. The man had been growing in confidence year on year, but this latest action had set Damon back eleven years. That legal firm was history—but that was the least of his worries now.

Needing space to think, he shifted lanes so he could take the long, straight road out of town. He got what he deserved—which was all the time in the world to work on his frustration as he battled with the sluggish evening traffic—but at least his mind cleared and he made a couple of calls. He had one possible ally, and he'd call in every card he'd got if it would make things right with Lizzie.

He'd told her to get some sleep?

Who the hell did he think he was?

Should she sleep? Sleep and dream? See all those faces in that courtroom again? He knew they haunted her. And he'd left her to deal with it on her own, so soon after the shock of receiving that lawyer's letter. To hell with that!

Swinging the wheel, he turned and headed back the way he'd come. Half an hour later he was finally getting somewhere—both in the car and with the project he had in mind. He was already calling Lizzie's number by the time he joined the traffic heading back into London.

'Where are you?' he demanded when she picked up.

'Where am I? Eating.' She sounded surprised to hear from him.

He could hear plates clattering in the background. 'Eating where?'

The silence continued until impatience was banging like cymbals in his head. 'Where *are* you, Lizzie?' he repeated tensely.

'In an Italian restaurant close to home—'

He cut the line and gunned the engine.

Some things were worth getting a speeding ticket for.

She'd been moving food around her plate for so long the waiters had started glancing anxiously at her. They had a reputation to uphold. The food at this restaurant was supposed to be the best in London outside of Italy. It certainly smelled good, but Lizzie hadn't managed more than a mouthful, and even that seemed to stick in her throat.

The wine helped, but she waved away the offer of another glass with a polite, 'No, thank you.'

What she *should* have done was tell Damon to come here, so they could talk things over before she did anything as rash as going back with him to Greece. It would have been easier here, surrounded by strangers in a busy restaurant.

'Penny for them…'

Breath shot out of her lungs. 'Damon?'

Framed in the doorway, Damon looked like a dark angel on a mission to seduce. Everyone in the busy restaurant obviously agreed with her, as every head had instinctively turned his way.

'May I join you?' he asked.

Who was going to stop him? She was as transfixed as every other sentient adult in the place. He looked vital and dangerous and a whole lot tastier than the pizza she'd been moving around her plate.

'Please.' She indicated the seat opposite hers in the secluded booth.

Within moments of him settling waiters were swarming.

'What are you doing with that pizza?' He stared with disapproval at her plate. 'Were you planning to re-sole your shoes with it, or maybe save it for a midnight snack? We'll have two more of whatever this was,' he added, smiling at a waiter. 'It smells delicious. And a bottle of your best red, some olives, and a plate of antipasti to pick at... maybe some prosciutto and melon, grilled veggies, and a bowl of meatballs—'

'Damon!'

He put a restraining hand over hers. 'I'm a big man with a huge appetite, and I didn't realise how hungry I was until I walked through that door and smelled the food.'

Blood rushed to her cheeks. Damon was a game-changer. She should have remembered that. She tried not to blink or react at all when he nestled his legs comfortably against hers. Space was the problem. Space would always be the problem with Damon. And the booth was an intimate, secluded oasis—ideal for people who wanted a little privacy with their meal.

'Damon—no!' she said as his expression changed from genial, when the waiter was around, to something else as he studied her face.

'What do you mean, no?'

The tug at the corner of his mouth was the only warning Lizzie needed that things weren't going to go to plan. At least not to *her* plan.

'I'm not going to hear any more of these trust issues, am I?' he demanded. 'Because I've got something for you.' He settled back. 'And there's someone who wants to speak to you before I hand it over.'

Her heart started thumping as Damon brought out his phone.

He punched in a number on speed dial. 'Is that okay with you?' he asked, glancing at the phone in his hand as he waited for the call to connect.

'Depends on who it is,' Lizzie admitted.

Damon's expression brightened as the person he was calling answered the phone. 'Thea?'

Damon had *Thea* on speed dial? Lizzie blenched. Change she could cope with—but change this fast was something else again.

'What's going on?' she demanded, before taking the phone.

'Chill!' Thea exclaimed. 'I heard you. Don't be angry with Damon. I've got something to tell you.'

'Obviously...' Lizzie tried to sound bright, and only succeeded in sounding tense and concerned.

'Don't sound so worried,' Thea said, reading Lizzie with her usual ease.

'I'm not worried,' Lizzie said, still tense.

'You're going to like this—I promise,' Thea said confidently.

Right now, Lizzie doubted it. 'Just tell me what it is,' she prompted, forcing a smile into her voice.

'Surprises are always the best, aren't they?' Thea enthused, giggling and obviously surrounded by her friends.

'I *do* love surprises,' Lizzie agreed, trying not to sound as if surprise right at this moment equated with a visit to the dentist.

'But that all depends what the surprise *is*, doesn't it, Mama?'

'Do you always have to be so smart?'

As Thea broke into peals of laughter Lizzie shot a keen look at Damon, trying to read his face.

'Damon's got it,' Thea announced, almost choking on her giggles. 'Let him show you the surprise. He wanted to get you something to say sorry, and I told him what you'd like. You *will* give him a chance to say sorry, won't you? Like in the last scene of all the best movies?'

'What have you done?' Lizzie mouthed, staring at Damon, who merely shrugged.

'Sorry—I have to go now!' Thea yelled. 'We're having movie night at school.'

Hence the reference, Lizzie thought as she clutched the phone, wishing she could give Thea a hug instead.

'Won't be long until school breaks up for summer— and then we're off to Greece again,' Thea announced with excitement. 'Night-night!' she exclaimed, before Lizzie could ask any more questions.

And with that the line was cut and Thea was gone.

Thea and Damon were not only in contact with each other, they were arranging holidays together now...

'You should have told me,' she said quietly. 'You *have* to keep me in the loop, Damon.'

He huffed agreement. 'I guess I'll get there eventually.'

'Damn right you will,' Lizzie said, getting up to leave the booth.

Damon grabbed her wrist, stopping her. 'Our food's on its way—'

'So?' She stared angrily at his hand on her arm until he removed it.

'Sit down,' he murmured, almost winning her over with a smile. 'I want to give you the gift I told you about.'

'It will have to wait,' she said coolly. 'I need time to—'

'To do *what*, Lizzie? You've had all the time in the world, as far as I can tell.'

She ground her jaw and then sat down again. 'This had better be good.'

'I hope you think so,' Damon agreed as he delved into the pocket of his jacket.

When he pulled out a battered ring case she was speechless.

'I want you to have this—whatever you decide to do next.' He pushed the black velvet box across the table towards her.

She hardly dared touch it.

'Thea would never forgive me if I didn't sort this out for you,' Damon explained. 'I felt so bad about the incident with the violin that I asked Thea how I could make up for it, and she said with this. She said she'd promised to get it back for you one day, and that this was her chance to make good on her word. It was the first time she called me Dad,' he added softly.

Lizzie closed her hand around the ring case. There was so much to take in.

'To be exact,' Damon added wryly, changing the mood and brightening it, 'Thea told me to, "Go get it, Dad. And remember this is just your *first* test."'

'That *does* sound like Thea,' Lizzie admitted as she caressed the ring case with her fingertips.

'Aren't you going to open it?'

'I'm not sure I dare.'

'I'm sure you do dare,' Damon argued softly. 'There's nothing you don't dare, from what I remember. If there's one thing I've learned about you, Lizzie, it's that you've got more guts than most people. So open the box and wear the ring. Think of your mother when you wear it. Think how happy she'd be to know that you've got it back. And remember this isn't a gift from me to you—this is a gift to you from Thea. Let the ring be the symbol of our new start...all three of us. It will make Thea happy to see you wearing it, and I think it completes the circle. Don't you agree?'

I'll heal you, he'd said, Lizzie remembered as Damon opened the ring case and took out her mother's ring.

She thanked him when he slipped the simple band onto her finger. 'Thank you' seemed inadequate for something like this, but she said it anyway.

'Don't thank me—thank Thea,' he said as she stared down at the distinctive ring with its three tiny seed pearls set snugly in the golden band.

'Thank you,' Lizzie repeated softly, lifting her gaze to meet Damon's.

'You don't have to thank a man who loves you for anything,' he insisted, smiling into her eyes.

The short time that remained before school was out for summer was spent packing up the bedsit and putting everything Lizzie cared about into storage. The rest went to the thrift shops that Thea loved so much—though Thea did keep back a few battered articles.

'We're not necessarily staying on the island for good,' Lizzie had warned.

She and Damon had started over. They hadn't slept together or even kissed since the night of the ring and Damon telling her that he loved her. The tension between them was ferocious, but it was all part of making that fresh start, he'd said.

Lizzie had thought she knew how she wanted things to go, which was slowly, but the more she saw of Damon the more she wanted to let the past go—to learn from it, certainly, but never to let it rule her again.

Damon's private jet took Lizzie and Thea to the island, where he was waiting for them on the Tarmac. Thea had no inhibitions and flung herself into her father's arms.

Thea had always embraced life wholeheartedly, Lizzie thought, glad that she could. Life required a healthy dose of courage, and self-belief never went amiss. Thea would need those qualities if she was to give confidence to others in her turn.

'The ring worked like the magic charm I said it would!' Thea exclaimed to Damon, with a happy glance at Lizzie.

Resting his sunglasses on top of his head, Damon smiled into Lizzie's eyes. 'So you're still wearing it?'

'Always,' Lizzie whispered.

Putting his arm around both of them, Damon escorted them to his SUV and saw them safely settled inside. The drive to the beach house was tense—but for all the right reasons, Lizzie thought as she sat up front with Damon. She tried not to look at him, not to register him at all, conscious that their daughter was sitting behind them and noticing everything. But she was entirely, acutely, lovingly aware of him.

There were more surprises to come. Damon didn't take them to the beach house, but to his old family home.

'I swopped houses with my parents,' he explained. 'My mother has always lusted after the beach house, so I asked Thea which house *you'd* prefer and she said this one.'

Lizzie was speechless—and not the slightest bit put out that Damon had sprung the surprise, because this *was* her true dream home.

'There's still a studio where you can paint, and a music room for Thea, but you can change things around any way you want,' Damon explained. 'No pressure for either of you. You can come here whenever you like, or don't come at all. The house is in your name, Lizzie. I signed it over to you. Lawyers can be useful sometimes,' he added with a wry smile.

'It's mine?' Lizzie exclaimed. 'But you can't—'

'I can and I have,' Damon assured her. 'I know a house can't make up for all the years you spent on your own, but I hope it goes some way to saying that I love you both, and that I want you both in my life. And you, Lizzie, will have something of your own now—something to sell or to keep or to do whatever you want. All expenses are fully covered, of course—'

'No.'

'Mama!'

'I can't accept that.'

'Why not?' Thea demanded.

'Are you two in league?' Lizzie found it hard to be angry with Thea, who had never once complained when they were short of money.

'If you mean, do we want to work together for your happiness, Thea and me, then the answer to that has to be yes,' Damon assured her. 'And there's one more thing I have to ask you.'

'Ask away. You might as well get it all off your chest,' Lizzie conceded.

She was stunned when Damon dropped to one knee at her feet.

'I never thought I'd feel the need to do this,' he said, 'but I do. I *so* do. Will you marry me, Lizzie? Will you spend the rest of your life with me?'

Damon had taken hold of her hand, and now he took hold of Thea's hand.

'Can we be a family at last—a *happy* family?' he added for Thea's benefit. 'We've still got a lot of work to do,' he admitted with his usual bluntness, 'but when we work to the power of three I don't know who's going to stop us, do you?'

It took her a moment to take everything in, but then Lizzie went to her knees in front of Damon. 'I certainly won't stand in your way,' she teased him softly.

He laughed.

And when Thea knelt to join them Lizzie said, 'For all of us, my answer to your question is absolutely *yes*.'

He'd waited to make Lizzie his bride for long enough, Damon informed Lizzie the next morning, so they would get married on the island that same week by special licence—with Thea as their bridesmaid and Iannis and Stavros as their witnesses.

'I hope you don't mind that I've already made plans,' Damon said as the two of them lay entwined in bed.

'There are some plans I'm quite happy for you to make without any direction from me,' Lizzie teased him lightly. 'Though I did think you meant that you couldn't wait for our wedding night.'

'That too,' he said, brushing her hair aside to kiss the angry tiger cub. 'And also this—'

'What?' she said as he leaned over the side of the bed.

Opening a drawer in the nightstand, Damon brought out a small jeweller's box. 'Wedding and engagement ring all in one,' he explained. 'I hope you're all right with that?'

When Lizzie opened the box she was speechless. The band was exquisite. Chased gold, with a flawless emerald cut diamond set in the centre of it, the ring was spectacular. It was everything she would have chosen for herself, way back when fairytales had been her usual night-time reading, but it was the inscription inside the ring that really choked her up.

For the love of my life.

And there was a date. Damon had charted their love from the first night they'd met.

'Full circle,' he said.

'For ever,' Lizzie agreed.

Drawing her into his arms, Damon removed the ring box from her fingers and placed the symbol of their love on her hand.

EPILOGUE

ALL OF LIZZIE's dreams came true under a cobalt blue sky on a sugar sand beach, barefoot in the arms of the man she loved.

Stavros and Iannis had got together with their wives to ensure there was a flower-strewn canopy where their wedding ceremony would be held, and guests came from all over the island to see Lizzie in a simple gown that slipped over her head and clung to her body like a delicately embroidered, diaphanous second skin.

She was sure the flimsy ankle-length gown must have cost Damon a fortune, though he'd completely blown her mind by supplying her with an entire rail of dresses to choose from.

'No reason why my bride should suffer because I can't wait to marry her,' he'd said.

'Don't look so worried. I found half of them in a thrift shop,' Thea had added, with a mischievous glance at her father.

'Yeah,' Lizzie had agreed wryly, 'a thrift shop named—'

'Does it matter where they came from?' Damon had interrupted. 'They've been bought with love. Accept them.'

Now she'd sold her first painting she might just do that, Lizzie thought. Who would have known that her happiness-infused watercolours of the island would sell so well?

The Internet made everything immediate, and she might only have been back on the island for a short while, but her head was buzzing with ideas for paintings and it seemed to Lizzie that she'd found a fresh calling—better than washing dishes, though the only downside was that her nails were now customarily rimmed with paint.

As everyone cheered the newly married couple Thea joined in with the local band on an improvised stage to salute them with a resoundingly popular solo.

'Maybe I *will* be a violinist, after all,' she told Damon and Lizzie, before racing off to join the friends she would be staying with during her parents' honeymoon.

Whatever their daughter wanted to be was all right with them, Lizzie thought as she shared a glance with Damon. They both wanted the same thing for Thea, and that was for their daughter to do what she wanted to do and be happy doing it.

'I guess I'll have to work harder at this family thing than I ever had to work at business,' Damon admitted as he brought Lizzie into his arms.

'You better had—'

'I will,' he promised softly, in a way that made her body yearn. 'Starting now…'

'*What*—where are you taking me?' Lizzie demanded as Damon carried her through the line of cheering guests. 'What about our wedding reception?'

'Our wedding has been unconventional, and the same goes for our wedding reception,' Damon informed her. 'The feasting will continue without us. We'll be back in a week's time for a celebratory party with our friends—'

'And where are we going in the meantime?' Lizzie asked.

'Some call it paradise,' Damon told her solemnly as he strode towards the waiting helicopter. 'I just call it bed.'

'I'm good with that,' Lizzie agreed.

'*Agapi mou*, you're the love of my life,' Damon assured her with a soft, husky laugh. 'And I need at least a week to prove that to you before the rest of our happily married life can continue—or I will surely die of frustration.'

'Me too,' Lizzie said, nestling close in the arms of the man she adored.

* * * * *

THE GIANNAKIS
BRIDE

CATHERINE SPENCER

CHAPTER ONE

ONLY 6:46 on Tuesday, with a fine May sunrise tinting the sky over Athens a pale, translucent peach. Yet for Dimitrios Giannakis, the day was already old and too grimly familiar. He hadn't needed to hear the medical team's latest bulletin when they met for their regular early-morning consultation. One look at their faces had told him all he needed to know.

Seated in his office now, Dimitrios regarded the telephone on his desk with the kind of loathing a man might show if he thought a pit viper was about to uncoil itself from the instrument and settle in his lap. This was not a call he wanted to make. Would, in fact, have done almost anything to avoid it if he'd had any choice in the matter. But the tragic fact was, he'd run out of options. Brianna Connelly was his last hope—or, more accurately, Poppy's last hope. And when it came to his daughter, Dimitrios allowed nothing, especially not his injured male pride, to come between her and what she so desperately needed.

Of course, the odds of Brianna agreeing to his request were slim to none. She'd made it clear enough, more than four years ago, where her priorities lay: in the glossy, artificial world of high fashion, which paid homage only to youth and beauty. But he had to ask. Was willing to beg, if necessary, to give his little girl a fighting chance.

The sweep second hand on his watch inched toward seven, making it almost nine the previous evening on Canada's west coast. As good a time as any to do what had to be done.

Jaw clenched, he lifted the handset from its cradle and punched in the number for Brianna's penthouse apartment, which, fortunately, was where his sources told him she was currently to be found. Time was of the essence, and by tomorrow she could be on location in some inaccessible corner of the Sahara, Iceland or the Australian Outback. Hers, after all, was a face and a body greatly in demand worldwide, and she too inexhaustibly ambitious to reject any assignment which might further her career.

The phone rang three times before her answering service picked up and asked him to leave a message. Glowering, he swiveled his chair to face the window. "It's Dimitrios Giannakis, Brianna. It's urgent that I speak to you as soon—"

"Dimitrios?" Her voice, slightly husky and disturbingly erotic, intercepted, caressing his ear like a kiss.

Steeling himself against the sensory impact, he said curtly, "Good. You *are* there."

If he hadn't known better, he might have thought her small intake of breath signaled dismay or regret, but whatever the cause she recovered quickly and replied with matching brevity, "Obviously. What can I do for you?"

For years now he'd prided himself on being his own man, able to conquer the world and bring it to heel on his terms. The idea of groveling to anyone, least of all a woman he despised, almost made him retch. But fate had zeroed in on his one weak spot, his daughter, and although he'd have gone to his grave before he asked anything for himself, as his child's advocate, he had no choice but to swallow the bitter taste in his mouth and turn to the one person in the world who might possibly be able to help her. Alienating Brianna Connelly within seconds of contacting her was hardly the route to take.

Bearing this in mind, he attempted to soften his approach. "How are you, Brianna?"

How are you, my lovely?

Happier than I ever thought it possible to be....

Slamming shut the door on memories that were particularly inappropriate at this moment and pointless at any time, he waited for her reply.

She laughed, a brittle, uncertain sound. "Considering we haven't exchanged more than ten words in years, Dimitrios, I hardly think you care one way or the other about my state of health. Nor would I have thought we shared anything in common since my sister's death. So why don't you cut to the chase and tell me what you're really after? I have an early flight tomorrow and need to get a good night's sleep."

He should have known it was still all about her. Some things never changed.

But some things did, and swinging back to his desk again, he picked up Poppy's framed photograph, taken just six months earlier, before illness had left her little face looking so pinched and wan. Grimacing with distaste, he did what he had to do. "Very well. I have a favor to ask of you, and I warn you now, it's huge."

Four years ago, Brianna had vowed never again to set foot in Greece, and except for the time she'd attended Cecily's memorial service when she'd quite literally flown in and out of Athens on the same day, she'd stood by that promise. Yet within forty-eight hours of his latest call, not only was she in the country, she was on Dimitrios Giannakis's doorstep, deposited there by his uniformed chauffeur who'd been waiting to meet her when she landed at Eleftherios Venizelos International Airport in Spata. Changing her original travel plans had been easy enough. Her suitcases had stood already packed for her much-anticipated, month-long hiatus in Bermuda, and the clothes she'd packed—casual summertime outfits for the most part—would serve her equally well in Athens.

"I'm perfectly capable of getting myself from the airport to a hotel," she'd said, when she'd relayed her arrival date and time to Dimitrios.

He, however, had vetoed any such idea. "You will be met," he informed her flatly, "and you will be accommodated in my house where you will be pampered and cared for throughout your stay. It's the very least I can do. I am, after all, deeply in your debt."

His *house?* The word didn't come close to describing the residence confronting her now, and she hadn't even seen the inside yet. Perched on a low rise of cliff above the Aegean, and surrounded by lush gardens, its soaring white stucco exterior blushing in the sunset, the place was intimidatingly grand. Palatial, even—and Brianna wasn't exactly unused to luxury. But then, what else had she expected? She knew from experience that Dimitrios wasn't a man to do things by half.

She'd have laughed at the irony of the thought if she hadn't been so tense she could hardly breathe. Although she would never admit it, the prospect of seeing him again, let alone living under his roof, terrified her. He'd shredded her heart once and it had taken the better part of four years for it to heal. She wasn't keen on having him trample all over it a second time. Yet proximity gave opportunity for just such an outcome, especially under the present emotional circumstances.

"Well, you could have said no," her longtime agent and friend, Carter Maguire, had pointed out, when Brianna explained the reason she had to cancel all assignments in the immediate future.

To Dimitrios, yes. But how did any woman turn her back on a critically ill three-year-old?

His estate lay a few miles south of Rafina. The chauffeur, a taciturn man who'd uttered not one word during the thirty-minute drive from the airport, dumped her luggage beside her, reached forward to yank on the bell pull hanging by a chain beside the front door, then without waiting to see if anyone answered, climbed back behind the wheel of the Mercedes-Benz and drove away.

Over the fading sound of the departing car, she heard footsteps approach from inside the house and braced herself. The moment of truth had arrived. If she could weather this first meeting with Dimitrios, the worst would be over.

But the man who opened the door was too short, too genial, too bald and about twenty years too old to pass for her brother-in-law. With a mile-wide smile, he ushered her across the threshold. "*Kalispera,* Despinis Connelly, *kai kherete!* Good evening and welcome! We have been expecting you and are all so happy you have arrived."

We? She cast a nervous glance around the vast, marble-floored entrance hall, expecting Dimitrios to appear momentarily, but found nothing beyond a profusion of flowering shrubs in jardinieres, and a floating staircase leading to the upper floors.

The man hauled her suitcases inside. "I am Alexio," he informed her cheerfully. "I and my wife, Erika, we run the household staff. She is waiting to meet you in the courtyard with a light refreshment, and later will show you to your room. Meanwhile, I will have your luggage taken care of."

"Thank you," Brianna said. "You're very kind."

"*Parakalo.*" He inclined his head. "You're welcome. Dinner will be served at nine o'clock, after Dimitrios returns."

"He's not here?"

Alexio's smile dimmed. "He's at the clinic with the little one," he explained, escorting her to the far end of the hall and through open glass doors to an inner courtyard. "He stays most evenings until she falls asleep. Most likely he will be home within the hour."

More flowering plants, a wall fountain and comfortable wicker furniture graced the tiled courtyard, making it a haven of shady tranquility, but the woman waiting to greet her wasn't quite as affable as Alexio. Although polite enough, Brianna saw reserve in her eyes, felt it in the cool touch of her hand as Alexio performed the introductions.

"You will wish to sit for a few minutes and relax after your long journey," his wife said, indicating a frosted pitcher of iced tea and bowl of fruit on the table.

Although pleasant enough on the surface, her words emerged less as an invitation than a command. Brianna, though, had been granted a short reprieve, and she wasn't about to waste it. She couldn't avoid Dimitrios indefinitely, but she could seize the chance to freshen up and look her best before she had to face him again. "That's very thoughtful of you, but I've been sitting for most of the last twenty-four hours and actually would like nothing more than to relax in a hot bath."

The woman switched her gaze to Alexio and muttered something in Greek. He responded by fanning his hands, palms down, and said quietly, "Do not fuss yourself, Erika." Then, addressing Brianna, attempted to ease the unmistakable tension in the air. "My wife is worried that she has yet to unpack your suitcases and prepare the clothes you wish to wear to dinner."

"Please don't be," Brianna told her. "I'm used to traveling and can manage perfectly well on my own."

Erika didn't quite sniff in disdain, but she came close. "Dimitrios will not like it. He has instructed us to treat you as if you are royalty."

"I'll make sure he knows that you have. Now, if you'll please show me to my room…?"

"This way, then."

As Brianna might have expected, the suite she'd been assigned outshone anything the best hotel in Athens could provide. Large and airy, it had a sitting alcove at one end beyond which a deck overlooked the sea and sprawling rear gardens whose centerpiece was a huge saltwater infinity pool. The finest linens draped the bed. A mirrored dressing room connected to a bathroom completely outfitted in travertine marble. Here was a place to which she could retreat, should things become too heated and unpleasant with Dimitrios.

"If I've overlooked anything you might need, be so kind as to let me know," Erika said woodenly, preparing to leave with Alexio, who'd followed them upstairs with the suit-cases.

Brianna cast an eye over the flower arrangements set at various points about the room, the carafe of iced water and upturned crystal glass on a tray, and remembered the array of toiletries in the bathroom. "I can't imagine there is. Nothing, that is, except—"

"Yes?"

"You mention changing for dinner. Exactly how should I dress?"

"Decently," the woman replied. "In keeping with the standards of this home."

Shocked speechless by such rudeness, Brianna simply stared at her. Apparently just as taken aback, Alexio prac-tically shoved his wife out of the room and closed the door on her before turning to Brianna again. "Erika, her English is not always the best," he offered apologetically. "What she means to say is that dinner is more…civilized than breakfast or lunch. A pretty dress will do very well, but when Kyria Giannakis was alive…" He shifted uncomfort-ably from one foot to the other. "Her ideas of what was seemly and proper did not always coincide with her husband's."

"I understand perfectly," Brianna said, and she did. Cecily had never been one to abide by anyone's rules but her own. If her behavior the last time she and Brianna had spent time together was any indication, she'd probably taken delight in flouting her husband's wishes at every turn.

Small wonder then that Erika was so hostile. She probably expected Brianna to be no better than her late twin, and who could blame her? After all, they had been identical, at least in looks, to the point that some people had never learned to tell them apart.

Especially not Dimitrios.

He was waiting in what she supposed was the living room, although "grand salon" better suited the proportions and furnishings of the long, elegant space to which Alexio directed her, just over an hour later. His hair still damp from a recent shower, Dimitrios stood in profile just outside a pair of French doors standing open to the night, a glass of amber liquid cradled in his hand, and Brianna's first thought on seeing him was that she'd overdressed for the occasion.

He wore a long-sleeved white shirt but no tie, and his trousers, though beautifully tailored, were light gray, his shoes Italian leather loafers. She, on the other hand, had put on the only dinner dress she'd brought with her. Of black silk jersey, which traveled well and took up almost no room in a suitcase, it draped softly over one shoulder, left the other one bare, and fell almost to her ankles. Platinum hoops studded with tiny diamonds swung from her ears and she'd pinned up her hair in a sophisticated swirl on top of her head. That, in combination with the three-inch heels of her strappy black sandals, left her standing close to six feet tall. Even so, when he crossed the room to greet her, he loomed over her by a good three inches, and she had to tilt her head to meet his dark gaze.

She thought she was prepared. That nothing he said or did could touch her. That she could withstand anything he threw at her—his scorn, his hostility—and that they would bounce off the hard shell of her indifference and return to him a hundredfold. But seeing him again flung her headfirst back into that painful abyss of longing she'd fought so desperately to overcome.

He was still so lean and hard and sexy that her mouth ran dry at the sight of him. She'd forgotten how big he was, how his thick black hair curled a little, no matter how severely he tried to tame it. She'd forgotten how beautiful he was, and how his mouth curved in a half smile when he was amused and trying not to show it. She'd forgotten how it felt to be the woman who was the object of his attention.

"Well, Brianna, I never thought so much time would pass before we met again, nor that it would be under such trying circumstances," he said, shaking her hand.

The last time she'd seen him—apart from a fleeting encounter at Cecily's funeral—he'd held her in his arms and begged her to stay the night with him in his stateroom. He'd been naked, his aroused flesh, hot and urgent, pressed against her, even though they'd made love as recently as fifteen minutes earlier. It had taken every last ounce of willpower for her to leave him.

It took even more to feel his fingers close so impersonally around hers now, and not tremble from the contact, brief though it had been. "I hope I got here in time."

"For dinner? Yes. We won't sit down to eat for a few minutes yet."

"That's not what I meant, Dimitrios. I was referring to your little girl. How is she?"

"Poppy's condition remains unchanged." He turned to where various decanters stood on a side table alongside a silver ice bucket containing an open bottle of champagne. "May I offer you something to drink?"

"I don't know," she said. "Am I allowed alcohol?"

She hoped she was. Normally not much of a drinker—an occasional glass of wine was her limit—just then she was rattled enough to latch on to anything that might fortify her.

"Let's ask the expert," he said, and flung an inquiring glance over his shoulder. "What do you think, Doctor? May she have a little champagne?"

Footsteps, light as a dancer's, fell into the silence following his question, and a moment later the figure of a woman somewhere in her late twenties or early thirties appeared from the shadows of the moon-washed terrace beyond the French doors. "I don't see why not. A glass or two of wine isn't going to make any difference one way or the other."

"Glahss," she'd said, her well-modulated voice overlaid with a distinctly English accent.

Approaching Dimitrios, she held out her own empty crystal flute. "In fact, I wouldn't mind a refill myself, if you're offering. Might as well take advantage of a night off. It doesn't happen often enough to go uncelebrated."

Blond, petite and elegant in a pencil-slim black skirt and pale-pink blouse, she barely reached Dimitrios's shoulder. Beside her, Brianna felt like an Amazon.

Dimitrios cupped her elbow and favored her with a smile so warm, it was a wonder the woman didn't melt on the spot. "My dear lady, you may have as many refills as you please." Then, managing to tear his attention away long enough to spare Brianna a cursory glance, supplied, "This is Doctor Noelle Manning, Brianna. She's the head of the transplant team looking after my daughter. I decided it was a good idea for you to meet her as soon as possible, since she's obviously much better able than I am to answer any questions you might have. And this," he continued, swinging his gaze back to the diminutive Noelle with all due speed, "is my late wife's sister, Brianna Connelly. You might have heard of her."

He made it sound as if Brianna topped the FBI's Most Wanted list, but if Noelle Manning noticed, she chose not to comment.

"Both heard of and seen in all my favorite magazines. Hers is not a face easily forgotten." The doctor smiled and extended her delicate little hand. "I'm sure I don't have to tell you how pleased I am to meet you, or how much is riding on your decision to come here."

In the course of her career, Brianna had met more than a few dukes, princesses, reigning monarchs and celebrities. None had left her feeling as tongue-tied and awkward as this tiny, self-assured woman. "Thank you," she managed, trying not to stumble over her reply. "I hope I'll be able to help."

"We'll find out soon enough."

"When will you begin the tests?"

"We'll give you a few days to recover from your journey, then get started." She steered Brianna to a couch beside the fireplace, took a seat on the one across from it and, tilting her head, asked, "How much do you know about the procedure, Brianna?"

"About as much as I know about my niece's illness, which is next to nothing."

"Brianna has other priorities," Dimitrios remarked, pouring the champagne. "Aplastic anemia and bone marrow transplants don't fall within her range of interests."

"How would you know?" Brianna shot back, the barely concealed contempt she'd noted in his voice cutting as sharply as a knife sliding between her ribs.

He sauntered over to hand them their drinks, then dropped down on the couch next to Noelle Manning, close enough that his knee almost touched hers. "I know my daughter will turn three in another month, and this will be the first time you've met her."

"And I explained the reason for that when you phoned."

"I know only what you choose to tell me."

"I think we all understand that time has a habit of slipping away from us," Noelle interrupted smoothly. "What matters is that you're here now, Brianna, and Dimitrios is very grateful for that." She pinned him with a forthright stare. "Isn't that right, Dimitrios?"

"Yes," he admitted, looking a little shamefaced. "You're our last hope, Brianna."

"Well, not quite," Noelle amended. "There's always the chance of an anonymous donor being found, but that could take a very long time, and Poppy…"

She didn't finish. She didn't have to. Her meaning was clear enough. Time wasn't on Poppy's side.

"I'm quite willing to begin the tests tomorrow," Brianna said. "In fact, I'd prefer to. Surely the sooner we get started, the better?"

Noelle shook her head. "Donating bone marrow isn't exactly a walk in the park, Brianna, and it would be unprofessional of me, if not criminally negligent, to allow you to go ahead without first making sure you have a thorough understanding of all that's involved."

"If it's a matter of money—"

"It has nothing to do with money," Dimitrios cut in sharply. "Your expenses will be covered."

"But I can afford—"

"So can I."

He was impossible. Arrogant, intransigent and just plain unpleasant! Why she'd once thought, even for a minute, that he was a man she could love, escaped her.

Pointedly ignoring him, she met Noelle's calm gaze. "Can we discuss this at another time? Privately?"

"Of course. I was about to suggest exactly that. Tomorrow, if you're up to it, although I understand if you'd rather wait another day. Crossing ten time zones in twenty-four hours is a bit much."

"I've been doing it for years and trained myself long ago to sleep on airplanes."

"Then it's a date. Say about noon? I'll be through surgery by then."

"Noon will be fine."

"Good. You'll arrange for your driver to bring her to the clinic, won't you, Dimitrios?"

He grunted assent and stared moodily into his glass. Unperturbed, Noelle smiled and raised hers. "Cheers, then. Here's to you, Brianna, and a long and happy relationship with your niece."

About to swallow a mouthful of whatever it was he was drinking, Dimitrios almost choked on it instead.

CHAPTER TWO

HE WAS behaving like a boor, knew it and couldn't help himself. And all because she hadn't changed, and watching her, noticing again the perfect posture, the graceful movement of her body, was driving him crazy.

He'd hoped that, like Cecily, she was beginning to lose her looks. Fat chance. If anything, she was more beautiful than ever. The same long, luscious legs and narrow, elegant hands. The same flawless ivory skin and thick, shining fall of ebony hair. The same amazing ice-blue eyes, whose clear, heavily lashed glance could paralyze a man's mind and leave him drooling like an idiot.

Erika served lamb for dinner. Flavored with rosemary and roasted on a spit over an open fire to succulent tenderness, it was one of his favorites, but that night, he could hardly keep it down. Brianna, of course, ate with her customary restraint, refusing the potatoes and helping herself to only a small portion of the meat, although she made inroads on the salad. She barely touched her wine and passed on the honey-and-fig compote dessert. Only Noelle ate with any relish, packing away a surprising amount of food for such a little woman.

After the meal they returned to the living room, and

although neither guest took him up on his offer of metaxa, they both accepted coffee. "What's it like, being a world-famous model?" Noelle asked, settling herself kitty-corner from Brianna on the couch.

"Very hard work, very long hours and not nearly as glamorous as most people think."

"Sounds a bit like my life."

"Hardly," Brianna said, with exactly the right degree of charming modesty. "I wouldn't presume to compare the two. Unlike you, I don't have any special skill or expertise. I've certainly never saved a life."

"You might. And that you're willing to try puts you on a pedestal in my eyes. As for your not having any special skills, I rather doubt that's true. It must take enormous patience and stamina to meet the artistic and, I imagine, often conflicting demands of photographers and couturiers."

Brianna gave an elegant little shrug, a studied response designed to draw attention to her upper body, he was sure. Why else would she have chosen to wear a dress that left one shoulder bare? "On occasion, yes."

Clearly fascinated by a way of life so far removed from her own, Noelle tucked her legs under her and settled more snugly into the couch. "What drew you to modeling in the first place?"

"My mother got us started when my sister and I were still in diapers, and it more or less took on a life of its own from there. While other children our age played in the sandbox or learned to ride a bike, we traveled from one junior beauty pageant to another."

"She must have been very proud of you."

"She marketed us ruthlessly," Brianna said flatly.

For a second Dimitrios thought he heard an edge of bitter resentment in her reply, then decided he must have been mistaken. She might not have had any choice when she was still a minor, but as an adult, if she didn't like what she did for a living, she could have chosen something else. She wasn't completely without brains, was she?

"And did it very successfully," he remarked, trying to keep his scorn under control. "Admit it, Brianna. You and Cecily became international celebrities before you were in kindergarten."

"Because, as you very well know, Dimitrios, there were two of us and we looked identical. *That's* what made us special."

"Now there's only you, but you seem to be doing just fine on your own."

"Losing a sister is never easy," Noelle said, flicking him a cautionary glance, "but it must have been particularly difficult to lose a twin. You were very close, I'm sure."

"When we were children, yes."

That was just one lie too many for him to stomach. "Oh, come on, Brianna! You were thick as thieves when I met you."

She turned a slow stare his way. "If you believe that, it just goes to show how little you knew either one of us."

"I was married to Cecily, remember?"

"I'm hardly likely to forget."

"Of course you aren't," he jeered, knowing that by continuing to goad her, he was pushing his luck, but unable to stop. "After all, look how you aided and abetted her in getting me to the altar."

Her mouth dropped open in shock, the delectable curve

of her lower lip stirring memories of a time when he'd explored it at erotic leisure. But he wasn't fooled. He knew better than most how she and her twin had impersonated one another when it suited their purpose.

Recovering, she said, "I dropped everything to come here at a moment's notice because you asked me to, Dimitrios. I can leave just as quickly."

"This isn't about you, Dimitrios, it's about Poppy," Noelle reminded him, electing herself mediator of a situation fast deteriorating past a point of no return. "Let's not forget that."

"Of course not." He ventured to meet his sister-in-law's icy-blue stare. "Forgive me, Brianna. I'm worried sick about Poppy, but that hardly justifies my belaboring you with it."

"I understand." Again, she tilted one shoulder in that tempting little shrug. "I'd have come sooner, if I'd known."

"You're here now, and that's what matters." Noelle set her cup and saucer on the coffee table and unfolded her legs from beneath her. "And, pleasant though it is sitting here and being spoiled, I'd better be off and catch up on my sleep. I enjoyed meeting you, Brianna."

Smiling, Brianna rose in one fluid movement. "I enjoyed it, too."

"I'll see you tomorrow, at noon?"

"I'm looking forward to it."

"Excellent! Walk me out, Dimitrios?"

"Sure."

Noelle waited until they reached her car and were well out of earshot of anyone in the house, before rounding on him. "Tell me, Dimitrios Giannakis, just how badly do you want your daughter to get well again?"

"More than anything in the world, as you very well know."

"Then I suggest you keep your tongue and your temper on a very short leash. Your behavior tonight was inexcusable."

"You might not think so, if you knew the history between Brianna and me."

"I don't give a rat's behind about your history! The only person I care about is Poppy, and I will not sit idly by and watch you systematically sabotage what might turn out to be her best chance of recovery."

"Brianna isn't all she seems."

"Really? I consider myself a pretty good judge of character and she struck me as a very nice, sincere woman."

"You didn't see past the beautiful face."

"I'm not the one hung up on her looks, Dimitrios. You are. And I strongly recommend you get over it."

"Easier said than done," he grumbled, helping her into her car. "She's a carbon copy of her sister."

Noelle laughed. "Identical twins usually are, dear!" she said and, engaging the gears, roared off into the night.

No sooner had they disappeared outside than Brianna escaped upstairs to her room. She and Dimitrios were like oil and water, never meant to mix. If Noelle Manning hadn't been there to referee, they'd have been at each other's throats by now. But they had to find a way to get along, and she could only hope a good night's rest would leave them both more kindly disposed toward each other by morning.

Erika or one of her minions had turned down the bed, switched on a reading lamp and left two English-language magazines on the nightstand. The French windows in the sitting area stood open, their filmy white drapes pulled back and hanging still as mist at each side. Over the arm of the love seat lay a shawl of softest mohair. A sterling silver tray holding an exquisite bone china hot chocolate pot and mug waited on the coffee table. Regardless of whether or not she approved, Erika was obeying to the letter her instructions to treat the guest like royalty.

But then, from what Brianna had seen, *palatial* was the key word at the villa Giannakis. She'd barely been able to concentrate on the evening meal, she'd been so bowled over by the magnificence of the setting. His dining room must have been fifteen by thirty feet, with a marble-tiled floor and priceless Savonnerie rug. Original artwork worth a king's ransom hung on the walls.

The table, large enough to seat twenty with ease, consisted of a square slab of beveled glass supported by pillars fashioned after Doric columns. Five chairs upholstered in rich cranberry fabric lined each side. A fabulous old carved sideboard and sleek sterling candelabra completed the decor, resulting in a marriage of antique and modern; of classic elegance and good taste.

A sharp departure from her penthouse which, although overlooking the strait separating the mainland from Vancouver Island, and furnished with its own kind of elegance, didn't compare to this place, which oozed comfort and opulence at every turn. And yet she'd have given anything to be back there now, mistress of her own fate.

But that wasn't an option. She was here in Dimitrios's home, if not exactly a prisoner, then certainly not a cherished guest, either.

Too keyed up to sleep, Brianna kicked off her shoes,

tucked the shawl around her shoulders and stepped out on her deck. Moonlight spilled over the sea and dappled the garden with shadows. Apart from the soft sigh of waves on the beach below, the night was utterly quiet, utterly peaceful—until a rap at the door shattered it, that was.

"Brianna," Dimitrios announced, too loudly for her to pretend she hadn't heard him, "it is I."

How painfully formal and grammatically correct, she thought wryly, refusing to acknowledge the frisson of apprehension his voice inspired. "If you've come to continue needling me," she began, opening the door, "you can take yourself and your—"

"I have come to apologize. Again. And to ask if we can forget the past, not just for Poppy's sake, but for yours and mine. This business of donating bone marrow amounts to more than a few minutes in a doctor's office. The tests are exhaustive, and I have no wish to make your time here any more unpleasant than it has to be."

"Well, if tonight's any example…"

"It's not. I'm afraid I'm never at my best after I come back from the hospital, but that scarcely excuses my taking out my anxiety on others, especially not you." He offered his hand. "May we please start over?"

She could cope with his hostility, his bad behavior. Let him snipe and rant until the earth stopped turning, if he chose. He couldn't hurt her that way, not anymore. But in his present conciliatory mode, he was downright dangerous. Enough that the resentment she'd harbored all these years suddenly seemed not so well-founded, after all, and how stupid a conclusion was that when all the evidence pointed to the contrary? "I'm not sure it's possible," she said, struggling to shore up her sagging defenses.

Taking her by surprise, he slid his fingers around her wrist in a warm, close grip. "Can we at least talk about it, and try to find a way?"

She wrenched her arm free and stepped back, horrified by the way her pulse leaped at his touch.

She'd have done better to stand her ground because he took her retreat as an invitation to march right into the room and close the door. It was all she could do not to run for cover behind the love seat. Trying not to hyperventilate, she clutched the cashmere shawl tightly at her throat.

The suite was generously proportioned. Even allowing for what the furniture occupied, there was still almost enough floor area left for a Las Vegas chorus girl to put on a show. Yet he seemed to swallow up the space until it shrank to the size of a shoe box. "What's the matter, Brianna?" he inquired silkily, closing in on her. "Are you afraid I might kiss you—or just afraid you might like it too much to try to stop me?"

"Neither," she replied, and suppressing a tug of something suspiciously like desire, she drew herself up to her full five foot nine in an attempt to stare him down.

She might as well have spared herself the effort. "Really?" he purred. "Why don't we find out?"

His arm snaked around her waist and pulled her close. The feel of his body against hers sent the blood thrumming through her veins. The lightning rod that was his mouth brought back in vivid recall the memory of the first time he'd kissed her, and where it had led: to a rendezvous in his stateroom, and an introduction to the pleasures of love-making, of sex, that had spoiled her for any other man.

But she remembered, too, what came afterward. The betrayal, the abandonment, had almost killed her. Although she'd honored her modeling assignments, smiling through her pain, covering up the dark circles under her eyes, everyone had noticed something was wrong. Rumors that she was ill—anorexic, bulimic, on the verge of a breakdown—had circulated like wildfire and almost destroyed her career.

You've got to show them you're still on top, Carter had urged. And she had. Because her career was all she had left. Dimitrios had robbed her of everything else.

She couldn't let him do it again.

Lifting her hands, she pushed against the solid wall of his chest with all her might. "That might be your idea of starting over, but it's certainly not mine."

He released her willingly enough. "Forgive me for allowing my baser instincts to get the better of me," he said, aloof disdain written all over his cold, beautiful face. "Believe me, I know better than anybody that what happened between us in the past is long ago over and done with, and nothing either of us can say or do will ever change that."

"At least we're agreed on one thing."

"More than one, I hope. I'm calling for a truce, Brianna, because the future—Poppy's future—is all that matters now." He wiped a hand down his face, and all at once weariness softened the severe cast of his mouth and left him looking achingly vulnerable. "They tell me what's happened to her isn't my fault, but I blame myself anyway. If I'd been a better father, paid closer attention to her, she might not be in such bad shape now."

Touched despite herself, Brianna said, "I'm sure you were, and are, an exemplary father, Dimitrios."

"No." Restlessly, he paced to the French doors and stared out. "I ignored her symptoms. She had what appeared to be a cough and a cold, and I did nothing about it for the better part of two months. It wasn't until I noticed she had bruises that couldn't be accounted for that I insisted on a more thorough investigation into the possible causes."

"Surely you'd consulted a doctor before that?"

The question was out before she could contain it, and he swung around, his face a mask of hurt and anger. "Of course I did! Within a week of her cold first appearing. I'm not a complete imbecile."

"Then if indeed there's blame to be assigned, surely it lies with her doctor?"

Again the fire went out of him. "It lies with me," he muttered, dropping down on the love seat. "It's a parent's job to protect his child. He should instinctively sense when something's not right, and maybe I would have, if I hadn't been away half the time, looking after business."

"But, Dimitrios," she said, "that's what fathers do. They go out and make a living so that their children have a decent roof over their heads, food on the table and clothes on their backs."

"There's a big difference between working to live, and living to work."

"I'm not sure I understand."

He cast her an oddly cynical glance. "Ambition can consume a person—and you ought to know."

"What's that supposed to mean?"

A muscle twitched in his jaw. "Nothing," he said, averting his gaze. "Just that, in your line of work, you have to…stay on top of your game."

"Well, yes. But don't you think that's true of anyone who wants to succeed, regardless of what they do?"

"Not if winning becomes more important than anything else. Because somebody always ends up paying. In my case it happened to be my daughter."

"You give yourself too much credit, Dimitrios. You aren't responsible for Poppy's illness. It happened despite you, not because of you. None of us ever has total control of the world around us. Sometimes fate plays a dirty trick and all we can do is find a way to live with it."

He pinned her in a mesmerizing stare. "Are you speaking from personal experience?"

Not five minutes earlier he'd said that the past was over and done with and the future was all that counted. But the way he was looking at her now was *all* about the past. It hung between them, as vibrantly alive as if it had happened just yesterday. The memories tore at her, making her ache for what might have been. And for the man she'd thought he was.

"Brianna?"

He felt it, too. It was there in the sudden deepening of his voice when he spoke her name. It swirled in the air between them—an awareness so acute she felt herself melting in its heat.

"Yes," she said, hating that she sounded so breathless. "I learned to move on when dreams I held dear didn't materialize."

"Any regrets? Ever wish you'd held on to those dreams, instead of letting them go?"

Cecily's triumphant voice echoed down the years. *Face it, Brianna, it's over. He tried both of us and chose me. We were married, just last week. Sorry there wasn't time to send you an invitation....*

Hardening her heart, Brianna said, "No. Do you?"

"Hell, yes," he said grimly. "I wish I could have given

Poppy a mother who cared. But there are some things money can't buy."

"Are you always so uncomplimentary about my sister?"

He flung another forthright gaze her way. "What do you want me to say, Brianna? That she was the best wife a man could wish for? Well, sorry to disappoint you, but there's a limit to how far I'm willing to go to preserve your illusions. The plain fact is, marrying Cecily was the second-biggest mistake of my life."

"What was the first?"

"You were," he said, surging to his feet and towering over her. "You and that damnable cruise to Crete. I should never—" He blew out an exasperated breath and raked his hand through his hair.

"Well, don't stop now. You never should have what?"

"Never mind! I've already said too much." He strode to the door and yanked it open. "Thank you again for coming. Get some rest. You're going to need it."

And having stirred up memories of the most painful period of her life, he left her.

So much for leaving the past in the past....

They'd stopped in Athens en route to London and Vancouver; a two-day rest between flights only. At least, that was the original plan, until the invitation was hand-delivered to their suite at the Grande Bretagne, the evening before they were scheduled to leave.

In marked contrast to Brianna's uninterested reaction, Cecily had almost fallen over herself with glee. "It sounds divine! I want us to accept, I really do! If you won't go for yourself, do it for me." She'd pinned on her most beguiling smile. "*Please,* Brianna? *Pretty* please?"

"Honestly, Cecily, I'd rather not. This is the first break we've had in months, and I'm ready for a rest. But there's no reason you can't go, if you're all that keen. We're not joined at the hip."

"You know full well having both of us there is the coup they're after. One of us doesn't have the same cachet."

"For heaven's sake, we're professional models, not a circus act."

"And all you ever think about is work." Cecily's tone crossed the line from wheedling to whining. "If you're so damned eager to take a rest, why can't you do it floating around the Mediterranean on a luxury yacht? What's so hard to take about that?"

"We don't know anyone else, for a start. These people so anxious to have us on board aren't friends, Cecily, they're collectors whose idea of scintillating dinner conversation is dropping the names of the celebrities they've rubbed shoulders with."

"And we're highly collectible!"

Brianna sighed. They'd argued this point more times than she cared to count, and were never going to agree. "We're a couple of reasonably pretty women who look so much alike, most people can't tell us apart. They might recognize our faces, but they haven't a clue who or what we're really about, and nor do they care. We're nothing more than novelties."

"Maybe it'll be different this time. Maybe these hosts enjoy meeting new people and showing them a good time."

Tired of riding the same pointless merry-go-round yet again, Brianna had welcomed the arrival of their manager, Carter Maguire, who occupied the suite next door. As usual after a successful assignment—and this last had been a triumph both on the runway and at the photography shoots—he'd brought a bottle of champagne. Her relief, though, was short-lived when he told them that he, too, was to join the yachting party. Was, in fact, largely responsible for the three of them having been invited in the first place.

"Too bad you wasted your time," Cecily informed him petulantly, when she heard. "Brianna's refusing to go. Thinks I should put in a solo appearance."

"Out of the question." Calmly he uncorked the champagne and filled three flutes, handed one to Cecily and shooed her out to the balcony. "Go enjoy the view, and leave me to talk to her." When she was well out of earshot, he faced Brianna. "This isn't so much an invitation as a command performance, sweet pea. These people are big names in the fashion industry and we need the contacts. You've been at the top for a long time now, but we're in danger of losing that spot, and I think we both know why." He cast a quick glance over his shoulder. "Cecily's screwed up a few times too many, and word's getting around that she's not reliable. That business in Bali last month made big headlines."

The reminder of her sister's drunken display at a night club made Brianna blush all over again. "I know. People don't forget that kind of thing in a hurry."

"Especially not in this business. And not to put too fine a point on it, but time isn't exactly on your side anymore. You'll be twenty-four in August. The next couple of years are critical—for all of us." He'd given her the lopsided grin she knew and loved so well. "Come to that, I'm no spring chicken myself. The way I see it, when you decide to call it quits, I will, too."

"That's ridiculous, Carter! You're only fifty-three, and

there are hundreds of models who'd give their right arms to have you represent them."

"Not interested." He shook his head. "When I've worked with the best, why settle for the rest? There'll never be anyone like the two of you, Brianna—or at least, there never used to be. Now…" He shrugged and raised his eyebrows in a way that spoke more eloquently than words.

Cecily wandered back into the room at that point and helped herself to more champagne. "Straightened her out yet, Carter?"

"I'm not sure." He turned a smiling glance on Brianna, but the message in his eyes was sobering. "Have I?"

She knew how much she and Cecily owed him. Until he came into their lives, they'd been pawns; children at the mercy of a mother who'd exploited them for their appearance, without any regard for their moral or intellectual well-being. She'd looked at her daughters and seen only dollar signs. The money they brought in, she spent. On herself.

Brianna and Cecily had grown up on a litany of familiar refrains.

I don't care if your feet hurt in those shoes….

Forget about joining the library. Reading books isn't going to pay the rent….

And always, as regularly as one season followed another: *You owe me…. I could've gotten rid of you and had some sort of life for myself, but I didn't. I carried you to term…raised you all by myself because your dumb-ass father fell off a ladder and broke his neck before you were even born, and left not a red cent of insurance to provide for his brats….*

The ultimate irony, of course, was that "the brats" had inherited their father's looks, as was evident from the one photograph, taken on his wedding day, which their mother had for some reason chosen not to throw away.

Fortunately, when the awkward teenage years had arrived and "the brats" weren't quite as saleable, she'd handed over the job of marketing them to an agency, and Carter had come into their lives. It had taken him less than an hour to ascertain their mother's measure and half that time to draw up a contract giving him sole control of their professional future.

Through his intervention, they'd received a decent education. He hired a lawyer and a financial consultant to protect and invest their earnings against the day when they might not be in demand as models any longer, or decided they'd rather pursue a different career. He became the family they'd never known, the one person in the whole world they could always rely on.

And now, for the first time, he was asking for something in return. How could she refuse him, especially for so small a favor?

"Yes, you've convinced me," she said. "Lazing around on board a luxury yacht for two or three weeks isn't such a bad idea, after all."

Nor was it, until Dimitrios Giannakis taught her the folly of trusting a stranger, and broke her heart in the process....

She hated the kind of people functions such as the one on the yacht attracted: women in desperate search of a rich husband, and if he happened to be ninety and so frail he could drop dead at any minute, so much the better; men who drank too much and felt their wealth and importance entitled them to paw any women who caught their fancy. She'd fended off dozens in her time, revolted by their excesses, enraged by their arrogance and condescension. She was not impressed by their studiously acquired tans, their expensively capped teeth, their hair implants. She had nothing but contempt for their boastful swaggering. Did they think what showed on the surface defined who they really were? Did they ever look at her and see past the glamorous veneer to the person underneath—one with a working brain and a heart that felt hurt and embarrassment just as keenly as anyone else?

But Dimitrios Giannakis was different. Slightly aloof and rather amused by the jostling for attention, the artificial laughter, the superficial conversation, he appeared content to socialize mostly within his own exclusive circle of friends and acquaintances. Yet when called upon to mingle, he did so with grace and charm. An acknowledged billionaire in his own right, he was rumored to be enigmatic, reserved, powerful and, when occasion called for it, utterly ruthless.

Not a man to lock horns with, from all accounts, but definitely one to admire from a distance for his cosmopolitan sophistication, his wit and, yes, his extraordinary male beauty to which even she, accustomed as she was to the most handsome of the species, was not immune.

He stood a good head taller than anyone else on board. Had a cleft in his chin, eyelashes an inch long and a mouth designed to stir a woman to outrageous fantasies. By mid-afternoon, his square, clean-cut jaw was dusted with a five-o'clock shadow. His high, patrician cheekbones were surely the legacy of some royal ancestor.

Below the neck he was no less impressive. His body, whether clad in an elegant dinner jacket or swimming trunks that defied gravity and clung to his lean hips by sheer willpower was, in a word, perfection. Strong, lean, sleekly muscled and, like his rare smile, dauntingly sexy, it epitomized masculine virility at its most potent.

She caught his attention when she sat across from him at dinner on the verandah deck, on the fifth night. Between courses, a few couples danced under the stars. Cecily sat at another table, engrossed in the leader of a rock band who was busy plying her with flattery and probably too much alcohol, but Carter was keeping an eye on her.

Not in the least interested in the latest celebrity gossip among those remaining at her own table, Brianna had smothered a yawn and glanced up to find Dimitrios's amused gaze fixed on her face.

"Do I take it," he murmured, his English so fluent only a trace of accent betrayed his Greek heritage, "that you find the conversation less than enthralling?"

"Oh, dear!" she said ruefully. "Does it show?"

"I'm afraid so." He rose and extended his hand. "Allow me to come to the rescue."

She'd have liked to say she wasn't in such dire straits that she couldn't rescue herself, but hypnotized by his faint smile and the hint of dark mystery in his eyes, she responded without a moment's hesitation. Docile as a lamb, she placed her hand in his.

Love at first sight? Until she met Dimitrios Giannakis, she hadn't believed in it. Fifteen minutes in his arms, with her body pressed close to his and his breath ruffling her hair, and she decided differently.

And paid a terrible price for doing so.

CHAPTER THREE

THE private clinic where she was to meet with Noelle Manning was in Kifissia, a northern suburb of Athens, just over half an hour's drive west of Rafina. The road wound over Mount Penteli, a fairly sparsely populated area of pine-scented forests, with the occasional very grand house interspersed among acreages whose little old cottages were as much a part of the landscape as the grape vines and olive trees planted on the land. Traffic was light, consisting mostly of agricultural vehicles, although once the Mercedes passed a truck carrying massive slabs of marble.

Set in spacious grounds on a quiet crescent high above the city, the clinic rose sleek and white against a backdrop of leafy green trees and brilliant blue sky. A receptionist in the lobby took her name and spoke briefly into an intercom. Within minutes Brianna was escorted to Noelle's consulting room on the second floor, where the doctor wasted no time getting down to business.

For the next hour she outlined the various stages of testing a potential donor to determine if she fulfilled all the requirements for a traditional bone marrow harvest, explaining each step with the succinct clarity of a true expert in her field.

"Naturally, we've combed the international registry of unrelated donors hoping to find a perfect tissue match, but so far we've unfortunately come up empty-handed," she concluded. "And since time is very much of the essence in Poppy's case, we're faced with settling for what we call an alternative donor such as a parent, who offers a half match. Poppy's mother is deceased—"

"Yes, but what about Dimitrios?"

"He's been tested, but is unable to help his daughter." Noelle lowered her glance to the open folder on her desk and closed it with gentle finality. "Obviously, I can't discuss the details with you. Professional confidentiality and all that, you understand."

"Of course."

"We're very lucky that Poppy's mother happened to have an identical twin. If it turns out that you're a suitable donor and you're willing to go through with this procedure, Brianna, you really will be giving your niece the gift of life."

"I'm absolutely willing. Nothing you've told me today has changed my mind about that."

"Do you have any questions?"

"Yes. What comes next?"

"I'll book you for a complete physical assessment—and I do mean 'complete'. By the time that's over, there'll be nothing about your health, past or present, that we won't know. We do this for two reasons. One is to make sure you're a suitable donor, free of infectious diseases—this being a fairly significant factor in your case, given the amount of foreign travel your work involves—and the other is to protect you. We gain nothing by saving one life if, in doing so, we compromise another. Once we've cleared those hurdles, we'll begin the actual protocol as I've explained it to you."

"All right, then. When can we get started?"

Noelle smiled. "I love your enthusiasm and certainly don't want to say or do anything to diminish it, but this whole undertaking has been sprung on you out of the blue, and I must therefore insist you take some time to absorb just what it involves."

"How much time?"

"A few days. A week maybe."

"But why? You've told me everything I need to know."

"No. I've told you what to expect in terms of the surgical procedure as it affects you, should you prove to be a suitable donor."

"Why do I get the feeling the other shoe's about to drop?"

"Because that's the easy part. It's what comes, or might come next, that's not so predictable." She rested her forearms on her desk and fixed Brianna in a candid gaze. "Sometimes a transplant just doesn't work. Should this happen with Poppy, it's imperative that you understand it's not your fault. Assuming you pass all the tests with flying colors, I'll be booking you for a couple of sessions with our staff psychologist, just to be sure you're prepared in the event of a negative outcome. Also, once you're approved as a donor, I'll ask you to sign a consent form. It's not legally binding and you're free to back out at any time—"

"I won't back out, Noelle. I'm committed to doing this for that poor child." Brianna leaned forward urgently. "Give me the form and I'll sign it now."

"Hear me out, please," the doctor said, holding up her

hand as if she was directing traffic. "There's more. Once you've signed that document, we'll start Poppy on a round of conditioning chemotherapy."

Brianna sank back in her chair, the information so unexpected and shocking that she felt sick to her stomach. She had a modeling friend, a stunningly beautiful young woman, who at only twenty-three had been diagnosed with leukemia. Although she was now in remission, she'd said more than once that the cure was worse than the disease.

"For heaven's sake, *why?*" Brianna cried, tears stinging her eyes. "Poppy's just a little girl—not much more than a baby—and she doesn't have cancer. Why do you have to do something so horribly drastic?"

"To destroy her abnormal cells and make room for your healthy replacement."

A logical procedure from a medical point of view, Brianna supposed. Still… "How long will it take—the treatment, I mean?"

"About a week, although the aftereffects last significantly longer, but you may be sure we'll do our best to keep her as comfortable as possible throughout that time."

"Does Dimitrios know about this?"

"Of course. I consult with him every day."

"It must be killing him!" *And I'm not making it any easier, doing battle with him over every perceived slight.*

"He's had a hard time coming to terms with it, certainly, but given the alternative, he's presented with little choice. However, the reason I'm bringing this up with you now, Brianna, is that the conditioning therapy also kills off the patient's immune system. It's therefore critical for you to understand that *if* you were to change your mind after this point, Poppy will almost certainly die or suffer serious delays in further treatment." She pushed a thick folder across her desk. "And that's why I won't let you sign anything today. I want you to go away, read this information package and weigh what I've told you before you make any final decisions."

"Poppy doesn't have time for that."

"We're talking about two weeks at the most, and Poppy is relatively stable right now."

"So stable she's in a hospital, instead of at home!"

"To protect her from exposure to infection. Even something as simple as a cold could set her back and prevent a successful transplant. Obviously, that's not a risk any of us is prepared to take."

"No, of course not." She hesitated a moment before continuing, "I'm not sure how much you know of my relationship with my sister, but you've probably gathered from remarks made at dinner last night that I've never actually met Poppy, and I'd very much like to put a face to this child who's depending on me for so much. Is it at all possible for me to visit her?"

"I don't see why not, as long as Dimitrios has no objection." Noelle glanced at the clock on her desk. "He usually stops by over the lunch hour, so is probably with her now. Why don't we go and find out?"

Brianna thought she knew all about heartache and heartbreak, but the next twenty minutes or so taught her she hadn't begun to plumb the depths of either. Not only was Poppy hospitalized, she was in isolation—what Noelle chillingly referred to as "a sterile environment"—which meant not only that she had no other children nearby to keep her company, but also that everyone going into her room first had to follow a strict hygiene regimen.

"Doesn't it frighten her, being surrounded by people whose faces she can't really see?" Brianna asked, donning the required gown and mask.

"You tell me," Noelle responded, approaching an observation window set in the wall connecting the nursery with the outer room. "Does that look like a frightened child to you?"

Following, Brianna looked through the glass, and what she saw on the other side made something deep and powerful clutch at her heart. Dimitrios sprawled in a rocking chair, reading to Poppy whom he cradled in his lap as easily, as naturally, as if it had been designed for the express purpose of holding a sick child.

His broad shoulders filled the width of his chair; his long legs, elegantly clad in finely tailored black trousers, poked out from the folds of a pale-yellow gown. Above his mask, his dark brows rose in comical dismay. Wide with feigned astonishment, his gaze swung from the book and came to rest on Poppy, and even with the barrier of glass separating them, Brianna heard her laughter.

Climbing his torso, she planted her bare little feet on his thighs and reached for the brightly colored balloon bouquet floating almost to the ceiling and anchored by ribbons to the back of the chair. From her vantage point, Brianna could see only the back of the child's head, covered with thick black hair just like her own. And soon it would be gone, falling away in clumps....

Again tears threatened, but she blinked them back and managed a shaky smile when she saw that Dimitrios had glanced up and was gesturing for her and Noelle to join him.

Poppy turned at the sound of the door opening, and for a moment, Brianna froze. Even allowing for illness robbing her of so much, the child was exquisite, her delicate little face dominated by enormous eyes the exact same shade of blue as her own and Cecily's—but with an innocence to them that Cecily had lost at a very early age if, indeed, she'd ever possessed it at all.

"*Kalimera*," Dimitrios said. "Hi. This is a surprise."

Until that moment Brianna had deliberately thought of Poppy as his daughter, or the little girl, or the child, or even, may God forgive her, "the patient." It had been, she supposed, her way of distancing herself from a set of circumstances still more painful to contemplate than they had any right to be. But now, suddenly, the words she'd avoided using were the only ones with real meaning. Closing the distance between herself and the chair, she dropped down to be at eye level with Poppy and said, "I thought it high time I met my niece. Hello, beautiful! I'm your auntie Brianna."

Whether or not she really understood what that meant was doubtful, but after surveying Brianna for a long, quiet moment, Poppy smiled and reached out her arms to be held. Almost choking with emotion, Brianna looked to Dimitrios to gauge his reaction.

In one lithe movement, he was out of the chair. With a jerk of his chin, he invited her to take his place, and when she was comfortably seated, passed her niece to her. Brianna felt the warm little body, the painfully fragile bones, the soft skin. She felt the sweet damp draft of breath against her cheek, the trusting clutch of tiny fingers at the side of her neck.

A fresh tide of emotion rolled over her. Her entire being

filled with something so visceral, so elemental, it left her breathless. Only once before had she known such an instant connection with another human being, and, as swiftly as she had the first time around, she fell in love again. Hopelessly, helplessly. And this time, forever.

I'm finally where I belong, she thought, dazed by sudden blinding insight. *Not on a runway or on location for a glamorous shoot, but in a simple rocking chair, with a child in my arms. Modeling might have been my occupation, but motherhood is my true vocation.*

Swallowing hard, she closed her eyes and held on: to Poppy, and to the tears she didn't want her niece to see; to the hope that she could be the one to give this little soul the gift of life; and most of all, to the chance to make up for the years she had missed being an aunt to this adorable child. When, after struggling for an interminable minute or so, she could finally breathe again, she set the rocking chair in gentle motion and began to hum a lullaby, which she neither knew how nor when she'd committed to memory. And as if she'd finally come home, Poppy relaxed and let her head settle drowsily against Brianna's shoulder.

"If I didn't know better, I'd say she recognizes you," Dimitrios said, his voice as rough sounding as if his throat had been scraped raw with coarse brown sugar.

Brianna's eyes flew open in shock. "Do you think she's mistaking me for Cecily?"

His laugh emerged, harsh, abrupt and brimming with bitter irony. *"Ohi!* Not in a million years! For a start she was only eighteen months old when her mother died. Not only that, Cecily never crooned to her or held her like that, and I'm pretty sure she never rocked her to sleep. She left that kind of job to Erika or the latest nanny."

Running her hand in slow, comforting strokes up Poppy's delicate spine, Brianna whispered, "What *did* she do for her, then?"

"Dress her up like a doll or something you'd stick on the top of a Christmas tree, and parade her before visitors to impress them. Smother her with kisses and endearments if there happened to be a captive audience on hand to applaud her. *Pretend* she cared," he finished, with such unvarnished disgust that Brianna shuddered.

It all sounded so horribly familiar; so reminiscent of her and Cecily's own blighted childhood, when their mother would deliver an award-winning performance as Parent of the Year if the "right" people were there to witness it and there was the chance she could further her ambitions to make money from her daughters. The difference, of course, was that Cecily hadn't done it for money. She hadn't needed to. She'd married it, instead.

"If that's how she felt, she never should have had a baby in the first place."

"No. You'd have been a much better choice," Dimitrios said, so quietly that Brianna wasn't entirely sure she'd heard him correctly.

But the glance he turned on her, intense and full of dark remorse, made her heart leap in her breast and sent a thread of warmth stealing through her body. But *Be careful!* her head cautioned. *He seduced you with words once before and you learned to your cost that, in the end, they meant nothing. Don't fall for the same old ploy a second time.*

From her post by the door, Noelle coughed lightly, as though to remind them of her presence and, crossing the room, lowered the high rail on the side of the hospital crib and took Poppy from Brianna. "This little one's had enough excitement for now and is falling asleep," she said, very much the doctor in charge. "The more rest she gets, the better, so let's leave her to nap undisturbed."

She placed Poppy gently on the mattress and drew a soft blanket over her lower limbs. Robbed of the warmth of that sweet little body, Brianna crossed her hands over her breast in a futile attempt to stem the emptiness that filled both her arms and her heart. *She should have been our baby,* she thought, anguished. *Mine and Dimitrios's. She'd never have had to make do with Erika or a nanny if I'd been her mother.*

Noelle touched her arm kindly. "If Dimitrios doesn't mind, you can come back later, but I have to ask you to leave her for now."

"I don't mind," he said. "It'll be a change from her having to make do with me all the time."

"Is there no one else in the family who comes to see her?"

"We have no other family," he replied with grim finality.

Poppy rested on her stomach with her head turned to one side. Her lashes lay thick and dark as soot on her pale cheeks. Her thumb had found its way into her sweet little rosebud mouth. Her little bottom rose and fell gently with each breath she took.

Brianna lingered for one last look at the new love of her life. *You do now, sweetheart,* she telegraphed fiercely. *You have me, and together you and I are going to beat this disease, and I'm going to be there to watch you grow up strong and healthy.*

Dimitrios was so silent and so obviously preoccupied as they rode the elevator to the main floor and walked out to the clinic's sun-filled forecourt where Spiros waited in the

Mercedes, that the last thing she expected was for him to stop her as she was about to climb into the car and say, "I don't know about you, but I'm ready for something to eat. How about we stop somewhere before you head home?"

Taken aback, she said, "You're inviting me to have lunch with you?"

"Why not?"

"Well, for a start, we might have agreed to put our differences behind us, but that doesn't mean we particularly like each other much."

"Are you so convinced of that, Brianna," he asked gently, "or is it just wishful thinking on your part?"

Both his tone and his question stopped her short. For the past several years she'd clung to the belief that he was a liar and a cheat. It had made losing him a little more bearable. After all, she prided herself on having some brains, and what woman in her right mind wanted to tie herself to a man incapable of fidelity?

Since her arrival on his doorstep, though, and from a couple of rather ambiguous remarks on his part, not to mention that unpremeditated, devastating kiss, she was no longer sure of anything. Last night, when the first doubts crept in, she'd told herself her imagination was in overdrive. Today, she'd been forced to confront a reality so stark it left nothing to the imagination.

Like it or not, she and Dimitrios were allies against a fearsome, wicked enemy. Although they were both hurting, his pain ran deeper; deep enough that he was regarding her now with a dark, almost pleading urgency that tugged at her heart.

But could she trust her heart, this time around? Could she trust *him?*

Sensing her reluctance, he said, "I'm inviting you to have lunch, Brianna, not asking you to sell me your soul, and I promise not to have your food poisoned."

"It never occurred to me that you might," she said, shaking off her doubts. "And yes, I'd very much like to have lunch with you, as long as your driver doesn't mind being kept waiting."

"I pay Spiros to be where he's needed, when he's needed. He can take us to the taverna I have in mind, or we can walk, if you'd rather. It's not too far."

Finding herself in the back seat of the Mercedes with a Dimitrios who, despite the anxieties plaguing him, grew more appealing by the second, was a bit too potent a mix for her to swallow. "It's such a lovely day, why don't we walk?"

"I hoped you'd say that." After a quick word with his driver, he cupped her elbow and steered her down the curving drive to the tree-shaded street. "Sure the heat's not too much for you?" he inquired solicitously, glancing at her cheeks, which she knew were flushed.

She was burning up, but not for the reason he thought. His touch electrified her, sending a tide of warmth riding up her neck and reviving more buried memories.

Time spun backward to another hot afternoon under a blue Greek sky. Clad in a black bikini, she reclined under an awning, on the deck of the 325-foot yacht lying at anchor in a quiet bay in the Cyclades, some sixty miles south of Athens. And Dimitrios Giannakis, a man she'd met only a few days before was tracing seductive patterns over her exposed midriff and murmuring sweet nothings in her ear.

And at the end of it all, they really were "nothings," she

reminded herself, shutting out the image. He hadn't meant a word he'd said, and she'd be a fool to read too much into the present situation. He was, after all, a sophisticated man, accustomed to moving in the upper echelons of society. Impeccable manners were as much a part of him as his black hair and beguiling smile. Taking a woman's arm as she crossed the street came as naturally to him as breathing. Or lying.

They stopped at a charming little taverna several blocks from the clinic. Tucked away on a side street, it opened at the back to a large courtyard shaded by a vine-covered pergola. About a dozen tables clustered around a fountain set in the middle, but only two were occupied, the lunch hour crowd having already been and gone.

Without consulting her, he ordered two salads and a bottle of Boutari Moschofilero. "Still your favorite Greek wine, I hope?" he queried, tipping the rim of his glass to hers, after the waiter had poured.

"Yes," she admitted, unable to stem a little glow of pleasure that he'd remembered.

"And you still don't care for ouzo?"

"Definitely not."

He fixed her in another unwavering gaze. "It's nice to know some things haven't changed, Brianna."

But some things have, she told herself sternly. *Don't let him seduce you into forgetting that.*

Their waiter reappeared and set down a basket of bread still warm from the oven and a small appetizer tray of olives and grilled octopus.

Welcoming the interruption as a chance to turn the conversation into safer, less personal channels, and hoping she sounded a lot more nonchalant than she felt, she said,

"I'm not familiar with this part of Athens. It's really quite lovely."

"Yes."

"I noticed on the way here that we passed a number of rather grand villas."

"Yes."

"Some reminded me of Victorian manor houses in England."

"Yes."

"Noelle's English, isn't she?"

"Yes," he agreed, still holding her captive in his stare.

"What made her decide to work in Greece?"

"The weather's better here?"

More unhinged by the second, she snapped, "Stop making fun of me—and stop saying 'yes' all the time."

"Okay. I don't know why Noelle chooses to work here, although I expect it's because she's free to work in any country that's part of the European Union. What I do know, and what matters to me, is that she's recognized as being one of the best in her field, the clinic's as high-tech as anything you'd find anywhere else in the world, and only the best is good enough for my daughter. Any other questions?"

"No."

"Good," he said, allowing himself a small, satisfied smile. "Then let's stop pretending either of us gives a damn about the neighborhood or Noelle's reasons for practicing medicine here instead of in England, and talk about something else."

"Like what?"

"Like us," he said. "As in you and me. And let's start with you."

CHAPTER FOUR

HE ACHIEVED the result he was hoping for, surprising her enough that she almost dropped her wineglass. Recovering herself just in time to set it down on the table, she raised startled eyes to his, classic deer-in-the-headlights shock registering on her lovely face.

Good. Perhaps by keeping her on edge, he could unearth a few fragments of truth from all the lies. It was well past time.

Hesitantly she said, "What do you want to know?"

"Everything, but we can begin with this morning. Now that you have a more complete picture of what you'd be letting yourself in for, how serious are you about going ahead with testing as Poppy's donor?"

"I haven't changed my mind, if that's what you're afraid of. In fact, I'm more determined than ever."

"Even though, if you turn out to be a suitable match, you'd end up with surgical scars on those elegant hips of yours? Won't do much for your career, will it, if you can't strut your stuff in a bikini?"

"I haven't modeled bikinis in years, but even if that wasn't the case, I hardly equate a couple of little scars with saving a child's life. You might not respect how I earn my living, Dimitrios, but I'm not quite as shallow as you seem to think."

"But you *are* ambitious. We both know that. You don't let anything come between you and your career."

"That's hardly a fair comment! There's a difference between being professional and being driven to the point that everything else runs second."

She sounded so aggrieved that, if he hadn't known better, he'd have thought she actually believed the rubbish she was spouting. Steeling himself not to soften, he said, "I could argue the point, but let's not go down that road, at least not right now. Instead tell me why you're so eager and willing to help a child you previously refused to acknowledge."

"I already explained I didn't know Poppy existed until your phone call last Tuesday."

"You don't seriously expect me to believe that, do you?"

A flush accentuated those classic cheekbones. "I don't care whether you believe me or not," she said, her eyes shooting icy, pale-blue sparks. "I'm *telling* you that the last time I spoke to Cecily was right after you married her. It was also, you might recall, the last time I spoke to you, as well—until the other day. And I have no reason to lie."

"Are you saying you didn't even know your sister was pregnant?"

"That's right. Apart from the lawyer's letter telling me she'd died, I knew nothing about her life with you. You were hardly forthcoming, after all. Even at her funeral, we didn't exchange more than the barest civilities. And contrary to what other twins might experience, Cecily and I didn't share telepathic communication."

He cradled his wineglass and regarded her thoughtfully.

"In a sick sort of way, I suppose that makes sense. Cecily didn't broadcast the news that she was expecting. In fact," he finished bitterly, "she didn't deal well with pregnancy at all."

Picking up on his black tone, she said, "What do you mean?"

"She tried to terminate it at twenty weeks."

"No!" Again he'd caught her off guard. Her flush drained into shocked pallor. "For heaven's sake, *why?"*

"She didn't like what it was doing to the shrine that was her precious body," he spat, the acrid taste of disgust lingering in his mouth.

"Oh." She dampened her lower lip with the tip of her tongue. "What changed her mind?"

"I did," he said, reliving the scene in all its ugly detail. "Very emphatically."

You can't make me go through with it.

Yes, I can, Cecily. And I will.

How? By keeping me under lock and key for the next five months? Appointing that benighted housekeeper of yours my prison guard?

If I have to, yes.

You don't have the right. It's my body, not yours.

But it's my child.

I hate you, Dimitrios!

I'll survive—and so will that baby....

Brianna cleared her throat. "Do you think," she began tentatively, "her trying to, um, bring on a miscarriage, is in any way responsible for Poppy being so ill now?"

"I've asked myself the same question a thousand times, and I'm told by those who ought to know that the two aren't related, but..." He shook his head, the doubts still plaguing him. "I should have kept a closer eye on Cecily. Monitored where she was going, who she was seeing. Made sure she didn't drink alcohol or worse yet, dabble in recreational drugs."

Reaching across the table, Brianna put a sympathetic hand over his, and this time he was the one taken by surprise. Up to that point, he'd initiated all physical contact between them, and, fragile though her overture was, he liked it. He liked it very much. And that was something he had to guard against.

"Don't," she said. "This was not your fault, Dimitrios. Do not blame yourself for Cecily's bad behavior."

"How do you know it wasn't my bad behavior that drove her to such extremes?"

"Because I knew Cecily. Better than you did, probably. We lived together for almost twenty-four years, remember, and it doesn't surprise me one iota that losing her figure struck her as a disaster on a par with the sinking of the *Titanic*. She was always very…" She shrugged, searching for the right word.

"Vain?"

"Conscious of her image," she amended. "It's not surprising, you know. We'd both been brought up believing how we looked was all that mattered. And I'm sorry to say, Cecily believed it. Not only that, I know for a fact that if she decided she was going to party with the wrong crowd, she'd have found a way to do it, regardless of any steps you took to prevent it."

"Are you speaking from personal experience?"

She withdrew her hand and sat back in her chair, seeming to regret having revealed so much. "She was my sister and I loved her, but…" She sighed and looked off to one side. "Look, I don't mean to sound disloyal, but for your peace of mind you need to understand that she was always…willful."

"What about you?" he asked. "Are you as much alike on the inside as you were on the outside?"

"I can be stubborn," she admitted. "When I make up my mind, I tend to stick to it."

"I guess I should be glad. Because of that, Poppy might have found a donor."

She bathed him in the kind of glance that, once upon a time, before he'd disciplined himself to separate sex from sanity, would have reduced him to a mass of raging testosterone. A soft, urgent, melting glance which, even now, he found dangerously distracting. "I might have been motivated by purely humanitarian reasons at the beginning, Dimitrios, but that changed when I actually met Poppy, when I looked into her eyes and held her in my arms." Her breasts rose in a heartfelt sigh—another distraction he didn't need. "My heart is engaged in a way I never expected. I've never before formed such an instant bond with another person."

He couldn't help himself. He had to ask. "Never, Brianna?"

Some of the animation faded from her face. "Hardly ever," she hedged. "And never with a child. Until this morning, I didn't know…"

"What?" he persisted, when she lapsed into silence.

Clearly undecided about how to answer, she bit her lip, then sat straighter in her chair, very much the posture-perfect model. "How remarkable children are. I mean, look at all Poppy's going through—being away from you and the people she knows and loves, having needles stuck in her all the time, not having other children to play with. Yet she was laughing and smiling and—"

She choked up suddenly, and he saw tears shining in her eyes. "I'm sorry," she mumbled. "I don't mean to go all weepy and emotional on you."

"No need to apologize. I have my moments, too."

She swallowed hard. "How do you do it, Dimitrios? How do you manage to hold it together when you see her?"

"Because I have to. Because if there's one thing I've learned through all this, it's that children are amazingly resilient and accepting and brave, and the least I can do is follow their example."

Again she grabbed for his hand, and this time curled her fingers around his. "I want to help you, not just by testing as a donor. I want to be with you both—see it through with you. Please let me. Please don't shut me out just because we were once…close."

"'Close,' Brianna?" He freed his hand and poured more wine into his glass. "We were *lovers,* until you abruptly decided otherwise."

She reared back in outrage. "Well, what else did you expect?"

"A truthful explanation for your very sudden departure would have been nice." He paused. "And if you couldn't do it then, how about now?"

Her eyes grew wide with astonishment. "You really want me to spell it out for you, after all this time?"

"It's never too late to set the record straight, and I'm tough. I can take rejection. What I can't tolerate are lies. So explain to me, please, why you bothered pretending you wanted to build a future with me, when all along you planned to jump ship at the first opportunity? Why didn't you just come right out and tell me your precious modeling career meant more than anything I had to offer?"

"Because that wasn't the reason, you jerk! I wanted you more than I've ever wanted anything in my life, even if I do now ask myself why, but I left because there were some things I refused to share with my sister, your bed being one of them."

He gave his head a disbelieving shake, sure he'd misunderstood. "What did you just say?"

"Oh, please! Stop pretending you don't know what I'm talking about. We made love in your stateroom. You wanted me to stay the night. I wouldn't, because I didn't want to start a feeding frenzy of gossip among the crew and passengers if we were found out. So I went back to my own quarters, but I couldn't sleep. That's the kind of effect you had on me, Dimitrios. I was intoxicated by you. Floating on air."

"You had a funny way of showing it."

Ignoring his snide interruption, she continued doggedly, "I finally decided to go up on deck and watch the sunrise. And that's when I saw Cecily leaving your cabin."

"Did you?" he said. "And did you ask her what she was doing there?"

"I didn't have to. She was only too happy to tell me what marvelous stamina you had, what an incredible romp between the sheets you'd given her."

"And you believed her."

Suddenly not sounding so confident, she muttered, "Why wouldn't I?"

"Because she was lying, Brianna," he informed her dully, none of the exhilaration he should have known filling him. Instead he felt hollow, empty. So much time wasted, so many mistakes piling one on top of another, and all because of a misunderstanding that need never have occurred in the first place. "As you'd have found out soon enough if you'd had the guts to shove her back through my door and made her repeat her allegations to my face."

"You're the one lying. I *saw* her. She'd been in your room."

"Sure she had. Tried climbing into my bed, as well, pretending to be you. It was dark enough that she might even have gotten away with it, if I hadn't picked up a whiff of tobacco on her breath."

"Did you confront her?"

"No," he said sarcastically. "I jumped up and down like a crazed ape, beat my manly chest and bellowed to the whole of Crete how lucky I was to have the Connelly twins fighting over me." He stopped and drew an irate breath. "What do you take me for? Of course I confronted her!"

"Well, what did she say?"

"That you'd asked her to keep me occupied so that you could sneak off and catch a flight out of Heraklion without my knowing."

Ashen-faced, Brianna stared at him. "But why would she bother concocting such an elaborate story for me? What advantage did that give her?"

"Use your head, woman! She wanted rid of you, because she was jealous, and she knew damned well your pride would never allow you to challenge me and thus expose her deception."

Rallying, she countered, "It's easy for you to make that claim now, when it's too late for anyone to prove otherwise."

"I'm not in the habit of lying, Brianna, and if it's a confession of guilt you're after, I freely admit I slept with her the very next night after you left," he acknowledged calmly. "A big mistake on my part, certainly, and I'm not proud of it, but a man tends to react badly when he's been dumped by the woman he planned to spend the rest of his life with. Pour enough booze into him, and if there's someone else more than willing to take her place, and she happens also to be a carbon copy of the original, well…" He shrugged. "It's called the rebound factor. Maybe you've heard of it."

"It strikes me as a bit more than that. After all, you ended up marrying her a couple of months later, and not a moment too soon, judging by Poppy's age."

She looked so crushed that, just briefly, he regretted having spoken so forthrightly. But she wasn't the only one who'd paid a high price, anymore than he was the only one who'd made mistakes.

"Because she was pregnant," he said. "Look, Brianna, I could tell you I never loved her the way I loved you, that I cursed myself a thousand times over for being such a bloody fool, and it would all be true, but none of that changes the fact that you and I, not Cecily, were mostly at fault. She seized an opportunity, but we're the ones who gave it to her because we didn't trust one another enough."

"We hadn't known each other long enough to develop any trust."

"Perhaps not, but if we'd really been as deeply in love as we thought we were, I'd have fought for you anyway and hoped like hell I wouldn't live to regret it. But I didn't. I let you go."

Again she glanced aside. "I'm to blame, as well. I ran

away because it was easier than facing what I thought was the truth. I should have known better. I just never dreamed Cecily could be so…so destructive."

"Because you didn't really know her as well as you thought. Nobody did. All we ever learned was what she allowed us to see. She was like an iceberg, with seven-eighths, the most treacherous part, hidden."

"Hindsight's a wonderful thing, isn't it?" she said miserably.

His cell phone interrupted, sparing his having to comment. Just as well. He might have said something he'd live to regret. *"Me sing khorite,"* he murmured, noticing the name showing on the display screen. "Excuse me. I have to take this call."

She nodded and, rising from her chair with her trademark grace, wandered over to examine the flowers growing near the fountain. "What?" he barked into the phone, royally ticked off with himself for not being able to tear his glance away from her long, elegant legs and slender hips.

"Where the devil are you?" Pavlos, his PA, shot back. "The meeting's due to start in ten minutes."

"What meeting?"

"The one slated to make you another cool two million euros or more, provided, of course, you're still interested. The one which has the consortium from Shanghai cooling its heels in the executive lounge and wondering if you really exist or are just a figment of an overactive Greek imagination. Need I go on?"

"Skata, Pavlos," he muttered. "I forgot all about it."

"Not surprising, I guess, all things considered. You've got a lot on your mind right now."

"More than you can begin to guess," he groaned. "Keep the visitors occupied with the video presentation until I can get there, will you? I'm still in Kifissia, but I'll be there as soon as I can. Traffic's building, so I'll leave my car here and take the Metro. I should be there within forty minutes."

Seeing he'd ended the call, Brianna returned to the table. "Everything all right?"

"*Ohi.* I have to go, but you stay and enjoy the rest of your meal and the wine. I'll take care of the bill on my way out. If you're up to exploring a bit more, you might want to browse the boutiques farther down the road." He pressed his phone into her hand. "You know how to use one of these. Spiros is on speed dial. When you're ready to leave, give him a call and let him know where to pick you up."

She caught his sleeve as he went to turn away. "Just a minute—"

"I don't have a minute, Brianna," he interrupted, making no effort to curb his impatience. "I know we were in the middle of something, but it'll have to keep until another time because I need to leave. Now."

"Just tell me before you go. Is it Poppy? Has something happened? Because if it has and you're headed back to the clinic, I'm coming with you."

He'd have had to be pretty jaded not to recognize the concern in her eyes and voice. Feeling low as dirt for snapping at her without cause, he squeezed her hand and said more gently, "It's not Poppy. It's business. But thanks for caring. Look, I'll see you later, okay, and we'll pick up where we left off. Meanwhile, try to enjoy what's left of the afternoon."

She watched him walk away, six feet plus of utter competence and self-assurance. Never a wasted word or motion.

Never an awkward pause as he fumbled for just the right word. Never a clumsy move.

She, however, was a mess. She'd been on an emotional roller coaster for the better part of three hours. And the last sixty minutes had, in some ways, been the most shocking.

She'd known for a long time that Cecily envied her; that what she herself saw as an equal partnership between sisters had, in Cecily's mind, become a competition between rivals, one that recognized no boundaries between their professional and personal lives. But that she'd go to such extremes, that she'd deliberately sabotage her sister's budding love affair…?

On the other hand, was it really so surprising? Casting her mind back, Brianna recalled a number of occasions during the last few months they'd shared an apartment, when she'd been singled out for special assignments which hadn't included her sister, but she'd missed them because Cecily either "accidentally" erased voice mail messages, or conveniently "forgot" to pass them on.

"She's spiraling into self-destruction, and she'll take you down with her if you're not careful," Carter had raged, after one particularly unfortunate incident. "Do yourself a favor and get set up in your own place before she succeeds."

But Brianna hadn't believed him. Hadn't *wanted* to believe him. "We might have our differences, but at bottom, we love each other," she'd insisted. "Cecily would never deliberately hurt me."

Now, when it was too late, she knew differently. What had begun as a slow, almost imperceptible erosion of her relationship with her sister had degenerated into outright betrayal during that cruise through the Greek islands. Yet it could all have turned out so differently if only, as Dimitrios had so astutely pointed out, they'd trusted each other. Instead they'd been too dazzled with stardust to see the danger lurking on the sidelines and guard themselves against it.

And yet it had been there all along, if only she'd recognized the signs. That first night, as the yacht set sail from the mainland and headed south to the island of Crete, their hosts had thrown an extravagant cocktail party. There were thirty-six guests gathered on deck, at least twenty-five of whom, including her and Cecily, were either famous faces or famous names on both sides of the Atlantic. The remaining eleven were a blend of wealthy sophisticates and corporate power moguls.

Of the latter, the most influential by far was the cultured Dimitrios Giannakis, whose empire, one of the group she and Cecily were with confided, ran the gamut from charter airlines to oil to real estate.

"Is he married?" Cecily had inquired, almost tripping over her own feet in her eagerness to catch a closer glimpse.

"No," the man replied on a well-bred snort of laughter. "But trust me, it's not for want of offers."

Perhaps if she herself hadn't fallen so completely under his spell, Brianna might have paid closer attention to Cecily's growing displeasure at being overlooked by the man who was undoubtedly the most eligible bachelor in Europe.

Swamped with regret for what might have been, Brianna pushed aside the remains of her lunch. She and Dimitrios had started out with such dreams. Found such bliss together, albeit for too short a time. Why hadn't they gone the extra distance and believed in each other?

Instead they'd fallen victim to one of the oldest games in the book: the fury of a woman scorned. Cecily had got what she'd been after from the start, and Brianna had lost a sister in the process. She'd never seen Cecily again, except for the occasional photograph plastered on the front page of some tabloid or other on display in the supermarket: "Former supermodel Cecily Connelly, wife of Greek billionaire Dimitrios Giannakis, at a party in Cannes…hobnobbing with the jet set in Monte Carlo…skiing in the Swiss Alps."

Cecily was always dazzling the camera with her famous smile. There was never any mention of a child. And a grim-faced Dimitrios, if he was there at all, invariably remained at arm's length from all the hoop-la.

Brianna never bought the tabloid. She never read the article. She turned away, even so small a reminder of what had been stolen from her, enough to darken her day.

CHAPTER FIVE

WALLOWING in remorse for things it was much too late to change, left Brianna too unsettled to endure the rest of the afternoon under Erika's hostile surveillance. She needed to be around people who didn't regard her as a necessary evil; with strangers who'd judge her on her own merits. So she took Dimitrios's advice and explored the streets of Kifissia.

The boutiques were lovely. If she'd been in a more frivolous mood, she could have spent a small fortune on exquisite clothes. One ensemble in particular caught her eye. A voile dress printed with pale, overblown roses in shades of pink and mauve on an ivory background, it floated over the back of an antique chair set on a circular dais in the showroom window. The hem of its voluminous skirt fell in graceful folds to where a matching hat with a wide brim lay on the silver-gray carpet, next to a pair of exquisite ivory silk pumps.

Brianna's experience with the garment industry was such that she recognized fine clothes when she saw them, and this was a gem; a special-occasion dress designed by someone with a true eye for elegance and style. But she had weightier matters on her mind, and the only special occasion in her near future was a date with a team of doctors in a private clinic. So, with a last fond glance at the dream of a dress, she continued down the street and found herself outside a shop catering to babies and small children.

The door stood open and, on impulse, she stepped inside. Stuffed toys, hand-made quilts, pint-size furniture and other nursery accessories vied for space with adorable dresses, beaded socks, dainty little shoes and lace-trimmed sun hats. Delightful outfits of the kind that Poppy should have been wearing, rather than the hospital gowns that presently comprised her entire wardrobe. But she lived in such a protected environment, she couldn't cuddle a plush teddy bear or a favorite doll. If an object couldn't be wiped off with germicidal solution morning, noon and night, it didn't get past the door to her room. Even the book Dimitrios had been reading to her had laminated pages.

Until that moment Brianna had been drawn more by idle curiosity and wishful thinking than by any serious intention of shopping for her niece. With so many restrictions in place, there hadn't seemed much point. But faced with such an abundance of riches, as it were, she suddenly found herself asking, Why not? If ever a child needed and deserved a little spoiling, that child was Poppy. Surely there was something here, some inoffensive, pretty thing that could soften the barren confines of her room without compromising her health?

The shop owner approached, and after ascertaining that the woman spoke English, Brianna explained, "I'm looking for a gift for my three-year-old niece, but it can't be clothing or anything like this." Regretfully, she picked up a gorgeous velvet rabbit with long, silky ears. "She's hospitalized, you see—and in isolation."

"She is in the children's wing of the Rosegarth Clinic?"

"I'm afraid so, yes."

"Ah." The woman clicked her tongue sympathetically. "Then certainly she needs something to make her smile when you're not there, but it must be something which will not expose her to risk of infection, yes?"

"How did you know?"

"Because you're not the first to come here, my dear lady. Many families with children at the Rosegarth end up at my door, hoping to find just the right gift to cheer up their sick little ones." She indicated a row of glass-domed porcelain figures, some perched on swings, some skating on mirrored surfaces, others riding on painted carousel horses or Ferris wheels, and all mounted on sturdy metal bases. "These are very popular. They're actually battery-operated music boxes with colored lights that rotate as the figures move. They can be kept out of reach of the patient, but still be enjoyed. I also have a wide selection of pretty mobiles—butterflies, humming birds, swans and such— which also sell very well."

Given a choice, Brianna would have left with enough packages to fill the trunk of the Mercedes, but when Spiros came to collect her, she'd managed to confine herself to one bright-red Ferris wheel music box, and a mobile of irides-cent butterflies. "Although I'll probably be back again before long," she warned the saleswoman as she left the shop.

It was after five by then, and the traffic exiting the city was horrendous. What had been only about a thirty-five-minute drive that morning took almost twice as long in late afternoon, making it close to half past six before she finally arrived on Dimitrios's doorstep a second time.

Erika answered the door. "We were beginning to think you were lost," she said, her glance suggesting she'd have been just as glad if that had been the case. "Dimitrios has been waiting well over an hour for you to show up."

"What for? You told me yesterday that he always spends the evening with Poppy at the hospital."

"As a rule, I do," he said rather curtly, emerging from what appeared to be some sort of library to the right of the front door, "but I thought you might like to come with me tonight, seeing that your visit was cut short this morning. Since you've been out all afternoon, though, you're probably too tired and would rather not bother."

"I'm not in the least bit tired. As for seeing her again, I'd love to, because I went shopping and bought her a gift."

"That's thoughtful of you, Brianna," he said, his tone softening slightly, "but we're pretty restricted on what we can take in."

"I know," she said. "Noelle explained all about that, but look, this will be acceptable, don't you think?" Carefully, she unwrapped the music box and held it up for his inspection. "See, it even has a glass dome covering it that can easily be cleaned, and if it was put someplace where Poppy could see it but not touch it…? Then there's this mobile. I thought it might hang near the window where it would catch the sunlight. What do you think?"

"They might work," he allowed, "and there's no question but that she'd get a kick out of them. You obviously went to a great deal of trouble to find something she'd really enjoy."

"Which is a lot more than the other one would have done," Erika muttered grudgingly. "Will you be back for dinner, Dimitrios?"

"Yes." He glanced at Brianna again. "How hungry are you? Can you hold off until about nine, or would you like a snack before we leave?"

"I can wait."

"Then let's get going, or Poppy'll be asleep before we arrive."

He hustled her outside, not to the Mercedes, as she'd expected—it, along with Spiros, had disappeared again—but to a low-slung black sports car built for comfort and speed. Erika watched them leave, her expression stony with disapproval.

"That woman doesn't like me," Brianna observed, as both housekeeper and villa disappeared from view.

Zooming past the gates that marked the boundary of his estate, Dimitrios made a sharp turn to the road and shifted into high gear. "You can't blame her. You remind her of Cecily."

"Well, if she had an ounce of brains…!" Annoyed with herself, because this was an irritation she'd lived with all her life and she ought to be over it by now, Brianna abruptly halted in midsentence.

"Please don't stop now," he urged, not taking his eyes off the road. "Get it off your chest, whatever it is."

"All right. Cecily and I were two individuals who happened to look alike, but too many people, including you, seem to believe we were—are—interchangeable."

"I soon learned differently. To my cost, I might add."

"And that's another thing! I know better than anyone that Cecily had her faults, but I'm getting sick and tired of hearing other people criticize her. Regardless of what she did or didn't do, she was still my sister. More to the point, she was Poppy's mother, and for that reason alone she deserves a modicum of respect, because no child should have to grow up never hearing a kind word about the woman who gave birth to her. You might be glad Cecily's out of your life, Dimitrios, but I was deeply saddened by her death. Believe it or not, there was a time when she was sweet and kind and loving."

"Before Crete, you mean?"

"No," Brianna admitted, quelling a sigh. "Her decline began long before then. The pity of it was, I didn't recognize it soon enough to put a stop to it."

He spared her a swift glance. "Just yesterday, you told me not to blame myself for the way she ended up. I suggest you take your own advice. And for the record, I did my best to be a good husband, Brianna, and I would never criticize Cecily to Poppy. I tried to make it work between us, if for no other reason than that I don't deal well with failure. It's not in my nature to accept defeat."

"Because you're a control freak," she said.

"Maybe I am, but one thing I learned the hard way is that even I can't control love. I couldn't conjure it up on command, and in all truth, I'm not sure it would have made any difference if I had been able to. You probably don't want to hear this either, but the fact is, Cecily wasn't looking for a husband, she was looking for a meal ticket."

"And what were you looking for, Dimitrios?"

"You," he said candidly. "I was looking for you. And by the time I realized the carbon copy didn't measure up to the original, the damage was done. Now I'm looking for ways to undo it."

She wasn't sure how to respond to that remark, and he didn't seem inclined to elaborate. "Well, at least you have Poppy," she finally said.

"And I thank God for that every day. But what do you have, Brianna? Is there someone special in your life?"

Not about to confess she'd practically lived like a nun since their breakup, she said, "I wouldn't say 'special,' no. My work and the amount of traveling it involves isn't exactly conducive to a long-term commitment."

"So the career *does* takes precedence over all else."

The edge of scorn in his voice was unmistakable. "If it did," she replied hotly, "I wouldn't be here now, would I?"

He shrugged. "Possibly not."

"There's no 'possibly' about it! Maybe I couldn't save my sister from self-destructing, but I'm not about to stand by and watch her daughter die if I can do something to prevent it."

"So what are you saying? That you're here out of guilt or a sense of obligation?"

"Perhaps in the beginning. But certainly not now."

"Why? What's changed in the past twenty-four hours?"

"Everything," she said. "I've fallen in love with my niece."

"For how long? Until she's healthy again, at which point you'll disappear from the canvas and that'll be the last we see of you?"

Was this love-hate pendulum what he meant by a truce? If so, she wanted no part of it. "That is *not* what I said. Stop putting words in my mouth."

"Then what, exactly, are your intentions?"

She gave an involuntary chirp of laughter. "For heaven's sake, Dimitrios, you're not interviewing a prospective suitor."

His lips twitched in an answering smile. An unfortunate response, she decided, hastily looking away. His mouth was a seduction in itself, and when it came to making love, he knew how to use it. And that was definitely not something she wished to be reminded of, especially not when she was trapped beside him in the intimate confines of his car. "I'm going to make a hell of a father-in-law, aren't I?" he said.

"I hope so," she replied, sobering. "With all my heart, I hope we're both going to see the day that Poppy walks down the aisle, a beautiful bride."

"You plan on being there for that, as well, do you?"

"Count on it. I can't take her mother's place, but I can and will do the next best thing."

"I'll hold you to that," he said.

They'd reached Kifissia by then, and the streets were just coming to life as dusk fell. The aroma of roasting meat and garlic and hot olive oil drifted from the open doors of tavernas, displacing the lingering scent of Penteli's pine-drenched air. Groups of people sat outside, their laughter and conversation vying with the music of the bouzouki players wandering among the tables.

Gradually, though, the noise diminished, muffled by the trees lining the streets, and when Dimitrios at last turned onto the steep crescent where the clinic stood and pulled up in the forecourt, a hush hung over the land. Stepping out of the car, Brianna caught the faint whiff of some sweet-smelling night flower. Palm trees swathed the parking area in dense shadow. Overhead, the sky had turned a soft violet. Although the hospital windows glowed softly in the encroaching dark, the raucous noise and bustle and bright lights of Athens might have been a continent away, instead of just a few miles.

They found Poppy almost asleep, but at the sight of Dimitrios, she climbed up and reached for him over the high rails of her bed. "Papa!" she whimpered.

Scooping her into his arms, he paced the room with her, all the while crooning softly in her ear. Eventually she grew quiet. Her little fist relaxed, its fingers spreading like pale petals against his tanned neck. Her head drooped against his chest. Her eyes fell closed. And Brianna had to turn away, so affected by the sight that her heart ached as if squeezed in a vise.

Quietly she left the room. Now was not the time for a stranger bearing gifts to intrude on such a special moment. Nothing money could buy held a candle to the bond between this big, strong man and his tiny, fragile daughter. Leaving the music box and mobile on a table next to her purse in the anteroom, she walked to the window and stared unseeingly at the gardens below.

She didn't turn when she heard him leave Poppy's room. She didn't want him to see the tears clinging to her eyelashes. But, joining her, he noticed anyway. Without a word he put his arms around her and drew her to him. The last time he'd done that, handling her as tenderly as if she were made of spun glass, had been with the murmured promise of a future together.

This time all he said was, "I know."

"Does it ever get easier," she asked, when she was able to speak again. "Coming here and seeing her so alone and ill, I mean?"

"No. But you get used to the pain."

"I don't think I will. I'm not strong like you."

"You'd be surprised, Brianna, at how much a parent will endure to help his child."

Not very much in my sister's case, she thought sadly, shaken by a sob she couldn't stifle. It was all very fine to lay the blame for Cecily's behavior at someone else's feet, but the fact remained, she'd left her baby to be brought up by a housekeeper, and shown such disregard for her own life that it ended before her daughter had laid down any lasting memories of the woman who'd brought her into the world. What sort of legacy was that?

"Enough now," Dimitrios scolded. "I'm taking you home. Poppy's asleep for the night and you're exhausted. Tomorrow's Saturday. We'll come back in the morning when she's more alert and you can give her your gifts then."

Still with his arm around her waist, they left the clinic.

Soon enough, they'd left Kifissia, too, and were following the twisting mountain road back to Rafina. "Doesn't it bother you, having to drive so far to see her?" Brianna asked, breaking a silence which had lasted almost fifteen minutes.

"No. I like being on the coast. Sailing's one of my passions—at least, it used to be, when I had the time and inclination to enjoy it. And it's better for Poppy to grow up away from the city. The air pollution in Athens grows worse every year."

"Did Cecily like Rafina?"

He let out a soft snort of laughter. "What do *you* think, Brianna?"

"She might have found it a little…isolated."

"She loathed it," he said, "although for the first year she pretended it was just what she wanted. But toward the end, she spent hardly any time there at all."

Puzzled, she said, "Where did she go?"

"I had an apartment in the city, in Kolonaki, which I've since sold. She stayed there."

"Alone? She didn't take Poppy with her?"

"She didn't take Poppy. And she wasn't alone."

Shocked speechless by the implication in his words, she stared at him.

"That's right," he said. "She had company. Of the male kind."

"Why didn't you divorce her?"

"I didn't care enough to bother. I—"

The car, until then purring smoothly along the unfolding ribbon of road like a sleek, well-bred cat, suddenly rebelled. For no apparent reason, the engine simply gave up the ghost. The only sound to break the silence was the soft hiss of the tires, and Dimitrios cursing as he wrestled with the steering wheel.

Somehow, before it lost all forward momentum, he managed to bring the vehicle to the shoulder of the highway and set the emergency brake. "Son of a bitch!" he remarked pleasantly.

"What happened?"

"Well, I'm not out of gas, so that eliminates one possibility." He dimmed the headlamps but pressed a button on the dash. "And the hazard lights work, which suggests the problem isn't electrical, so my guess is some other computer part has failed. Not that I pretend to be any sort of auto mechanic, you understand."

"So what do we do now?"

"I call Spiros to come and collect us." Lifting the car phone from its cradle, he accessed the number, spoke briefly, and hung up. "Done. Ten minutes, fifteen tops, and we'll home."

"What about this car?"

He angled his body toward her and slung a casual arm over the back of her seat. The blinking yellow hazard lights made him appear more shadow than substance, but the heat of his body was very, very real. "It'll be towed in for repair."

"I see." She cleared her throat, all too aware of the solitude of their situation. The last house they'd passed lay several kilometers behind them. "So what do we do until Spiros gets here?"

"We wait." His voice grazed her ear. His warm breath drifted over her face. "And pass the time the best way we know how."

Her lungs just about seized up on her. "I don't think we should be doing this, Dimitrios," she protested feebly.

"Why not? If you were telling me the truth earlier, I'm not poaching on another man's territory."

Blink, blink, blink went the hazard lights, regular as a heart monitor. Except her heart wasn't keeping time. It was leaping around behind her ribs like a mad thing. And other parts of her, parts well below her waist, were stirring in ways that left her taut with forbidden delight.

"Perhaps not, but the fact remains, you're my brother-in-law," she gasped, turning her face aside and pushing him away with one hand. Big mistake! He was all firm, heated masculine flesh and steely muscle beneath his shirt.

He placed his forefinger at the side of her jaw and effortlessly turned her face to his again. "And now I'm a widower. By my reckoning, that frees both of us to listen to our hearts. I can't speak for yours, *karthula mou*, but mine is telling me this is long overdue."

His mouth nudged hers, masterful, persuasive, and no

amount of frantic rationalizing on her part could turn it into a brotherly peck. His hands shaped her face, mapping every curve, every hollow, with the minute attention to detail of a blind man.

"Why don't we stop pretending we don't know where this is leading?" he murmured.

She wished she could tell him it wasn't going anywhere, but the inescapable fact remained that what was happening had slipped right off the friendship scale and veered altogether too close to love of the man-and-woman, Adam-and-Eve kind. He was blatantly, flagrantly, seducing her. Sending time spinning backward. Reviving old yearnings and leaving them screaming for satisfaction.

His fingers stroked down her neck, dipped inside the top of her blouse, close enough to bring her nipples surging to life, but not enough that she could actually accuse him of fondling her breasts.

He was stealing her soul. Making her forget she was supposed to hate him. She should have slapped him. Jumped out of the car and waited on the road for Spiros to rescue her. Instead she melted. Enthralled past all reason, she cast off any thought of self-preservation. The kind of magic he wove was too rare, too blissful, to resist. He reminded her of things she'd ignored for a very long time; in particular that, beneath her glossy exterior, she was a very lonely woman who'd been aching and empty for far too long.

Her hand slid up his chest to his neck. Her fingers tangled in his hair. She clung to him, her body yearning toward him, a moan of raw need rising in her throat. If the console separating their two seats hadn't made it virtually impossible, she'd have climbed into his lap.

The blaze of approaching headlights cut across the scene, a timely interruption that snapped her back to reality before she made a complete fool of herself. Oh, she was hopeless, pathetic, to have succumbed so quickly, so easily, to temptation.

"Thank God!" she breathed, recognizing Spiros at the wheel of the Mercedes as it made a U-turn in the road and came to a stop behind them. She groped for her purse lying at her feet and made a grab for the door handle in her haste to get away from Dimitrios.

But at the last minute he reached over and stopped her. "Run as far and as fast as you like, Brianna, but what just started here isn't finished, not by a long shot."

"Nothing started," she panted.

"You think not, *karthula mou?*" he inquired, his own breathing as ragged as hers. "Then I suggest you think again."

CHAPTER SIX

DINNER turned into an onerous affair. The conversation was stilted, the atmosphere charged with tension, the superbly presented butterflied scampi and chilled white wine flavored equally with sexual awareness and disapproval.

Brianna sat across from Dimitrios with what seemed like an acre of table separating him from her. A safe enough distance, she'd have thought. But its glass top unfortunately provided him with an unimpaired view of every inch of her, from the tip of her black sandals to the top of her head. If she crossed her ankles, he noticed. If she tugged at her skirt or scratched her knee, he saw.

"You don't seem to be enjoying your meal, Brianna," he remarked, watching as she rearranged the food on her plate. "Why not? I know how much you like shellfish."

"You do?"

"Of course," he said, his lazy gaze traveling the length of her and back again. "I remember everything about you."

No doubt including the fact that she'd been a virgin when she met him and hadn't known an orgasm from an aubergine!

He'd wasted no time teaching her the difference, and if

his scrutiny now was any indication, seemed bent on fur-
thering her education as soon as possible. His camera eyes
captured everything they saw and recorded it in the steel
trap that was his mind. Smoldering eyes that burned
through her clothes and seared her flesh.

At the other end of the spectrum, Erika stood in the
corner, vengeful as a crow in her severe black blouse and
ankle-length skirt. Ready to defend him should he come
under attack, she kept her cold, beady gaze fixed accus-
ingly on Brianna. With good reason, because Brianna
hadn't merely submitted to his overtures in the car, she'd
responded to them willingly. Eagerly. And she knew her
cheeks glowed like neon signs advertising her guilty secret
for all the world to see.

Not that it was any of Erika's business.

*She acts as if she's his mother and I'm some hussy
who's set her sights on him,* Brianna thought balefully.
*What does she think? That I pinned him down in the back
seat of the Mercedes and had my way with him when Spiros
wasn't looking?*

Finally even Dimitrios had had enough of his housekeeper's surveillance. "*Efharisto,* Erika, that'll be all," he
said, after the main course had been cleared away and
coffee served. "We can manage by ourselves now."

With one last inimical glare at Brianna, the woman
departed, leaving behind a silence so fraught with electricity that it was almost worse than her hovering presence. A
minute passed. Stretched to two, then three. Dimitrios
rested his elbow on the upholstered arm of his chair,
stretched out his long legs, and continued his leisurely observation.

Schooling herself not to fidget, Brianna scoured her

mind for some pithy conversational gambit that might distract him, but "Lovely weather we're having," didn't quite cut it. So, reminding herself of the adage that it was better to keep her mouth shut and be thought a fool, than to open it and remove all doubt, she focused her attention on the dancing candle flames reflected in the table top. And still the silence stretched, taut as a bow string.

At last, when she was about ready to drain her glass of wine in one gulp, then do the same to the bottle, he said, "You're upset."

"My goodness," she retorted acidly, "how did you guess?"

"With me?"

The temptation to lie and say "yes" nagged at her, but there'd been enough untruths in the mess between them, and even if she was willing to deceive him, she refused to deceive herself. "No. With me."

"Why? Because I kissed you and touched you, and you couldn't deny it's exactly what you wanted me to do?"

That, and a whole lot more than she cared to admit. But the real problem was less easily defined because he touched her in other ways that had nothing to do with the physical. "No," she confessed. "Because I'm in danger of repeating a mistake which cost me dearly the first time around, and that's something I promised myself I wouldn't let happen a second time."

"What mistake is that?"

"That once again, I'm on the point of leaping headfirst into an involvement with you, without considering the risks."

"What if I were to tell you there are no risks this time? That all I want is to put right what went wrong between us before, and pick up where we left off?"

Desperately trying to shore up her crumbling defenses, she said, "You didn't give me that impression yesterday. You were openly hostile."

"Perhaps I was, at first. But then…" He didn't exactly sigh; he wasn't that kind of man. Instead he exhaled and gave a shrug that drew her attention to his broad shoulders. "Since we're talking truth at all costs, I admit I was looking to find flaws in you where once I'd seen only perfection. I hoped you'd changed, that you were beginning to lose your looks and had nothing underneath. No warmth, no heart, no humanity. I hoped that the giving, passionate woman I fell in love with really was nothing more than the cold-blooded tease I had reason to believe she'd become, and that seeing you again would reinforce what I'd been telling myself for years: that I was well rid of you."

"Well, in a way, you got your wish because the plain fact is, I'm not the same as I was when we first met, and nor are you," she pointed out. "Life happened, Dimitrios, and it's changed us. We can't go back to the way we once were, any more than a smashed china plate can be glued back together without showing any cracks. So what's the point of pretending otherwise?"

"The point," he said, "is that, despite everything, it's not too late for us. We're not china plates, we're two intelligent, consenting adults with no ties to other partners. To the best of my knowledge, nowhere is it written that as such, we're not entitled to a second chance."

This wasn't part of the plan. In fact, it was in direct contradiction to everything she'd resolved. He was part of her past, and not one overflowing with happy memories. Yet his kiss in the car, and now the way he was looking at her, and the tone of his voice—somehow they were managing to erase all that old, tired grief and revive a joy and anticipation she'd only ever experienced with him.

Schooling herself to caution, she said, "I rather think the only reason you feel that way is that you're facing a terribly difficult situation, and it would help if you weren't doing it alone."

"I'm not alone, Brianna, and if all I need is support, I can find it in my large network of friends, and a household of loyal staff."

"I didn't mean…that kind of alone."

"You think I've lived like a monk since Cecily died?" His mouth curved in bitter amusement. "I might be widowed, *koritsi mou,* but I've still got a pulse. If all I want is sex, I don't have to import it from North America."

"Then why are you pursuing me? You already know I'll do whatever I can to help Poppy."

"You know why, Brianna. Because we belong together and we always have. Do I want to make love to you? Of course I do, badly enough that I'd take you right here on this table, if you were willing. But you're not so naive as to think a relationship is only about sex. And *that's* the point I'm trying to make. I want a relationship. Not just any relationship, but one with you."

"Would you still be talking this way if I told you I've decided against going ahead with the tests? That I've changed my mind about becoming a donor for Poppy?"

"But you haven't," he said. "And you won't. You're not that kind of person, which is another reason I'm falling for you all over again."

"What if it turns out that I'm not a suitable match?"

"Then we'll keep looking for someone who is. And if I have my way, we'll do it together. I can't keep you here against your will, and if your career matters too much to give it up, I'll let you go. But I'm warning you now, I won't make it easy for you. I'll do my damnedest to make you want to stay."

One by one he was systematically destroying every barrier she'd erected against him. Beset on all sides, she buried her face in her hands, not knowing which way to turn. Her career wasn't the issue. She could kiss that goodbye and never miss it if, in its place, she found true love and fulfillment as a wife and a mother.

But desire, passion, yearning? How did she subdue their voracious demands and relegate them to their proper place? How separate them from the more enduring dimensions of a relationship, like friendship and trust and common values? Heaven knew, the temptation to cast caution to the winds and fling herself into an affair with him was strong. But if, once their carnal appetites were satisfied, she found there was nothing of substance left, what then? How would she survive losing him a second time?

She heard his chair scrape back, felt him gently prying her hands away so that he could look her in the eye. "You don't have to give me an answer now," he said. "I won't pretend I'm a patient man because I'm not. When I want something badly enough, I go after it with all I've got. And make no mistake about it, Brianna. I want and need you in every way a man can want and need a woman. Four years ago, I recognized you as my soul mate and it's taken no time at all for me to realize that's still the case. But until you decide you feel the same way about me, I won't press you for an answer. All I ask is that you give some unbiased thought to the idea of us as a couple, and know that my feelings for you aren't going to change, no matter what your final decision might be."

"And in the meantime?"

"Oh, I'm not going to make it easy for you," he admitted, beguiling her with his smile. "I never said I'd be content to sit on my hands and not take action. I intend to woo you at every turn. But tonight, I'll settle for this."

He drew her to her feet and tilted up her chin with his thumb. His eyes, their irises dark gray ringed with black, their lashes casting a dense inky shadow in the candlelight, tracked her face, feature by feature.

His lips followed, sampling the hollow beneath her cheekbones, the corner of her jaw, the bridge of her nose. His mouth flirted with hers but never quite settled, a feast for her starving soul, cruelly held just beyond reach.

The last of her resistance in tatters, she clutched fistfuls of his shirt front. "Dimitrios," she begged, the persistent throb of frustrated desire tormenting her.

He traced the outline of her mouth with his fingertip. Slid it between her parted lips and out again, a boldly unmistakable promise made more erotic by the urgent thrust of his flesh which neither his slim-fitting trousers nor the silky fabric of her dress could disguise.

Heaven alone knew what she might not have done or said next, had his cell phone not interrupted the moment. "Under any other circumstances," he muttered, his breathing almost as strangled as hers, "I would ignore this, but with Poppy…"

"I understand."

"I know you do." Flipping open the phone, he glanced at the display screen and turned pale beneath his tan. Tonelessly, he said, "It's Noelle."

Brianna's heart missed a beat, and far from escaping when opportunity presented itself, as had been her original intention, she stood rooted to the spot. The hands of a marble wall clock showed seventeen minutes after ten. At that hour, whatever the reason for the doctor's call, it couldn't be good.

Dimitrios paced the length of the room to the glass doors opening onto the terrace, the phone clamped to his ear. "No," Brianna heard him say. "We're just finishing dinner. What…? Oh, that! With everything that's happened lately…no, of course I haven't forgotten, it just got pushed to the back of my mind…. I haven't asked her, but either way, I'm still depending on you to be there, Noelle…. Don't be silly, I'm always available to speak to you, you know that. Absolutely…. Good night."

He slapped the phone closed and turned back into the room, his face the picture of relief.

"I take it Poppy's fine?" Brianna ventured.

"Yes." He shook his head ruefully. "I'm not sure I am, though. First, I forget an important business meeting this morning, one that had been arranged months ago. And now, another couple of important dates have crept up without my realizing. See the effect you have on me?"

"Dates?"

"If you can call them that, yes, though they're as much a social obligation as anything. I offered my place as the venue for a garden party being held next Sunday to honor the people who've supported the Rosegarth with private donations throughout the year. The annual fund-raising gala that is open to the general public takes place the following Saturday. I always support both, but this year's events hold special significance for me, as you can imagine. If it weren't for the generosity of other people, there'd be no clinic here in Athens and I'd have had to take Poppy to another country for treatment."

"And you'll have Noelle for moral support both times. That's nice."

She thought she'd done a pretty good job of hiding the unreasonable burst of jealousy welling up within her, but something in her voice must have given her away because he skewered her in a sharp glance. "She agreed to stand in as hostess next weekend, yes, and I offered to be her escort at the gala. I made these plans weeks ago, before I knew you'd be here, but in case you're wondering, there's nothing romantic going on between me and Noelle. We've known each other for quite some time, but it's only recently, since her involvement with Poppy, that we've become close friends."

"I see."

"I hope you do," he said, an edge of steel in his words, "because I had my share of emotional game playing with Cecily, and I'm not interested in going another round with you. I don't lie, Brianna, and I don't expect you to lie, either. For what it's worth, Noelle was calling to let me off the hook on both occasions, especially the garden party. But as you won't know many people, I told her to leave things as they stand. I don't see a problem with that, but if you do, I won't press you to attend. For my part, though, I've made a commitment and I intend to keep it."

"I'd like to be there," she said, ashamed. In her own way, she was as much a mass of insecurities as Cecily had been, and for the same reasons. Valued by her mother for her looks and what they earned. The trophy girlfriend, desired by men for her glamour. But until Dimitrios, never loved for herself; for the woman inside the body, the brain behind the face.

"You're sure?"

"Yes. And I'm sorry I responded badly just now. It was a stupid, knee-jerk reaction."

He caught her hands and pulled her to him. "Old habits die hard, and we've both been burned. But sweetheart, dragging all that old baggage with us will kill any chance we have of a successful future together."

"You're right, but sometimes that's easier said than done." She leaned against him. Felt the strong, unhurried beat of his heart. Everything he said made sense, so why was it, now that they'd cleared up the misunderstandings of the past, that she persisted in looking for flaws? "You know, Dimitrios, for all that I've defended her to you, I'm still having a hard time getting past what Cecily did. I knew she resented me at some level, but I had no idea she'd take it that far."

"*Mana mou,* I don't say this to hurt you, but Cecily resented anyone she perceived as having more than she did, whether it was to do with money or business or relationships. No matter how much you gave her, how much she already had, it was never enough. She couldn't stand knowing someone else might have more. That was reason enough for her to try to take it away and keep it for herself."

Deep down Brianna knew that to be true. "You're right again," she said bleakly. "I guess I just haven't wanted to admit it."

"You always gave her the benefit of the doubt. It's what families do for one another. And that's why it cuts so deep when family betrays you. Trust me, I ought to know."

"What do you mean?"

His expression changed. Grew guarded; forbidding almost. "It's a long story that can wait for another day. Go to bed, Brianna. You look worn-out."

He went to drop a kiss on her cheek, but just as the fragments in a kaleidoscope could assume a different pattern with the merest twist of the wrist, so her connection with him underwent swift change. In the brief second before he'd masked it, she'd glimpsed pain in his eyes, and a loneliness that matched her own.

Unable to help herself, she cradled his face and turned it so that their parted lips met. And meshed. And lingered.

At first he resisted. Held her firmly by the shoulders and tried to step away. But his determination was no match for hers. She wrapped her arms around his waist, hung on tight and refused to let him go.

He tasted of coffee and wine and sexual hunger kept severely in check; a potent aphrodisiac that shot straight to her bloodstream and surged through her veins like wildfire. With an inarticulate whisper, she sank against him, pressing her breasts to the solid plane of his chest and tilting her hips so that her body nested against his where he was most susceptible.

He almost weakened. His hand slid down her spine to cup her bottom and hold her hard and fast. His fingers plucked at her skirt, inching it high enough to give him access to the smooth bare skin of her thigh.

She felt a shock of damp warmth at her core. A trembling weakness in her limbs. An aching in her breasts. A bone-deep hunger that had waited years too long for satisfaction.

And then it was over. Cool night air replaced the heat of his mouth, his hands. "I'm trying my utmost to do the decent thing and abide by your rules," he ground out savagely, "but if you persist with this, I'm going to take you right here on the floor, and if you wake up tomorrow full of regret, you'll have only yourself to blame."

"I thought you wanted me," she quavered.

"I've always wanted you, Brianna, and not just because I desire you sexually. I want you in my life and in my daughter's. I want you to wear my ring and bear my children. In other words, *khriso mou,* I'm in this for the long haul. When you can tell me you feel the same way, we'll make love, but not before."

She bit her lip, humiliated. "I don't make a habit of throwing myself at men."

"That's good to know, because I'd break the neck of any man I saw as competition, and I don't relish the idea of spending the rest of my life behind bars. Greek prisons aren't known for their creature comforts." He turned her around and gave her a smart swat on the behind. "I'll see you at breakfast. Now get to bed before my baser instincts get the better of me."

In the week following, they established a routine that allowed them to take care of business, maintain an uninterrupted schedule of visits with Poppy and still leave enough time for their unhurried rediscovery of each other.

Each day, he drove them both into the city and dropped Brianna off at the clinic where she spent sweet, tranquil hours with her niece. Sometimes she read to her, or sang, or wound up the music box, or set the mobile in motion. Other times she'd carry her to the window and they'd wave to people in the gardens below and wait for Dimitrios's car to turn into the forecourt. And sometimes, she'd simply sit and watch her as she slept, and pray that she'd be able to save this precious child's life.

Whenever they could steal time for themselves, Dimitrios showed her Athens. Not just the popular sights, but places the tourists seldom discovered. Tiny tavernas tucked away behind bougainvillea-draped walls, that served wonderful intimate dinners by candlelight. Narrow streets lined with ateliers full of exquisite paintings and sculptures by little-known artists who loved what they created more than they cared about fame and fortune. Out-of-the-way little churches in dusty squares, where old women knelt on their bony knees and prayed for their dead husbands and new-born great-grandchildren.

To preserve the privacy she and Dimitrios treasured, Brianna hid behind large concealing sunglasses. With her hair tied back, and her casual skirts and tops and flat-heeled sandals, she blended in with the crowd, another unremarkable woman wandering the city with her man. Only once did a photographer recognize her, and Dimitrios made short work of him.

One morning, he took her to his corporate headquarters, just off Syntagma Square, and introduced her to his colleagues. Not surprisingly, that day she caused a stir.

"Did you see their faces?" she exclaimed, afterward.

"They'd better get used to it, is all I can say, because if I have my way, they'll be seeing a lot more of you."

They were alone in the elevator at the time, and he seized the opportunity to back her up against the padded leather wall and kiss her so thoroughly that she turned liquid with pleasure.

If the warning *ping!* of the doors opening to admit another passenger hadn't interrupted the moment, what might have happened next didn't bear thinking about. Bad enough that she was all rosy and breathless, with her nipples visibly advertising their presence under her cotton blouse.

"You're so bad!" she muttered, slipping her sunglasses

in place as they left the building and stepped out into the midday sun.

He grinned unrepentantly. "Small wonder, my dear. The novelty of my self-imposed chastity is taking a terrible toll."

For her, too. His smile, his touch, his kiss, his every glance, filled her with a riot of sensation. She melted in the warmth of his smile. Went weak at the knees when he kissed her. Ached for him in the lonely luxury of her bed.

Yet she worried they were hurtling along at too fast a pace when they should have been taking the time to be sure, *really* sure, they were getting it right this time. Because it was no longer just about the two of them. Poppy was part of the mix, and she'd already lost one mother. She didn't deserve to lose another. No child did.

On the Thursday she met again with Noelle and began the round of preliminary tests at the clinic. For the next two days, she was weighed, measured and X-rayed. Poked and prodded by an endless stream of technicians and doctors who took endless blood samples. Quizzed about everything from her childhood ailments, to her diet, to possible allergies, to her menstrual cycle.

"I warned you we'd be thorough," Noelle said with a smile.

And with every passing hour, Brianna and Dimitrios grew closer. Whatever the interruptions during the day, they always made time to be together last thing at night. Walking the beach after dark, stolen kisses and touches that set her on fire, and hard-won restraint: these formed the foundation of their new understanding, the pattern of their renewal, even though every inch of her body screamed for the ultimate intimacy, the easing of a perpetual ache that only he could bring.

When they'd first met, she'd fallen in love with his cosmopolitan tastes, his sharp intelligence, his wit and charm. She'd been seduced by the deep, exotic purr of his voice, and his masculine beauty. By his passion and sensitivity.

This time she loved him for all that and more. For laying bare all the misunderstandings and lies that had come between them, and for taking the time to court her, just as he'd promised he would. Most of all, though, she loved him for the father he'd become.

He stole her heart with his gentleness with his little girl; with his patience and tenderness. She loved how his big hands cradled Poppy's little body; how he snuggled her against his shoulder. She loved his tone of voice, his face as he watched her sleep, his pain when she cried. Everything to do with his daughter made Brianna want to put her arms around him and give him comfort and support however she could. With her body, her heart, her soul, her life.

Somehow she resisted, knowing it was too soon. There was too much else going on and all of it so steeped in emotion that it was hard to separate sex from stress; empathy from love. She had to be cautious. He'd broken her heart once. She'd never survive his doing it a second time.

"You're going to wear yourself to a shadow worrying about the two of them, if you're not careful," Erika informed reprovingly.

But her words, Brianna noticed, lacked the bite of a week ago. "I can't help it, Erika," she replied. "They both mean too much to me. In any case, you worry, too. I know you do."

"Because I belong with them. But how long before you

grow tired of the whole business and walk out, just like the other one did?"

"I'm not my sister, Erika, and I don't play fast and loose with other people's lives, especially not a child's. I love that little girl as if she were my own."

"Hmm," came the reply on a disparaging sniff. "Time will tell, I suppose."

The next morning, though, she scooped up the last hot breakfast scone and deposited it on Brianna's plate before Dimitrios could reach for it.

"I do believe you're winning her over," he remarked, sotto voce, as the housekeeper went to refill their coffee cups.

From the other side of the breakfast room, Erika said sharply, "I heard that!"

But there was no real sting in her tone. In fact, when she turned back to the table, the hint of a smile played over her mouth.

Moved by the small gesture of acceptance, Brianna realized that this was what real families were all about— affectionate teasing and loyalty and devotion and the willingness to give one another a chance. Why hadn't Cecily recognized the gift she'd been given, and grabbed hold of it with both hands?

Brianna knew why. Because her poor sister had never learned how to love unselfishly. She and Brianna had only ever known the fickle approval of a parent perennially dissatisfied with her lot in life. To their mother, they'd always been either a burden or the means to an end; something she could exploit to her own advantage. If the desired results didn't bring her the rewards she felt she deserved, her children paid the price. And Cecily had continued along the same path with Poppy, showering her with attention when it suited and ignoring her when it didn't.

Well, no more, Brianna decided, as she lay in bed that night. The destructive pattern of behavior ended here.

"I've made my decision, Dimitrios," she announced, the next morning. "About us. And if your offer to make me a permanent part of your life still stands, I'd very much like to see if we can make it work."

CHAPTER SEVEN

HE REGARDED her solemnly. "So soon? Are you sure?"

"Yes, I'm sure."

"You've really thought it through?"

"I've really thought it through," she confirmed, somewhat disconcerted by his measured response. She'd expected a little more enthusiasm. Unbridled ecstasy, even. After all, picking up where they'd left off four years earlier had been his suggestion, not hers.

"In case I haven't made it clear," he said, holding her in his serous gaze, "I'm not looking for an affair. I want you as my wife."

As proposals went, this one left something to be desired, enough that she looked at him blankly, wondering if she hadn't heard him correctly. "Your what?"

"My wife, Brianna. As in *Kyria Dimitrios Giannakis*."

No mistaking it, this time. He couldn't have made himself any clearer if he'd had it emblazoned in gold on his forehead.

Elation fizzed through her veins, heady as champagne. Dimitrios, her husband? She'd buried that particular dream a long time ago, yet here it was, resurrected from the ashes. A modern-day miracle.

If something sounds too good to be true, Carter's voice whispered in her head, just as it had often enough in the past, *take care, because it probably is. Look for the hidden agenda, Brianna. Don't be so ready to take everything at face value.*

But she turned a deaf ear. He'd been referring to business; to the dog-eat-dog world of international modeling. This was different. This was about matters of the heart. About love and commitment. What for so long had seemed a hopeless fantasy had suddenly turned into a reality, and she wanted to jump up and dance with sheer happiness. She wanted Dimitrios to catch her in his arms and swing her off her feet and smother her in kisses.

Instead he remained seated, spelling out his terms with the uncompromising exactitude he no doubt brought to his corporate acquisitions.

Except…she wasn't a corporate acquisition. Was she?

Her skin prickled as if a cold wind had drafted up her spine. Reining in her initial uprush of delight, she said, "I wouldn't have it any other way, Dimitrios. I'm really not interested in being your live-in mistress."

"You'll be taking on a husband with a ready-made family, not to mention a new country and a whole new life that leaves no room for your celebrity career. I want more children, Brianna, and I expect my wife to be a hands-on mother."

"Well, just in case *I* haven't made it clear to *you*," she retorted, adopting an equally direct manner, "I consider being a wife and a mother far more of a career than walking the runways of Milan and Paris. But while you might not hold that world in very high regard, let me point out in its defense that it taught me a lot about dedication, patience, and self-discipline. As I see it, they're qualities which should meet your exacting standards at the same time that they stand me in very good stead as a wife and mother."

His beautiful, sexy mouth twitched. "Yes, ma'am! If I spoke out of turn, consider me well and truly chastised."

"Furthermore," she went on, really hitting her stride, "marriage is a contract between equals, not a favor conferred by one party on the other. Marrying you won't make me your chattel, Dimitrios, it'll make me your partner."

"I agree. I just want you to be sure you can live with my expectations. I settled for less than I wanted with Cecily. I won't settle again. One failed marriage is enough. I want you to be happy, Brianna, but—"

"There's no doubt in my mind that in becoming your wife and Poppy's mother, I'd be gaining far more than I'd be giving up," she said, torn between understanding and resentment. "Far more, in fact, than I ever dared dream about or hope for. I've only ever loved one man, Dimitrios, and that man is you. But if that's not enough to convince you that I know what I'm getting myself into, then perhaps you're the one who's not sure."

His dark eyes gleamed with amusement. "Oh, I've never been more certain of anything my entire life. But I feel obligated to point out that I can be difficult. Some might even say high-handed."

"How about downright bossy, not to mention arrogant?"

"I'm Greek. It's the nature of the beast, at least in my case."

"I've noticed."

"You think you can handle me?"

"About as well as you can handle me, which is to say it'll be enough of a challenge that life will never be dull."

At that, he broke into a smile that took her breath away.

His gaze softened. Grew dark with emotion. He pushed his chair back from the table so abruptly it crashed to the tiled floor. "Come here, woman," he ordered, his voice rich as molasses, and hauled her into his arms. "This bossy, arrogant Greek wants to kiss his bride."

He did. At very great length, and with all the fire and passion she could ask for.

Later that morning as they drove the familiar streets of Kifissia to the clinic, he mentioned that a catering crew would be spending the day at the villa, setting up for tomorrow's event.

She laughed. "You mean to say Erika and Alexio are going to let strangers run loose all over the place?"

"They oversee everything, but it's too big an affair for them to manage by themselves. To give them a break, we'll have dinner in Rafina tonight."

"Why?" she objected. "I don't mind cooking, and I'm happy to spend a quiet evening at home with you."

"That's the whole point. It won't be quiet, and the kitchen will be off-limits."

"Oh, I hadn't thought of that. Well, just for the record, you don't have to wine and dine me every night of the week."

He grimaced slightly. "Keep reminding me of that, will you? It's not something I'm used to."

"Cecily needed constant entertainment, I know."

"Oh, yeah. And if I wasn't able or willing to provide it, she went looking for someone who was."

"You never told me who was with her, the night she died."

"Nobody I knew. They might have been part of her new circle of friends, or perfect strangers. She wasn't choosy about the company she kept when it came time to party.

The police report stated only that there'd been a fire in a night club and she was among those who hadn't made it out alive, most likely because, as the autopsy showed, she'd consumed enough alcohol to put someone twice her size under the table."

"It'll be different with us, Dimitrios. I know most people think a model's life is all about wearing fabulous clothes and flying first class from one exotic location to another, but in my case at least, the truth is somewhat different. I'm a real homebody at heart, and never more content than when I can shut my front door on the rest of the world, put on a comfortable old pair of sweatpants, and curl up by the fire with a good book."

"Don't," he said roughly. "Don't make me regret the years I've wasted with you any more than I already do."

"We'll make up for them. We've already started."

He reached over and squeezed her hand. "I guess we have. But speaking of work, do you have outstanding assignments to complete or contracts you need to honor?"

"As a matter of fact, I don't. Carter managed to get someone else to stand in for the work I had coming up, and we were planning to look over some new offers when I went home, but as far as I'm concerned, the only thing I plan to sign in the near future is the consent form for the transplant. Speaking of which, do you have any idea when we'll get my test results?"

"Later in the week, according to Noelle. Listen, Brianna, if you turn out to be a match and the transplant goes ahead, you realize what it means, don't you? You'll be back on your feet in about a week, but Poppy's going to take months to recuperate."

"I know, and I'm sick at the thought of what she faces."

"Me, too. But what I'm getting at is that it's taken me a long time to find my way back to you. Will you think me very selfish if I ask you to marry me as soon possible?"

"How soon is that?"

He turned into the clinic forecourt and killed the engine. "You're not a Greek citizen, so there'll be some red tape to cut through, but I have connections in all the right places that can speed up the process. I'd say we could set a date for a couple of weeks from now. We'd have to postpone the honeymoon, obviously, but the wedding itself can be anything you want."

"I want you." She swiveled in her seat and let her gaze roam over him. She'd never tire of looking at him, she thought dreamily. Nothing time could affect would lessen the perfect bone structure that blessed him with such elegantly sculpted features. Even in old age, he'd be beautiful. "You and Poppy," she said, curving her hand over his thigh. "All the rest is just window dressing."

"Stop that," he scolded, removing her hand and dropping it firmly in her own lap. "I'm a well-respected corporate giant in these parts, not some hormone-driven teenager with an overload of testosterone. Much more temptation of the kind you're dishing out, though, and I won't be responsible for my actions."

"And here I thought you couldn't wait to have at me." She sighed in mock regret. "How long must I wait?"

Choking back a laugh, he glanced at his watch. "About another twelve hours or so, if it's up to me. But regardless of when, I guarantee it'll be someplace a lot more comfortable and private than the passenger seat in my car. Now take my mind off your delicious body and tell me what you have planned for the rest of the day."

"I thought I'd be with you and Poppy."

"I hoped so, too, but a client I've been trying to hook up with for a while now is in Athens just for the day, before he flies to the Orient, which means there'll be no spiriting you away for a romantic lunch while Poppy takes her nap."

"In that case, I might go shopping. You've probably noticed I didn't bring many clothes with me. This sort of thing…" She indicated her plain white cotton skirt and silk-screened T-shirt. "The quality might be good, but it was never intended for a high-society garden party, but I saw something in a boutique the other day that would be perfect. I think you'll like it."

The look he turned on her made her quiver inside. "Haven't you figured out yet that what's inside the clothes is all that matters to me?"

"Still, the last thing I want is to embarrass you in front of your friends and associates."

"Brianna, *mana mou,* you couldn't embarrass me if you tried." Stopping her as she went to open the car door, he leaned over and dropped a kiss on her cheek. "That's for Poppy, and this—" he kissed her again, a lovely, hot, open-mouthed kiss that sent shock waves of delight shimmering all the way to the soles of her feet "—is for you. Consider it a down payment on what I owe you. Have fun shopping, treat yourself to a nice, relaxed lunch, and I'll see you later."

She didn't immediately go up to Poppy's room after he left. She went instead to sit by the courtyard fountain, wanting to savor the moment and let the taste of joy linger on her tongue. How different everything looked through the eyes of a woman in love. The sky reflected a deeper, more intense blue, the flowers a more brilliant palette of scarlet and purple and gold, the lawns a richer shade of emerald. If she was able to make Poppy well again, all truly would be right with the world.

The dress—*her* dress—was still in the window when she arrived at the boutique just ahead of the siesta hour, but recognizing her from a magazine spread she'd done in Paris earlier in the year, the owner, Elene, was more than happy to hang a Closed sign on the door and accommodate her.

"Thavmasios!" she gushed, rolling her eyes dramatically when Brianna emerged from the fitting room in a swirl of pale roses and fine silk voile. "Not many women have the height and body to carry such an ensemble, but on you, Despinis Connelly, it is perfection."

Turning slowly before the three-way mirror to get a better view of how she looked from the back, Brianna had to agree. The entire outfit might have been made with her in mind. The draped bodice molded softly to her shoulders and breasts. The skirt fell in graceful folds from its high empire waist almost to her ankles. The hat was nothing less than a work of art. Its wide sweeping brim, anchored to the crown with one large, perfect cream satin rose, imparted a demure air of mystery to her face. Even the high-heeled ivory shoes were the correct size.

"You are pleased?" Elene eyed her anxiously.

"More than you can begin to imagine," Brianna assured her. "I fell in love with this dress over a week ago, and was afraid it might have sold before I came back. It's one of a kind, I'm sure."

"Indeed, yes. Everything you see here is unique. You needn't concern yourself that you'll come across a duplicate on someone else. But if you are undecided, I have other designs I can show you."

"I decided the minute I saw it. It's perfect for the garden party I'm attending tomorrow. But I would like to look at a few other things, in particular something suitable for evening. Next weekend, I'm also going to the Rosegarth Clinic fund-raising gala. Perhaps you know of it?"

Elene nodded energetically. "Everybody in Athens knows of it, and you're right, it is a very chic, sophisticated affair. I have had a steady stream of clients coming here, hoping to find just the right gown. Please slip into a kimono, make yourself comfortable, and enjoy a glass of champagne while I bring out a few items for your consideration."

Some forty minutes later, Brianna climbed into a taxi, loaded down with an assortment of gorgeous items tenderly wrapped in tissue paper and secured with ribbon in shiny black shopping bags and boxes bearing the boutique's discreet silver logo. She had her evening gown, her garden party outfit, a pair of satin dancing shoes, two other dinner dresses she hadn't been able to resist, and a selection of delicious lingerie lavishly trimmed in French lace.

Dimitrios showed up at the clinic soon after she returned. For an hour or more, they played with Poppy, helping her assemble the brightly colored plastic interlocking building blocks Brianna had found in the toy shop.

After her evening meal, they followed the usual bedtime story ritual. Not until she was asleep for the night did they leave, a heartrending experience that never grew any easier, no matter how often they did it. She was so little, so helpless, so trusting, with no idea of the ordeal awaiting her if the transplant went ahead. And if it didn't, if Brianna turned out not to be a suitable donor…well, that just didn't bear thinking about.

"The day I walk out of this place with Poppy in my arms, we're going to celebrate for a week," Dimitrios vowed, with a last, anguished glance at his daughter's sweet face.

"It's going to happen," Brianna promised, sharing his pain. "And I'll be right there beside you when it does."

He gripped her hand so tightly she winced. "I'm counting on it, sweetheart, more than you can begin to know."

They collected her purchases from the lobby where she'd left them and headed out to the car. "I take it you found what you were looking for," he observed dryly, loading the bags and boxes into the trunk and making an obvious effort to shake off his black mood. "As a matter of interest, did you leave any merchandise for the next customer, or have you bought out the entire shop?"

"I bought what I deemed to be necessary. I'll leave you to decide if I made the right choices."

"Heaven help me, I'm marrying a clothes horse," he moaned.

"Yes, you are," she said cheerfully. "But you knew that when you asked me to be your wife."

That night, he took her for dinner to the Rafina Yacht Club where his fourteen-meter sloop was moored, and the first part of the evening was nothing less than idyllic. They sat at a table by the window and sipped champagne by candlelight. Outside, the moon carved a rippled path over the water and tipped the tall masts of the sailboats with silver.

Brianna wore one of her new outfits, a deep-purple knit cotton dress cut along straight, simple lines. She accessorized it with silver stud earrings, a narrow silver bracelet, her heeled black sandals and a black clutch purse.

Dimitrios, as always, was immaculate in dove-gray Armani trousers, white shirt and navy blazer.

"I'll take you sailing one of these days, when things settle down a bit," he promised. "As they presently stand, though, I'd just as soon be on dry land and able to get to the clinic in a hurry if I need to."

"Yes, of course," she said. "I understand perfectly."

"We'll have a good life, Brianna. You won't regret marrying me."

And that was when the evening fell apart. An older couple, passing by on their way to join a large party at the next table, recognized his voice and stopped. "Dimitrios?" the woman said.

In less time than it took to blink, all the warmth and animation in his face drained away. "Hermione," he returned stiffly, half-rising to his feet in a reluctant show of courtesy. "Mihalis," he added, acknowledging the man with a nod so brief, he might as well not have bothered.

"Yios." The man's eyes, black as coal but with none of its inherent propensity for warmth, skimmed over Brianna. Switching to heavily accented English, he said, "Did I just hear you say you're getting married again?"

"That's right."

"And this is your future wife?"

"Right again."

"So history repeats itself, right down to an exact replica of the original bride. We had heard Cecily's twin was in town and now we know why. Let's hope you don't drive her to an early grave, as well."

Dimitrios grew so forbiddingly still, he might have been turned to stone. The woman, Hermione, however, let out a shocked, "Mihalis!"

Mihalis silenced her with a quelling glare and turned a cheerless smile on Brianna. "Our deepest sympathies, my dear, and all the luck in the world. I'm afraid you're going to need it." Then, overriding his companion's visible distress, he led her away.

Unmoving, Dimitrios watched them leave, his fists clenched at his sides, his eyes stormy, his face the color of old parchment except for two faint strips of color riding his high cheekbones, and his entire body vibrating with rage.

"Dimitrios," Brianna whispered urgently, "who were those people?"

Very slowly he uncurled his fingers, expelled a long breath and resumed his seat. He raised his eyes to hers.

"My parents," he said.

CHAPTER EIGHT

HE'D shocked her, as he'd known he would. Her lovely mouth fell open before she could bring it under control and press it closed again. "Your parents? Dimitrios, you told me they were dead!"

"No," he said. "I told you I have no family but Poppy, and nor do I."

She shook her head. "I don't understand. You just said that man is your father."

"A biological error on his part, I'm sure."

"He spoke as if he hates you!"

"That's because he does."

"But if he's your father! And what about your poor mother…?" Eyes clouded with dismay, she fumbled for her water glass. "I thought she was going to burst into tears."

"But she didn't," he said. "She behaved exactly as she's always behaved around him. Like a downtrodden wife with no right to her own opinions or feelings. I can only suppose she enjoys being molded to the underside of his heel. Eat your fish, Brianna. It's growing cold."

She pushed her plate aside, the grilled red mullet barely touched. "I've just lost my appetite."

"Would you like to order something else? Dessert, perhaps? They make a wonderful almond brandy cake here."

"No. I'd like you to explain what just happened."

"I'd have thought that was self-evident."

"Stop stonewalling, Dimitrios," she snapped, displaying exactly the kind of fire and spirit his mother had never dared fling at his father. "I'm not some stranger poking my nose in where it doesn't belong, I'm the woman you say you want as your wife, and if that's the case, I deserve to know what I'm letting myself in for."

She was right, of course. An explanation wasn't just in order, it was overdue, and better she hear it from him than someone else. "*Endaxi*. Okay." Abandoning his own meal—he'd lost his taste for his grilled octopus, too. His father tended to have that effect on people—he said, "How about coffee and brandy first?"

"Coffee would be nice, but I'll pass on the brandy. You go ahead, though."

He waited until they'd been served, and rolled a mouthful of the very excellent Metaxa Golden Reserve over his palate to erase the lingering aftereffects of his father. "So what would you like to know?"

"Everything," she said promptly.

"Well, you're already aware, of course, that I'm filthy rich."

"Not that it matters to me one way or the other," she said dryly, "but yes, I have noticed."

"So has Mihalis. And that's the problem."

"He didn't look to me as if he's suffering any. The diamond in his pinky ring just about blinded me."

"Ah, but what galls him is that if my tastes also ran to

gaudy, ostentatious jewelry, I could afford a bigger, better, flashier diamond than his."

Again she shook her head. "I'm not following you, Dimitrios. This isn't about jewelry, so why don't you start at the beginning and tell me what's really going on?"

"All right. My father made his first million when he was twenty-one. By the time I was born, eight years later, he'd increased that amount ten times over, and I grew up watching him wield his assets like a weapon to control everyone around him. I saw my mother change from a vivacious, beautiful woman to a passive, listless creature unable to decide what color shoes to wear, without consulting him first. I grew to despise him and pity her, and I'm not sure which I found more distasteful."

"Your mother struck me as a very gentle soul, Dimitrios," Brianna said softly, "and from the little I saw, I think it breaks her heart that she's alienated from you."

"That's her choice."

"Perhaps, but it's a choice no woman should have to make. Is there no possibility of a reconciliation between you?"

"Not as long as my father's alive. He'd never permit it."

"Why not? Surely he must be proud of you? You're smart, successful, respected."

"*Despite* him, not *because* of him, and that's the real problem in a nutshell, Brianna. I learned at a very early age that there are no free lunches with my father. Sooner or later, for every so-called 'favor' he conferred, he'd present me with a bill which was more than I was prepared to pay. So I severed the family ties and struck out on my own."

"I'd have thought that would make him proud of you."

"Wrong, wrong, wrong, *karthula mou!* Certain I couldn't possibly succeed without the almighty Mihalis

Poulos to back me, he waited for me to fail and come crawling back to him."

"Poulos? Where did Giannakis come from?"

"My maternal grandmother. I changed my name when I turned eighteen. Anyhow, when I proved him wrong and succeeded past anything he ever envisioned, he punished me by becoming my biggest, most ferocious business competitor who'd strip me of every euro I own if he could."

"Obviously, he hasn't succeeded."

"Fortunately not. My brain is even more agile than his and I remain one step ahead of him at all times."

"Then you can afford to be generous and drop a vendetta which serves no purpose except to hurt your mother."

"I could." He swirled the brandy in its glass and took another mouthful. "But I won't."

"Why not?"

"Because I'm a proud man, Brianna," he said flatly. "I don't beg, I don't forgive easily, and I never forget."

She regarded him pensively a moment. "What about Poppy? Doesn't she deserve to know her grandparents?"

The old, familiar rage rose up, turning the brandy sour in his stomach. "You just saw the kind of man my father is. Do you really think he gives a rat's ass about my child?"

"He never goes to see her? Never asks about her?"

"Never."

"Your mother, either?"

He let out a bark of laughter as bitter as bile. "Haven't you heard a word I've said, Brianna? My mother daren't even sneeze without his say-so."

"I don't understand any of this." She slumped in her seat, the picture of dejection. "Families are supposed to unite in times of trouble. Look how it brought us together again."

"You have a heart, Brianna. Underneath my reputedly hard-bitten, ruthless tycoon exterior, so do I. I can't say the same for my father."

"Even hard-bitten, ruthless tycoons are supposed to be putty in the hands of their grandchildren."

"In an ideal world, maybe. Not in mine."

She bit her lip. "No wonder you hate him."

"I don't hate him," he was quick to reply. "I refuse to expend the energy it would take. I simply ignore him."

As though to put the lie to his claim, a burst of laughter at his parents' table rolled through the room, and glancing over, he found his father's malevolent gaze fixed on him and Brianna. She noticed it, too, and flinched.

Once upon a time, in his reckless youth, he'd have reacted by hurling himself across the room and smashing his fist into that sneering face. Now he contented himself by trading stare for stare and said evenly, "Don't let him upset you, my darling. He's not worth it. Would you like more coffee, or something a bit stronger to get rid of the bad taste he's left in your mouth?"

She shook her head miserably. "If you don't mind, Dimitrios, I'd really like to get out of here."

"Of course." Reaching for her hand, he brought it to his lips. Across the room, his father watched, his lip curled in amused disdain.

While Dimitrios signed for the meal, Brianna escaped to the ladies' room and sank down on the bench before the mirrored vanity. Her face stared back at her, pale and shocked.

She'd come across her fair share of jealousy and dislike over the years. Professional sabotage, even. In the competitive, unforgiving world of high fashion, success inevitably bred some resentment among those less fortunate. But never had she been the target of the kind of vitriolic loathing Mihalis Poulos had leveled at his only son.

Dimitrios was right, she decided, taking a tube of lip gloss from her purse. The man was toxic and the less they had to do with him, the better.

Just then the door opened and Hermione Poulos slipped into the room. Since they were the only two women present, there was no possible way Brianna could pretend she hadn't seen her. But nor was there any point in lingering and making a tense situation worse, so capping her lip gloss, she dropped it back in her purse and stood up to leave.

Hermione, though, prevented her with an urgent hand on her arm. "*Parakalo,* Despinis Connelly," she practically whimpered, her big brown eyes filled with pleading, "may I have a word?"

Loyalty to Dimitrios told Brianna she should refuse and keep going, but short of pushing the poor woman aside, she had little choice but to stop. "I don't see that we have anything to say to one another, Mrs. Poulos. We certainly have nothing in common."

"We both care deeply about my son, you as the woman who is to become his wife, and I as his mother."

"I'm not sure he believes the latter."

Hermione blinked back the tears welling in her eyes. "He has told you that we are estranged?"

"I more or less figured that out for myself, but yes, he elaborated on the story. We have no secrets from each other."

"Then let me share another one with you that he might not be aware of. A father might qualify his love for his child, but a mother's love is unconditional and eternal. She might not always approve of the things he does or the choices he makes, but she will always hold her child close in her heart."

Not in my experience, Brianna thought.

"Perhaps," Hermione concluded, "one day, my dear, you will discover that for yourself."

Sympathy warring with impatience, Brianna said, "Why are you telling *me* this? Dimitrios is the one you should be talking to."

"I would, if he would listen, but that's not why I asked to speak with you." Her thin, desperate fingers tightened around Brianna's arm. "Tell me, please, how is Poppy? Will she ever be well again?"

"We're hopeful that she will, yes."

"She remains at the Rosegarth?"

"Yes."

"I wish that I could see her."

Impatience winning out over sympathy, Brianna said, "You could, if you chose, Mrs. Poulos. All you have to do is show up. There are no bars on her room. She's in hospital, not prison."

"Mihalis will not permit it."

"Your husband can't stop you, not if you really want to see her, so what you're really saying is that pandering to him matters more to you than giving your sick little granddaughter an hour of your time."

Hermione's mouth trembled and her hand fell away from Brianna's arm. "You make me ashamed," she quavered. "I wish I had your fortitude. But my husband—"

"Is a bully, Mrs. Poulos, and he gets away with it because you let him," Brianna replied bluntly. "Why don't you try standing up to him, for a change? You'd be surprised how much it would boost your confidence, not to mention your self-esteem. Who knows, it might even earn the respect of the son you claim to love so devotedly."

"It isn't easy."

"Not many things worth having ever are. It all boils down to how hard you're willing to fight for them. And now, if you'll excuse me, Dimitrios is waiting to take me home."

"You were in the ladies' room a long time," he remarked, as they headed back along the road to the villa. "I was beginning to think you were being held hostage."

"In a way I was. Your mother cornered me."

He stiffened, his hands suddenly gripping the steering wheel until his knuckles turned white. "I'm surprised my father risked letting her off her leash and out of his sight. What did she want?"

"To know how Poppy is."

"I hope you told her to mind her own business."

"I couldn't do that, Dimitrios. She was so upset and seemed genuinely worried. But I did suggest she could always visit Poppy and see for herself how she's doing."

At that, he hit the brakes with such force that the car nearly skidded off the road. "You did *what?*"

"I told her, if she was all that interested, she should go to the clinic and find out for herself."

"You had no right, Brianna!" he said, his words a whiplash of contained fury. "No right at all to interfere in something that's none of your concern."

"I thought Poppy was my concern," she shot back. "That by volunteering to donate bone marrow, I'd earned the right to make her my concern."

"One thing's got nothing to do with the other. I decide who gets to spend time with my daughter, not you."

"I see." She swallowed painfully, her throat so thick suddenly, it almost choked her.

"No, you don't," he snapped, stepping on the accelerator again and racing the last few hundred yards to the gates of his estate. "You don't have the first idea what's really going on here."

"Why don't you enlighten me, then, Dimitrios? Or does my being a model make me such an airhead that I couldn't possibly understand the intricate workings of your superior mind?"

He slammed on the brakes a second time and killed the engine. In the beat of silence that followed, she heard a gust of frustration escape his lips as he wrestled with his inner demons. Then, his anger at last subsiding, he turned to her in the moonlight and stroked a conciliatory hand down her cheek. "It's complicated, Brianna, okay? Let's just leave it at that. Look, we're home and it's a beautiful night. Don't let what happened at the club spoil things. Let's forget about my parents and take a walk on the beach, and talk about our wedding and the future."

All around them, huge urns of fresh flowers glowed like stars in the moonlight, ready for tomorrow's garden party. A striped tent stood on the far lawn. Chairs swagged in white linen clustered around small tables with floral centerpieces. Stephanotis and gardenias scented the air.

No question but that the setting was perfect. The Garden of Eden recreated to Dimitrios Giannakis's exacting standards, with not a petal out of place, and him its benevolent god, willing to dispense forgiveness for her sins with a touch of his almighty hand!

Bleak with misery and disappointment, she flinched

away from him. Did he really believe a walk on the beach would erase what had just taken place between them?

"What future?" she asked bitterly. "The one in which you issue the orders and I meekly obey them? No thanks, Dimitrios, I'm not that desperate for a husband! You can sneer at your father all you like, but the apple doesn't fall far from the tree, and underneath the charmingly civilized veneer you present to the rest of the world, you're exactly as manipulative and domineering as he is."

He started to reply, but she'd heard enough. Flinging open the door, she climbed out of the car and left him without a backward glance.

Erika met her at the front door. "You're crying, Brianna!" she exclaimed, a rare note of solicitude coloring her words. "Why? What's happened?"

"Ask your boss," she wailed, furious at her own weakness. "He's the one with all the answers."

"Is it Poppy?"

She shook her head and swiped at the accursed tears streaming from her eyes. "No, it's not Poppy."

"A lover's quarrel, then. I could see the pair of you were falling in love." Almost fondly, Erika cradled Brianna's chin in her work-worn hand. "They happen, but the making up is all the sweeter for it. The two of you will work it out, you'll see."

Overwrought, Brianna sobbed, "When did you suddenly decide you were on my side, Erika? I'm trouble, just like my sister, remember?"

"I have second sight," the old woman replied sagely. "I see more than appears on the surface. Dimitrios is right. You look like her, but there the resemblance ends. Dry your tears, *pethi mou,* and I'll make you some *tsai apo votana*—

some herbal tea to soothe your nerves. You're exhausted. Anyone would be in such trying times. You should get some rest. Everything will look quite different after a good night's sleep. Off you go now, before Dimitrios comes in and sees your pretty eyes all red and swollen."

But it would take more than well-meant home remedies to bridge the differences between her and Dimitrios, Brianna knew. Too pent-up to sit passively in her room, she paced the floor like a caged animal and finally, in desperation, flung off her clothes and climbed into her bathing suit.

Except for the distant murmur of voices in the kitchen wing, the house was quiet. Making her way downstairs, she slipped through the French doors leading to the rear terrace, and ran silent as a shadow along the path to the pool deck.

The moon had slipped behind the trees, but underwater lights turned the water into a swath of turquoise satin. Dropping her towel on a chaise, she plunged cleanly into the limpid depths and began a punishing crawl up and down the twenty-meter length.

Her thoughts kept pace with every stroke.

She'd have to move out of his house. First thing tomorrow, she'd pack up her stuff. Find a hotel close to the clinic. Visit Poppy when she knew he wouldn't be there, because she couldn't stand seeing him every day.

What a good thing he'd shown his true colors before it was too late. That he could invite her into his life one minute, then slam the door in her face the next, defied rational explanation.

But that he could speak to her so brutally…be so unfeeling toward the woman who'd given birth to him…!

Oh, he was horrible! She was *so* well rid of him!

In all fairness, though, she had to shoulder some of the

blame. She'd broken every promise she'd made to herself not to get involved with him again. Not to rush blindly into any arrangement that might compromise her hard-won peace of mind and heart.

Yet within a week, she'd agreed to marry him, a man with whom she'd spent little more than thirty days total, and most of those occurring years ago. He was a stranger, someone given to half truths and secrets. What else hadn't he told her? He could be a wife beater, for all she really knew. Be hiding a criminal past behind his exquisitely tailored suits and handmade leather shoes.

She was too willing to be dazzled by illusions of romance. Too easily taken in by appearances. Show her a pair of dark, Mediterranean eyes, a smile that could, when it chose, reduce tempered steel to a molten mass, and the body of a Greek god, and she was lost. A helpless heap of female hormone-driven need.

She shouldn't be allowed to roam free without a keeper. She was a fool.

He was a liar. He'd deliberately misled her.

And she had finally run out of energy. Her body ached, her lungs were bursting, her pulse racing, and her arms leaden weights she could barely lift. Depleted, she rolled over on her back, closed her eyes, and floated to the ladder hanging over the side of the deep end of the pool. Wearily, she grasped a rung, hauled herself onto the deck and made her way to the chaise where she'd left her towel.

As she bent to pick it up, a tall figure strolled out from the black shadow cast by a nearby palm tree. "Feel better?" Dimitrios inquired coolly.

Not about to admit he'd scared her so badly she almost fell back in the pool, she clutched the towel to her heaving breasts. "As a matter of fact, I do. Not," she couldn't help adding with unvarnished sarcasm, "that it's any of your business."

"When my fiancée disappears from my house without a word to anyone, I make it my business."

"Really?" she drawled with feigned insouciance, and tried to slide past him. "You must have mistaken me for someone who cares."

But he was faster, stronger and more merciless. He lunged forward, lethal as a tiger on its prey, and grabbed her squarely by the shoulders. He was, she realized belatedly, very angry.

"This is not how we settle our differences, Brianna," he informed her. "If I say or do something you don't like, you set me straight. You do *not* cut and run, ever again. Do you understand?"

Incensed, she spat, "Get your hands off me!"

"Make me," he said, his voice deadly, and plastering her wet, scantily-clad body against him, he snagged her dripping hair in one hand, yanked her head back and kissed her, his mouth open, searching. Demanding and taking.

He tasted of rich, mellow Metaxa and frustration. Unbearably erotic and dangerously intoxicating.

Hopelessly enmeshed in craving, she drank him in.

Some distant part of her brain that was still functioning told her she was flirting with disaster, and urged her to extricate herself from a situation fast spiraling out of control. Attempting to heed it, she went to shove him away. But her knees were buckling, a tightness was building between her thighs, and her hands had a mind of their own. They blundered inside his open shirt to rediscover the lovely, sculpted planes of his chest, the lean symmetry of his ribs. His skin was hot and smooth and irresistible.

The more she touched, the more she craved and the farther she strayed past the boundaries of self-preservation. She tested the washboard strength of his midriff—hard, powerful, just like the rest of him. An incorrigible demon of need made her whimper into his mouth.

She heard the sharp intake of his breath and knew she was lost; that in being too daring herself, she'd tacitly invited him to return the favor. His fingers skimmed the length of her torso to search out the sensitive triangle between her thigh and her hip. His thumb strayed inside the leg of her bikini. Circled insolently. Exquisitely. And found its quarry.

Against her will and every shred of common sense at her command, a spasm of tortured pleasure streaked through her. "I hate you," she moaned, her legs falling slackly apart.

"I know," he purred, and touched her again. "I hate you, too."

Rampant desire consumed her. Her entire body contracted in a flood that made an utter mockery of any show of resistance she might have wanted to portray. She was so ready for him, so desperate to feel him skin to skin, heat to heat, that she tore at his shirt like a mad woman.

With a muffled growl, he swept her off her feet and carried her into the palm tree's dense shadow which neither stars nor moon nor man-made light could penetrate. She heard the rustle and rasp of fabric and zipper as he shed his clothes. Modesty and self-preservation lost in the rapacious demands of a hunger at last acknowledged after too long a fast, she kicked off her bikini bottom, tugged loose the strings holding her top in place and flung it aside.

She reached for him, wanting to touch him as he'd

touched her. Intimately, audaciously. She wanted to close her hand around him and hear him groan in an agony of pleasure. She wanted to punish him as he'd punished her and leave his control hanging by a thread, his flesh so tight and yearning for release that he begged for mercy. All this ran through her mind in a molten stream of desire.

But he was not to be so easily subjugated. Closing in on her, hot and naked, he cupped her breasts in his palms and grazed his teeth lightly over her nipples. Teasing and taunting them, with his lips and his tongue until, defeated, she uttered his name on a soft cry, and dissolved in a wash of ecstasy that robbed her of her remaining strength.

He caught her as she collapsed, eased her onto the soft grass and drove into her in one long, hot urgent thrust that sent her over the edge a second time. She clawed at his back. Sank her teeth into the curved muscle of his shoulder. Wrapped her long legs around his waist and clung to him— anything to anchor herself to him as the world tilted on its axis.

He muttered in her ear, Greek and English words jumbled together in graphic exposition of how often he'd imagined this moment, of what she was doing to him. He called her darling and sweetheart, and told her she was the most beautiful woman on earth, and he the luckiest man.

He cursed her for making him come too soon, and within minutes grew hard inside her again and drove them both to new heights of delirium. And when the demons of passion finally were satisfied, she lay tangled with him, a breath of night-cool air teasing her limbs. The storm had passed and taken the anger with it.

The problem, though, still remained, and for all that she tried to dismiss it, it circled restlessly in her mind, tainting the warm afterglow of loving. Easing herself out of his arms, she stood up and went to retrieve her towel and bikini.

He stopped her with a hand around her ankle. "What are you doing?" he inquired lazily.

"Making myself decent again. I can hardly walk into the house stark naked, and nor can you."

"Is our truce so soon ended?"

"What just happened wasn't a truce, Dimitrios."

His fingers drew mesmerizing circles up her calf. "What would you call it then, *agape mou?*"

"A gross error of judgment," she said.

Sensing her disquiet, Dimitrios tightened his grip. "What is it, Brianna? Am I not the lover you thought I was? Did I disappoint you?"

"You know you didn't," she said. "But that doesn't change the fact that what just happened was a huge mistake."

CHAPTER NINE

VERY carefully he removed his hand and propped himself up on one elbow. Her lovely pale shape glimmered in the night, her skin like polished ivory against the dark lush growth of the shrubbery behind her.

"Are you worried I might have left you pregnant?" he asked gently.

"There's that, of course," she said, wrapping herself in her towel as though ashamed to let him see her naked body. "I'm not on the pill, and you didn't use anything."

"I wasn't expecting to make love to you. But, Brianna, what does it matter if you have conceived? A child born of love is cause for celebration, and we'll be married soon enough that no one need know we didn't wait until our wedding night to pledge ourselves to each other."

"A hasty marriage isn't the solution to everything."

"There's another problem I don't know about?"

"There is, and you know very well what it is."

No sweeping stuff under the rug with her, he thought wryly. She wouldn't let him get away with a damned thing. "You're still angry with me."

"My anger isn't the issue. It's yours that worries me. Deny it all you like, but this business with your parents is eating you alive. Put an end to it, Dimitrios, please. I've had enough in-fighting with my own family to last me a lifetime. Don't ask me to take on yours, as well."

If ruining the moment was her intention, she was succeeding admirably. All traces of passion as dead as last year's roses, he pulled on his pants and drew up the zipper. "And exactly how do you propose I go about doing that?"

"Swallow your pride and talk to your father. Declare a truce. If you could do that with me, you can do it with him."

"It'll be cold day in hell before I grovel to Mihalis Poulos, my dear."

"Come on, Dimitrios, be the bigger man," she persisted. "You need your family at this time. Poppy needs her grandparents."

"She has you and me and everyone else in my house. We are all the family she needs."

"What if your parents need her?"

"They do not. My father refuses to acknowledge her, and my mother—"

"Would defy him, if she knew she had your support. Instead you go through her to try to punish him and it's not working, Dimitrios, because he doesn't care. The only one hurting here is the person least able to arm herself against you."

"Leave it, Brianna," he said harshly. "Don't push me on this. My mind is made up."

Her sigh gusted into the night, rife with frustration. "Is this the example you want to set for Poppy, Dimitrios? To hold on to a grudge at any price?"

"If it's justified, yes."

"Even if she turns on you one day? You're human, after all. You make mistakes, just like the rest of us. What if you do something she decides she can't forgive? How will you live with yourself?"

"It won't happen. I won't allow it."

"You won't *allow*…?" She lapsed into a silence that hung in the air, an implicit threat. Then she spoke again. "What if I can't live with a man who thinks he's God?"

He didn't like what he heard in her voice. "Are you saying we're at an impasse, Brianna? That this is a deal breaker and if I don't give way on it, you won't marry me?"

"Yes," she said. "That's exactly what I'm saying."

"I don't deal well with ultimatums."

"Of course you do," she shot back scornfully. "As long as you're the one issuing them. And if, in the process, you trample all over a few hearts, well that's just the price of doing business, isn't it?"

"Whose heart am I trampling? Yours?"

"Sorry to disappoint you, but no. Mine is made of sterner stuff. I've lost you once and lived to tell about it. I can do it again, if I have to. Your mother, though, she's a different story. Between the pair of you, you and your father are going to end up putting her in her grave."

"So let me get this straight. Either I agree to your terms or you walk. May I ask where Poppy fits in the picture?"

"Exactly where she deserves to be—as my top priority. She isn't the problem here, Dimitrios. You are. In your own way, you're as dysfunctional a parent as Cecily was, and our mother before that."

No one else would have dared speak to him so bluntly, laying bare truths he didn't want to acknowledge. But she was different. She always had been. Beneath that delicate exterior lay a tempered-steel core of integrity that refused to be compromised. How could he not respect that?

He wiped a hand down his face. "You do realize this is emotional blackmail, pure and simple?"

"Of course," she returned blithely. "Surprising though you might find it, my IQ does register on the positive side of zero, which leaves me well able to put two and two together and come up with four."

Choking back a laugh, he said, "Okay, I'll make you a deal. Marry me, and I'll agree to try to sort things out with my mother—my *mother,* Brianna, not my father."

"When?"

"Is tomorrow soon enough?"

She edged away from the palm tree and onto the pool deck, her face a study in suspicion. "It's not like you to capitulate without a fight. Where's the catch?"

"There isn't one," he said, and following her, caught her around the waist. "I want you more than I don't want the alternative, that's all." And pulling her back into the shadows, he kissed her again.

At first she resisted him, holding herself stiff as a board.

"Be patient with me, *agape mou,*" he whispered against her closed lips. "Remember, I'm a work in progress."

She made a soft, helpless sound in her throat and wound her arms around his neck. Her mouth bloomed under his, hot and sweet.

His body quickened in a burst of need that staggered him. Bracing himself against the tree, he tossed aside her towel and yanked down his fly. In one swift move, he lifted her so that she straddled him, and slid to the hilt in her sleek and eager flesh.

She convulsed around him almost immediately; spasm after mind-numbing spasm that pushed him beyond anything mortal man could hope to withstand. Desperate to prolong the pleasure, to distract himself from the siren song that was her body, he doggedly recited to himself the months of the year. *Ianouarios…Fevrouarios…Martios….*

April made a fool of him. He came in a blinding rush, spilling into her endlessly, violently, until he had nothing left to give. Drained, and still buried inside her, he sagged at the knees and lowered them both to the grass, too depleted to support his own weight, let alone hers. "If you don't end up pregnant after that," he panted, when at last he was able to speak again, "then one or both of us needs to see a fertility specialist."

Her breast rose in a sigh. "I didn't mean to play Russian roulette again. You caught me off guard."

"I caught me, as well." He wrapped her more securely against him. "Not surprising, really. I'm making up for four years of lost time."

"It wasn't all bad. At least you ended up with Poppy."

He'd feared all along that sooner or later he'd have to share everything with her; that she deserved better than the laundered truth he'd so far given her. If golden opportunity was what he'd been waiting for, the one she'd just handed him couldn't be beaten. "And I wouldn't be without her," he began. "Until you came back, she was my whole life, but—"

She stopped him dead with an ear-splitting shriek as a jet of cold water sluiced over them. Too late, he realized that the in-ground sprinkler system had been turned off only where the tables and tent were set up. The rest of the grounds were receiving their nightly soaking.

Cursing, he rolled to his feet and took her with him. Another blast caught them in the crossfire, streaking over his pants and spraying the length of her spine. Grabbing her towel, he thrust it at her and shoved her toward the pool deck, then raced back to collect their remaining clothes. He didn't fancy having one of tomorrow's guests stumbling over her bikini or his boxers.

Joining her, he said, "Not exactly how I'd hoped to end the evening, but now you know how I keep my gardens so green and lush."

Drops of water spiked her eyelashes and clung to the ends of her hair like so many scattered diamonds. Her teeth were chattering, likely as much from shock as cold, and she looked thoroughly offended. "I thought someone had turned a hose on us."

"It'd take more than that to put out the fire between us, *agape mou!*" he laughed. "Come on, I'll sneak you in by the side door and up the back stairs. With any luck, you'll make it to your room without bumping into anyone."

"I can only hope," she said tartly. "I've had about as many surprises as I can handle for one night."

Close to an international crowd of a hundred showed up the next afternoon, among them several personnel Brianna had met at the hospital over the past two weeks. The vast majority of guests, though, were strangers, and although some did a double take, most managed to mask their surprise when Dimitrios introduced her as Poppy's aunt and his future bride.

"How very lovely to meet you," they murmured politely, giving her a discreet once-over.

And "What a refreshing return to normality for little Poppy, to have two parents again."

They didn't add, "Especially when one's a dead ringer for her late mother," but Brianna was sure that must be what they were thinking. Once out of earshot, they gathered in little cliques and exchanged knowing glances over their champagne flutes and teacups.

"I imagine you're finding this a bit of a baptism by fire," Noelle remarked sympathetically at one point. Petite, blond and elegant in lavender shantung, she looked more like a ballet dancer than the head of a prestigious transplant team, and was a perfect foil for Dimitrios's dark good looks. "Don't let it get you down, Brianna. Just be yourself and enjoy the afternoon."

Easier said than done, though. She and Dimitrios made a handsome pair and Brianna felt very much the third wheel, tagging along in their wake as they mingled with the crowd. Still, she made the effort, smiling and nodding in all the right places, but the strain must have shown because after a while, Dimitrios took pity on her and sent her off to the refreshment tent for a reviving cup of tea.

Not a good idea, as it turned out. Only a few people clustered around the linen-draped buffet table, among them four women, all Americans, were helping themselves to an array of tiny pastries and deep in conversation not meant for anyone else's ears, least of all hers.

"Marrying the identical-twin aunt takes keeping it all in the family a bit too far, if you ask me," one in robin's-egg-blue brocade declared.

"Not the smartest choice he could have made, I agree," another put in. "If she's anything like Cecily, he's in for a load of trouble he doesn't need, what with his daughter being so ill and all. Noelle's a much better candidate."

The third nodded conspiratorially. "Grist for the gossip mills, though. The buzz around Athens is he met both sisters at some sort of celebrity yachting party years ago, and this is the one he was really after, but Cecily put the moves on him and trapped him into marrying her instead."

"Just goes to show even Dimitrios Giannakis makes a mistake once in a while. Kind of gives hope to the rest of us mere mortals, doesn't it?"

"That's harsh," the remaining member of the quartet said. "If the rumors are true and this is a love match that's been forced onto the back burner all this time, I say good luck to them."

"And they'll need it. Sixty-seven percent of second marriages end in divorce, and I'd lay money on theirs being one of them," robin's-egg-blue brocade pronounced sanctimoniously.

Resisting an uncharitable urge to stuff the entire tray of pastries down the woman's throat, Brianna took aim and fired a shot of her own. "If saving face is at all important to you, you might want to keep that opinion to yourself," she said sweetly, her hand admirably steady as she accepted a cup of Earl Grey from the uniformed maid manning the sterling tea service. "Dimitrios and I, you see, plan to be one of the remaining twenty-three percent."

The collective gasp that followed indicated she'd scored a direct hit. It should have made her feel better, but it didn't. Rather, it underscored what she'd believed from the outset. She and Dimitrios were getting too far ahead of themselves.

Just that morning, on the way back from visiting Poppy, she'd tried talking him out of going public so soon with news of their engagement, if such it could be called. "It's not the time," she'd argued. "This afternoon's about honoring the people on your guest list. It's nor fair to steal their thunder."

He'd disagreed. "Face it, Brianna, when it comes to news like this, there's no such thing as the right time. It's going to cause a stir, no matter when we announce it. We might as well get it over and done with."

"But I'm not ready to broadcast it to the whole world."

"Why not? Are you still having second thoughts about us?"

"No," she said slowly. "It's more that I'm still getting used to the idea of us being a couple, and I don't want to share it with anyone else just yet."

"That's all very fine, sweetheart," he reminded her, "but you forget my father already knows. This is happy news, Brianna, the best, and I'm not about to stand back and let him taint it with his own particular brand of poisonous cynicism."

Against her better judgment, she'd allowed herself to be persuaded. But what she'd just overheard warned her that Mihalis Poulos didn't have a monopoly on poison. And once again Carter's advice came back to haunt her. *Take care, Brianna....*

We're rushing into this too fast, she thought miserably. *Too much is going on, and we're losing sight of the most important person here, who is Poppy. The minute this party's over, I'm going to talk to Dimitrios. I have to convince him to slow down.*

Her plan hit a snag when, with the sun casting long shadows over the garden, a white limousine purred up the drive and drew to a stop not far from where she and Dimitrios stood waving goodbye to the last of the departing guests. Noelle had been called back to the hospital just after five o'clock. Now it was almost seven, and well past the time for latecomers to show up.

Disappointed, because she desperately wanted to be alone with him and set a few things straight, Brianna said, "Are you expecting someone, Dimitrios?"

"*Neh.* I have a surprise for you. We'll be three for dinner tonight. Hermione is joining us."

"Your *mother?*"

"That's right. I called her this morning." He linked his fingers in hers. His eyes caressed her. His smile bathed her in warmth. "You see, *calli mou,* I do listen when you speak. I do try to please you every way I know how."

He was doing it again. Ambushing her with his compassion; disarming her when she was in battle mode. He was worse than a chameleon, she thought helplessly. One part of him was all about power and success and pride and ambition; the other, a testament to the generosity and kindness he shared only with a few select individuals, including her. How was she supposed to combat that?

"Well?" he said, nudging her gently. "Do we invite her in, or do I send her away again?"

She swung her gaze to the woman hovering beside the open door of the car, as though uncertain of her welcome. Brianna could only imagine the courage it had taken for her to get this far. "We ask her in, of course. And Dimitrios? Thank you."

"*Efharisto,*" Hermione murmured in an aside to Brianna, as Dimitrios attended to predinner drinks. "I know I am here only because of your intercession with my son."

They sat on the west-facing verandah in comfortable wicker armchairs, with a tray of *mezedes* on the table in front of them, the olives, chunks of ripe red tomatoes drizzled in oil, slivers of octopus in wine, tzatziki and deep-fried calamari a meal in themselves.

Candles flickered in brass hurricane lamps strung among the vines overheard and nested at the base of the potted hibiscus shrubs fringing the perimeter of the terra-cotta-tiled floor. Hidden somewhere out of sight in the garden, a lemon tree in bloom perfumed the air. Below the verandah, the lawns dropped down in a series of manicured terraces to the shore. The sun sat low on the horizon, its dying rays staining the sky pink and orange and mauve.

An idyllic setting for a family reunion long overdue, some might have thought, but it was spoiled by the nervous tension simmering in the atmosphere. Hermione's fingers lay knotted in her lap. Her foot in its expensive suede pump tapped an anxious tattoo on the terra-cotta tiles. Her eyes flitted from Dimitrios to the glass doors opening into the house, as though she was unsure whether she should stay and face whatever the evening brought, or leave now, while she still had the chance.

Brianna felt terribly sorry for her. "I'm glad he asked you here, and so glad you came, Hermione. I'm sure it wasn't easy for you to accept his invitation."

"Mihalis doesn't know I'm here," she said, with another furtive glance around. "He thinks I'm visiting a friend."

It was on the tip of Brianna's tongue to say she was surprised the poor woman was allowed to have friends. Luckily, Dimitrios returned to the table just then and spared her having to think of a more suitable reply.

"An occasion such as this calls for a special toast," he announced, plucking a bottle of Krug from a silver ice bucket and pouring into three spun-glass flutes. "*Kherete,*

Mother. Welcome. I can't recall the last time you and I sat down together and enjoyed a glass of wine."

"I can," she said. "It was the day you came home with an honors degree from the London School of Economics. I was so proud of you. I still am, Dimitrios. I always will be. Not that it matters to you one way or the other, I suppose."

He cleared his throat and studied the bubbles rising in his glass as if they were the most fascinating things he'd ever come across. "It matters, Mother, and I'm proud of you, too. I know it wasn't easy for you to come here tonight. I can't imagine Mihalis was any too pleased when he heard."

"Well, he hasn't heard, at least not yet, although I suppose I can't keep it from him indefinitely. But whatever the price I have to pay, it won't compare to what it's cost me to be alienated from my son and grandchild. So, if you don't mind, I'd like to propose a toast, as well." Eyes shining with suppressed tears, she raised her glass. "To the future. May it bring you both all the happiness you deserve. And to my dear granddaughter, that she may soon be well again and back home where she belongs."

Regaining his composure, he clinked the rim of his flute against hers. "Better yet, how about, to all four of us?"

I'm going to cry, Brianna thought, barely able to swallow her wine.

Across the table Dimitrios caught her eye. "And most especially to my beautiful fiancée, for her wisdom and patience. I'm a better man because of you, Brianna, *calli mou.*"

Dear heaven, what a talent he had for laying claim to her heart! What an abundance of charm! He knew exactly the right buttons to push to make her cast aside her doubts and think only of how lucky they were to have found each other again.

Hermione beamed through her tears. "So when is the marriage to take place?"

"As soon as possible. Yesterday, if it was up to me," Dimitrios said. "I lost this beautiful woman once already. I won't risk losing her again."

"I can see that you love her very much."

Reaching for Brianna's hand, he brushed his mouth over her knuckles. "She is my life," he declared, piercing her with a glance of such unbridled hunger that she blushed. "Even now, with things about as grim as they can get with Poppy, Brianna gives me hope of better times to come. With her by my side, I can face whatever the future holds."

"Which is exactly as it should be." Hermione blinked away a fresh onslaught of happy tears. "If you'll let me, I'd love to help with the wedding—unless your parents, Brianna…?"

"My father died when I was a baby, and my mother when I was nineteen," she said. "As for a wedding, I really haven't given it much thought. It doesn't seem terribly important in the greater scheme of things."

"Because of Poppy," Hermione said gently. "I under stand. But, *pethi mou,* your wedding day is important, too. You should be able to look back on it with pleasure for the happy memories it holds, not regret that it passed by without your noticing."

"Let's not forget whose wedding this is, Hermione," Dimitrios warned, all the old reserve back in his voice. "It's up to Brianna to decide what she wants."

"Well, yes…I didn't mean to push my way in where I don't belong."

She shrank back in her chair, looking so crestfallen that Brianna rushed to reassure her. "As mother of the groom, of course you belong, Hermione. And once we set a date, I'll be glad of your input."

Erika came to remove the appetizers just then, and a short time later brought in the main course. Conversation resumed on a more general note after that, easing the tension and lending an almost festive air to the occasion. But it all came to an abrupt end when a fracas at the front door heralded the uninvited and decidedly unwelcome arrival of a fourth member to the party.

Recognizing her husband's raised voice, Hermione turned ashen and froze with her fork halfway to her mouth. As for Dimitrios... Brianna cringed at the murderous expression on his face. Iron-jawed, he rose from the table, his eyes blazing, his fists clenched.

A moment later Mihalis Poulos erupted onto the scene, with Alexio trailing behind in a fruitless attempt to stop him. Ignoring him, Mihalis adjusted his heavy gold cuff links and tugged the lapels of his cream linen jacket in place. "What happened, son?" he drawled. "Did my invitation get lost in the mail?"

Dimitrios impaled him in a feral, unblinking stare. "Brianna," he said softly, "please take my mother inside and wait there for me."

She hesitated, torn about how she should respond. Instinct told her to throw herself between him and his father; to stop the inevitable and violent confrontation she knew was coming. Years of bitterness and resentment had finally come to a head. Tonight it would end, and only one man would emerge the winner.

She had little doubt who that would be. Mihalis was big,

but Dimitrios was bigger. Stronger. Younger by almost thirty years.

"Brianna," he said again.

"No." She edged around the table to grasp his arm. "Dimitrios, don't play into his hands. Don't let him goad you into doing something you'll regret."

He shook her off as easily, as casually as if she were a fly. "*Now,* Brianna. This is between Mihalis and me. We don't need an audience."

"You might need a lawyer, though. Hurt him badly enough, and you could wind up spending the next twenty-five years behind bars. How much use will you be as a father, then?"

Just briefly she thought she'd reached him. She felt, rather than heard his indrawn breath. Sensed rather than saw the sudden doubt assailing him.

But Mihalis hadn't missed a thing. "Now, there's the difference between you and me, *yios,*" he sneered. "I've never felt the need to hide behind a woman's skirts. No wonder your first wife ran around on you. She probably grew tired of having to fight your battles."

At that, Dimitrios let out a roar and lunged. The table flew over, smashing dishes and spreading a mess of orzo and olive-stuffed breast of pheasant everywhere. Shards of crystal glittered on the terra-cotta tiles.

Alexio yelped and ran back inside the house. And because she was too late to stop the carnage, Brianna did as she'd been asked in the first place and hurried Hermione away from the scene.

Erika met them in the hall. "Take her to the sitting room, Brianna," she ordered calmly. "This is not something either of you need to see."

"Is Alexio calling the police?"

Erika laughed grimly. "If you think Dimitrios can't deal with that man by himself, *pethi mou,* you still have much to learn about him."

Outside, something else fell with a crash. Wincing, Brianna said, "How about an ambulance, then? At this rate, they're both going to need one."

"Go." Erika ushered them firmly toward the big, formal sitting room, as serenely elegant with its ivory walls and silk-upholstered sofas as the terrace currently was in a shambles. "You don't care for brandy, I know, but I will bring you coffee, which you will sit and enjoy until Dimitrios joins you."

"This is my fault," Hermione whispered, shaking so badly Brianna was afraid she might collapse.

"No, *Kyria,* this is not about you," Erika declared. "This is between your husband and your son. It's been a long time coming and there's nothing you or the police or anyone else can do but let them settle their differences, once and for all."

She paused and tilted her head, listening. "And it would seem," she finished, "that they have done just that. I'll bring coffee for three, and a decanter of Morello cherry liqueur. Dimitrios enjoys it once in a while, as a change from Metaxa."

Brianna realized then that silence reigned outside, and the only sound was the inner thudding of her heart.

CHAPTER TEN

HE BRUSHED one hand against the other. It was done.

He should have felt vindicated. Purged. He didn't.

Grimacing, he turned back to the house. To the villa he'd built as a monument to his success. Twilight dusted its walls. Lights streamed from the windows, warm and yellow. But he felt only the coldness of another in a long list of empty victories. At the end of the day, what did any of them matter compared to a home, a wife, a healthy child. A family living in harmony and bound together by love. Ordinary, everyday pleasures which most people took for granted, but which he had never known.

The front door opened and the woman who'd been both mother, mentor and servant to him for the last nine years stepped out. "Coffee's waiting," she said, as if nothing untoward had occurred.

When he didn't reply, she came down the steps to stand next to him. "No point in brooding, Dimitrios. You did what had to be done. He left you with no choice. Now it's over."

"Yes," he said, but he'd seen the horror in Brianna's eyes before she took his mother away, and knew it wasn't quite over, not yet. "Where are they?"

"Waiting for you in the sitting room."

He nodded and touched her shoulder. "I'm glad you're on my side, Erika."

She slapped at his hand with rough affection. "Which other side is there, dolt? Get inside and speak with your women."

He found Brianna standing at the window, her fingers drumming lightly on the sill, her face unreadable. His mother huddled in the corner of one of the two settees facing each other in front of the fireplace, and she...

She was only fifty-eight, but underneath the expensive clothes, the stylish hairdo, and all that estheticians and cosmetics could do to preserve the illusion of youth, she looked old, beaten down, afraid, and he felt a pang of guilt that he'd stood by and done nothing to help her until now.

"He's gone and he won't be back, Mother," he told her, advancing into the room.

She regarded him anxiously. "Is he all right?"

"He didn't leave with a smile on his face, if that's what you're asking."

"I must go to him."

"No, you must not. You must stay here."

"Overnight, you mean?"

"For as many nights as it takes him to come to his senses." He helped himself to one of the demitasses on the library table and drained it in one gulp. Erika had made *metrios,* medium-sweet coffee, and for once he was glad of the sugar. He needed something to chase away the sour taste in his mouth.

"Dimitrios is right," Brianna said, coming forward. "At least here you'll be safe."

"Safe?" Hermione stared at them as though they were

both certifiably insane. "Mihalis would never hit *me*. He's never lifted a hand against me in his life."

"Abuse doesn't have to be a physical thing, Mother," Dimitrios said wearily. "There are other, more subtle ways to wear a person down."

She raised a few more feeble objections—she'd be putting them out, his father would be worried, she had no change of clothes, no makeup, not even a toothbrush. But in the end he overcame her objections and she allowed Erika to take her upstairs.

"Well," he said, as the door closed behind them and left him alone with Brianna, "no broken bones or blood, as you can see."

"Your shirt's torn," she said frostily.

He shrugged. "Shirts can be replaced."

"And husbands, fathers?" Her light-blue eyes bored into him, laser beams of disgust. "Are they disposable items, too?"

"I didn't kill or maim him, if that's what's worrying you, Brianna. I kicked him out. Sent him packing with his tail between his legs. His pride's badly dented, he's a little dusty, and his suit won't be fit to wear again, but he's in one piece otherwise."

"I see. And do you settle all your differences with your fists?"

"What the hell would you have had me do?" he inquired irascibly. "Stand idly by and let him terrorize my mother? Insult you—*again?*"

"Of course not. But couldn't you have reasoned with him? Did you have to be so violent?"

"Yes," he said. "I did. Because reason is only effective if the other party's willing to listen. And my father hears only his own voice. And because there comes a time when a man has to take a stand. For me, that time came tonight. He invaded my home. He threatened my household staff. He intimidated you and my mother. He behaved like a thug. Don't ask me to reason with a man like that."

"You could have called the police."

"And give him the satisfaction of thinking I couldn't deal with him myself?" Frustrated, he shook his head and, lifting the decanter of cherry liqueur parked on the tray next to the coffee cups, poured himself a hefty measure. "No, Brianna, this was between him and me, no one else."

"What if he charges you with assault?"

"His pride won't let him."

"Like father, like son," she muttered, her lovely mouth set in obstinate disapproval.

He downed his drink and poured another. He was tired and spattered with food. His body felt as if it had gone ten rounds with a sumo wrestler. His right hand was bruised, the knuckles scraped raw. "I don't have to defend myself to you, Brianna."

"No, you don't," she agreed loftily. "You can get drunk, instead. Excuse me for not wanting to stand here and watch."

She went to stalk past him, but he caught her and swung her round to face him, his fingers spanning her slender wrist in an iron grip. "Don't you dare walk out on me again."

She glared at him, outraged. "Don't you dare manhandle *me. Ever!*"

Aghast, ashamed, he released her and raised both hands in surrender. "Forgive me. I'm not at my best right now. Believe it or not, I don't make a habit of brawling."

She sighed and lowered her gaze. "I know that."

"Do you?"

"Yes," she said. "You were in an impossible situation. Most men would probably have reacted as you did."

"The point is, I'm not most men. I'm his son. That he's finally been called to account for his actions is something only I could accomplish. It's the old law of the jungle, Brianna. A case of the aging lion accepting someone younger and more powerful has taken over as king."

"You really believe he understands that?"

Dimitrios thought of the last look his father had turned on him, before he crawled into his car and was driven away. He'd seen a lurking respect in those black, indomitable eyes; a certain sick satisfaction, even, as though he'd finally proved to himself and the rest of the world that the man he professed to hate was worthy of being called his son. "Yes, I do. For all his faults, Mihalis is no fool. He knows when he's beaten."

"How do you suppose he found out where your mother was?"

"Most likely from the chauffeur who drove him here. He was the same man who brought my mother, and was waiting in the same car to take her and my father home again. His staff are as much under his thumb as she is."

"You never did explain how you persuaded her to break rank and visit you."

"I told her if she really wanted to reestablish a connection with me and my family, my door was open. She asked when would be a good time to stop by, I invited her to dinner tonight, and she came."

"Simple as that?"

He didn't tell her Hermione had burst into tears when

she heard his voice, or that it wasn't until then that he realized how much he loved her despite everything. That was something he himself had yet to digest. "Not quite. I was as surprised as you when she actually showed up. I thought she'd lose her nerve at the last minute."

"She must have known your father would find out, sooner or later."

"That was a risk she chose to take. I didn't browbeat her into it, and I didn't beg. That's not my style."

She chewed her lips thoughtfully. "So, what are you going to do about her now? She won't stay here, if that's what you're hoping. She believes her place is with her husband, no matter how he treats her. He's what she's used to. She'd be lost without him."

"I agree. But the dust needs to settle first." He raked his fingers through his hair and dislodged a sliver of olive. "Look, can we table this discussion until tomorrow? I need a shower in the worst way."

She let out an exclamation and peered at his damaged hand. "You need a first-aid kit more! If there was no blood involved in your little fracas with your father, what do you call this?"

"It's nothing. A scratch, that's all. We scuffled, and I...connected with the verandah wall by mistake."

"Right!" She rolled her eyes scornfully. "Go take your shower, for pity's sake. You're bleeding all over the rug."

"Will I see you later? We've had hardly any alone time today. I haven't even told you how lovely you look."

"You were so busy being the attentive host, I didn't think you'd noticed."

"How could I not have noticed, when you left every other woman in the shade?" He let his gaze drift over her in leisurely appreciation, amazed as always by her match-less elegance and beauty. "The dress, the hat, the shoes…." He made a circle of his forefinger and thumb. "Perfection!"

"I'm not wearing the hat now."

"I noticed. And if I have my way, you soon won't be wearing the dress or shoes, either."

"Forget it," she said, rolling her lovely eyes. "You've had enough excitement for one day."

But half an hour later, just as he'd finished shaving and went to leave his bathroom, he heard the quiet click of his bedroom door opening. Hastily slinging a towel around his hips, he went to investigate and by the light of a reading lamp next to the bed, caught Brianna tiptoeing toward the nightstand. She'd changed into a flame-colored robe cinched tightly at the waist, and loosened her hair so that it floated in a dark cloud around her shoulders, and her feet were bare.

"Ahem," he murmured.

The very picture of wide-eyed guilt, she spun around. "Oh," she said, and gulped when she saw his state of undress. "I did knock, but when you didn't answer, I thought you might still be in the shower."

"No. I'm done."

"Yes…well…" She averted her gaze. "I brought you this. I thought you might need it. Your hand looked…pretty badly swollen."

She thrust an ice pack at him, tugged the tie belt at her waist a little tighter and actually blushed when she saw his smile. He was tempted to tell her his hand wasn't the only thing swelling up. Points south of his waist weren't exactly hibernating, either. But she was so clearly agitated, he didn't have the heart to tease her.

She was shy, he realized, charmed. Uncertain of her welcome. This beautiful, spirited creature, the envy of women the world over and surely desired by any man who didn't have both feet in the grave, wasn't nearly as self-assured as she'd like him to think.

"Efharisto," he said gravely. "That was kind of you."

"You're welcome." She shifted from one foot to the other and cast a longing glance at the door. "Well then, I'll be going."

"Please don't," he said, and ghosting a hand down her spine, drew her to him and touched his mouth to hers.

She wilted against him like a flower left too long without water, and let out a sigh. "I shouldn't be here."

"Why not?"

"Your mother's asleep in a room just down the hall."

"If we're very quiet, we probably won't wake her."

"Oh, it's not that, Dimitrios, and you know it."

"What is it, then, *calli mou?*"

"I'm here because I couldn't stay away," she admitted forlornly, "even though I keep telling myself that jumping into bed together won't resolve the problems we face. I'm the one who insisted last night was a mistake, yet here I am, ready to repeat it. It's wrong. We need to get to know each other properly all over again, and only then…"

"Hush," he said, and kissed her a second time, dipping his tongue fleetingly into her sweet mouth. "This *is* getting to know each other properly all over again."

"I'd really like to believe that."

"What's stopping you, Brianna? What is it about me, about us, that you don't trust? Is it that I've asked you to marry me, but haven't yet put a ring on your finger?"

"No!"

"Because I intend to remedy that this week. I'd have done it sooner, but I've had a few things on my mind."

"I don't care about a ring!"

"Are you afraid I'll turn into my father and browbeat you into wifely submission?"

She almost smiled. "That's the least of my worries."

He drew his fingertip in a straight line from her throat to her cleavage, past her rib cage and over the firm, smooth curve of her belly to the juncture of her thighs. "Do I not stir you to ungovernable passion?"

Her eyes grew heavy with desire. Her breathing quickened and a shudder ran through her. "You make me crazy," she whispered.

He loosened the knot at her waist and parted the folds of her robe. Underneath, she wore a whisper of a bra and tiny panties; two nonsense strips of peach-tinted satin trimmed with lace that concealed nothing. Her nipples pushed hard as pebbles against the bra; her panties were warmly damp against his palm.

"How crazy?" he muttered at her ear.

She responded by stepping back a pace, stripping away his towel and running her hands down his flanks to cradle him.

He was already hard. Had been from the moment he'd discovered her in his room. And she seemed fascinated by his arousal, displaying a curiosity at once naive and bold. "You are so beautiful and strong and perfect," she breathed.

Her touch, delicate as butterflies, lethal as fire, almost finished him off before he'd begun, and he couldn't allow that. Swinging her into his arms, he carried her to the bed and lowered her to the mattress. He ached to feel her clench around him, to fuse his body with hers and find again the release only she could bring, but the satisfaction, though exquisite, would be all too brief, and it had been such a long, long time since they'd made love at leisure.

"First, we get rid of these," he said, making short work of the bra and panties.

She lay naked before him in the lamplight, and for the first time since she'd come back into his life, he was able to look his fill at her naked body. She was as beautiful as ever, her breasts still small and firm, the nipples tinted the same dusty rose he remembered from before, her hips flaring in a graceful, narrow curve, her waist so tiny he could span it with his hands.

The difference was there'd been no hesitation back then, no doubt. She'd reveled in his scrutiny, offering him all that she was, her hunger as urgent and all-consuming as his, her flesh pliant and willing. This time, caution warred with desire and she lay frozen beneath his gaze, her arms pinned at her sides, her thighs clamped together.

Patiently, persistently, he kissed every exposed inch of her: the slope of her breasts, the inner curve of her elbow, the arch of her instep, the back of her knees. And inch by inch, she melted under his ministrations. Most of her, at least, until, capturing her gaze, he said softly, "Open your legs, Brianna."

She blinked and swallowed, her mind clearly rebelling at the idea, but her body had a will of its own and when he blew a damp breath against the top of her thighs, they fell apart and gave him leave to do what he'd never done to her before. He put his mouth against her and seduced her with his tongue, sliding it between the satin folds of her flesh to search out the hidden nub at her center.

Her skin had the texture of gossamer, the sheen of a

pearl, and she tasted of honey and woman and passion on the verge of explosion. He delved deep with his tongue, once, twice, three times, and felt the tremors racing through her. Heard her shocked gasp fade into a long, low moan as she shattered, her body arching off the bed in mindless torment, her fists clutching at his hair.

He soothed her, stroking her, kissing her, and when she subsided into dreamy acquiescence, he seduced her again. And again, she climaxed, faster, harder this time. She clawed at his shoulders, trying to drag his body up to cover hers, to accept him between her legs, and all the while begging amid fractured sobs, "Please, Dimitrios...all of you...now, please...!"

"I have nothing here...no *profilaktiko,*" he said hoarsely, remembering too late that he never kept any in the house because if he was going to spend the night with a woman, she wasn't the kind he'd bring home to meet his daughter.

"I don't care!" Brianna cried, guiding him deep into the hot, wet temple of her body. "I *want* to have your baby!"

She didn't really mean it. Just yesterday, she'd worried she might get pregnant. So he'd be careful. He'd give her the satisfaction she craved, pleasure himself as much as he dared, then pull out at the last minute.

Just as it took two to come together in complete intimacy, though, so it took two to agree when the time was right to break apart. And she was of a different mind, one that rendered him blind to everything but the driving need to possess her. Fully and completely and forever.

"Thee mou!" he ground out, his lungs burning and the sweat beading his brow as she climaxed a third time. He was lost, a leaf caught in a raging river, helpless to direct

his own fate. Accepting defeat, he poured into her, gave her everything he had, everything he was. She'd stolen his heart years ago. She might as well have the rest of him.

When he could breathe again, he stroked a damp strand of hair from her face and said, "Someday we're going to take this slowly and make it last all night. Just don't ask me when. It could take years before I'm able to pace myself."

She smiled and closed her eyes. "May I ask you something else instead?"

"Anything, *calli mou.*"

"Are you going to kick me out of your bed now and send me back to my own room?"

"Not a chance. You belong here, with me."

"Oh, good," she said, and turning on her side, curled up against him and fell asleep.

He was gone when she awoke the next morning, but a glass of chilled orange juice stood on the bedside table, and a single perfect red rose lay next to her on his pillow, proof positive, if proof she needed, that last night hadn't been a dream.

She brushed the velvety petals against her cheek and inhaled their delicate fragrance. She couldn't recall the last time she'd slept so soundly or awoken filled with such joy.

Yesterday's petty anxieties seemed woefully unimportant in the light of the new day. Dimitrios was right. It was time to banish her insecurities. Time to let go all the black and bitter memories eating away at her. The sting of Cecily's betrayal, the pain of her death, were in the past, but Brianna and Dimitrios, they were the present and the future. Life wasn't perfect—that would only be the case when Poppy was well again—but it was good. It was filled with hope again.

Throwing back the covers, she put on her robe, took her juice and stepped through the glass doors that opened onto the deck running the length of his room. Like hers, it over-looked the sea and pool. To the left, a crew was at work dismantling the tent and carting away the tables, chairs and assorted debris from the garden party.

She felt like calling out, take away the gossip and the speculation, too. They had no place in her life. She was a woman in love; a woman who'd been well and truly loved by her man. Her mouth was swollen from his kisses, her body tender and aching in dark and secret places. She hated the idea of washing away the scent of sex and passion that clung to her skin, and wished the day would speed to an end so that she could be alone with Dimitrios and they could make love again.

But others needed her attention first. Poor Hermione waited downstairs, alone and unsure of what her future held. Poppy waited in her hospital crib for the aunt who'd become a permanent fixture in her young and troubled life. And perhaps today Noelle would have good news about the test results and they could move to the next phase of that precious child's recovery.

In fact, for a woman who'd surely spent a sleepless night, Hermione looked remarkably serene and relaxed when Brianna finally ran her to earth in the courtyard, enjoying a breakfast of fruit and yogurt.

"I've done a lot of thinking since speaking to you at the yacht club," she said. "You're so wise, Brianna, and I owe you so much. You made me see that I have enabled Mihalis by submitting to his demands, and the sad thing is we've all lost so many years because of my weakness. I realize now that if I want to see changes, it's up to me to initiate them. And so I've begun, starting with yesterday."

"By accepting Dimitrios's invitation to come here, you mean?"

"Yes. Uniting my family is my dearest wish, but a week ago, I didn't think I had the courage to do that. Now I know differently, although I won't pretend I wasn't horrified by the scene at dinner last night. It upset me dreadfully. No woman ever wants to see her husband and son go at each other like that."

"Your husband wasn't badly hurt, Hermione," she said, helping herself to the fruit and yogurt, "Just a little shaken up."

"I know. Dimitrios explained all that. We had a long, frank talk this morning, before he left for work. Neither of us held anything back. He's not always right, you know. No one ever is. And his father isn't always wrong. At bottom, Mihalis is a very good man, but he's proud, and so is Dimitrios, and that's been the biggest obstacle to their settling their differences. My mistake has been in letting them carry on this senseless feud for so long. I should have put my foot down years ago. Well, what is it they say? Better late than never?"

The woman has more backbone than I've given her credit for, Brianna thought admiringly, *although when it comes to putting her foot down, her tiny little size sixes won't make much impression on the men in her family.*

"So," Hermione continued, "I phoned my husband a little while ago and told him I will be visiting my grand-daughter this morning."

"And how did he take it?"

"Oh, he growled and muttered, just as I knew he would, then asked when he might expect me home. I said I'd be there sometime this afternoon, and that whether or not I stayed depended on how reasonable he was prepared to be."

Brianna couldn't help herself. She hiccupped with laughter. "You did not!"

"Yes," Hermione said placidly. "I did."

"And what did he have to say to that?"

"He growled and muttered some more, but in the end asked what he should tell Artemis, our cook, to make for dinner." She laughed then, too. "I chalked that up as one victory for me."

"Do you think it's going to be that easy to change him?"

"Of course not. Nor do I really want to change him all that much. I have loved Mihalis with all his flaws for the better part of forty years. I don't relish the prospect of finding myself married to a stranger at this late date. All I want is for him to show his son and granddaughter and you the good heart he so seldom lets anyone but me ever see. Did you know, for instance, that when he heard Poppy was hospitalized, he donated a huge sum to the clinic, anonymously?"

"Dimitrios said his father refuses to acknowledge Poppy."

"Dimitrios has never brought Poppy to meet her grandfather. The last time my husband and son sat down to a meal together and exchanged anything resembling civilities was almost nine years ago. They have been estranged ever since."

"But *you* met Poppy."

"I went to see her in the hospital when she was born. Mihalis refused to come with me. He would not give Dimitrios the chance to turn him away. And Dimitrios would not give his father the chance to reject his grand-daughter."

"A vicious circle," Brianna murmured, realizing what she should have known all along: that there were always two sides to every story.

"Precisely. One that has been in effect for a very long time, and since neither of these proud, stubborn men I love so dearly will break the cycle, then I have decided that I must. And thanks to you, my dear, I feel confident that I can do so. You are the kind of woman I once was. I intend to become that woman again."

"I'm glad," Brianna said, "and, Hermione, I'm so proud of you. Hopefully, between us, we can bring about some sort of lasting peace in this family."

Hermione covered her hand. "When women stand together, they're unstoppable, so if I fall back into my old, weak ways, I shall count on you to set me straight again."

"Consider it done." She finished the last of her yogurt, drank her coffee and laid her napkin to one side. "So, what next?"

"Dimitrios thought you'd want to see Poppy."

"Yes, I spend most mornings with her. I'm usually up earlier and he drops me off at the clinic on his way to work, but I slept in today."

"That's what he said, but he didn't want to disturb you. Instead, he left instructions for Spiros to drive you to Kifissia when you're ready, and suggested I might go with you. He'll meet us for lunch later and after that…" She shrugged and made a little face. "Then I go home and face the music."

"Does that worry you, Hermione?"

"I'm a little apprehensive, I suppose. This is new territory for me, after all. But my mind is made up. From now on, Mihalis will have to dance to my tune, at least some of the time. And knowing I have you and Dimitrios behind me, well, that makes all the difference. You're very good for him, you know."

Brianna thought of the night just past and felt a blush stealing over her face. The lovemaking had been amazing and wonderful and stupendous. But there'd been so much more to it than just sex. She and Dimitrios had reached a new depth of understanding, of commitment. There'd undoubtedly be more rocky times ahead, but for the first time she really believed that together they could overcome whatever life flung at them.

"He's very good for me," she said. "We're good for each other."

Hermione nodded. "Yes. A match made in heaven."

Yesterday Brianna had questioned that. Today she almost believed it.

CHAPTER ELEVEN

SHE floated on the same cloud of optimism throughout the following week. Although no word came through on the test results, Poppy was holding her own and thrived under the extra attention of a grandmother who came to see her most days.

From all accounts, Hermione was gradually chipping away at her husband's obstreperous insistence that she choose between him and their son. "He claims my first loyalty is to my husband," she confided to Brianna on the Wednesday, her brown eyes sparkling with something close to indignation. "He says that when I married him, I promised to be a dutiful, obedient wife. I pointed out that didn't translate into my becoming his doormat."

"I shudder to think how he responded to that!"

"Actually, he was so taken aback that at first he didn't react at all. Then he glowered as only he can, and grumbled under his breath that women today were too bold and didn't know their proper place in life. And I said I knew exactly my place—it wasn't under his heel, and suggested he get used to the idea."

Was this really the same timid mouse who'd crept into the ladies' room at the yacht club less than a week ago,

Brianna wondered. But then she remembered Dimitrios telling her that his mother had once been a vivacious, spirited woman, so perhaps the person she was looking at now was the real Hermione Poulos.

"Well, I've been working on Dimitrios, too, and trying to get him to soften his attitude toward his father," she said. "He puts up a good front of pretended indifference, but I suspect he's not as averse to the idea as he pretends to be."

Hermione sighed. "I suppose, if truth be told, they're both tired of being at odds. They just don't know how to bring about an armistice without losing face."

Regardless of the issues separating Dimitrios and his father, however, between Brianna and Dimitrios blissful harmony reigned. On the Thursday night they had a picnic dinner in the quiet cove below the villa. They sat on a blanket and toasted each other with champagne. They ate salad and wonderful Greek bread Erika had baked just that morning, and big fat prawns which Dimitrios grilled over an open fire. For dessert there were fresh figs and apricots and decadent little squares of baklava. And when the fire dwindled to glowing embers and the moon rose round and yellow over the sea, he withdrew a little box from the picnic hamper and slid a dazzling two-carat diamond and platinum solitaire on her finger.

"Now it's official," he declared, lifting her hand to his mouth. "You're mine and I'll never let you go."

If he sounded a tad too triumphant, as if he'd just pulled off a business coup that left his competitors eating his dust, she supposed it was understandable. After all, they'd traveled a rough, unhappy road to get to this point, but she was finally where she'd always wanted to be, wasn't she? So why quibble over a few words uttered in the heat of the moment? Still, she couldn't help saying lightly, "This ring designates me your fiancée, Dimitrios, not a corporate acquisition."

He drew her down on the blanket and ran a possessive hand over her body. "It signifies to the whole world that you're everything I want, *chrisi mou kardia.* Everything I need."

And with the night as witness, he showed her just how deeply he wanted and needed her, making love to her with such exquisite tenderness, such masterful finesse, that her silly doubts sank into oblivion. The moon rose higher, spilling over their naked bodies in tacit blessing. The waves rolled gently ashore, whispering approval. The entire universe narrowed to a few yards of sand still warm from the day's heat, and the only man she'd ever loved.

Hermione, of course, was thrilled to see the ring on Brianna's finger. Erika clucked like a proud mother hen. Alexio and even the taciturn Spiros beamed. Just briefly the dark cloud that had hovered over the villa for so long lifted, and the sun broke through again. There was to be a wedding, a bride, a celebration.

But first, there was the gala to get through on Saturday evening. The high point of the season before people fled the summer heat of Athens and left it to the tourists, it also marked Brianna's official debut into society as the future Kyria Dimitrios Giannakis.

As usual on weekends, Dimitrios planned to spend a good part of the day with Poppy, and looked floored when Brianna said she'd go with him. "You won't have the time," he objected.

"I don't see why not," she said. "I don't have anything else to do all day."

"You mean, you haven't booked an appointment?" Then, at her uncomprehending stare, "You know—to get yourself fixed up for tonight?"

"I can fix myself up, Dimitrios," she informed him, amused. "It's one of the perks of being a model. An occupational hazard that comes with the territory, you might say. Give me an hour to get ready and I promise I won't embarrass you."

"You could never embarrass me, but you never cease to surprise me, either. Most women I know would be spending the entire day at the spa to prepare for a night on the town."

"I consider the time better spent with you and my niece. In fact, if it weren't for such a good cause, I'd be happy to miss tonight's event altogether. I don't mind admitting, after last Sunday when I felt I was under a microscope, I'm not looking forward to a repeat performance tonight."

He caught her to him and dropped a swift, hard kiss on her mouth. "Last weekend we made headlines, *agape mou*. Now we're old news and someone else has center stage."

I hope he's right, she thought later, as she checked her appearance one last time in the full-length mirror in her dressing room. She knew she looked her best. She'd pinned up her hair in a sleek chignon, and her evening gown, a lovely, narrow-skirted creation in aquamarine satin lavishly decorated with tiny crystals, was a morale booster in itself. Sleeveless, with a deep vee neck and low-cut back, it needed no enhancement beyond her engagement ring and diamond-studded platinum hoop earrings, and she shouldn't have been lacking confidence. But remembering the American women who'd been so forthcoming with their opinions at the garden party, she couldn't suppress a grimace. If she came across the one in blue again tonight, she just might pinch her.

Some four hundred people thronged the halls and gardens of one of Kifissia's grandest Victorian-style villas. A wonderful old house, with a frescoed ceiling in the ballroom, a turret at one corner and wide porches, it provided just the right touch of formal elegance to suit the occasion.

Designer gowns and priceless jewels were much in evidence, as were many of the faces Brianna had seen at the garden party. As Dimitrios had predicted, though, she was less an object of curiosity than she had been the previous weekend. She found herself relaxing and enjoying the evening as they circulated during the cocktail reception and he introduced her as his fiancée to various friends and acquaintances.

"Wonderful news," people said warmly, and "Congratulations, Dimitrios," and "Much happiness to you both."

"You see," he murmured, during a brief lull. "All your pre-gala nerves were for nothing."

Not until they found their table at dinner and she noticed an empty seat on his left did she realize Noelle hadn't shown up. "I know," Dimitrios said, when she commented. "I forgot to mention that she phoned while you were getting dressed to say she's been delayed but she'll join us later."

"Later" turned out to be almost midnight. Brianna was dancing with one of the other men from their table, leaving Dimitrios deep in conversation with two others when

Noelle arrived. All three stood up to greet her. She smiled rather wanly, shook hands, then spoke briefly to Dimitrios. He shot her a look of consternation, took her arm and quickly led her out of the ballroom.

Brianna didn't need to be clairvoyant to guess that something was amiss. "Excuse me," she muttered, and, leaving her startled dance partner performing a solo waltz, worked her way through the couples on the dance floor and hurried in the direction the other two had taken.

By then they'd disappeared and it took her several more minutes before she found them. They were not in the big entrance hall where the champagne reception had taken place, nor were they in any of the various parlors on either side.

Noticing her, a sweet-faced older woman whom she'd met earlier pointed to a closed door toward the rear of the house. "If you're looking for Dimitrios, dear," she said kindly, "I believe I saw him go into the library with Dr. Manning."

In fact, they weren't in there, either, but she heard their voices from beyond a pair of French doors opening to a covered porch, and was about to announce her presence when the gist of their conversation stopped her dead.

"Well, Dimitrios," Noelle was saying, "it's not what we hoped for, when you first suggested approaching Brianna, but I warned you then that there are never any guarantees that a parent—or in this case, a parent's identical twin— will turn out to be an acceptable donor. It's disappointing, of course…."

Disappointing? As the impact of the news struck home, Brianna recoiled as if she'd been shot in the heart. *How about* devastating, *Noelle?* She screamed silently. *How*

about the fact that Poppy could die because I've failed her?
Will that be disappointing, too? Something we'll push to
one side, in order to get on with our lives?

Overcome with sorrow and despair, she clutched
blindly at the door frame, frantic to strike some sort of
bargain with God. She'd sacrifice her own health, give up
Dimitrios, never again ask to be loved or to know passion
and desire—anything and everything, if only Poppy could
be saved.

Noelle's voice intruded again. "No point in beating
yourself up, Dimitrios. You've known all along that the
best possible candidate is always a sibling. But even if you
and Brianna were to have a baby…"

Her words faded, lost in a burst of laughter from a
group of people strolling in the garden, but it hardly
mattered. The gist of what she'd been saying was clear
enough, and as a second wave of shock hit, Brianna
backed away from the scene, willing herself to believe she
must have misunderstood.

And much, much more afraid that she finally understood all too well.

No wonder Dimitrios had been so willing to make
amends, so quick to propose, so anxious to marry her as
soon as possible. No wonder he *needed* her so much! Idiot
that she was, she'd convinced herself he wanted her for
herself. Now it all made a different kind of sense, one that
had nothing to do with love—at least, not between her and
him. He wanted her DNA and another child, one only she
could give him.

Dear God, she might even already be pregnant!

And yet…if her having a child gave Poppy a fighting
chance; was, in fact, her *only* chance…? And if, regard-

less of *why* she conceived, Brianna loved the baby, as she knew she would, with her whole heart, for ever and ever, would it really be so wrong…?

No. What was wrong and would always be wrong was a relationship between a man and a woman built on deception. *I don't deal well with failure,* Dimitrios had once told her. *It's not in my nature to accept defeat.*

Well, he'd certainly proved that. Even she hadn't realized the lengths he was prepared to go to, to win. He was duplicity personified. The lies and half-truths rolled off his tongue with the same facile ease as the endearments he constantly showered on her.

Sickened, she turned to leave the room. She'd heard enough and had only herself to blame if her romantic idyll had ended so abruptly and inexorably. She'd refused to listen when every instinct told her to take a step back and be sure before she once again gave everything of herself to Dimitrios.

She had wanted to believe in happily-ever-after when she'd always known that endings like that only happened in fairy tales.

If it seems too good to be true, Brianna, it usually is….

Oh, Carter, she mourned. Why didn't I pay attention to the one man in the world who's never let me down?

From the verandah, Noelle's voice again penetrated her thoughts. "…is why I'm so late. I wanted to be sure there were no last-minute hitches before I spoke to you."

Brianna couldn't bear to hear another word. Not even bothering to steal away in secret, she opened the door and let it fall shut behind her.

"So there you have it. Not the news you were hoping for, but something better. A perfect match from an unrelated donor," Noelle said. "Congratulations are definitely in order. The future's looking very bright. First you and Brianna have found each other again, and now this. She's lovely, Dimitrios, and I'm very happy for both of you." She reached up and kissed his cheek. "So, go find her and give her the excellent news."

"Come with me," he urged. "She should hear it from you."

"I'd love to, but I have a patient I need to get back to, one whose prospects are, sadly, not nearly as favorable as Poppy's."

He caught both her hands in his and squeezed them. "I owe you everything, Noelle," he said earnestly. "How do I ever repay you for all you've done?"

"By being happy for a change. Heaven knows, it's been a long time coming."

He watched her leave, then turned back into the house, eager to find Brianna. But she was not, as he expected, at their table in the ballroom, nor was she on the dance floor. She sat alone on a hard wooden bench in the grand hall, close by the front doors, her spine poker straight, her face empty of the animation she'd shown earlier, her incredible blue eyes staring sightlessly ahead.

Crossing the floor, he dropped down beside her. "Brianna, what are you doing out here?"

"Waiting for you," she replied, the chill in her voice enough to send the temperature plummeting.

Nice going, Giannakis, he thought ruefully. She knocks herself out looking gorgeous for a fancy ball she never really wanted to attend in the first place, and you leave her to fend for herself among a bunch of strangers. "Look, I'm sorry I abandoned you, sweetheart. It was unavoidable, but

I'm here now, and the night's still young. Would you like to dance?"

"No," she said flatly. "I would like to leave."

"Okay…" Baffled, he observed her more closely. He didn't particularly want to stay, either. He wanted to be alone with her, and celebrate in private news that was better than anything they could have hoped for. But he didn't have to be a rocket scientist to recognize that at this point, and for reasons he couldn't begin to fathom, she was in no mood to listen to anything he might say, let alone celebrate with him. "Brianna, what's happened? Are you not feeling well? Has someone said something to upset you?"

A brittle laugh escaped her, but her eyes, he noticed, were suddenly sheened in tears.

"Never mind," he said hastily. "Talking can wait. Let's get out of here."

Ignoring the way she shied away from him as if he had the plague, he slipped his arm around her waist and propelled her outside, and down the wide front steps to the porte-cochere where the parking valets waited. During the few minutes it took for his car to be brought round, he kept hold of her. He might as well have been hugging a marble statue.

He ushered her into the car as if she were made of china, so persuasively concerned, so convincingly tender, that it was all Brianna could do not strike out blindly and rake her nails down his beautiful, deceiving face. Instead she huddled in her seat, as far away from him as she could possibly get. Turning to the window, she stared blindly out, seeing nothing as he drove through the streets of Kifissia.

Hearing nothing but Noelle's concise summation of a situation she herself hadn't begun to guess.

…there were no guarantees…you knew from the outset the best possible candidate is always a sibling…if you and Brianna were to have a baby…

And underscoring that elegant English accent, Dimitrios's dark exotic voice and her own rash, impassioned response.

…I have no profilaktiko….

…I don't care…I want to have your baby….

Furtively she wiped at the lone tear trickling down her face. He'd hurt her before, but never like this. She felt emotionally bruised, battered and betrayed. Flayed to the bone by his deception, every loving touch, every passionate encounter, every whispered endearment exposed for the lies they were. It had all been a big sham from start to finish. He'd bamboozled her into believing he loved her, when all he really wanted was to use her.

Except, she realized with another cold sense of shock, he'd never actually used the word *love*. Never once come right out and said, "I love you." Rather, he'd told her he wanted her and he needed her. And now she knew why. Knew it had nothing to do with love and everything to do with expedience.

They'd left the lights of the city behind and were headed down the eastern slopes of Mount Penteli when he finally spoke, and this time he sounded every bit as hard and callous as she now knew him to be. "Okay, Brianna, I've had about enough of the silent treatment. I can't fix the problem if I don't know what it is, so how about spelling it out for me?"

Struggling to keep her voice steady, she said, "There is no problem. I have decided I can't marry you, that's all."

"I see. And why is that?" he inquired evenly.

"Because I don't want a husband who sees me only as a means to an end."

"What the devil are you talking about?"

Tired of the games, she said, "I followed you tonight, when you went off with Noelle. I heard her tell you I didn't measure up as a donor for Poppy."

"Is that what this is all about?" He actually had the gall to laugh. "Sweetheart, it's not a question of your not measuring up, it's—"

"A question of how soon you can get me pregnant. Yes, I heard that, too.

"What?" There was no laughter this time, just well-feigned incredulity, which she didn't buy for a second.

"'The ideal donor is always a sibling,'" she recited in her best imitation of Noelle's precise English diction.

"And?"

"And I'm the only woman still alive who can give you a child whose DNA will match Poppy's. If that's all you ever wanted from me, why didn't you just say so in the first place, and spare us both this masquerade?"

By then they'd reached the coast and were just minutes away from the villa. "Let me get this straight," he said, slowing to let a cat cross the road. "You can't donate bone marrow to Poppy, but if you have my baby, we can use it in your place, instead?"

"That's right. I should be wearing your ring through my nose, not on my finger."

He turned into the drive, parked at the front door and killed the engine, but made no move to get out of the car. Instead he hefted the keys in his palm and stared through the darkened windshield at the moonlit walls of the house.

"Whatever happened to the idea of truth and trust between us, Brianna? You're the only woman I've ever loved. Why isn't that enough for you?"

"Because your idea of love isn't the same as mine. As for truth and trust, they're just a couple of five-letter words you throw into the mix whenever you think they might get you what you want."

"I wanted you," he said harshly. "I thought we had the ideal recipe for marital bliss. Sexual electricity, desire, passion, yearning—everything we had before, except *this* time, it was better because we believed in one another. And all the time, the same vital ingredient was missing. You never could quite bring yourself to accept that what we had was real. I'm surprised you're still here. Usually you don't bother to stop long enough to say why, before you decide to cut and run."

"Don't worry. I'll be gone tomorrow."

"Thanks for the warning. I'll try to come up with an explanation for Poppy when she asks about you."

"I won't desert Poppy. I love her dearly and I'd do anything in my power to make her well. And now, if you'll excuse me, I have some packing to do. I'll let you know which hotel I'm at, in case you need to reach me."

She flung open the car door, but before she could escape, he wrenched her back and pinned her to the seat. "Oh, no, you don't!" he snarled. "This is one time you'll stay and listen."

"I don't want to hear anything you have to say."

"I don't care! First, I have a piece of advice you'd do well to heed. The next time you decide to eavesdrop on someone else's conversation, do yourself a favor and make sure you listen in on everything before you leap to unwarranted conclusions."

"Thank you so much," she said acidly. "Anything else you feel compelled to share?"

"Yes," he replied. "I am not Poppy's biological father."

It was her turn to stare in disbelief. "What did you say?"

"I am not Poppy's biological father, I have no idea who is, and nor do I care. She is my daughter in every way that matters, and I would give my life for her. *That,* Brianna, is how I define love."

"But Noelle said—"

"That even if you and I were to have a child solely for the purpose of harvesting his or her stem cells, it wouldn't necessarily help Poppy and that, of course, is something I've known since the day I tested as a possible donor myself, and discovered not only that I wasn't a match but also that there was no way I could possibly be her biological parent. So you see, my dear, my proposal to you was never contingent on your acting as a brood mare. Oh, yes, and one last thing—I learned tonight that we've found an unrelated donor who's a perfect match for Poppy. That was the other piece of news Noelle wanted to convey. She'd have told both of us yesterday, when she also learned of your unsuitability. But rather than risk a second disappointment, she waited until she received absolute confirmation that the other person, a twenty-three-year-old medical student from Chile, is available. Apparently, he is and will be here on Tuesday."

He released her then and flung himself back in his seat. "You may leave now. Don't let me keep you from your packing."

CHAPTER TWELVE

THE house was silent as a tomb. Creeping up the stairs, Brianna let herself into her room and slumped onto the love seat. She wished she could cry. But she had nothing left inside. No tears, no hope and no heart. She and Dimitrios were finally over. Done. She'd heard the absolute contempt in his voice. Seen it in his face. Felt it in his touch.

Slowly, she pulled off his ring and placed it on the coffee table. She couldn't blame Cecily for this latest falling out. This time it was all her own fault. She'd been the one who lacked faith, and if she was as honest with herself as she'd told him he should have been with her, she'd admit she'd been second-guessing herself and him from the day she arrived. Now the only thing left for her to do was leave with dignity.

Or was it? Was anything ever really over as long as a person had life and the will to fight?

You're the only woman I've ever loved, he'd said, not in a moment of passion, but with anger fueling his words. Wasn't that reason enough not to give up on the best thing that had ever happened to her?

She had no answers, and knew only that if she wanted to find any, she had to put some distance between him and her. As long as his room was just across the hall from hers, it would be too easy to go to him. She knew what the outcome would be if she did: the same as it had always been with them. A matter of body over mind, of the driving hunger of the flesh silencing the saner voice of reason.

And they had made enough mistakes. There were only so many times that a man and a woman could keep trying to mend what was broken between them before all they had left were the tattered remains of what had once been beautiful but was now ruined past recognition.

Kicking off her satin dancing shoes, she stripped away her pretty gown and changed into a light cotton shift and sandals.

Opening her door, she saw a strip of light showing under his. Otherwise, the house lay in darkness. Quietly she stole along the upper landing, down the stairs and out into the sweet night air of early June. When she reached the gates, she turned left, away from Rafina, which lay to the north, and toward the village a few kilometers in the opposite direction.

Dimitrios ripped off his bow tie and yanked the top two studs of his dress shirt undone. Still he felt choked—on anger, on regret, on pride. Why couldn't she simply have come to him and asked him to explain, instead of automatically believing the worst of him? He thought they'd moved beyond that. Instead it seemed nothing he did would ever really redeem him in her eyes. At the first hint of trouble, he became again the man she believed had betrayed her before.

Well, to hell with her! He was tired of proving himself worthy of her love. Let her run back to her precious career.

He'd lived without her once before; he could do so again. He had his daughter, his loyal household staff, perhaps his mother. And if he needed a willing body once in a while, there were women enough who'd be glad to warm his bed.

But would they be enough to make him forget her, or would it always be *her* face he saw in his mind's eye, *her* body he thought of as he lost himself in some stranger whose name he'd have forgotten by morning? How long before the day came that he didn't think of her, or miss her with an ache that never went away?

Never. She was in his blood, a fatal, magnificent disease. And the cure he'd spend the rest of his life seeking, if he let her slip through his fingers a second time.

He couldn't let it happen. If he had to get down on his knees and plead with her to stay, he'd do it, and pride be damned.

Stepping out of his room, he saw a strip of light showing under her door. No time like the present, he decided. Tomorrow might be too late. Crossing the hall, he tapped gently, and when he received no reply, he turned the knob and went in.

He knew then why she hadn't answered. The room was empty.

Although it was well after midnight, the village teemed with life. Music and light spilled from open windows into the warm Mediterranean night. Children played in the street, dogs barked, babies cried. Men and women, husbands and wives, laughed and loved and scolded, daring to wring every last drop of flavor from life because it was worth it and in the end, the good balanced out the bad.

The four-kilometer walk had cleared Brianna's mind and swept away the anger and confusion. Standing now, a solitary spectator on the fringe of the scene, she knew that *this* was what she wanted. Not perfection. Not a trouble-free future with no dark clouds. She wanted the security of knowing she could be angry sometimes; of loving deeply enough to forgive; of trusting enough to believe what she and Dimitrios shared was strong enough to survive, not because they'd ironed out all their differences, but despite the fact that they didn't always see eye to eye.

She wanted all the rich flavors, all the subtle textures that made up a marriage. The sweet and the not-so-sweet. The rough and the smooth. She wanted him because without him, she was nothing. She needed him because she loved him. And there in that dusty road, surrounded by strangers, she at last realized what she had to do to keep him. She had to risk it all to have him.

She'd turned to go back the way she'd come, when the screech of brakes split the night. Parents scooped their children out of the path of impending danger and retreated to the safety of their doorways. But the speeding car had stopped at the far end of the road and a tall, familiar figure was climbing out.

A wonderful lightness filled her then, and slowly she started toward him. Then suddenly she was running and so was he, and they met in a breathless meshing of arms and mouths, and she was crying helplessly, and he was telling her he was sorry, that it was all his fault and he should have explained about Poppy sooner and he was nothing but a big, arrogant Greek fool with too much pride and not enough brains, and if she ever took off like that again without telling him where she was going, he'd put her over his knee.

Eventually the tumult passed and they drew apart. He took a deep breath and so did she. "Let's go home," he said, surely the sweetest words in the world.

"Yes," she said. "Please."

The next second he was carrying her to the car, while everyone in the village clapped and whistled, and the bouzouki music started up again, loud and exuberant.

"I thought I'd lost you," he whispered, holding her so tight she could hardly breathe. "When I saw you'd gone…Brianna, I once told you I don't beg, but I'm begging now. Don't leave me. Don't give up on us."

She wrapped her arms around his neck. "I won't," she told him, smiling through her tears. "Never again. I was coming back to tell you so, but then you were here and…"

"And I'm never letting you out of my sight again. If you want Poppy, you have to take me, as well. We're a package deal."

"And a bargain at half the price. I know that now."

They sat on the love seat in her room, and the first thing he did was slide the ring back on her finger. "Just to let the rest of the world know you're taken," he said, settling back with his arm around her.

After that, they talked far into the small hours of the night, hours longer than they'd ever done before. About how, after they'd made love by the pool after the garden party, he'd almost told her about Poppy not being his bio-logical child, and how later, he was glad he'd kept quiet because he'd tarnished Cecily's memory enough and he wanted to leave Brianna with some of her illusions intact.

About Poppy and what she faced in the coming months. About finally closing the door on the past. About how much they'd both always craved marriage and children and family. And most important of all, about priorities.

"I agree," he admitted, when she said the wedding should be put on hold. "As long as we're together, it can wait until everything else is sorted out. Assuming the transplant does go ahead without any complications, Poppy's facing a lengthy recuperation."

"There's also the small matter of you and your father getting past your differences and reaching some sort of truce. This ridiculous feud has gone on long enough, and you have to know how hard it is on your mother. Even though you and she have reconciled, she's still caught in the middle. Put an end to it, Dimitrios, for everyone's sake. You made your point. He got the message. Can't you please leave it at that and just sit down with him, man to man, and try to heal the wounds?"

"Hmm." He eyed her gloomily. "Are you going to make a habit of always being right?"

"Only when it can't be avoided," she said, snuggling deeper into the curve of his arm. "Which'll probably be most of the time."

She felt the laughter rumble deep in his chest. "Is there anything else I should know?"

"Just that I love you, I always have, and that will never change."

"That's all I ask," he murmured against her hair, and took her to bed to seal their bargain.

The passion consumed them, as it always had, but in its wake came a new serenity, a sense of absolute certainty that while trouble and sorrow might touch their tomorrow, their love would do more than survive. It would emerge triumphant.

She was where she belonged. At his side.

EPILOGUE

A COLD February rain dripped from the palm trees, but inside the villa walls, fires chased away the chill of the winter afternoon, and the scent of gardenias filled the rooms with summer.

In her bedroom Brianna fixed the coronet of rosebuds more securely in Poppy's hair, which had grown back thicker and more lustrous than ever after her chemotherapy. "You look adorable, my angel."

Poppy twirled before the mirror, sending the skirt of her pale-pink flower girl's dress flaring around her ankles. "I'm not an angel, I'm a princess."

Brianna exchanged a smiling glance with Hermione. "She's a miracle."

"One of many lately," Hermione replied fondly, "and I give thanks for them every day. You've done more than fill my son's life with love and happiness, Brianna. You've given me back my family. I never thought to see the day that Mihalis would stand up as best man for Dimitrios at his wedding." She dabbed at her eyes and gave a little laugh. "Dear me, I promised myself I wouldn't cry today, and look at me. I'm not even waiting for the ceremony to begin before I get started."

"Don't," Brianna begged. "You'll get me going, too, and we've shed enough tears in the past eight months to last us a lifetime."

Even on this, the happiest day of her life so far, the specter of those dark days after the transplant still haunted her. She still sometimes woke up in the middle of the night, terrified and soaked in sweat, tears streaming down her face, caught again in the nightmare of agony of watching Poppy suffer the nausea, the fever, the pain and debilitating weakness that were part and parcel of the cure.

She'd never forget the suspense of waiting for signs that the new bone marrow had migrated and was beginning to produce normal blood cells. For weeks on end, every time the phone rang, she and Dimitrios would freeze, fearing the worst.

The emotional highs and lows, the unending stress, had almost killed them. Yet it had made them stronger, too. "If we can survive this," he'd often said, "we can survive anything."

But whoever first said God never closed a door without first opening a window, had it right. One day she'd looked up from her post with Dimitrios beside Poppy's hospital crib, and seen Mihalis standing with Hermione on the other side of the observation window, his chin quivering and tears rolling down his face. Dimitrios had been a rock until then, but at that, he'd buried his face in his hands and his whole body had shaken with great, heaving sobs.

Heavens, yes. They'd all cried enough tears to fill a lake. They didn't need more today.

Fortunately, Carter knocked on the door just then, timing his arrival to prevent a complete emotional meltdown. "You're running late, ladies, and the groom's growing impatient."

"We're ready," Hermione said, letting him in. "Come along, Poppy, my darling. We'll go ahead and give Mommy Brianna a moment to collect herself."

Alone with Carter, Brianna managed a smile. "Thank you for being here, Carter."

"Try keeping me away! You're a picture, you know that? And I'm a damn fool to be giving away the best client I ever had. I hope that Greek god you're so crazy about realizes how lucky he is."

"We're both lucky," she said tremulously. "And you're a lot more than just my former agent, Carter. You've been my best friend for more years than I care to count, and I don't know how I'll ever repay you for all you've done for me."

"I do," he said, kissing her cheek. "Be happy. That's payment enough for me."

"You've got the rings?"

"Right here." His father patted his pocket, then cleared his throat and stepped closer. "Just wanted to say…well, I'm here and you're here and…well, that young woman upstairs, she's all right. You're both all right, and I'm…well, I'm here. If you need me. Which you probably don't."

"I need you, Dad," he said. "I always have."

"Huh. Well, it took some doing. You're a stubborn cuss when you put your mind to it, just like me, but— Stop sweating. You're making me nervous."

Dimitrios buried a grin.

A murmur from the sixty friends and associates filling

the hall had him looking up. His mother was coming down the stairs, holding his daughter by the hand, and suddenly he was so choked with emotion he could hardly swallow. The pale, listless little waif he'd worried about and fretted over for so long had turned into a sweetly rounded sprite whose cheeks were as pink as the rosebuds in her hair.

"Cut it out," his father muttered brokenly. "The men in this family don't cry in public."

Behind him, all the people who'd helped him come to this day—Erika and Alexio, Noelle and everyone else who'd given his daughter back her life, friends he hadn't known he had until he needed them and they were there for him—every last one rose from their ribbon-festooned chairs as the harpist tucked in the lee of the curving staircase segued from Debussy's "Claire de Lune," to Wagner's "Bridal Chorus."

And suddenly, there she was, his bride, his Brianna, descending the stairs with the innate grace she brought to everything she did, her hand resting lightly on Carter's arm, her ivory silk gown billowing around her, her lovely face shadowed by a gossamer veil.

He'd been wrong to think she'd lose her looks with age. Wrong to believe she'd have nothing left. Hers was a beauty carved from love, from compassion and deep generosity of spirit. It would cloak her features with softness, illuminate her from within, when she was old and gray and youth was but a memory. She would always be a beauty. His beauty, his life.

She was closer now, covering the last few meters that separated her from him, carving a graceful path through the rose petals Poppy was flinging enthusiastically before her.

He squared his shoulders and held out his hand. Her

fingers closed around his, warm and firm and sure. His father was crying; his mother, too. But Brianna was radiant, her smile for him alone.

He was home at last.

THE MARAKAIOS
BABY

KATE HEWITT

To Lauren, Thank you for your many
years of friendship. Love, K.

CHAPTER ONE

'WILL YOU MARRY ME?'

The question seemed to bounce off the walls and echo through the room as Marguerite Ferrars stared in shock at the face of the man who had asked the question—her lover, Leonidas Marakaios.

He gazed at her with a faint half-smile quirking his lips, his eyebrows slightly raised. In his hand he held a small black velvet box, and the solitaire diamond of who knew how many carats inside sparkled with quiet sophistication.

'Margo?'

His voice was lilting, teasing; he thought she was silent because she was so surprised. But, while that was true, she felt something else as well. Appalled. *Terrified.*

She'd never expected this—never thought that charismatic playboy Leo would think of *marriage.* A lifetime commitment, a life—and love—you could lose. And she knew the searing pain of losing someone—the way it left you breathless and gasping, waking up in the night, your face awash in tears, even years later…

The moment stretched on too long, and still she said nothing. She couldn't. Because she didn't dare say yes and yet no seemed just as impossible. Leo Marakaios was not a man who accepted refusal. Rejection.

She watched as a slight frown pulled his eyebrows together and he withdrew the hand holding the open velvet box to rest it in his lap.

'Leo…' she began finally, helplessly—because how could she tell this impossibly arrogant, handsome, charismatic man no? And yet she had to. Of course she had to.

'I didn't think this would be *that* much of a surprise,' he said, his voice holding only a remnant of lightness now.

She felt a surge of something close to anger, which was almost a relief. 'Didn't you? We've never had the kind of relationship that…'

'That what?' He arched an eyebrow, the gesture caught between wryness and disdain.

She could feel him withdrawing, and while she knew she should be glad, she felt only a deep, wrenching sorrow. This wasn't what she'd wanted. But she didn't—couldn't—want marriage either. Couldn't let someone matter that much.

'That…led somewhere,' she finished, and he closed the box with a snap, his expression turning so terribly cold.

'I see.'

Words stuck in her throat—the answer she knew she had to give yet somehow couldn't make herself say. 'Leo, we've never even talked about the future.'

'We've been together for two years,' he returned. 'I think it's reasonable to assume it was *going somewhere*.'

His voice held a deliberate edge, and his eyes were blazing silver fire. Or maybe ice, for he looked so cold now—even contemptuous. And moments ago he'd been asking to marry her. It almost seemed laughable.

'Together for two years,' Margo allowed, determined to stay reasonable, 'but we've hardly had what most people would call a "normal" relationship. We've met in strange cities, in restaurants and hotels—'

'Which is how you wanted it.'

'And how you wanted it too. It was an *affair*, Leo. A—a fling.'

'A two-year fling.'

She rose from her chair, agitated now, and paced in front of the picture window that overlooked the Île de la Cité. It was so strange and unsettling to have Leo here in her apartment, her sanctuary, when he'd never come to her home before. Restaurants and hotels, yes—anonymous places for emotionless no-strings sex…that was what they'd *agreed*. That was all she could let herself have.

The risk of trying for more was simply too great. She knew what it was like to lose everything—even your own soul. She couldn't go through that again. She *wouldn't*.

Not even for Leo.

'You seem upset,' Leo remarked tonelessly.

'I just didn't expect this.'

'As it happens, neither did I.'

He rose from where he'd been sitting, on the damask settee she'd upholstered herself, his tall, rangy figure seeming to fill the cosy space of her sitting room. He looked wrong here, somehow, amidst all her things—her throw pillows and porcelain ornaments; he was too big, too dark, too powerful…like a tiger pacing the cage of a kitten.

'I thought most women wanted to get married,' he remarked.

She turned on him then, another surge of anger making her feel strong. 'What a ridiculous, sexist assumption! And I, in any case, am *not* "most women".'

'No,' Leo agreed silkily. 'You're not.'

His eyes blazed with intent then—an intent that made Margo's breath catch in her chest.

The sexual chemistry between them had been instantaneous—electric. She remembered catching sight of him in a hotel bar in Milan two years ago. She'd been nursing

a single glass of white wine while she went over her notes
for the next day's meeting. He'd strolled over to the bar
and slid onto the stool next to hers, and the little hairs on
the back of her neck had prickled. She'd felt as if she were
finally coming alive.

She'd gone back with him to his room that night. It had
been so unlike her—she'd always kept herself apart, her
heart on ice. In her twenty-nine years she'd had only two
lovers before Leo, both of them lamentably forgettable.
Neither of those men had affected her the way Leo did—
and not just physically.

From that first night he'd reached a place inside her
she'd thought numb, dead. He'd brought her back to life.
And while she'd known it was dangerous she'd stayed with
him, because the thought of *not* being with Leo was worse.

Except now that was a reality. She'd thought an affair
with Leo would be safe, that he would never ask more of
her than she was prepared to give. But here he was asking for marriage, a lifetime, and her response was bone-
deep terror.

Which was why she could not accept his proposal.

Except she had a terrible and yet thrilling certainty that
he had a different proposal in mind now, as he came towards her, his gaze turning hooded and sleepy even though
that lithe, powerful body she knew almost as well as her
own was taut with suppressed energy and tension.

She licked her lips, felt the insistent thud of her heart,
the stirring of blood in her veins. Even now her body
yearned for him.

'Leo…'

'You surprise me, Margo.'

She gave a little shake of her head. 'You're the one who
surprised *me*.'

'Clearly. But I thought you'd be pleased. Don't you want to get married?'

He sounded so reasonable, but she saw a certain calculation in his eyes, and he ran one hand up and down her bare arm, so gooseflesh broke out in the wake of his touch.

'No.'

'Why not?'

His easy, interested tone jarred with the fingers he continued to run up and down her arm, and with that sleepy, knowing gaze.

'I'm a career woman, Leo—'

'You can be a *married* career woman, Margo. This is the twenty-first century, after all.'

'Oh? And how would that work, exactly? You live in central Greece—the middle of nowhere. How am I supposed to work from there?'

For a second she thought she saw a gleam of something like triumph in his eyes, but then it sparked out and he gave a negligent shrug of his shoulders. 'You could commute. The flight from Athens to Paris is only a few hours.'

'Commute? Are you serious?'

'We could work something out, Margo, if that's all that's stopping you.'

There was a note of challenge in his voice, and she realised then what he was doing. Leonidas Marakaios was a powerful and persuasive man. He was CEO of the Marakaios Enterprises, a company that had started with a few olive groves and a cold press and was now a multibillion dollar company—a man of the world who was used to getting what he wanted. And he wanted her. So here he was, breaking down her defences, discarding her arguments. And the trouble was she was so weak, so tempted, that it might actually work.

She turned away from him to take a few steadying

breaths without him seeing how unsettled she was. In the darkness of the window she could see her reflection: a too pale face, wide eyes, and a tumble of long dark brown hair that fell nearly to her waist.

When Leo had shown up twenty minutes ago she'd been in yoga pants and a faded tee shirt, her face without a lick of make-up, her hair down. She'd been silently appalled. She'd always been careful that he saw only the woman she wanted him to—the woman the world saw: sexy, chic, professional, a little bit distant, a little bit cool. All their meetings had been stage-managed affairs; she'd swept into a restaurant or hotel room in full make-up, a sexy little negligee in her bag, insouciant and secure.

He'd never seen her like this: vulnerable, without the mask of make-up, the armour of designer clothes. He'd never seen her agitated and uncertain, her *savoir-faire* slipping from her fingers.

'Margo,' Leo said quietly. 'Tell me the real reason.'

Another quick breath, buoying inside her lungs. 'I told you, Leo. I don't want marriage or what it entails. The whole housewife routine bores me to death.' She made her voice cold—careless, even.

Steeling herself, she turned around to face him and nearly flinched at the careful consideration in his eyes. She had a horrible feeling she wasn't fooling him at all.

'I just said you don't need to be a housewife. Do you think I want to change you completely?'

'You don't even know me, Leo, not really.'

He took a step towards her, and again she saw that intent in his eyes, felt an answering flare inside her. She had, she realised, just given him a challenge.

'Are you sure about that?'

'I'm not talking about sex.'

'What don't I know, then?' He spread his hands wide, his eyebrows raised. 'Tell me.'

'It's not that simple.'

'Because you don't want it to be. I *know* you, Margo. I know your feet get cold in the middle of the night and you tuck them between my legs to keep them warm. I know you like marshmallows even though you pretend you don't eat any sweets.'

She almost laughed at that. 'How do you know about the marshmallows?' Her dirty little secret, when it seemed as if every other woman in Paris was stick-thin and ate only lettuce leaves and drank black coffee.

'I found a little bag of them in your handbag once.'

'You shouldn't have been looking through my things.'

'I was fetching your reading glasses for you, if you remember.'

She shook her head—an instinctive response, because all those little details that he'd lobbed at her like well-aimed missiles were making her realise how intimate her relationship with Leo really had been. She'd thought she'd kept her distance, armoured herself—the elegant Marguerite Ferrars, keeping their assignations in anonymous places. But in truth reality had seeped through. Emotion had too, as well as affection, with the glasses and the marshmallows and the cold feet. Little signs of how close they'd become, how much he'd begun to mean to her.

And she saw all too clearly how he would chip away at her defences now—how he would seduce her with knowing words and touches until she'd say yes. Of course she'd say yes. Because she was already more than halfway to loving him.

For a second—no more—Margo thought about actually accepting his proposal. Living a life she'd never thought to have, had made herself never want. A life of happiness but also of terrible risk. Risk of loss, of hurt, of heartbreak. Of coming apart so she'd never put the pieces of her soul back together again.

Reality returned in a cold rush and she shook her head. 'No, Leo.'

That faint smile had returned, although his eyes looked hard. 'Just like that?'

'Just like that.'

'You don't think I—*we*—deserve more explanation?'

'Not particularly.' She'd made her voice indifferent, maybe too much, because anger flashed in his eyes, turning the silver to grey.

He cocked his head, his gaze sweeping slowly over her. 'I think you're hiding something from me.'

She gave a scoffing laugh. 'You would.'

'What is that supposed to mean?'

'You can't believe I'm actually turning you down, can you?' The words tumbled out of her, fuelled by both anger and fear. 'You—the Lothario who has had half the single women in Europe.'

'I wouldn't go quite that far. Forty per cent, maybe.'

There was the charm, almost causing her to lose that needed edge of fury, to smile. 'No woman has ever resisted you.'

'You didn't,' he pointed out, with what Margo knew was deceptive mildness.

'Because I wanted a fling,' she declared defiantly. 'Sex without strings.'

'We never actually said—'

'Oh, but we did, Leo. Don't you remember that first conversation? We set out the rules right then.'

She saw a glimmer of acknowledgement in his eyes, and his mouth hardened into a thin line.

It had been an elaborate dance of words, their talk of

business concerns and obligations, veiled references to other places, other people—every careful remark setting out just what their affair would and wouldn't be. Both of them, Margo had thought, had been clear about their desire for a commitment-free relationship.

'I didn't think you wanted to get married,' she said.

Leo shrugged. 'I decided I did.'

'But you didn't at the beginning, when we met. You weren't interested then.' She'd felt his innate sense of distance and caution, the same as her own. They had, she'd thought, been speaking the same language, giving the code words for no commitment, no love, no fairytales.

'People change, Margo. I'm thirty-two. You're twenty-nine. Of course I'd think of settling down…starting a family.'

Something clanged hard inside her; she felt as if someone had pulled the chair out from under her and she'd fallen right onto the floor.

'Well, then, that's where we differ, Leo,' she stated, her voice thankfully cool. 'I don't want children.'

His eyebrows drew together at that. 'Ever?'

'Ever.'

He stared at her for a long, considering moment. 'You're scared.'

'Stop telling me what I feel,' she snapped, raising her voice to hide its tremble. 'And get over yourself. I'm not scared. I just don't want what you want. I don't want to marry you.' She took a breath, and then plunged on recklessly. 'I don't love you.'

He tensed slightly, almost as if her words had hurt him, and then he shrugged. 'I don't love *you*. But there are better bases for a marriage than that ephemeral emotion.'

'Such as?'

'Common goals—'

'How romantic you are,' she mocked.

'Did you want more romance? Would that have made a difference?'

'No!'

'Then I'm glad I didn't wine and dine you at Gavroche, as I was considering, and propose in front of a crowd.'

He spoke lightly enough, and yet she still heard an edge to his voice.

'So am I,' she answered, and held her ground as he took a step towards her. She could feel the heat rolling off him, felt herself instinctively sway towards him. She stopped herself, holding herself rigid, refusing to yield even in that small way.

'So this is it?' he said softly, his voice no more than a breath that feathered her face. His silvery gaze roved over her, seeming to steal right inside her. 'This is goodbye?'

'Yes.' She spoke firmly, but he must have seen something in her face, for he cupped her cheek, ran a thumb over her parted lips.

'You're so very sure?' he whispered, and she forced herself to stare at him, not to show anything in her face.

'Yes.'

He dropped his hand from her face to her breast, cupping its fullness, running his thumb over the taut peak. She shuddered; she couldn't help it. He'd always affected her that way, right from the beginning. A single, simple touch lit a flame inside her.

'You don't seem sure,' he murmured.

'We have chemistry, Leo, that's all.' She forced the words out past the desire that was sweeping through her, leaving nothing but need in its wake.

'Chemistry is a powerful thing.'

He slid his hand down to her waist, his fingers splaying across her hip. Sensation leapt to life inside her, low down, sparks shooting through her belly.

'It's not enough,' she said through gritted teeth.

She ached for him to move his hand lower, to touch her with the knowing expertise her body had once revelled in. Still she didn't move, and neither did Leo.

'Not enough?' he queried softly. 'So you want love, then?'

'Not with you.'

He stilled, and she made herself go on—say the words she knew would hurt them both and turn him from her for ever. She had to…she couldn't risk him breaking down any more of her defences. She couldn't risk, full stop.

'I don't love you, Leo, and I never will. Frankly, you were just a fling—something to while away the time. I never intended for it to be *serious*.' She let out a laugh, sharp and high, as Leo pulled back his hand from her hip. 'Honestly—a *proposal*?' She made herself continue. 'It's almost funny… Because I'd actually been planning to end it when we met in Rome next week.' She took a quick breath and went on recklessly. 'The truth is, I'm seeing someone else.'

He stared at her for a long, taut moment. A muscle flickered in his jaw, but that was all. 'How long?' he finally asked, the two words bitten off and spat out.

She shrugged. 'A couple of months.'

'*Months*—?'

'I didn't think we were exclusive.'

'I've always been faithful to you,' he said in a low voice.

'I never asked you to be,' she replied with another shrug.

She could hardly believe she was actually fooling him—didn't he see how she trembled? And yet she knew he was taken in. She saw it in the way everything in him had gone dangerously still.

Then a cold little smile played about his mouth.

'Well, then, this really is goodbye,' he said, and before she could answer he pulled her towards him and kissed her.

She hadn't been expecting it, the sudden press of his mouth on hers, knowing and sure, a delicious onslaught that had her insides flaring white-hot even as her mind scrambled frantically to resist.

But Leo had always been impossible to resist, and never more so than now, when he was utterly, ruthlessly determined to make her respond to him. His tongue slid inside her mouth as his hands spanned her waist, fitting her to his muscled body perfectly.

She kissed him back, gave herself up to the rush of sensations that left her dizzy with longing. The feel of Leo's hands on her body was so intense it almost hurt—like touching a raw nerve. He slid his hands under her tee shirt, discarding the flimsy bit of cotton with ease. And then her yoga pants were gone too. She kicked them off, needing to be naked, too enflamed by desire to feel either exposed or ashamed as she stood before him, utterly bare, her breath coming in pants and gulps.

Leo stood in front of her and slowly unbuttoned his shirt. She saw a predatory gleam in his eyes, but even that could not cool her desire. Was this his revenge? His punishment? Or simply his proof that she desired him still? Whatever it was, she'd take it. She'd welcome it. Because she knew it would be the last time she'd hold him in her arms, feel him inside her.

He shrugged his shirt off. The crisp white cotton slid off his shoulders, revealing his taut six-pack abs, the sprinkling of dark hair that veed towards his trousers. With a snick of leather he undid his belt and then kicked off his trousers, and he too was naked.

He came towards her, taking her in his arms in a way

that was possessive rather than sensual. When he kissed
her she felt branded. Perhaps she always would.

He backed her towards the window, so her back was
against the cold glass, and then without a single murmur
or caress he drove inside her.

Even so she was ready for him, her body expanding
to fit around his length. She wrapped her legs around his
waist and pulled him inside her even more deeply, her head
thrown back against the glass so she felt suspended between this world and the next, caught in a single moment
of memory and desire.

The tension and pressure built inside her, a tornado that
took over her senses, and at its dizzying peak Leo took
her face in his hands and looked her straight in the eyes.

'You won't forget me,' he said, and it was a declara-
tion of certainty, a curse, because she knew he was right.

Then, as her climax crashed over her, he shuddered into
her and withdrew, leaving her trembling and weak-kneed
against the window. She watched, dazed and numb, as he
dressed silently. She could not form a single sentence, not
even a word.

She watched him walk to the door. He didn't speak,
didn't even look back. The door closed with a quiet, final-
sounding click. Slowly she sank to the floor, clutching her
knees to her chest as the aftershocks of her climax still
shuddered through her.

Leo was gone.

CHAPTER TWO

LEO STRODE FROM Margo's apartment, his body still shuddering from their lovemaking—but no, he couldn't call it that. *Never* that.

With one abrupt movement he lobbed the little velvet box into the nearest bin. A foolish waste, perhaps, but he couldn't bear to look at that wretched ring for another moment. He couldn't stand the thought of it even being in his pocket.

He drew a deep breath and raked a hand through his hair, willing back the emotion that had nearly overwhelmed him in Margo's apartment. All of it. She was out of his life. He need never think of her again.

It wasn't as if he'd loved her, he reminded himself. Margo had been right about that. He had liked her, yes, and they'd certainly shared an explosive sexual chemistry. She'd seemed the obvious choice when he'd decided it was time he married.

Six months ago, just after their mother's death, his brother Antonios had resigned as CEO of Marakaios Enterprises and Leo had taken his place. It was what Leo had wanted his whole life, what he had striven for as a young man, working for the father who had never even noticed him. Who had chosen Antonios instead of him, again and again.

But he was over that; he'd made peace with Antonios, and his father had been dead for ten years. His mother too was gone now, and all of it together had made him want to marry, to start a family, create his own dynasty.

But Margo doesn't even want children.

Why hadn't he known that? Why hadn't he realised she was so faithless, so unscrupulous? *Theos*, she'd been *cheating* on him. He could hardly credit it; they'd seen each other every week or two at least, and their encounters had always been intense. But she had no reason to lie about such a thing.

And when he thought of how he'd asked her to marry him, how he'd tried to convince her, persuade her with gentle reason and understanding because he hadn't been able to believe she didn't want him... Leo closed his eyes, cringing with the shame of it.

Well, no more. He wouldn't marry. Or if he did it would simply be for a child. He would not engage his emotions, would not seek anything greater than the most basic of physical transactions. And he would never see Margo again, Margo of the cold feet and the marshmallows...

His face twisted with regret before he ironed out his features and strode on into the night.

Margo's stomach lurched for the third time that morning and she pressed one hand against her middle, closing her eyes and taking a deep breath. This stomach bug was both insistent and annoying. She'd been feeling nauseous for over a week, although she'd thankfully never actually been sick.

'Are you all right?'

Margo looked up to see Sophie, her colleague and fellow buyer at Paris's exclusive department store Achat, frowning at her.

They'd worked together for six years, starting as interns, Sophie with her freshly minted college degree and Margo doing it the hard way, having worked on the shop floor since she was sixteen. They'd both moved up to being assistants, and now they were buyers in their own right. Margo was in charge of the home department; Sophie covered accessories. Both of them were completely dedicated to their jobs.

'I'm fine. I've just been feeling a little sick lately.'

Sophie raised her eyebrows, a teasing smile playing about her mouth. 'If it was anyone but you I'd be worried.'

'What is *that* supposed to mean?' Margo asked, a note of irritability creeping into her voice. She had been out of sorts for a month now, ever since Leo had left her alone and aching.

It was for the best—it had to be—but she couldn't keep herself from feeling the hurt. The emptiness.

'I mean,' Sophie answered, 'that I'd think you were pregnant. But you can't be.'

'Of course I'm not,' Margo answered sharply.

Sophie knew her stance on relationships and children: one night over a bottle of wine they'd each confided their intention to have single, solitary, *safe* lives. At least that was how Margo had viewed it; she suspected Sophie just wanted to play the field.

'I'm on the mini-pill,' she stated, and Sophie raised her eyebrows.

'You haven't forgotten to take it, then?'

'No, never.'

Margo frowned at her computer screen and the image there of a selection of silk throw pillows, handcrafted in Turkey, that she was considering for Achat's exclusive range. Her mind was racing back to that night a month ago, when she and Leo had had their memorable farewell.

But she'd taken a pill that morning, and one the next day. She hadn't missed anything.

'Well, then, it's probably just a stomach bug,' Sophie said dismissively.

Margo barely heard her.

The next morning she'd taken it a bit later, she recalled. She hadn't been able to sleep after Leo had left, her mind seething and her body aching, so she'd taken a herbal sleeping tablet some time in the middle of the night. It had knocked her out, which had been a blessing at the time, and she had slept for eight hours, waking around eleven, which was only three hours after she normally took the pill…

She couldn't be pregnant.

But what if those few hours had made a difference? Allowed enough of a window…?

She let out a laugh, then, a trembling, near-hysterical sound that had Sophie looking up from her laptop across their shared open-plan office.

'Margo…?'

She shook her head. 'Just thinking how ridiculous your suggestion was.'

And then she turned back to her computer and worked steadily until lunchtime, refusing to give her friend's teasing suggestion a single second of thought.

Her mind was filled with a static-like white noise even as she focused on the Turkish pillows of hand-dyed silk, and at lunchtime she left her desk and hurried down the Champs-Élysées, walking ten blocks to a chemist that wasn't too close to Achat's offices.

She paced the length of the shop, making sure no one who knew her was inside, and then quickly bought a pregnancy test without meeting the cashier's eye. She stuck the paper bag in her handbag and hurried out of the shop.

Back at the office, she went into the bathroom, grateful that it was empty, and stared at her reflection, taking comfort from the elegant, composed face in the mirror. Her mask. Her armour. For work she wore nothing more than some eyeliner and red lipstick, a bit of powder. Her hair was in its usual sleek chignon and she wore a black pencil skirt and a silver-grey silk blouse.

The shade suddenly reminded her of the colour of Leo's eyes.

But she couldn't think about Leo now.

Taking a deep breath, she fumbled in her bag for the test and then locked herself in one of the stalls. She read the directions through twice, needing to be thorough, to focus on the details rather than the big picture that had been emerging ever since Sophie had made her suggestion.

Then she took the test and waited the requisite three minutes, staring at the face of her watch the whole time. As the second hand ticked to twelve for the third time she turned the test over—and stared down at two blazing pink lines.

Positive.

She was pregnant…with Leo's baby.

For a moment she couldn't think, couldn't breathe, couldn't even see. She doubled over as the world swam and darkened all around her. Then she took a few shallow breaths and straightened. She wrapped the test in a paper towel and shoved it deep in the bin, washed her hands and retouched her make-up. She would not think about this yet. She couldn't.

She went back to her office, ignoring a curious look from Sophie, and sat at her desk and worked non-stop until six. She took phone calls, she attended a meeting, she even chatted and joked a little with colleagues.

But all the time she could hear the buzzing in her head. She felt as if she were watching herself from a distance, applauding how effortlessly she was handling it all. Except she wasn't really…because inside she could feel the beginnings of panic ice over her mind and her belly.

She was pregnant with Leo's baby.

'Do you want to go for a drink?' Sophie asked as Margo rose to gather her things at six.

'I don't think…' Margo began, intending to put Sophie off, but then she hesitated.

She couldn't bear the thought of returning to her apartment and spending the evening alone—not with this bomb of knowledge still ticking inside of her, waiting to detonate.

'Why not?' she amended as lightly as she could, and slipped on her blazer.

It was a warm evening in early September, and the office buildings of Paris's centre were emptying out onto the wide boulevard of the Champs-Élysées. They walked to a wine bar on a narrow side street, one of their favourites, and sat outside at a rickety table so they could watch the world go by.

'Red or white?' Sophie asked as she moved to go inside and order their wine from the bar.

Margo hesitated, and then shook her head. 'I'll just have a glass of sparkling water. My stomach is still a little queasy.'

Sophie stared at her for a moment and Margo held the stare. She'd come out with Sophie tonight to avoid being home alone with this new knowledge, this new *life* inside her, but she wasn't ready to tell her friend yet.

'Very well,' Sophie said, and went inside.

Margo sat back in her chair and blindly watched people stream by, heading home or to a bar like this—people with plans, with jobs and busy lives…

Hours ago she'd been just like them—at least on the surface. To the world she presented an image of the confident, sophisticated career woman who had everything she wanted. She'd always known it was nothing more than a flimsy façade, but no one else had.

And now the façade was about to crumble. Because she was pregnant. Pregnant with a baby…a child of her own…

Instinctively her hand crept to her still flat stomach. She imagined the little life nestled inside her, the size of a grain of rice and yet with a brain and a beating heart. *A baby…*

'So what's going on?' Sophie asked as she returned to the table and handed Margo her glass of water.

Quickly Margo dropped her hand from her middle. 'What do you mean?'

'You've been acting strange all afternoon. Almost as if you were in a daze.'

'I've been working.'

Sophie just gave her a look; she knew her too well for Margo to dissemble. She took a sip of water to stall for time.

'Is everything all right?' Sophie asked quietly, abandoning her usual flippancy for a sincerity that made Margo's eyes sting.

She didn't have many friends. She had acquaintances and colleagues, people on the periphery of her life, but no one had ever been at its centre. She hadn't allowed anyone to be, because loneliness was safer. And maybe it was all she deserved.

If you'd married Leo he would have been there.

But she couldn't think that way because she'd made her choice. She couldn't change her mind now, couldn't wonder or wish for something else.

'Margo?' Sophie prompted, real concern wrinkling her forehead.

Margo took a deep breath. 'Actually…I really am pregnant.' She hadn't been planning on admitting it, but now that she had it was such a relief to share the burden, even if Sophie looked as dazed and shocked as she'd felt a few hours ago.

'Seriously? But…'

'I took a test at lunchtime.'

Sophie shook her head slowly. 'I didn't even know you were seeing anyone seriously.'

'I wasn't. It was…casual. He lives in Greece.'

'And…? Have you told him?'

Margo let out a trembling laugh. 'Sophie, I told you, I just found out at lunchtime.'

'Right.' Sophie sat back in her seat and took a sip of wine. 'So you're still processing it, I suppose?'

Margo passed a hand over her forehead. Telling Sophie had made her pregnancy seem more real, and she felt a bit shaky as a result. 'I don't think I've even started.'

'Well,' Sophie said, 'I didn't think you wanted children.'

'I didn't. Don't.'

Sophie raised an eyebrow and Margo realised her hand had strayed once more to her middle. She let out another uncertain laugh and dropped it.

'I don't know what I want,' she said quietly, and felt everything inside her lurch at this admission.

'What about the father, this Greek guy? How long had you been with him?'

'We were together for two years—'

'Two *years*?' Sophie's jaw dropped. 'Why didn't you ever *tell* me, Margo?'

'I…' Why *hadn't* she told Sophie about Leo? Because, she supposed, she had been afraid to allow Leo to seem that important to her, and yet she was afraid it had happened anyway. 'It was just a fling,' she said lamely.

Sophie laughed in disbelief. 'Quite a long-term fling.'

'Yes, I suppose… In any case, our…relationship is

finished. Completely.' Margo stared down at her glass of water. 'It didn't end well.'

'If you're thinking of keeping the baby, he should still know,' Sophie pointed out.

Margo couldn't keep herself from wincing. How on earth could she tell Leo now? Considering what she'd said to him the last time they'd been together, he might not even believe the baby was his.

'I can't think about all this just yet,' she said. 'It's too much. I have time.'

'If you're *not* going to keep it,' Sophie replied warningly, 'the sooner you decide the better. For your own sake.'

'Yes…'

A termination, she supposed, might seem like the obvious answer. And yet the most fundamental part of herself resisted the possibility, shrank away from it in horror.

She hadn't expected that. She hadn't expected pregnancy to awaken anything in her but dread and fear. And yet she couldn't deny the faint stirrings of hope, as ephemeral as a will-o'-the-wisp, that had gathered inside her. A *baby*. A second chance.

'You do have *some* time,' Sophie allowed, reaching over to pat her hand. 'Don't make any rash decisions, in any case.'

'I won't,' Margo promised, but already her mind was spinning, spinning. If she actually decided to keep the baby she would have to tell Leo. And how on earth would *that* work? Would he believe her? Would he want to be involved?

She left Sophie an hour later and took the Metro back to her apartment on the top floor of an eighteenth-century townhouse on the Île de la Cité. As she stepped into the little foyer, with its marble table and antique umbrella stand, she felt some of the tension leave her body, uncramp her shoulders. This was her home, her haven, lovingly created over the years and the only real one she'd ever known.

She ran a bubble bath in the claw-foot tub and sank gratefully into its warmth, closing her eyes and trying to empty her mind for a few moments. But thoughts crept stealthily back in. *A baby.* How would she manage with her job? Childcare in Paris was expensive, and she was entitled to only sixteen weeks of maternity leave. Even though she made a decent salary she didn't think she'd be able to keep her apartment *and* pay for the full-time childcare she'd need.

But far more concerning, far more terrifying than the financial implications of having a child, were the emotional ones. A baby…a human being she would be entirely responsible for, a person who would be utterly dependent on her…

A person she could love. A person she could lose. *Again.*

And then, of course, there was Leo. She didn't even know if he would see her or listen to anything she had to say. And if he did…would he want to be involved in her child's life? And if so…how much? How would they come to a custody arrangement? And was that what she wanted for her son or daughter? Some awful to-ing and fro-ing between parents who as good as hated each other?

Exhaustion crashed over her and she rose from the tub. She couldn't think about all this yet. She certainly couldn't come to any decisions.

As the days and then the weeks slipped past Margo knew she had to decide soon. Sophie had stopped asking her what she was going to do, but at work she could see the silent question in her friend's eyes and knew she was concerned.

And then the sickness really hit. The faint nausea that

had been plaguing her for a few weeks suddenly turned into something else entirely, something horrendous that left her barely able to get out of bed, and unable to keep anything down.

Lying alone in her bed, unable to do anything but crawl to the toilet, she realised how alone she was. She had so few friends in the city. Sophie wanted to help, but as a single working woman her resources and time were limited.

Margo knew all too well how short a step it was to destitution, to tragedy, when you were on your own. When there was no family, no safety net. If she was going to keep this baby she couldn't do it on her own. She couldn't risk it.

After suffering for a week, she managed to drag herself to the doctor for some anti-nausea medication.

'The good news,' the doctor told her cheerfully, 'is that nausea usually means a healthy pregnancy. That baby is here to stay.'

Margo stared at him, his words reverberating through her. He had no idea, of course, how conflicted she was about this child. Except in that moment she realised she wasn't conflicted at all. This baby was a gift—a gift she'd never expected to receive. And she knew then—realised she'd known all along—that of course she was keeping her child.

And of course she would have to tell Leo.

CHAPTER THREE

'SOMEONE'S HERE TO see you, sir.'

Leo glanced up from his laptop at his assistant Elena, who stood in the doorway of his office on the Marakaios estate. He'd been going over some figures for a new deal with a large North American restaurant chain, and it took a few seconds for Elena's words to penetrate.

'Someone? Who is it, Elena?'

'A woman. She wouldn't give her name, but she said it was urgent.'

Leo frowned. His office was on the family compound in central Greece—the middle of nowhere, as Margo had so acerbically reminded him. He didn't get unexpected visitors to his office here. *Ever.*

'Well, why on earth wouldn't she give her name?' he asked as he pushed back from his chair.

'I don't know. But she's well-dressed and well-spoken. I thought perhaps…'

Elena trailed off, blushing, and Leo took her meaning. She'd thought this woman might be one of his lovers. Only he hadn't taken a lover in months—not since he'd last seen Margo.

And he very much doubted *Margo* had come all the way to Greece to see him.

Leo's mouth twisted cynically at the thought. It had

been over four months since he'd seen her—over four months since he'd walked out of her apartment with that ring in his pocket. Four months since he'd let himself think of her. That part of his life was over.

'Whoever this woman is, Elena, I find it decidedly odd that she wouldn't give her name.'

'She seemed very insistent...'

With a sigh, Leo strode to the door. 'I'll see her, then,' he said, and walked briskly out of his office.

It wasn't until he reached the foyer and saw the woman standing there amidst the leather sofas and sleek coffee tables that his step slowed. His heart seemed to still. And an icy anger came over him like a frozen shell.

He folded his arms. 'If I'd known it was you I would have told Elena to send you away.'

'Please, Leo...' Margo said quietly.

She looked awful—gaunt, with dark shadows under her eyes. She wore a black wool coat that made her ivory skin look pale...too pale.

Leo frowned. 'What do you want?'

'To talk to you.' She glanced at Elena, who had gone back to her desk and was ostentatiously busying herself, but was of course listening to every word. 'Privately.'

Leo opened his mouth to tell her they had nothing to say to one another, but then he paused. He didn't want to have this conversation in public—didn't want anyone, even his assistant, to know his private affairs.

With a terse nod he indicated the corridor. 'Come to my office, then,' he said, and without waiting for her to follow he turned and strode back the way he had come.

He watched as Margo came in and carefully closed the door behind her. She looked bruised and exhausted, as if a breath of wind would knock her right over.

'You don't look very well,' he said flatly.

She turned to him with the ghost of a smile. 'I don't feel very well. Do you mind if I sit down?'

He indicated one of the two chairs in front of his desk and she sank into it with a sigh of weary relief.

'Well?' Leo asked, biting off the single syllable. 'What do you want?'

She looked up at him, and he felt a ripple of uneasy shock at the resignation in her eyes. It was so different from the way he'd usually seen her—all elegant polish and sassy sophistication. This was a different Margo... one with a layer stripped away.

'Leo,' she said quietly, 'I'm pregnant.'

He blinked, the words taking him totally by surprise.

She said nothing, waiting for his reply.

'And how does this concern *me*?' he asked coolly.

She held his iron gaze. 'The baby is yours.'

'And you know that *how*? Do I need to remind you of what you told me four months ago?'

'No.' She hesitated, her gaze moving away from his. 'The other...man...he can't be the father,' she said at last.

A rage so fierce it felt like an earthquake shaking his insides took hold of him. *'Don't,'* he said in a voice like a whip-crack, 'talk to me of him. *Ever.*'

'This baby is yours, Leo.'

'You can't know that.'

She sighed, leaning her head back against the chair. 'I *do* know it,' she said wearily. 'Utterly. But if you like I'll have a paternity test done. I can prove it beyond a doubt.'

He stared at her, shaken more than he wanted to admit or reveal that she sounded so certain. 'I thought you didn't want children,' he said, after a long, taut moment.

'I didn't,' she answered.

'Then I'm surprised you didn't just deal with this on your own,' he snapped.

She put a hand to her throat, the gesture making her seem even more fragile. Vulnerable.

'Is that what you would have wanted?'

'No.' He realised he meant it utterly. A child…*his* child, if she wasn't lying. Yet how could he trust a word she said? 'Why have you come here and told me?' he asked instead. 'Do you want money?'

'No, not particularly.'

He laughed at that—a cold, sharp sound. 'Not *particularly*?'

'I admit having this child will be hard for me financially. But I didn't come here to ask for a hand-out. I came because I thought you should know. You'd want to know.'

He sank into his chair, the reality of it crashing over him as he raked his hands through his hair. '*Theos*, Margo. This is a lot to take in.'

'I know. I've had three months to process it—'

'You've known for that long and you are only telling me *now*?'

Colour touched her cheeks faintly. 'I've been very ill. Extreme morning sickness, apparently.'

'Are you taking medication?' he asked sharply, and she nodded.

'It helps a little.' She sighed and shifted in her seat. 'The truth is, Leo, I didn't know how you would respond, or if you'd even see me. And I wanted to tell you in person. But with being so sick I couldn't face travelling all this way until now.'

He nodded. It all sounded so very reasonable and yet he still felt angry. He should have known. He should have had the choice to be involved from the beginning. And now…?

'If this is indeed my child,' he told her, laying his hands flat on the desk, 'there is no question of my not being involved.'

'I know.'

'And I don't mean some weekend arrangement,' Leo continued, knowing he meant it even though he was still reeling from her news. 'I won't be the kind of father who sees his child only on a Saturday afternoon.'

'No,' Margo agreed quietly. 'I don't want that either.'

'Don't you?'

He gazed at her narrowly for a moment. He still didn't understand why she was here. She hadn't possessed enough honour to be faithful to him, so why would she care whether he knew about his own child or not?

'I would have expected you to have had a termination,' he said abruptly. 'Or, if you wanted the child, to pass it off as this other man's.'

She winced at that. 'Clearly you don't have a very high opinion of me.'

'And you think I should?'

'No.' She let out a little defeated sigh. 'No, I don't.'

'So why didn't you do either of those things, Margo?'

It was the first time he'd said her name since he'd seen her again, and it caused him a sudden, surprising flash of pain. He clenched his hands into fists, then deliberately flattened them out, resting them again on his desk.

'Because I am not, no matter what you think, completely without morals,' she replied with a bit of her old spirit. 'I want my child, and I want my child to know its father.' She took a deep breath. 'And more than that I want my child to have a loving, stable home. A home where it knows it's safe, where its parents are, loving and protecting. *Always.*'

Her dark brown eyes seemed to glow with an inner fire, an utter conviction.

'And how,' Leo asked after a pause, 'do you suppose *that* is going to work?'

'That's the other thing I want,' Margo said, still holding his gaze, her eyes like burning coals in her pale face. 'I want you to marry me.'

In another situation, another life, Margo might have laughed at the way Leo's expression slackened with surprise. He hadn't been expecting that—and why would he? The last time he'd seen her she'd sent him away with a scornful rejection, told him lies of infidelity that she'd known would make him hate her. And here she was now, with a proposal of her own.

'You must,' Leo said, his voice like ice, 'be joking.'

'Do you think I'd come all the way to Greece just to make a joke?' Margo asked quietly.

Leo stood up, the movement abrupt. He paced in front of the window that overlooked the Marakaios olive groves, now stark and bare in winter, which produced Greece's finest olive oil.

'Your *proposal*,' he said, his teeth clenched and the word a sneer, 'is offensive.'

'I mean it sincerely—'

He cut her off, his voice now low and pulsating with fury. 'The last time I saw you, you told me you didn't want marriage or children.'

She gestured to the gently swelling bump that was just barely visible under her coat. 'Things have changed.'

'Not that much. Not for *me*.'

'Don't you want to know your own child?'

'Who says I won't? Who says I won't sue for custody?'

Her stomach plunged with fear at that, but she forced herself to stay calm.

'And do you think that would be in the best interest of our baby, Leo?'

He sat back down in his chair, raking his hands through

his hair. With his head lowered she could see the strangely vulnerable nape of his neck, the momentary slump of his shoulders, and everything in her ached.

'I'm sorry, Leo, for springing this on you,' she said quietly. 'I've thought long and hard over these last few months about what is best for our baby, and I've come to the conclusion that it's to live in a stable home with two parents.'

It hadn't been an easy decision to make, but Margo's own sorry history made her wary of going it alone as her mother had. Just like her, her mother had had no friends, no family, no safety net. And she'd lost everything.

Margo would not subject her child to the same risk.

He lifted his head, his eyes flashing although the set of his mouth was grim, bleak. 'Even two parents who don't love each other? Who have absolutely no reason whatsoever to respect or trust each other?'

She flinched slightly. 'I respect you, Leo.'

'You've had a funny way of showing it, then.'

She should tell him, Margo knew, that she'd made up the other man. Any hope of a marriage that was amicable at least was impossible with that perceived betrayal between them. But she was afraid Leo wouldn't believe her if she told him now, and even if he did believe her he would want to know why she had told such an outrageous and damaging lie. The answer to that question was to admit her own fear, and that was something she was not ready to do.

'I know you don't respect *me*,' she said.

She clenched her hands in her lap and fought another wave of nausea. The sickness had eased a bit in the last few weeks, but she still felt as if she had to drag herself through each day.

'I know you don't trust me. I hope that maybe, in time, I can win back both your respect and your trust. But this

marriage would be for the sake of our child, Leo. To give
our baby the opportunity of a stable home. And even if we
don't love each other we'll both love this child.'

'So you're willing to enter a cold, loveless union, all
for the sake of a baby you professed to not even want?'

Another deep breath and she met his gaze without a
flinch. 'Yes.'

'I don't believe you.'

'Why would I be here, then?' she asked quietly.

'You want something. Are you in trouble? Did this other
man throw you over? Do you need money?'

'I told you before, I'm not asking for a hand-out.'

'You also said,' Leo reminded her ruthlessly, 'that having this baby would be a struggle financially.'

'A struggle, yes, but not impossible. I could do it. I've
thought about doing it,' she continued, determined to make
him believe her, even if he didn't—*couldn't*—understand
her motives. 'I thought very hard about raising this child
on my own and not even telling you I was pregnant.'

'And yet you now want me to *trust* you?'

'I *didn't* choose to do that, Leo,' Margo said, her voice
rising. She strove to level it; giving in to temper now
would not help her cause. 'I knew that you needed to know,
and that our child needed more. Two parents. Stability,
safety—'

'You don't think you could give this child those things
on your own?'

'No. Not for certain. I don't…I don't have a lot of
friends, and no family. This baby needs more than just
me. He or she needs a father.'

'If I *am* the father.'

'Please…'

She closed her eyes, waves of both nausea and fatigue
crashing over here. Coming all this way, dealing with the

plane and the rental car and the endless travel, had completely exhausted her.

She summoned what little strength she had left and made herself continue. 'Let's not argue. I want to marry you for the sake of our child. I'm not expecting you to love me or even like me after—after what I did, but I do hope we might act amicably towards each other for the sake of the baby. As for...' She dropped her gaze, unable to look him in the eye. 'As for the usual benefits of a marriage... I'd understand if you chose to look elsewhere.'

Leo was silent and Margo risked a look up, wondering if he'd taken her meaning.

'Am I to understand,' he asked, his voice toneless, 'that you are giving me permission to violate my marriage vows?'

'It would be a marriage of convenience—'

'But still a marriage.'

'I'm trying to make this more amenable to you—'

'To sweeten the deal?' He cut across her, his voice hard. 'It still tastes rancid to me.'

'Please, Leo...' She swallowed, hating the fact that she had to beg.

Maybe he was right. Perhaps she should go back to Paris, raise the baby on her own. Leo could be the sort of weekend father he claimed he didn't want to be. Plenty of couples did it—why not them?

Because she was afraid of going it alone. Because she wanted more for her child. So much more than she'd had.

'You ask so *nicely*,' Leo said, his eyes glittering now.

He was furious with her, even after so many months apart. She wondered if his anger could ever be appeased. Perhaps if she told him the truth...if only he would believe it.

'I'm willing to live in Greece,' she continued, deciding she might as well say it all.

'Even in the "middle of nowhere"?'

'I'd leave my job at Achat. I'd want to stay home with the baby for the first few years, at least.'

'I thought the whole "housewife routine" bored you to death?'

Once again he was throwing her words back in her face, and she couldn't blame him. 'It's different now.'

'So you're saying you *want* those things? That life?'

He sounded incredulous—contemptuous, even—and bile surged in her stomach again. She swallowed past the metallic taste in her mouth. 'I'm saying that I am willing,' she answered. 'It's a sacrifice I'm prepared to make.'

'So I'd be marrying a martyr? What an appealing thought.'

'You'd be making a sacrifice too,' Margo replied. 'I understand that.'

'I still don't understand you,' Leo answered.

'Why is it so hard to believe I'd be willing to do this?' Margo demanded. She could take only so much of his sneering disbelief. 'Most women would.'

'And yet,' Leo reminded her softly, 'you *aren't* "most women".'

She closed her eyes, felt herself sway.

She heard Leo's sharply indrawn breath. 'Margo, are you all right?'

His voice was rough, although with impatience or anxiety she couldn't tell.

She forced her eyes open.

'I'm just very tired, and still quite nauseous,' she said levelly. 'Obviously you need time to think about my—my proposal.' Not the word she'd wished to use, and Leo's mouth twisted cynically when she said it. There had been too many proposals already. 'If you could let me know when you've decided…'

'Are you actually intending to return to France?' Leo asked sharply. 'You're in no condition to travel.'

'I'll spend the night at a local hotel,' she answered, 'and fly out of Athens tomorrow.'

'No.' Leo's gaze was cold and implacable as he gave his order. 'You'll stay here. I'll give you my answer to-morrow.'

Which made her feel like Scheherazade, wondering if she was to be beheaded in the morning. Not the way she would have wanted to think about her marriage, but she'd reconciled herself, or thought she had, to what life with Leo would be like. She'd told herself it was worth it, that anything was worth it if she could give her baby a stable, loving home.

Even if you and Leo will never love each other?

Some sacrifices, she reminded herself grimly, were necessary. And maybe it would be better this way. Without the complication and risk of loving someone, you could never be hurt. Hopefully.

She rose from her chair, blinking back dizziness. Even so Leo must have seen something in her expression, for he reached forward and steadied her elbow with his hand. It was the first time he'd touched her in three months, since he'd made love to her against the window and then walked away.

'I'm fine,' she said, and shook off his hand. 'Just a little dizzy when I stand up, that's all.'

'I'll arrange for someone to show you to the guest suite,' Leo said.

He was frowning, although over her dizziness or the whole situation she didn't know. Couldn't think. He was right: she really wasn't in a fit state to travel.

She stood, swaying slightly, as Leo made arrangements on his phone. Then he ended the call and gave her one last, hard look.

'I'll see you tomorrow,' he said, and Margo knew it was a dismissal.

CHAPTER FOUR

A BABY. HE WAS going to be a father… If the child was truly his. Leo knocked back his third whisky and stared grimly out at the starless night. It had been eight hours since Margo had confronted him in his office, and he was still reeling.

He hadn't seen her in all that time. Elena had taken her to the house, and then his personal staff had seen to her comforts. He'd called his housekeeper Maria to check on her, and she'd told him that Margo had gone to her room and slept for most of the afternoon. He'd requested that a dinner tray be taken up to her, but Maria had told him it hadn't been touched.

Anxiety touched with anger gnawed at his gut. If the child was his, he wanted to make sure Margo was staying healthy. Hell, even if the child *wasn't* his, he had a responsibility towards any person under his roof. And he hadn't liked how pale and ill Margo had looked, as if the very life force had been sucked right out of her.

Restlessly Leo rose from the leather club chair where he'd been sitting in the study that had once been his father's, and then his brother Antonios's. And now it was his. Six months into his leadership of Marakaios Enterprises and he still burned with the determination to take the company to a new level, to wield the power his father and brother had denied him for so long.

A lifetime of being pushed to the sidelines, being kept in the dark, had taken its toll. He didn't trust anyone—and especially not Margo. But if the child was his...then why *not* the cold marriage of convenience she'd suggested? It was what he'd determined he'd wanted after she'd turned him down. No messy emotion, no desperate searching for love. He just hadn't expected Margo to be his convenient bride.

Grimly Leo turned back to the whisky bottle. What she'd suggested made sense, and yet everything in him resisted it. To live with a woman who had been unfaithful, who had *rejected* him, and who was now viewing their marriage as the altar upon which she'd sacrifice herself, her hopes and dreams... It was a bitter pill to swallow—and yet what was the alternative? To come to some unsatisfactory custody arrangement and not be nearly as involved in his child's life as he wanted?

If the child was his.

If it was then Leo knew he had to be involved. He wanted to be the kind of father his own father hadn't been to him. Loving, interested, open. And he wanted a family—a child, a wife. Why not Margo? He could control his feelings for her. He had no interest in loving her any more.

He could make this marriage work.

Margo had thought she wouldn't be able to sleep, but she was so tired that she'd fallen into a deep and thankfully dreamless sleep the moment her head had hit the pillow, after Leo's housekeeper had shown her to her room.

When she awoke it was dark and the room was chilly, the curtains open to the night sky. Margo rolled over in bed, feeling disorientated and muzzy-headed, as if she were suffering from jet lag or a hangover, or both. She heard a knock on the door, an urgent *rat-a-tat-tat* that made her think it was not the first knock.

She rose from the bed, pushing her hair out of her face, and went to answer the door.

The housekeeper Maria stood there, with a tray of food. The salad, bread, and lentil soup looked and smelled delicious, but Margo's stomach roiled all the same. She didn't think she could manage a mouthful.

'*Efharisto*,' she murmured, and reached out to take the tray.

But Maria would have none of it. She shook her head and bustled into the room, setting the tray on a table in the corner. Bemused, Margo watched as she drew the curtains across the windows and remade the bed, plumping the pillows. She turned on a few table lamps that were scattered about the room and then looked around, seemingly satisfied with how cosy she'd made it in just a few minutes.

'*Efharisto*,' Margo said again, and Maria nodded towards the food.

'*Fae*,' she commanded, and while Margo didn't recognise the word she could guess what it meant. *Eat.*

She gave the housekeeper a weak smile and with another nod Maria left the room.

Margo walked over to the tray and took a spoonful of soup, but, warm and nourishing as it was, her stomach roiled again and she left it.

Now that the cobwebs were clearing from her brain she remembered every excruciating detail of her conversation with Leo. His disbelief and his contempt, his suspicion and anger. And now she was stuck here, waiting to see if he would marry her.

Shaking her head at her own stubborn folly, she crawled back into the bed and pulled the covers over herself. She wouldn't back out of her offer. She cared too much about this child inside her—this child she'd never expected to have, never dared want.

This child she would sacrifice anything for to ensure it had a better childhood, a better life, than she had had. To keep her, or him, safe.

She slept again and when she woke it was dawn, with the first grey light of morning creeping through a crack in the closed curtains. She dozed for a little while longer and then finally got up and went to shower, to prepare herself to meet with Leo and hear his answer—whatever it was.

At eight o'clock Maria knocked on the door and brought in a breakfast tray. Margo didn't know whether to feel like a pampered princess or a prisoner. At some point, she realised, Maria must have removed the untouched tray from the night before. She must have been sleeping at the time.

'*Efharisto*,' she said again, and Maria gave her a stern look.

'*Fae*.'

'Yes—I mean, *ne*.' Margo smiled apologetically. 'I can't keep much down, I'm afraid.'

Maria clucked at that, but Margo didn't think the older woman understood her. She bustled about a bit more, pouring coffee and juice, taking the lids off jam and butter dishes. Finally she left and Margo gazed in dismay at the lavish breakfast Maria had left. The smell of the coffee made her stomach lurch.

For the housekeeper's sake she tried to eat some yogurt with honey, but after two spoonsful she left it aside and then paced the room, wondering if she should go in search of Leo or wait for him to summon her.

She'd paced for several minutes, restless and anxious, until she realised she was being ridiculous. Had she lost all her spirit since coming here? She might be tired and unwell, and afraid of Leo's response, but she'd faced far worse obstacles than this and survived. Her strength in the face of adversity was something she clung to and prided herself on.

Determinedly she strode to the door and flung it open—only to stop in her tracks when she saw Leo standing there, looking devastatingly handsome in a crisp white shirt and grey trousers, his ink-dark hair still damp and spiky from a shower. He also looked decidedly nonplussed.

'Going somewhere?' he enquired.

'Looking for you, actually,' she replied crisply. 'I'd like your answer, Leo, because I need to get back to Paris. My flight is at two o'clock this afternoon.'

'Cancel it,' he returned. 'You won't be returning to Paris. Not right now, at any rate.'

She stared at him, as nonplussed as he'd been. 'Excuse me?'

His eyes flashed and his mouth thinned. 'Which part of what I said didn't you understand?'

Margo gritted her teeth. Yesterday she might have donned a hair shirt and beaten her chest in grief and repentance, but clearly that hadn't been enough for Leo. She didn't think she could endure a lifetime of snide remarks, all for a crime she hadn't even committed.

Except you told him you did.

'Perhaps,' she suggested, with only a hint of sharpness, 'we could discuss our future plans in a bit more detail?'

'Fine. I was coming to get you, anyway. We can go down to my study.'

'Fine.'

Silently she followed him down the terracotta-tiled corridor to the sweeping double staircase that led to the villa's soaring entrance hall. Yesterday she'd been too overwhelmed and exhausted to take in any of her surroundings, but today she was keenly aware that this grand place was, in all likelihood, her new home. It seemed, based on what Leo had said about cancelling her flight, that he was going to agree to marry her.

And from the plunging sensation in her stomach she knew she wasn't sure how she felt about that.

He led her to a wood-panelled study overlooking the villa's extensive gardens. This late in November they were stark and bare, but Margo could imagine how lush and lovely they would be come spring. Would she walk with her baby out there? Bring a blanket and lie on the grass, look up at the clouds while the baby gurgled and grabbed its feet?

'Let me cut to the chase,' Leo said, and Margo was jolted out of her pleasant daydream to the current cold reality.

He stood behind a huge desk of carved mahogany, his hands braced on the back of a chair, his expression implacable.

In the two years they'd been together she'd seen his lazy, knowing smiles, his hooded sleepy gazes. She'd seen him light and laughing, and dangerously, sensually intent. But she hadn't seen him like this—looking at her as if she were a difficult business client.

Well, if he could be businesslike, then so could she. She straightened and gave him a brisk nod. 'Please do.'

'I will marry you—but only on certain conditions.'

Margo took a deep breath and let it out evenly. 'Which are?'

'First, we drive to Athens this afternoon and you undergo a paternity test.'

It was no more than she'd expected, although the fact that he believed the baby might not be his still stung. This, at least, was easy to comply with. 'Very well.'

'Second, you resign from your job immediately and come and live with me here in Greece.'

So he wanted complete control of her and their child? She couldn't say she was really surprised. 'Fine.'

'Third, you agree to have a local doctor of my choosing provide you with medical care.'

Her temper finally started to fray. 'I think I'm capable of finding my own doctor, Leo.'

'Are you?' He arched an eyebrow, coldly sceptical. 'Because you came here looking dreadful.'

'Thanks very much, but my looks have nothing to do with my medical care or lack of it,' Margo snapped.

How much of this was she supposed to take? Maybe, she thought with a surge of reckless fury, the answer was none of it. She'd come to Leo as a supplicant, truly believing that their child should know his or her father. Trusting that she was making the right decision in seeking to provide the kind of stable home life she'd never had…no matter what the sacrifice to her.

If Leo was going to snipe at her constantly, was that really an environment she wanted to raise her child in? The kind of relationship she wanted her son or daughter to emulate?

But the alternative was too bleak to consider. Raise her baby alone, a single mother without a safety net. No parents, no relatives, no one who could help or support her besides a few friends like Sophie, who didn't even want children themselves. One wrong choice or an accident away from destitution, from losing everything. *Again*.

'Leo,' she said, keeping her voice even, 'if you're going to snipe at me about everything this whole negotiation process will be very unpleasant.'

Leo's mouth hardened. 'I'm just trying to be clear.'

'You are. Abundantly.'

A muscle flickered in his jaw. His gaze was the colour

of a sea in winter, slate-grey and utterly icy. 'I'm not finished with my conditions.'

'Fine,' she said wearily. 'What are the rest of your conditions?'

'You don't work while you're pregnant—or while our child is small. I want my child to have a mother who is fully present and available.'

'I've already said I would give up my job for a few years,' she reminded him. 'And anyway, considering I'll be stuck in the middle of Greece, a career is hardly an option for me at the moment.'

'Our marriage might be made for convenience,' Leo continued relentlessly, 'but it won't be *that* convenient. When you are healthy, and recovered from the birth of our child, I want you in my bed.'

Her stomach plunged again, with that weird mixture of anticipation and dread. 'I thought you could hardly stand the sight of me?' she said after a second's pause. Her voice sounded husky.

'We have chemistry,' Leo answered. 'Why should I look elsewhere when I have a woman to see to my needs right there at home?'

'Are you *trying* to be as offensive as possible?'

'Just stating facts,' Leo answered in a bland voice. 'And here's another fact: if you ever cheat on me again I will divorce you. Immediately. And I will gain complete custody of our child.'

Margo stared at him for a moment, saw the steely glint of challenge in his eyes, the hard set of his mouth.

Her hands clenched into fists at her sides. 'No.'

'No? You mean you can't even *pretend* you're going to be faithful?'

'I'll be faithful to you, Leo,' Margo said, her voice very even despite the maelstrom of fury and pain she felt whirling through her. 'But if you ever threaten to take my child away from me again I will leave you and I will never come back. I will go where you will never find me, and you will never see either of us again—' She broke off, her nails digging into her palms, her chest heaving.

'That's a lot of nevers,' Leo remarked tonelessly.

'You started it.'

'I wonder why you are so fierce and protective,' he answered, his silvery gaze sweeping slowly over her, 'when you made it abundantly clear the last time we met that you didn't even *want* children.'

'People change.'

'And yet I wonder if you really have?'

She shook her head, her anger subsiding, replaced only by weariness. She sank onto one of the chairs in front of his desk. 'Are there any other conditions?'

'None we need to discuss at present.'

She looked up. 'Good. Then I have a few of my own.'

She almost laughed at the look of shock that blazed across his features. Did he think her so weak and spineless that she would accept all his conditions without naming her own? Or perhaps he was simply that confident of his own strong position.

She thought of his threat—no, his *promise* to claim full custody if she was unfaithful, or even if he just thought she was unfaithful. His position was strong and hers was weak, because she knew her threat to leave him and go where he could never find her was just that: a threat. Empty. Meaningless.

Leo would always find her.

'So what are your conditions?' he asked, folding his arms.

'First, that you never threaten me again.' She glared at him and he gazed back, unsmiling.

'What you call "threat" I call statement of fact.'

'Nevertheless.'

He shrugged. 'What are the others?'

Margo almost dug her heels in and argued the point, but she was so very, very tired. 'I have sole care of our child. No nannies or nurses.'

He inclined his head in acknowledgement. 'You'll have no argument from me. I said I wanted you to be present and available.'

'Even though you don't respect or trust me?' Margo couldn't help but jibe.

Leo pressed his lips together, and then bit out, 'I trust you to be a good mother to our child.'

And despite all his sneers and orders it touched her that he thought that. Because the truth was she wasn't sure she thought it herself. She *wanted* to be a good mother, God knew, but she certainly hadn't had the best example. And she had too many regrets when it came to loving a child. Losing a child.

'What else?' Leo asked.

'Any decisions regarding our child's welfare are made jointly. I won't have you laying down the law when it comes to our baby.'

His jaw set. 'It seems reasonable to discuss things,' he said after a pause.

Margo cast around for more conditions, but she couldn't think of anything. This was all so unknown, so unbelievable. She had no idea what her marriage, her *life* would look like. *But at least it would be safe.* Her baby would be safe.

'Good,' she said finally, with a nod. 'Then I have no more conditions…at present.'

'I'm glad we've come to an agreement,' Leo answered, inclining his head. 'We'll leave for Athens this afternoon.'

'I will have to return to France at some point,' Margo warned him. 'I have to give notice and deal with my apartment.'

She swallowed, the realisation of all she was leaving behind hitting her with sudden force, making her breathless. The career she was so proud of. The friends she'd made. The home she'd created for herself—her sanctuary and haven, the only place she felt she could be herself. All of it gone.

But it's worth it. It has to be worth it.

'When you are fit to travel,' Leo said, his tone implying that *he* would be the one to make the decision, 'you may return to France and deal with your job and apartment.'

His imperious tone, as if he were giving her permission, grated on Margo's already raw nerves. 'Who do you think you are,' she demanded, 'to order me about in such a way? I *chose* to come here, Leo—'

'I'll tell you who I am,' Leo cut across her, his voice quiet and deadly. 'I'm your husband.'

'Not yet,' Margo answered, her voice just as quiet, just as deadly. 'And at the rate you're going maybe not ever.'

He took a step towards her, his eyes narrowing to silver slits. 'Do you *really* think,' he asked, 'that I'd let you go now you are carrying my child? *If* it is my child.'

'Oh, enough with that, Leo—'

'We'll know the truth by tomorrow,' he answered. 'And then we'll be married.'

CHAPTER FIVE

THEY DIDN'T SPEAK during the three-hour drive to Athens. His hands clenched on the wheel, Leo slid a covert, sideways glance towards Margo. She sat very still, one hand resting on the handle of the door, her face pale and composed.

She seemed a little better than she had yesterday, but she still looked tired and washed out. She wore a sweater dress of magenta wool that clung to her shape, making him realise just how much weight she'd lost—although he could still see the gentle swell of her small baby bump. *His* baby.

He was, of course, going to insist on the paternity test, and yet Leo felt in his gut that the baby was his. Margo wouldn't have agreed to everything so readily if she'd had any doubt. Which made him wonder how she could be so certain.

He hadn't given much thought to the other man in Margo's life; he'd simply shut the door on the whole idea and tried not to think of her—or him—at all. Now, however, he wondered—and he realised they needed to address it.

'This other man,' he said abruptly. 'Are you still with him?'

She turned to him, the ghost of a sad smile curving her lips. 'Do you think I'd be here if I was?'

'I have no idea.'

She let out a small sigh. 'No, Leo. We're not together.'

'When did you break it off?'

She didn't answer and his hands clenched harder on the steering wheel, his knuckles turning white.

'Well, Margo? It's not that hard a question. I need to know if this guy is going to resurface in our lives, because I assure you—'

'Oh, this is ridiculous,' she said, and closed her eyes. 'Leo, there *is* no other man. There never was.'

He turned sharply to stare at her. Her eyes were still closed; she was leaning her head back against the seat. 'You expect me to believe that?'

'Not really, but it's the truth.'

'Why did you lie to me before, then?' he demanded.

Again she didn't answer, and he wondered if she were scrambling for some plausible excuse.

'Because,' she finally said softly, her eyes still closed, 'I knew it was the one thing that would send you away for good.'

Leo blinked, stung by this almost as much as he'd been by her alleged infidelity. 'You mean my proposal of marriage was so abhorrent to you that you needed to *lie* to get rid of me?'

'You're putting it in the worst possible light, but, yes, I suppose that's true.'

The sheer rejection of it, as brutal as his father's had been, left him speechless.

He stared straight ahead, flexing his hands on the steering wheel. 'And yet here we are, about to get married.'

She opened her eyes and gazed at him bleakly. 'Yes. Here we are.'

'I don't understand you, Margo.'

'I know.'

'If, four months ago, the idea of marrying me was so

disagreeable, why did you come back? Plenty of children live with single or divorced parents. You could have managed. I wouldn't have forced you to marry me. We could have come to a custody arrangement.' He hesitated, and then continued. 'We still could.'

'Is that what you want?'

'I don't know.' He shook his head, thoughts whirling through his mind like leaves in an autumn wind. Margo's rejection of him hurt more than he wanted to admit. And yet…she'd come back. She'd chosen to be here. They could still find a way ahead, for the sake of their child.

And the truth is, you still want her.

Underneath his anger the old desire burned just as bright, just as fierce.

'Leo…there's no reason we can't be amicable with each other, is there?'

She laid her hand on his arm, her fingers long and slender, the touch as light as a butterfly and yet still seeming to reach right inside him and clench a fist around his heart.

'We can be friends,' she continued. 'A convenient marriage doesn't have to be a cold one.'

Friends—when she'd either cheated on him or lied in the worst possible way in order to avoid marrying him? Friends—when she clearly viewed marriage to him as a *sacrifice*? The desire he'd felt was no more than that: desire. Lust.

He pulled his arm away. 'I don't think so,' he answered coolly. 'I think it's best if we keep this businesslike.'

She turned her head towards the window. 'And will we be "businesslike" in bed?'

'We've never had a problem with that aspect of our relationship,' Leo answered. He'd keep his physical feelings for Margo separate from any potential emotional complications. 'And we won't once we're married.'

They were on the outskirts of Athens now, with the raised mount of the Acropolis visible on the horizon. They didn't speak until they'd reached Leo's apartment in Kolonaki.

Margo had never been to Leo's city home before. Now she walked around the elegant rooms that took up the top floor of a nineteenth-century townhouse. The living room and dining room had been knocked together to create a large open space scattered with black and white leather sofas and tables of chrome and glass.

A huge canvas of wavy green lines and white splotches was the only colour in the whole room. She stood in front of it, wondering if this was the kind of modern art Leo liked. It had probably cost a fortune, and it looked as if it had been painted by a five-year-old.

'A masterpiece made by my nephew Timon,' he said as he came to stand beside her.

'I didn't know you had a nephew.'

There was, she realised, so much she didn't know about him. She knew what he liked in bed, and what kind of food he liked to order in, and that he preferred classical music to jazz. She knew he shaved with an old-fashioned straight razor and that the only cologne he wore was a splash of citrus-scented aftershave. She knew what a woman would know of a lover, but not of someone she loved. Not of a husband.

'Yes, my sister's son.'

'Is he an aspiring artist, then?' she asked, with a nod to the canvas.

'I suppose you could say that. He's three.'

Margo let out a surprised laugh. 'And I was just thinking this painting looked like it was done by a five-year-old and had probably cost a fortune.'

'Luckily for me, it cost nothing. My interior designer wanted me to spend a hundred thousand euros on some modern atrocity and I said my nephew could do something better. He did.' He glanced briefly at the huge canvas. 'I quite like it, actually. It's meant to be the olive groves, when the trees blossom in spring.'

'I like it too,' Margo answered. 'Especially now that I know it's done by your nephew.'

For a moment, no more, it felt like the way things had used to be, or even better. Easy, relaxed… A faint smile curved Leo's mouth as he stared at the painting, and Margo felt her wilting spirits lift as hope that they might in fact be able to have an amicable marriage after all unfurled inside her.

Then Leo turned away.

'I've put your things in the guest bedroom. You can refresh yourself and then we'll go to the doctor.'

The guest bedroom was as sumptuous as the rest of the apartment, with a huge king-sized bed covered in a cream silk duvet and an en-suite bathroom with a sunken marble tub. Margo was tempted to run a bath and have a soak, but she knew Leo would be waiting, watching her every move, and the thought made her too uptight to relax, even in a bubble bath.

She washed her face and hands instead, and put on a little make-up, no more than concealer to cover the dark shadows under her eyes, and a little blusher and lipstick to give her face some colour.

'Have you eaten today?' Leo called through the closed door. 'Maria told me you didn't have supper last night, nor breakfast this morning.'

So Maria was her keeper and his spy? Margo tried not to let it rankle. 'I can't manage much food,' she answered. She took a quick breath and opened the door.

Leo stood there, scowling.

'You need to keep up your strength.'

'I would if I could, Leo, but I can't keep anything down.'

'I thought the medication you were prescribed helps?'

'It does,' Margo answered. 'But I still have to be careful.' She tried for a smile. 'I've eaten a lot of melba toast. It's the one thing my stomach can stand.'

'Melba toast?' he repeated.

Margo shrugged. 'My doctor said I should start to feel better soon.'

'I don't even know how far along you are.'

'Seventeen weeks. The baby is due in the end of April.'

He looked startled by that news, and Margo wondered if the actuality of a baby—a living person coming into their lives—had just become more real to him.

But all he said was, 'We should go.'

'I'll just get my coat.'

Leo insisted on driving to the doctor's, even though it was only a few blocks away.

'You look as if a breath of wind could knock you over,' he informed her, and Margo told herself he was actually being considerate, even if it came across, as did everything else, as both a command and a criticism.

The doctor's office was plush and well-appointed, and they were seen immediately. Margo perched on top of the examination table, feeling shy and rather exposed with Leo in the room, standing in the corner, practically glowering.

The doctor, a neat-looking woman with a coil of dark hair and a brisk, efficient manner, took them both in with a single glance. 'Would you prefer to be seen alone?' she asked Margo in clipped English.

Leo looked taken aback. Clearly he'd expected the doctor he'd chosen to leap to do his bidding, just as everyone else did.

'No,' Margo answered, 'but maybe you could sit down?' She raised her eyebrows at Leo, who took a seat without a word.

'Now, let's see.' The woman, who had introduced herself as Dr Tallos, flipped through the forms Margo had filled out in the waiting room. 'You believe you're seventeen weeks along? Have you had an ultrasound?'

'Not yet. I was scheduled for one at twenty weeks.'

'Well, we can do one now, just to make sure everything's all right,' Dr Tallos said briskly. 'If you'd like?'

A tremor of both fear and excitement rippled through Margo. 'Yes, all right.'

'Let's get that done first, then, shall we?'

'What about the paternity test?' Leo asked, and the doctor shot him a narrowed look while Margo flushed at the obvious implication.

'We can establish paternity by a simple blood test. I'll draw blood from both of you after we've established the baby is healthy.' She raised her eyebrows at him, her expression and voice both decidedly cool. 'If that's all right with you?'

A blush touched Leo's cheeks and Margo almost felt sorry for him. The doctor didn't know their convoluted history.

'That's fine,' he said, and sat back in his chair.

A nurse wheeled in a machine with a screen and wires, and Margo lay back on the examination table.

'Do you mind?' Dr Tallos asked, and lifted her dress all the way up to right underneath her breasts, pulling her tights down to reveal the soft white swell of her belly.

Now she felt really exposed, lying there like a beached whale with her belly on view. She couldn't so much as sneak a glance at Leo, but she felt his presence, his tension.

'This will be a little cold,' Dr Tallos murmured, and squirted a clear gel onto Margo's bare stomach.

It wasn't just cold, it was icy, and she shivered.

'Here we go.' She started pressing a wand into Margo's belly, hard enough to make her wince.

'That's hurting her,' Leo said sharply, and both Margo and Dr Tallos turned to him in surprise.

'It's a bit uncomfortable,' the doctor said, 'but I promise you it's not hurting anyone.'

Leo didn't look convinced, and Margo said quietly, 'I'm all right, Leo.'

'There we are,' Dr Tallos announced, and they all turned to look at the fuzzy shape on the screen.

Margo blinked, trying to connect what looked like nothing more than a few blobby circles into a shape that resembled a baby.

Then Dr Tallos started pointing things out on the screen. 'There's the head, and the stomach, and you can see fingers and toes—look.'

And almost as if by magic Margo could see it: the curled up bud of her baby unfurling as he—or she—stretched out arms, kicked tiny legs.

'Kicking up a storm,' Dr Tallos said cheerfully. 'Do you feel anything?'

Margo shook her head. 'Not yet.'

'Well, don't worry, you're sure to in the next few weeks. And there's the heart, beating away.' She pointed to the flickering image on the screen, pulsing with life. 'Let me turn up the volume and you can hear it.'

She twirled a knob on the ultrasound machine and all at once the room was filled with a sound like the galloping of a horse, an insistent swoosh that had both Leo and Margo's jaws dropping in amazement.

'I've never heard such a sound,' Leo said softly.

He looked gobsmacked, as if someone had hit him on the head, and Margo knew how he felt. That rushing sound had knocked her for six too. It was so *real*.

'Baby is measuring seventeen weeks, just as you said,' Dr Tallos continued as she pressed some keys to take measurements. 'Everything looks well. It's a bit early to tell the sex, but we'll schedule a more comprehensive ultrasound for twenty weeks. Now...' She flicked off the machine and removed the wand from Margo's stomach before handing her a paper towel to wipe off the gel. 'I'll give you a moment to clean yourself and we'll do the blood test.' She turned to Leo with raised eyebrows. 'I'm assuming that's still required?'

He hesitated, and Margo jumped in. 'Yes, it's required,' she said. She would not have Leo casting any more aspersions or doubt.

Fifteen minutes later they'd left the doctor's office, with their promise to call with the results of the paternity test tomorrow.

It was strange, walking along the city street together, crossing the wide boulevard lined with cafés and upscale boutiques.

'Wait just a moment,' Leo said, and ducked into a gourmet deli.

Margo waited on the pavement, the brisk December wind buffeting her.

He came out a few minutes later, a paper bag in hand. 'Melba toast,' he said, and Margo, quite suddenly, felt near to tears. 'Margo, what is it?' he asked.

She sniffed and shook her head. 'Nothing. I'm just emotional because I'm pregnant. And being at the doctor's office...hearing the heartbeat...'

Leo frowned. 'That was a good thing, was it not?'

'Yes. Yes, of course it was.'

And yet hearing that heartbeat had also terrified her—because what if it stopped? What if the next time she had an ultrasound she heard nothing but yawning, endless silence? She was used to expecting, and experiencing, the worst. She couldn't bear for it to happen again, and yet she still braced herself for it.

'Here.' Leo opened the bag of melba toast and handed her a piece. 'Eat something. You'll feel better.'

But his kindness only made her feel worse; it opened her up so she felt broken and jagged inside. She'd told him she'd wanted an amicable marriage, but now she wondered if Leo's coldness, even his snideness, would have been easier to handle. These little kindnesses hurt her, made her realise how much they'd both given up—and all because she hadn't felt strong or brave enough to risk the real thing.

But it was too late for regrets, she reminded herself as she took a piece of toast and munched obediently. And it was better this way. If she kept telling herself that perhaps she'd start to believe it.

Leo watched as Margo ate a piece of toast, her shoulders hunched against the winter wind, her face pale and composed now, although he could still see the sheen of tears in her dark eyes, turning them luminous and twisting his gut.

He didn't want her to cry. He had been angry and alarmed when he'd thought the doctor had hurt her during the ultrasound. He felt worse now, seeing her near tears. He still had feelings for Margo—feelings he had neither expected nor wanted to have. *Feelings which had led him to agreeing to this marriage.*

For the last four months he'd refused even to think of her. She'd been as good as dead to him. And since she'd come back into his life twenty-four hours ago he'd made sure to keep both his distance and his composure. But he hadn't been keeping either. He saw that now. He'd been fooling himself—punishing her with snide or sarcastic comments because it was easier than grabbing her by the shoulders and demanding to know why she'd left him. Or maybe just kissing her senseless.

Who cared what her reasons had been? She was here now.

And she rejected you once. Why shouldn't she again?

But he didn't need to punish her any more. Perhaps he never should have, if she really was telling the truth when she said there hadn't been anyone else. He could at least be amicable. Amicable and no more.

'We should get back,' he said. 'You look like you need a rest. And I need to arrange the wedding details.'

Margo's step faltered. 'The wedding? Already?'

'We'll marry tomorrow afternoon in a civil service here in Athens. Pending the paternity results, of course.' Margo looked dazed by that news, but he continued, an edge to his voice. 'Surely, considering our circumstances, you don't expect the whole church and white dress affair?'

Fire flashed in her eyes. 'Are you *really* so old-fashioned and chauvinistic?'

'How is that *either* of those things?' Leo demanded. 'We're getting married for the sake of this child, Margo—not because we love each other or even want to be with each other.'

He was saying it for his own sake as well as hers, and somehow that just made him even more furious. 'A church wedding would be a mockery.'

'And a white dress would too, I suppose?'

'This isn't some criticism of you,' Leo answered. 'It's simply a statement of fact and what our marriage really is. What it will be.'

'Fine,' Margo answered, her eyes still flashing. 'Fine,' she said again and, dropping the remnants of her toast in the bin, she walked past him towards the car.

CHAPTER SIX

SHE COULDN'T SLEEP. Margo had tossed and turned in the guest bedroom for several hours before she'd finally given up trying. It wasn't the bed—it was one of the most comfortable she'd ever slept in. And it wasn't that she wasn't tired, because she still felt exhausted. Even so her mind seethed with half-formed questions and thoughts, and they spun around in her brain until she decided to make herself some herbal tea in an attempt to help her sleep.

She reached for her dressing gown and the box of ginger tea she'd brought with her; it was one of the few things she could stomach. Tiptoeing out of her bedroom, not wanting to disturb Leo, she made her way to the kitchen.

The rest of the day had passed uneventfully enough: she'd had a nap and a bath while Leo had worked in his study. And at around dinnertime he'd knocked on her door and told her he was planning to order food in, asked her what she'd like.

It had reminded Margo painfully of the weekends they'd spent together in this hotel or that, drinking champagne and eating takeaway, making love. Weekends stolen from reality, and yet so precious to her. Weekends when she'd felt carefree and alive in a way she never had before—or since.

She'd thought those weekends had kept her safe, kept

her from being emotionally engaged. Emotionally vulnerable.

Now she knew she'd been a fool. And she was still being a fool, because every moment she spent with Leo made her feel more raw. More afraid.

The meal they'd shared tonight had been utterly different from those earlier ones. They'd sat at either end of a huge dining room table, a modern-looking thing of carved ebony, and Margo had picked at her plain pasta while Leo had eaten souvlaki and answered emails on his smartphone. Neither of them had spoken.

This, then, was her future. Silent meals and endless tension.

Would it have been different if she'd said yes to Leo's proposal? Or would they have ended up here anyway, because they'd never loved each other? At least, Leo hadn't loved *her*. And what she'd felt for Leo had been only the beginnings of something, a tender shoot that had been plucked from the barren soil of her heart before it could take root and grow.

She hadn't let herself truly love Leo because loving someone meant opening yourself up to pain, heartache and loss. She'd learned long ago that people left you. Her mother, her foster parents, her sister. *Oh, God, her sister.*

Margo closed her eyes and willed back the rush of memory and pain.

Leo wouldn't leave her. He had too much honour for that. And as for this child... She pressed a hand to her middle and closed her eyes. *Stay safe, little one*, she prayed silently. *Stay strong.*

She made a cup of ginger tea, cradling the warm mug in her hands, and curled up on a window seat in the living room. The huge bay window overlooked Kolonaki's wide boulevards and narrow side streets, now illuminated only by a few streetlights and a thin crescent moon high above. In the distance she could see the Acropolis, its ancient buildings lit at night, a beacon for the city.

She took a sip of tea and tried to settle her swirling thoughts, but they were like leaves in a storm and the moment she tried to snatch at one another blew away. She closed her eyes and leaned against the window frame, tried instead to think of nothing at all.

'Is everything all right?'

Margo opened her eyes to see Leo standing in the doorway, dressed only in a pair of navy silk pyjama bottoms that rested low on his trim hips. The sight of his bare chest, all sleek rippled muscle, the sprinkling of dark hair vee-ing down to the waistband of his pyjamas, made her heart lurch and the breath stop in her lungs. She knew how hot and satiny his skin could be. She remembered the feel of that crisp hair against her seeking fingers. She knew the intimate feel of his whole body pressed against hers, chest to breasts, hips bumping, legs tangled.

She stared at him, willing herself to speak, not to want. 'I couldn't sleep,' she finally managed, her voice coming out in little more than a croak. 'I made some tea to help me settle. I'm sorry if I disturbed you.'

'I couldn't sleep either,' he said, and to her shock he came to sit down beside her on the window seat, his hip nudging her toes. 'Why couldn't you sleep?' he asked quietly.

'Why couldn't *you*?' Answering his question with one of her own was easier than admitting all the fears and worries that were tumbling through her mind.

'It's a lot to process,' Leo said after a moment. 'A baby, marriage... Just over twenty-four hours ago I wasn't anticipating either.'

'No, I suppose I've had more time to deal with it.'

He glanced down at her bare feet and then wrapped one warm hand around her foot. Everything in Margo jolted hard, almost painfully, at the feel of his strong hand curled around the sensitive arch of her foot, his fingers touching her toes.

'Your feet are cold,' he said, and drew them towards him, tucking them under his leg just as he had so many times before, when they'd been together.

Margo simply sat there, rigid with shock, with both of her feet tucked under his legs, everything in her aching.

'When you found out you were pregnant...' Leo asked slowly. 'How did it happen? How did you feel?'

Margo tensed, wondering if this was some kind of trap. Was he attempting to remind her once again of how non-maternal she'd been? Because she knew that. Of course she knew that, and it fed her fear.

'Why do you ask?'

'I just want to know. I feel like I've missed a big part of this.'

'I'm only four months along, Leo,' Margo said, but she relaxed slightly because she believed him. This wasn't a trap. Not with the sincerity she heard in his voice and her feet tucked under his legs.

'I had no idea at the start,' she began. 'I was on the pill, as you know. I didn't even miss taking one.'

'Then how did you get pregnant?'

'The day after...' She swallowed, felt a blush heat her cheeks and hoped Leo couldn't see in the dark. 'The day after I saw you I slept in. I took the pill three hours later than I normally would.'

'And that was enough to keep it from working?'

With a self-conscious laugh she patted her little bump. 'Apparently the mini-pill has to be taken at exactly the same time every day—although I didn't know things were quite that strict until it was too late.'

'You must have been shocked.'

'I was in a complete daze. I…I didn't know what I was going to do.' She hesitated in making that admission, afraid that Leo would use it against her, but he just nodded.

'That's understandable.'

'So for a while I didn't do anything. And then I felt so sick I *couldn't* do anything but drag myself through each day. When I went to the doctor to get some medication for my nausea he said something—just a throwaway comment about how such sickness usually meant the baby was healthy. "Here to stay," is what he said. And I knew that he was speaking the truth. That this baby was here to stay…that my inertia had been out of—well, out of fear,' she said.

Suddenly she realised just how much she was revealing. But she hadn't talked about this to anyone, and it felt good to unburden herself a little. Or even a lot.

'Fear?' Leo frowned. 'What are you afraid of?'

So many things. 'Of what the future would look like,' Margo answered, knowing she was hedging. 'Of how it would work. And of how you would take the news—what it would mean.'

'And so you decided to ask me to marry you?' Leo said. 'I still don't understand *that*, Margo.'

She swallowed, her throat feeling tight and sore. 'I grew up without a father,' she said after a brief pause. 'I didn't want the same for my child.'

He was silent for a moment. Then, 'I don't actually know anything about your childhood.'

And there was a very good reason for that. 'We didn't share many confidences, really, during our…' She trailed off.

'Our fling?' Leo filled in tonelessly.

'Yes.'

Even though her toes were still tucked under his warm thigh she felt a coolness in the air, tension tauten between them. It was a timely reminder of just what they'd had together…and what they had now.

'You want this baby,' Leo said slowly, a statement.

He lifted his head to look her straight in the face, and even in the darkness she could see the serious, intent look on his face, although she didn't know what it meant.

'Yes, I do.'

'You've changed in that, then?'

She took a deep breath and nodded. 'Yes.'

'Why?'

She stared at him, knowing he deserved to know at least this much. 'I didn't want children before because I was afraid,' she said slowly. 'Afraid of loving someone…and losing them. Or of getting it wrong. Parenting is a huge responsibility, Leo. The biggest.'

'But one you feel ready to take on now?'

'With your help.'

Except she didn't feel ready, not remotely. She felt inadequate and afraid and guilty. Because she wasn't sure she deserved another chance with someone's life.

'I *will* help you, Margo,' Leo said. 'We can do this. Together.'

She smiled even as she blinked back tears. She wanted to believe him. She almost did.

'I hope the tea helps you sleep,' he said, nodding towards her cup.

Margo knew he was about to leave and realised she didn't want him to.

'Leo…thank you,' she said, her voice both hurried and soft.

He stopped and turned to look at her in surprise. 'What are you thanking me for?'

'For…for being kind.'

He let out a huff of sound—almost a laugh. 'I don't think I've actually been very kind to you, Margo.'

'I know you were angry. I know you thought I'd cheated on you—maybe you still do. But even so you've agreed to marry me, and you've—you've shown concern for my welfare. I do appreciate that.'

He gazed at her for a long, fathomless moment before rising from the window seat. 'That's not very much, really.'

'I'm still grateful.'

It seemed as if he were going to say something else, something important, and Margo caught her breath… waited.

But all he said was, 'Get some sleep,' before returning to the darkness of his bedroom.

Leo stretched out on his bed and stared up at the ceiling, as far from sleep as he'd ever been. So much had happened today, tender little moments that had left him feeling uneasy and raw. It would be easy, he realised, to let himself care about Margo again. Let himself fall in love with her.

Let himself be rejected. Again.

Whatever had kept Margo from being with him before, it was still there. He didn't know what it was—the conversation he'd just had with her had left him wondering, uncertain. He'd seen a new vulnerability and fear underneath Margo's glossy, confident sophistication, and it had shocked him. It had made him realise there was depth and sadness to the woman with whom he'd had a passionate affair. The woman he was going to marry tomorrow.

The results of the paternity test were nothing more than a formality; he knew the baby was his. He knew Margo knew it. And with a baby and a marriage they could, in time, begin to build something together. Maybe not a grand passion or love, but something good and real and strong.

Then he reminded himself with slamming force of how she'd refused to marry him just four months ago, when they'd still been having their *fling*. She still clearly viewed their marriage as a sacrifice. How could he build on *that*— and, even if he could, why would he want to?

He'd had enough of trying to win people's trust or affection. For his entire childhood he'd been desperate for his father to notice him, love him. But Evangelos Marakaios had only cared about his business, and about handing it to his oldest son. In his mind Leo had been nothing more than spare—unneeded, irrelevant.

When his father had died Leo had hoped that his older brother Antonios would include him more in the family business, that they would have a partnership. But Antonios had cut him off even more than his father had, making him nothing more than a frontman, the eye candy to bring in new business without actually having any serious responsibility.

All that had changed six months ago, when Antonios had finally told Leo the truth. Evangelos had been borrowing against the company, making shoddy and sometimes illegal investments and running everything into debt. He'd hidden it from everyone except Antonios, confessing all when he'd been on his deathbed. Antonios had spent the next ten years hiding it from Leo.

He'd finally told the truth when prompted by his wife Lindsay and by Leo's own furious demands. And, while Leo had been glad to finally learn the truth, the knowledge didn't erase ten years of hurt, of anger, of being intentionally misled. His father and his brother, two of the people most important to him, had lied to him. They hadn't trusted him, and nothing they'd done had made Leo believe they loved him.

After so many years of trying to make them do both, he was far from eager to try the same with his soon-to-be wife.

He let out a weary sigh and closed his eyes, willed sleep to come. Enough thinking about Margo and what might have been. All he could do was take one day at a time and guard his heart. Make this marriage what they'd both agreed it would be: businesslike and convenient, and, yes, amicable. But nothing more.

Never anything more.

CHAPTER SEVEN

IF BRIDES WERE meant to look radiant on their wedding day, Margo thought, she fell lamentably short. She still had the exhausted, washed-out look she'd been sporting since the nausea had first hit, and she was, according to Leo's plan, going to get married this afternoon.

Sighing, she dragged a brush through her dark hair and wondered which of the two outfits she'd brought would be better to get married in—a sweater dress or jeans?

She didn't actually want the whole white wedding affair that Leo had mocked yesterday, but even so it felt pathetic and sad to be married like this, in the clothes she'd travelled in, looking like death barely warmed over.

With a sigh, she pulled her hair back into a neat ponytail and went in search of Leo.

She found him in the dining alcove of the kitchen, where the wide windows overlooked the small garden at the back of the townhouse. He'd made breakfast: toast and coffee, yogurt and fruit.

'I know you probably can't manage anything,' he said, gesturing to all the food, 'but I thought I'd make it just in case.'

'Thank you,' Margo murmured and sat down.

She spooned a little fruit and yogurt into a bowl and stirred honey into the centre.

Leo rose from the table and a few seconds later brought back a mug of ginger tea.

Margo blinked in surprise. 'How—?'

'You left the box of sachets in the kitchen. It seems like something you can keep down.'

'Just about the only thing.'

'Don't forget melba toast.'

'Right.'

She took a sip of tea and tried to still her swirling thoughts. Leo's consideration made her feel both restless and uneasy. It would have been easier to deal with his businesslike briskness, even his coldness, but this kindness… it reached right inside her. It made her ache with both regret and longing.

'Why are you doing this, Leo?' she asked.

'Doing what?'

'This.' She gestured to the breakfast dishes. 'You're being so…considerate.'

He gave her the ghost of a smile. 'Is that a bad thing?'

'No, but…'

'I don't want to fight all the time, Margo. That's not good for either of us, or our child.' He hesitated and then said, 'The doctor's office called this morning with the results of the paternity test.'

So that was the reason for his kindness and consideration. 'So now you know.'

'And you knew all along.'

'I told you there wasn't anyone else, Leo.'

'I believe you.'

He didn't look particularly pleased, though, and Margo wondered if the truth had hurt him as much as her lie had. Could he ever understand the desperate fear that had driven her to act as she had? She didn't even want him to.

'The marriage ceremony is at the town hall, at two

o'clock,' he said after a pause. 'We can drive back to the estate afterwards.'

'All right.'

'We need two witnesses for the ceremony,' he continued. 'I thought I'd ask two of my staff from the Athens office.'

'Fine.'

It wasn't the way she'd ever anticipated getting married —a cold ceremony in a bureaucrat's office in a country she didn't know—but then she'd never anticipated marrying at all. She'd expected to live her life alone, the way she had since she was twelve and she'd lost everyone. *She'd lost Annelise.*

Leo glanced at the rumpled sweater dress she'd worn two days in a row. 'Do you have something to wear to the wedding?'

'I wasn't planning to get married today,' she reminded him. 'I have this or jeans.'

He frowned and took a sip of coffee. 'Then we'll go shopping this morning for something suitable. If you feel up to it?'

She almost asked him why they should bother, but then just nodded instead. Leo had said arguing would be unpleasant for both of them, and she agreed. She would do her part in keeping things civil, even if his kindness had a strange way of hurting her.

Half an hour later they were strolling down Voukourestiou Street, home to many designer boutiques. Leo led her into the first one, a soaring space of airy lightness, with a white leather sofa where shoppers could rest and a few select garments hanging from silver wires suspended from the ceiling.

Margo glanced at the elegant gowns in bemusement, for she had no idea what kind of dress she was supposed

to get married in. But this was a business arrangement, so
a business outfit seemed appropriate. She saw a pale grey
suit at the back of the boutique and nodded to it.

'How about that one?'

Leo frowned. 'That doesn't look much like a wedding
dress.'

'This isn't much of a wedding,' she answered.

His frown deepened. 'We might be marrying in a civil
ceremony, but it is still very much a wedding. We will still
very much be married.'

He nodded towards a dress of cream silk with an empire
waist and a frothy skirt glittering with beaded crystals.

'How about that one?'

It was a feminine, frou-frou kind of dress—so unlike
her usual tailored wardrobe. Margo hesitated, because
while it wasn't something she would normally wear, she
did like it. It was different. It wasn't armour.

She gave a quick nod. 'All right. I'll try it on.'

Moments later she stared at herself in the mirror, surprised at how the dress softened her. The warm cream of
the material actually brought a bit of colour to her face,
and complemented her dark hair and eyes. The sales assistant had brought her a matching pair of shoes—slim
heels with a small diamante on each toe. They went perfectly with the dress.

'Well?' Leo called.

'You're not supposed to see it before the ceremony,'
Margo called back. 'But I think it will do.'

At the cash desk she offered to pay for it, but Leo silenced her with a single look as he handed over his credit
card. He'd been the same when they were dating: he'd paid
for all their meals and hotels, despite Margo's insistence
that she could pay her way. She hadn't minded, because
she'd still felt safe. Still kept him at a distance.

This felt different. This was a wedding dress—the start of a new life that would be utterly intertwined with Leo's.

'We should go back to the apartment,' he said as he accepted the dress, now swathed in a designer hanging bag. 'You should rest before the ceremony.'

A few hours later Margo's stomach was seething with a whole different kind of nausea, now caused by nervousness. She'd showered and put on her new dress and heels, coiled her hair into its usual elegant chignon. The dress's high waist hid her small baby bump, for which she was grateful. She'd rather not have some sanctimonious city official looking at her disapprovingly.

'Are you ready?' Leo called, and she gave her reflection one last, swift look.

In less than an hour she would be married. She would have made vows that would bind her to Leo for ever.

'I'm coming,' she called, and walked out of the bedroom.

Leo's eyes widened as he took in her appearance, and then he gave one nod. 'You look very nice.'

It was a rather 'milquetoast' compliment, but Margo saw the way colour touched his cheekbones. She felt awareness—physical awareness—sweep through her in an electrifying wave.

'You look nice too,' she said, which was a serious understatement.

In a dark grey suit and silvery-grey tie he looked amazing. The colour of his tie made his eyes look even more silver, seeming to blaze in his swarthy face, and his dark hair was brushed back, the strong lines of his cheekbones and jaw emphasised by the cut of his suit.

'We should drive to the town hall,' he said. 'And then

we can leave directly from there. I need to get back to the estate to work.'

Margo nodded. No matter how incredible Leo looked, this marriage was still no more than a business arrangement. 'I'll get my bag.'

They drove in silence to the town hall, with tension stretching and snapping between them, or at least that was how it felt to Margo. She knew the civil marriage ceremony would be short and simple, but she would still be making promises to Leo. To herself. To their baby. Promises she intended to keep. Which made her heart race and her hands go clammy. There would be no going back from this.

The town hall in Athens was an impressive building in the centre of the city; the marriage ceremony was to be held in a small room on a top floor, with only a few people in attendance. The two staff from Leo's office greeted him with bland faces, although Margo imagined they had to be curious as to why their CEO was getting married in such a quick and pragmatic way. Thank goodness her bump wasn't visible, although of course it would be soon enough.

The official cleared his throat and began, and within a few minutes it was over. Margo had barely had to say a word.

Leo slid a ring of white gold on her finger; she stared down at it in surprise.

'When did you…?'

'I had it couriered,' he answered, and for some reason it hurt her—the thought that someone else had bought her wedding ring.

It was stupid, of course, but then she'd been so emotional lately. In any case, Margo knew she'd have to get used to these little things and remind herself that they weren't slights. She hadn't wanted romance, so she shouldn't expect it. Its absence surely shouldn't hurt her.

Just like the fact that he hadn't kissed her shouldn't hurt. It was simply the way it was. And so they walked out of the town hall into the bright winter sunshine, and then to the car.

They drove out of Athens as husband and wife, with not one word or person to mark the occasion.

Leo drove in silence for nearly an hour, his mind seething with thoughts he didn't want to articulate. The ceremony had been both simple and brief, which was how he'd expected and wanted it to be, and yet somehow he felt as if he were disappointing Margo. Disappointing himself.

It had hardly seemed appropriate to have a big church wedding, and yet... It had been a very small ceremony for a big step such as they were taking.

He glanced at the ring she'd slid onto his finger, her fingers seeming so fragile and cold on his. *Married.* He was a husband now, with responsibilities to his wife and child. Responsibilities he'd bear gladly, and yet he still felt their weight.

And one of those responsibilities was introducing Margo to his family. He hadn't considered the ramifications of marrying quickly and bringing Margo back to his villa immediately after. He'd simply wanted to control the situation, to have it on his terms.

Now he realised two of his sisters, Xanthe and Ava, who lived on the estate with him, would be wide-eyed and speculating when he brought back his sudden and obviously pregnant bride.

His older brother Antonios had done virtually the same thing—coming back from a business trip to North America with his unexpected bride, Lindsay. Antonios's iron will had assured Lindsay was made welcome, but even so Leo had seen how hard it had been on her, for a variety of reasons. And she hadn't even been pregnant.

He didn't want the same rocky start for Margo.

Flexing his hands on the steering wheel, he glanced at her, looking so pale and weary. 'My sisters will be at the estate when we return,' he began, and she turned to him sharply.

'Sisters? I didn't even know you *had* sisters.'

'Three, and one brother.'

'Your brother I know about. He was CEO before you?'

'Yes.' He'd told her that much at least, although he hadn't even hinted at the strains and sins that had marred their relationship. 'Two of my sisters live on the estate. They will want to meet you.'

'They weren't there before when I came?'

'No, they were visiting Parthenope, my third sister. She lives with her family near Patras.'

'Timon's mother?'

'Yes.'

Margo expelled a shaky breath. 'And what about your parents?'

'They're both dead.'

'I'm sorry.' She glanced at him, her eyes dark. 'When?'

'My father ten years ago, and my mother six months ago.'

Her eyes widened. 'When we were together?'

'Yes.'

He hadn't told her. There was so much he hadn't told her. And for the first time Leo acknowledged how Margo had had a point, claiming their relationship hadn't been going anywhere. He'd kept inside its careful parameters as much as she had. It was only when he'd become CEO that he'd decided he should marry and have an heir, and Margo had seemed the obvious choice. The right choice.

And now it had all happened just as he'd wanted…and yet not at all as he'd expected.

'They won't be pleased, will they?' Margo said after a moment. 'To welcome a surprise sister-in-law, and one who's pregnant?'

'They'll be surprised,' Leo allowed.

Margo let out a huff of laughter. 'I should say so. Did they even know you were—that we were—?'

'No.' He shifted in his seat. 'I never told anyone about us.'

She eyed him curiously. 'And yet you asked me to marry you?'

'I know.' He hesitated, and then continued a bit stiffly, 'I realise now how surprising my proposal must have been. Regardless of how you felt about it, it had to have been a shock.'

'It was.' She took a breath. 'Why…why did you ask me, Leo? If you didn't love me?'

'It felt like the right time to get married. I'd just been made CEO and I was conscious of needing an heir, stability. And as we were already together…'

'It was convenient?'

She let out another huff of sound, although whether it was a laugh or something else Leo couldn't tell.

'Well, that's what it is now. *Convenient.*'

'In any case,' Leo continued, 'I want to make sure my family accepts you as mistress of the household. You'll have my full support—'

'I don't want to displace anyone.'

'As my wife, you will have a role—'

'I know.' She leaned her head back against the seat and closed her eyes. 'I know. And I will rise to that particular challenge, I promise you. Just…just give me some time—please?'

'What about *your* family?' he asked, deciding it was wiser, or at least safer, to leave the topic of his own family for now. 'Is there anyone you want to tell? You could invite them to come—'

'No,' she cut across him flatly, her face turned to the window. 'There's no one.'

'Your parents?' Belatedly he remembered she'd said she'd grown up without a father. 'Your mother, at least?'

'I haven't seen her since I was twelve.'

'Really?'

Perhaps he shouldn't have been shocked. In the last few days he'd sensed a sorrow, even a darkness, in Margo's past that he'd never noticed before, perhaps because she'd been careful to hide it.

'Why not?'

She twitched her shoulders in a shrug. 'She wasn't a very good mother.'

It was clear she didn't want to talk about it, and Leo decided not to press. There had been enough emotional upheavals today.

'I'm sorry,' he said, and she bowed her head, a few tendrils of hair escaping her ponytail to rest against her cheek.

'So am I,' she said, and she sounded so sad that Leo felt an answering emotion rise in him in an unstoppable tide.

For a moment he considered pulling the car over, pulling her into his arms. Making her feel better.

But then she raised her head, set her jaw, and that moment passed almost as if it had never happened at all.

They didn't speak until they reached Amfissa.

CHAPTER EIGHT

MARGO FORCED HERSELF to relax as Leo turned the car up the sweeping drive that led to the Marakaios estate. She'd seen it all before, of course, when she'd driven up here in her rental car just two days ago. But then it had just been a house, grand and imposing; now it was her home.

As he pulled the car up to the front of the sprawling villa she noticed the other buildings surrounding it. The Marakaios estate was actually a complex, almost a little city.

'What are all the other buildings?'

'The office, a guesthouse, staff housing, a private villa where I used to live before I moved to the main house.'

'When was that?'

'When I became CEO.'

Which seemed to have been a life-changing moment, with his moving and then thinking of marrying.

'Why did your brother step down?'

'He wanted to move into investments,' Leo said, and the terseness of his reply made Margo wonder if there were more to it than that. She really knew so little about this man, her *husband*. So little about his life, his family.

And some of his family were coming out of the house right now: two tall, dark-haired women with the same striking good looks as Leo. Margo was intimidated by them already, and they hadn't even seen her yet, or her bump.

As Leo climbed out of the car the first one addressed him in a torrent of Greek, her hands on her hips. Distantly Margo considered that perhaps she should learn her husband's native language. Lessons, at least, would fill her empty days until the baby was born.

Leo came round to open the passenger door as his other sister joined them, unleashing her own incomprehensible diatribe. Leo didn't answer, just extended a hand to Margo.

She rose from the seat, still in her wedding dress, and as she stood the material caught on the door and tugged tight, outlining her small bump. Both sisters stopped abruptly and sucked in their breaths.

'*Kalispera*,' Margo said, and pinned on a bright and utterly false smile.

One of the sisters turned to Leo and began speaking again in rapid Greek. He held up a hand to silence her. 'Speak English, please, Xanthe. You're perfectly capable of it. My wife does not speak Greek.'

'Your *wife*—' Xanthe said, and her mouth dropped open.

She looked, Margo thought, appalled.

'Yes. My wife. We married today and, as you can see, we are expecting our first child in a few months.' He placed a hand on Margo's lower back, propelling her forward. 'Xanthe, Ava—please meet Margo Ferrars, Margo Marakaios now.'

She smiled weakly.

'Margo—my sisters.'

'I'm pleased to meet you,' she said, and they both nodded stiffly. Margo couldn't really blame them for the lack of welcome; they were clearly completely shocked. Still, it stung.

'Come inside,' Leo said, and drew her past his sisters into the villa.

Maria bustled up to them as soon as they stepped inside the door, and Leo spoke to her in Greek before turning to Margo with a grimace of apology. 'Maria doesn't speak English, but I've told her we're married.'

Margo nodded. She couldn't tell a thing from the housekeeper's expression, but she felt too overwhelmed and exhausted to care. It had been an incredibly long day, and she didn't have the energy to deal with any of these strangers.

'Leo,' she said, 'I'm tired, and I'd like to rest.'

It was only a little past seven, yet even so Margo knew she couldn't face an evening with Leo's family. Was she neglecting her responsibilities, even her vows, so soon? So be it. Tomorrow she would try to be the Stepford Wife he seemed to want. Today she needed to recover.

'Of course. I'll show you to your bedroom.'

Margo felt the silent stares boring into her back as she followed Leo up to the bedrooms. He went down a different corridor than before, and then ushered her into a sumptuous room decorated in pale blue and ivory.

'This is your bedroom. I have an adjoining one.' He gestured to a wood-panelled door in the corner, by the window.

So they wouldn't be sharing a bedroom. Margo didn't know how she felt about that, and in her exhausted state didn't feel like probing the tangle of her own emotions.

'Thank you,' she murmured, and took a few steps into the bedroom.

'You must let Maria know if you would like anything,' Leo said. 'And I'll be right next door if you need something in the night…'

She swallowed painfully. A lump had risen in her throat and it was hard to speak around it. It was their wedding night and they would be sleeping apart. She knew she shouldn't expect, much less want anything else.

'I'll be fine,' she said, and he nodded, one hand on the doorknob, seeming reluctant to leave her.

But he did, and Margo sank onto the bed and dropped her head into her hands. She felt more alone, more isolated, than she had in a long, long while—and considering the lonely course of her life, the loss of both her mother and Annelise, that was saying something.

She missed her apartment desperately, with its cosy, familiar furnishings, its sense of safety. She missed her life, the job that had given her security and purpose, her friends like Sophie, who might not have known that much about her but had still been *friends*.

She should text Sophie and tell her everything that had happened… But Margo didn't think she had it in her to weather Sophie's undoubtedly stunned and concerned response. No, she'd sleep. And maybe in the morning it would all look a little bit better.

At least their wedding night, wretched as it was, would be over.

Leo sat alone in his bedroom and stared moodily out of the window. He'd endured a barrage of questions from his sisters, who had wanted to know how he'd met Margo and why he'd married her.

'You might have noticed she's carrying my child,' he'd said tersely.

Xanthe had rolled her eyes. 'It's the twenty-first century, Leo. Illegitimacy isn't the stigma it once was.'

'I'm a traditional man.'

But he hadn't simply married Margo because she was pregnant with his baby, he acknowledged now. That might have been the impetus, but the truth was he'd wanted to marry her. He'd wanted her four months ago and he wanted her now.

And now it was his wedding night, and he was sitting here alone, drinking his second whisky, when what he really wanted was to take Margo into his arms and feel her softness against him…

Muttering a curse, Leo finished his whisky in one burning swallow. It was going to be a long, long night.

When Margo woke up the next morning she felt a lump of dread in her middle, as heavy as a stone, at the thought of facing the day and Leo's sisters, his staff…facing this whole strange world that she was now a part of.

She lay in bed and blinked up at the ceiling as wintry sunlight filtered through the curtains and illuminated the room's luxurious furnishings. For a girl who had been a breath away from growing up on the streets, she really had landed in a soft place indeed.

Resolutely Margo swung her legs over the side of the bed. After the usual moment of dizziness passed, she rose. She might not be looking forward to today, but she would meet it. She'd certainly faced far worse. And no matter how uncertain of her or unfriendly Leo's sisters might be, this was her new life. She had to accept it. Embrace it, even.

With that in mind, Margo put on her last remaining outfit, jeans and a jumper, and headed downstairs.

She could hear Leo's sisters' voices from the dining room as she came downstairs. They spoke in Greek, but Margo didn't need to know the language to understand the gist of what they were saying. Agitation, hurt and anger were audible in their tones.

She took a deep breath, squared her shoulders, and entered the room. '*Kalimera.*' Her knowledge of Greek extended only to greetings and saying thank you, but she hoped she was at least showing them she was trying.

Xanthe and Ava fell silent, forcing smiles to their lips. Margo sat at the opposite end of the table from Leo and busied herself with putting a napkin on her lap. She could see yogurt, fresh fruit and pastries on the table, and coffee, tea and juice on the sideboard. She wasn't very hungry but, wanting something to do, began to fill her plate.

'Good morning,' Leo answered her in English, and from the corner of her eye Margo saw him give a pointed look to his sisters. 'Did you sleep well?'

Margo felt a ripple of surprise from his sisters, and knew they were wondering why Leo should ask such a question. It would soon be clear to everyone that they had not shared a bedroom.

Leo must have realised it too, for his mouth tightened and he took a sip of coffee.

'I slept very well, thank you,' Margo said quietly.

They sounded like polite strangers. His sisters' eyes were on stalks.

'I thought perhaps after breakfast I could show you around the estate a bit,' Leo continued, his tone stiff now with formality. 'If you feel up to it?'

'That would be good.'

They sounded as if they were ironing out the details of a business merger—which was, Margo supposed, essentially what they were doing. If Leo wanted their marriage to be businesslike, then she supposed he wouldn't mind his sisters knowing it.

'Leo hasn't told us anything about you,' Xanthe said after a few moments of strained silence, when all Margo did was toy with her food and stare at her plate. 'Where are you from?'

She looked up and met Xanthe's speculative gaze with what she hoped was a friendly smile. 'I lived in Paris.'

'I love Paris!'

Ava jumped in quickly, and Margo wondered if the sisters would actually be welcoming towards her after all.

'It must have been very hard to leave.'

Margo glanced at Leo, whose face was as bland as ever. 'A bit,' she allowed, 'but I have other things to think about now.'

She rested one hand on her small bump, which unintentionally but effectively silenced all conversation. Both Xanthe and Ava excused themselves a few minutes later, leaving Leo and Margo alone with about an acre of polished mahogany between them.

'I'm sorry things seem a bit awkward,' Leo said after a moment. 'They'll come to accept you in time.'

'Maybe,' Margo allowed. 'I don't suppose it really matters.'

'Doesn't it? This is your home now, Margo. My family is your family. I want you to feel a part of things. I want you to *be* a part of things.'

'I know.' She toyed with a piece of melon and then laid down her fork. 'I'll hold up my end of the bargain, Leo.'

To her surprise he threw his napkin down and rose from the table. 'I don't want to talk about bargains,' he said. 'Let me know when you are ready to begin the tour. I'll be in my study.'

Mystified, Margo watched him stride out of the dining room. She'd annoyed him, obviously, but she didn't know how or why. Sighing, feeling the day stretching out in front of her would be very long indeed, she ate a bit of yogurt and nibbled on a pastry before rising herself and going to find Leo.

He'd told her he would be in the study, but she couldn't remember where it was—although she certainly recalled the interview she'd had in there just two days ago. She pressed a hand to her forehead, amazed at how much had changed in such a short time. Her whole life had been up-ended.

After opening and closing a few doors that led to various impressive reception rooms, she finally found the study. Leo sat behind the desk, one hand driving through his hair, rumpling it in a way that would have made him seem endearing if he hadn't had such a scowl on his face.

Margo knocked on the already open door and Leo looked up. His face cleared, but only just.

'Did you eat something?'

'A bit. I'm fine.'

He hesitated, then said, 'Things will get better. As you settle in.'

'I hope so. Although I'm not sure what you want sometimes, Leo. You almost seemed angry back there, talking about our marriage as a bargain, and yet *you're* the one who said you wanted to keep it businesslike.' The words spilled out of her, even though she hadn't intended to say them.

'I know,' Leo said, and drummed his fingers on the desktop.

Margo waited for him to elaborate but he didn't.

'I just want us to be on the same page,' she said quietly. 'Whatever page that is.'

'I think it will take time to decide what page that is,' he said finally. 'But in the meantime we can deal with practical matters.' He nodded towards her jeans and jumper. 'You need clothes and toiletries. We can order some things online, or go into Amfissa—'

'I'd like to get my things from Paris,' Margo answered. 'I'll need to speak to people at work, put my apartment on the market.'

'There's no need to sell your apartment. I can certainly afford to keep it, and it might be nice for us to have a permanent place in Paris.'

She blinked, surprised by his generosity. It was a far cry from the conditions he'd given her the last time they'd been in this room. 'Are you—are you sure?'

'Yes. Why shouldn't we keep it?' He stared at her for a moment and then said, his voice gaining an edge, 'Not *everything* about our marriage has to be a sacrifice, Margo.'

'I didn't mean it like that—'

'No? Sometimes when you look at me you seem as if you're steeling yourself.' He rose from the desk, shrugging on his suit jacket. 'It seems strange that it is so difficult for you to spend time with me now when we had two years together. But perhaps when you said you were planning to end it you spoke the truth, whether there was another man or not.'

He spoke with such bland indifference that it took Margo a few seconds for his meaning to penetrate. 'Leo, I thought it was you who didn't want to spend time with *me*. You've been angry with me for months, and I understand why—'

'I'm not angry.'

'No? If I look like I'm steeling myself,' Margo said, her heart starting to beat hard at this sudden, unexpected honesty, 'it's because I'm bracing myself for whatever mood you're in—whatever you're going to say. Sometimes… sometimes it feels like you're still punishing me for leaving you.'

He stared at her for a long moment, his eyes like shards of ice in his fathomless face. Margo waited, her breath held.

'I'm not punishing you,' he said at last. 'Not any more. I admit when you first came here…when I believed you'd been unfaithful…I may have been acting out of anger, or even spite.' He sighed, the sound weary. 'A petty, useless emotion if ever there was one. But I don't want to act like that any more. We need to move on, Margo, and make this marriage something we can both live with.'

'Which is?'

'That I don't know yet. But hopefully we'll find out in time.' He moved past her towards the door. 'Now, let me show you the rest of the villa.'

She followed him through the house as he showed her various rooms: a formal living room and a smaller, cosier TV room, the large dining room where they'd had breakfast, and another less formal room for family meals. A music room, a library, a second kitchen for parties... Margo started to feel overwhelmed. The house was huge. And Leo wanted *her* to be its mistress.

'What exactly do you want me to do, Leo?' she asked as they left the second kitchen.

He turned to her with a frown. 'What do you mean?'

'I mean what are my responsibilities? You mentioned that you wanted me to be in charge of your household...'

'I only meant that as a courtesy to you and your position here. I don't expect you to have *duties.*'

Which made her feel more confused than ever. 'I don't understand...'

'Margo, we're married. You're the—'

'Mistress of the house? The chatelaine? Yes, I understand that.'

'You can do as much or as little as you like. If you want to consult with Maria about meals, or housekeeping, or anything, you're more than welcome. If you want to redecorate, go ahead. I'm trying to give you freedom, not a burden.'

'Thank you,' Margo said after a moment, because she didn't know what else to say.

She might have established her career in acquiring household items for a large department store, but even so she wasn't about to bring her skills to bear here. She doubted his sisters would appreciate her changing so much as a cushion. As for meals... Her cooking skills had always been limited. She couldn't imagine planning meals for everyone.

And yet...

This was her life. She needed to own it.

'Do Xanthe and Ava both eat in the main house?' she asked. 'Will we have meals with them every day?'

'They come and go. Neither of them really work, although Xanthe does a little PR for Marakaios Enterprises. Ava travels to Athens frequently. I suspect she's seeing someone there, but she's quite close-mouthed on the subject.'

So she'd have both women underfoot...watching and judging her. Margo pressed a hand to her middle to suppress the lurch of queasiness that prospect gave her.

Leo, of course, noticed.

'Are you well?'

'I'm fine, Leo. I'm actually feeling a bit better today than yesterday.' A good night's sleep and no more travelling had helped in that regard. 'But I do need some more clothes and things.'

'I can take you into Amfissa this afternoon for some supplies. And, if you'd like to make a list, I'll arrange for whatever possessions you want to be sent here from your apartment in Paris.'

'All right,' Margo said. And although she didn't like the thought of some stranger rifling through her things she had the sense to know that another long trip would exhaust her, and she appreciated Leo's kindness.

He took her upstairs, where he pointed out Xanthe and Ava's bedrooms, in a separate wing from theirs. And then he hesitated before opening the door to a slightly smaller bedroom next to hers.

'I thought, when the times comes, this could be the nursery.'

She glanced at the beautiful yet bland room, decorated in pale greens and creams.

'You can completely redecorate it, of course. Have you...?' He cleared his throat. 'Have you given some thought as to whether you'd like to know if it's a boy or girl?'

Shock rippled through her at the question; it raised a host of images and possibilities in her mind. Pink frilled dresses or blue romper suits. And whatever this child was—boy or girl—*they* would be the parents. Together they'd be raising this person, putting this tiny being at the centre of their shared lives.

'I don't think I've let myself,' she said slowly.

'What do you mean?'

She swallowed, not wanting to admit how fearful she was, about so many things. How even now she was terrified of losing this child, of something going terribly wrong.

'So far I've just wanted to make sure the baby is healthy,' she said. 'Do *you* want to find out?'

'I haven't thought about it,' Leo answered, rubbing his jaw. 'But I think...yes. If you do. It could help us prepare. Make it more real.'

Again she thought of the swooshing sound of the baby's heartbeat, the reality of this life inside her, so small and vulnerable, so *important*. 'Yes, I suppose it would.'

'Dr Tallos has recommended a local obstetrician,' he said. 'You're meant to have an ultrasound in three weeks.'

'Just before Christmas.'

And what a wonderful Christmas present that would be—the promise of a healthy baby, boy or girl.

Something must have shown in her face, for Leo stopped to look at her seriously, and then took her chin in his hand, his touch light, his gaze searching.

'Margo, what is it?'

'What do you mean?'

'You seem…afraid.'

Her throat tightened and she tried to smile. 'I just don't want anything to go wrong with the baby.'

'Why do you think something might?'

Because she knew what it was like to lose someone precious. One day Annelise had been there—soft and smiling and warm, with her button-black eyes and her round cherubic cheeks—and the next she'd been gone. There had been nothing left but emptiness and heartbreak.

'Margo…' Leo said again, and he sounded alarmed.

She knew she must have an awful expression on her face.

She stepped back, away from his hand. 'I'm a first-time mother,' she reminded him as lightly as she could. 'I'm bound to be nervous.'

But judging by Leo's frown she didn't think she'd fooled him into believing that was all it was.

CHAPTER NINE

A WEEK PASSED and Margo started to think she and Leo were finding that same page. Things had settled, more or less, into a routine: Leo worked most of the day and Margo drifted. She didn't mind it for now, because with her nausea and her exhaustion drifting through each day was about all she could manage.

But as the days passed, and her nausea thankfully started to abate, she knew she needed to find some focus. Some purpose.

Xanthe and Ava had thawed towards her a little, which made life less tense if not exactly easy. And her things had arrived from Paris. Besides her clothes and toiletries she'd requested that some of her personal items—paintings and ornaments and books—be shipped to Greece. It felt both comforting and strange to arrange her things in the bedroom that still didn't feel like hers. They were dotted around the yawning space like buoys bobbing in an unfamiliar sea.

Still, life marched on, and Margo knew she needed to march with it.

She drove into Amfissa one afternoon and wandered the streets, window-shopping. She went into a shop that sold nursery furniture and gazed in wonder at the array of cradles and buggies—at a whole arsenal of parental tools with which *she* would one day need to be equipped.

When she came back down the sweeping drive that led to the main villa of the Marakaios estate Leo came out of the house, standing on the portico as he glowered at her.

She hadn't even cut the engine before he was striding over to the driver's side and opening door.

'Where were you—?'

'In Amfissa. I told Maria.' She'd managed to learn enough Greek, and Maria knew enough English, to communicate with the housekeeper.

'By yourself?'

Leo sounded incredulous and Margo only just kept from rolling her eyes.

'Leo, I'm a grown woman—'

'You're also pregnant—'

'Pregnancy is not a disease.'

'You've been suffering from extreme morning sickness, Margo, and I've seen how dizzy you can get. What if something had happened?'

She quelled the lurch of alarm she felt at that thought. Just when she'd been coming to grips with her own fear Leo had managed to rake it all up again.

'I can't just stay in the villa, Leo, like some knocked-up Rapunzel in her tower. I'll go mad.'

She heard a snort of laughter from behind her and turned around.

'Knocked-up Rapunzel?' Leo repeated, a smile tugging at his mouth. 'That presents quite an image.'

Margo smiled back. She'd missed this kind of banter so much. The jokes and the teasing…the *lightness*. She needed it to combat the darkness she felt so often in herself. 'Well, that's how I feel. And I don't even have tons of beautiful blonde hair to compensate.'

'Your hair is beautiful,' Leo said.

And just like that he dropped the banter, replacing it with an intent sincerity that made Margo's heart judder.

'I always enjoyed watching you when you unpinned it in the evening.'

All at once she had an image of Leo, gazing at her as she reached up to undo the chignon she normally kept her waist-length hair in. She pictured the hotel room, the candlelight casting flickering shadows across the wide bed. The moment's intimacy and expectation, the sheer eroticism of it...

It felt like a lifetime ago—and yet it also felt very real. She could remember exactly how it had felt when her hair had cascaded down her back and Leo had reached for her, taken her into his arms and pushed the heavy mass aside to kiss the tender nape of her neck...

She swallowed hard, not sure if she wanted to revel in the moment spinning out between them or move past it.

In the end Leo chose for her.

'I understand you needing to get out. But your mobile phone doesn't even work here—'

'Then perhaps I should get a new one. I can't be a prisoner, Leo.'

'I don't want you to be. I'll order you a phone today. I should have done it before. I'm sorry.'

She nodded wordlessly, still caught in the thrall of that moment, that memory.

'I was thinking,' Leo said abruptly, 'we should have a party. To welcome you properly and introduce you to the community. If you feel up to it.'

'I'm feeling much better. I'd like that.' Maybe a party would help her to meet people and finally start feeling a part of things.

* * *

Somewhat to Margo's surprise, Xanthe and Ava were excited about the party. They set a date, and contacted caterers, and sent out invitations to everyone in the local community.

And they took Margo shopping.

She resisted at first, because the thought of the two women fluttering around her like butterflies while she tried on dresses was alarming, to say the least. But they insisted and she finally gave in, driving with them into Amfissa one afternoon a few days before the party.

'You're not quite ready for maternity wear,' Ava said, casting a critical eye over Margo's neat bump. 'How far along are you, anyway?'

'Just over eighteen weeks,' Margo said.

The nausea had almost completely gone, and she was starting to feel a little more energetic and look a little less gaunt.

'You're so *thin*,' Xanthe said, envy audible in her voice. 'It seems like all Parisian women are thin. Do you ever eat?'

'Not lately,' Margo admitted, 'but normally, yes.'

Suddenly she thought of the mini-marshmallows she'd kept in her bag—her secret vice—and how Leo had known about them.

'You're smiling like a cat who just ate the cream,' Ava noted.

Margo shook her head. 'Just…remembering something.'

Which made the sisters exchange knowing looks.

And then Xanthe asked abruptly, 'So what is going on between you and Leo? Because obviously…' she gestured towards Margo's bump '…you've been together, but…' She trailed off as Ava gave her a quelling look.

Margo sighed. She'd come to realise that Ava and Xanthe were good-natured and well-intentioned, if a little interfering. They deserved the truth, or at least as much as she could tell them without betraying Leo's confidences.

'We were together. But things had…started to cool off. And then I became pregnant.'

'Accidentally?' Xanthe asked with wide eyes.

Ava snorted. 'Of course accidentally, *ilithia*.'

Margo recognised the Greek word for idiot; this wasn't the first time Ava had used it towards her younger sister and Leo, amused, had told her what it meant.

Ava turned to Margo. 'So you told Leo about the baby?'

'Yes. I never thought I'd have children, but—'

'Why not?' Xanthe interjected.

Margo hesitated. 'I suppose because I was focused on my career.' Which was no more than a half-truth. It was because she was afraid of loving and losing someone again—so desperately afraid.

Her hand crept to the comforting swell of her bump and Ava noticed the revealing gesture.

'Come on, let's try and find some dresses,' she said, and Margo was glad for the change in subject.

She spent a surprisingly enjoyable afternoon with both sisters once she'd got used to Xanthe's nosiness and Ava's bustling, bossy manner. She realised they were both fun to be around, and she could tell they actually cared about her. It almost felt like being part of a family—something she hadn't experienced since she'd been twelve years old, and even then not so much…

They finally all agreed on a dress of deep magenta that brought colour to Margo's face and complemented her dark eyes and hair. Its empire waist and swirling skirt drew attention away from her bump without hiding it completely.

'Understated, elegant, and just a little bit sexy,' Ava declared in satisfaction. 'Perfect. Leo will love it.'

And with a little thrill Margo realised she *wanted* Leo

to love it. She wanted to be beautiful to him again. A dangerous desire, perhaps, but still, caught in the happy glow of their shared afternoon, Margo didn't try and suppress it. Leo was her husband, after all. Why shouldn't she want him to find her attractive, desirable?

The night of the party, as she stood in front of the full-length mirror in her bedroom and gazed at her reflection, she wondered again just what Leo would think of her in this dress. She'd done her hair in its usual chignon but styled it a bit more loosely, so a few tendrils escaped to frame her face. She'd taken care with her make-up, making her eyes look bigger and darker with eyeliner and mascara, choosing a berry-red lipstick that matched her dress.

She looked, Margo thought, a bit more like her old self—the old Margo, who'd armed herself with make-up and designer clothes and stiletto heels. And yet she looked...softer, somehow. Her face was rounder, her bump was visible, and she didn't feel quite as guarded as she normally did.

Maybe living here in Greece with people all around her was softening her slowly. Changing her just a little. It was so different from the isolation she'd known for so long.

A knock sounded on the door that joined her bedroom to Leo's. He used it on occasion, to come and say good-night to her, or talk with her about various matters. He always knocked first—always kept things formal and brief.

Now Margo cleared her throat before calling for him to enter.

'Are you—?'

He stopped as he caught sight of her, and Margo's breath dried in her throat as she looked at him. He wore a tuxedo, something she'd never actually seen him in before, and the crisp white shirt and black jacket was the perfect foil for his swarthy skin and ink-dark hair. The strong, clean lines of his jaw and cheekbones made Margo ache to touch him. And when she saw the blaze of desire in his eyes she felt as if a Roman candle had lit up inside her, fizzing and firing away.

'I was going to ask you if you were ready,' Leo said, his voice turning husky, 'but you obviously are. You look beautiful, Margo. Utterly enchanting.'

Colour touched her cheeks, and when she spoke her voice was almost as husky as his own. 'Thank you. You look…incredible.'

She blushed even more at this admission, and Leo's mouth quirked in a small smile. Margo could feel the tension snapping between them, but for once it was a good, exciting kind of tension. Sexual tension.

'Shall we?' he asked, and held out his hand.

Nodding, Margo took it.

Even though they'd been living as man and wife for a couple of weeks, they'd hardly ever touched. In this charged atmosphere the feel of his fingers sliding along her hand and then curling over her fingers made heat pool deep in Margo's belly.

Leo drew her out of the room and down the stairs towards the guests who were already arriving and milling in the foyer; the extra staff hired for the night circulated with trays of champagne and canapés.

The pooling desire she'd felt was replaced by a sudden lurch of nerves at the sight of all the people waiting to meet her, and maybe to judge her.

Leo gently squeezed her fingers. 'Chin up,' he said softly. 'You look beautiful and you are amazing.'

She glanced at him swiftly, surprise slicing through her at the obvious sincerity in his tone. What was happening between them? This certainly didn't feel businesslike.

But before she could say anything, or even think about

it any further, he was drawing her down the stairs and towards the crowd.

It had been a long time since Margo had socialised; morning sickness had kept her from doing anything but the bare minimum. Now, however, wearing a gorgeous dress, feeling beautiful and even cherished on Leo's arm, she felt some of her old sparkle return. And people, she found, were happy to welcome her.

A few glanced askance at her baby bump, but she suspected that most had already heard and come to terms with the new, unexpected addition to the Marakaios family. As Leo's wife, she was accepted by the people unequivocally, and it made her both relieved and grateful.

She felt even more so when Leo held his flute of champagne aloft and proposed a toast. 'To my lovely bride, Margo,' he said, his clear, deep voice carrying throughout the whole villa. 'May you welcome her and come to love her as I do.'

Margo smiled and raised her own glass of sparkling water, but his words caused a jolt of shock to run through her. *Love her.* He didn't, of course. She knew that. And yet for the first time she wondered what it would feel like if he did. If she loved *him.* If they had a proper marriage— real and deep and lasting.

A moot question, of course, because even if she wanted to risk her heart by loving Leo there was no guarantee that he would love her back. There were no guarantees at all— which was why it was better this way. They'd reached a level of amicability that was pleasant without being dangerous. She shouldn't want or seek more.

By the end of the evening her feet, in the black suede stilettos she'd had brought from Paris, were starting to ache, and she was definitely starting to wilt. Leo seemed to notice the exact moment she felt ready to call it a night, for in one swift movement he came to her side, putting his arm around her waist.

'You look tired. Why don't we retire?'

'I don't want to seem rude…'

'Greeks love a party. They will stay here till dawn unless I kick them out.'

Her mouth twitched in a smile and she let herself lean slightly into Leo's arm. Not enough for him to notice, or for it to matter. Just enough to feel the heavy, comforting security of it. To feel safe.

'So, are you going to boot them to the door?'

'I'll leave that to the staff. I'm going to come upstairs with you.'

And even though she knew he didn't mean it in *that* way, she still felt a shivery thrill run through her.

To her surprise, Leo didn't leave her at her bedroom door as he usually did at night, but came into the room behind her. Margo hadn't expected that, and she'd already started to undo her hair—the pins had been sticking into her skull all evening.

Suddenly self-conscious, she lowered her arms—and then froze at the sound of Leo's husky voice.

'Don't stop.'

In an aching rush she remembered how he'd told her he liked to watch her unpin her hair. It felt even more intimate, even more erotic, now that she knew he liked it. Slowly, her heart starting to thud, she reached up and took the pins out of her hair one by one.

Leo didn't say anything, but she could hear him breathing…feel the very air between them tauten. The pins now removed, she gave her head a little shake and her hair came tumbling down her shoulders, all the way to her waist.

Leo gazed at her, his eyes blazing, and Margo stared back, every sense in her straining, her heart thudding hard.

'Margo…'

She heard a world of yearning in his voice and it made her tremble. She pressed a hand to her middle to stay the nerves that leapt like fish in her belly—and then realised they weren't nerves at all.

'*Oh*…'

'What?' Leo came towards her quickly, his voice sharp with concern. 'What is it?'

'I think…' Margo pressed her hand against her bump, a smile dawning across her face. 'I think I felt the baby kick.'

'You *did*?' Leo sounded incredulous, amazed, as if he'd never heard of such a thing.

Margo let out a little laugh as she felt that same insistent pulse of life. 'Yes! I just felt it again!' She looked up at him, beaming, as amazed as he was. 'It feels so *funny*. There's actually a person inside me!'

He laughed then, and so did she, and then he reached out a hand—before staying it. 'May I?' he asked.

Margo nodded. She reached for his hand, pressing it to her bump, her hand on top of his. 'Wait,' she whispered, and they both stood there, still and transfixed, barely breathing.

It seemed an age, but then finally it came again: that funny little inward thump.

Leo let out an incredulous laugh. '*Theos*, I felt it! I really felt it.'

She looked up at him, still beaming, but the wide smile slid right off her face as she saw Leo's own joyful incredulity turn into something else. Something sensual.

The breath rushed from her lungs as he reached out one hand and slid it through her hair so his fingers curved around the nape of neck, warm and sure and seeking. He drew her slowly towards him and she came, one palm resting flat against his chest so she could feel the thud of his heart, as insistent as her own.

And then he kissed her, as she knew he would, his lips brushing hers once, twice, in a silent question. Without waiting for an answer—an answer she'd have given with every part of her body—he went deep, his tongue sliding into her mouth as he pulled her more closely to him, fitting their bodies together as much as her bump would allow.

The feel of his lips on hers…his hands on her body… his touch made every sense she had flare painfully alive as need scorched through her. She slid her hands up to clutch at his lapels and opened her mouth to his kiss, his tongue, felt the raw passion inside her kindle to roaring flame.

And then the baby kicked again—that determined little pulse—and Margo froze. Her thoughts caught up with the sensations rushing through her and that little kick reminded her just why they were here in the first place. The only reason they were here.

Leo, as attuned as ever to her emotions, broke off the kiss and stepped back. Margo couldn't tell a single thing from his expression. His gaze dropped to her bump and she wondered if he too were reminding himself of the real and only reason they'd got married.

The silence stretched on, and Margo could not think how to break it. Her emotions felt like a maelstrom, whirling inside her; she couldn't separate one from the other, couldn't articulate how she felt about anything.

In the end Leo broke it with a single word. 'Goodnight,' he said quietly, and then walked to the door that joined their bedrooms.

Margo was still standing in the centre of the room, one hand pressed to her bump, another to her kiss-swollen lips, as she heard the door click softly shut.

CHAPTER TEN

LEO PACED THE length of his bedroom and willed the blood in his veins to stop surging with the furious demand to taste Margo again. To bury himself inside her.

He let out a shuddering breath and sank onto the bed, dropping his head into his hands. *He'd come so close...*

But then she'd frozen, and he'd felt her emotional if not her physical withdrawal. No matter how sizzling their chemistry had once been, Margo had still chosen to reject him. And the way she'd stilled beneath his touch had felt like another rejection.

His hands clenched in his hair and he considered opening the door between their bedrooms and demanding his marital rights. They were husband and wife, and he knew Margo desired him—whether she wanted to or not. She was feeling better and the pregnancy was healthy—why shouldn't they enjoy each other?

But, no. He would not share Margo's bed until she wanted him to be there. Utterly.

And yet the evening had started so promisingly. He'd loved seeing Margo at the party, looking bright and beautiful, as much her old self as ever, reminding him of how interesting and articulate and sophisticated she really was. And when she'd drawn his hand to her bump and he'd felt their child kick… It had been the most intimate thing Leo had ever experienced.

The kiss had felt like a natural extension of that intimacy. He couldn't have kept himself from it if he'd tried—which he hadn't.

So what had gone wrong? What had spooked Margo?

Then, with a wince, Leo remembered the toast he'd given at the party. *'May you welcome her and come to love her as I do.'* He hadn't thought of the words before he'd said them; they'd simply flowed out of him, sounding so very sincere. But he'd assured Margo he didn't love her—just as she didn't love him. Had his toast frightened her off?

Had he meant those words?

It was a question he strove to dismiss. Things had become muddied with Margo. Their business arrangement was morphing into something more amicable and pleasant. And yet…*love*?

No. No, he wouldn't go there. He'd suffered enough rejection in his life—starting with his father's determination to exclude his second son. He didn't need more of it from a woman who had already made it clear what she wanted from this marriage.

The same thing he wanted. The *only* thing he'd let himself want. A safe, stable life for the child they had created.

The next morning Margo came into the breakfast room and hesitated in the doorway. Leo saw uncertainty flash across her features and forced himself to stay amicable, yet a little cool. They'd had breakfast together every morning since they'd been here and today would be no different.

'Good morning.' He rose from the table to pour the ginger tea he'd requested Maria to brew every breakfast time. 'Did you sleep well?'

'Yes, thank you.'

Margo sat across from him and spread out her napkin on her lap. Leo thought she looked paler than usual, with dark smudges under her eyes.

She must have caught him looking for she smiled ruefully and said, 'Actually, not really.'

'I'm sorry to hear that.' He handed her the tea and then returned to his seat before snapping open his newspaper. 'It's always hard to sleep after a party, I find.'

Such bland, meaningless conversation—and yet it provided a necessary kind of protection, a return to the way things needed to be.

'It wasn't because of the party, Leo,' Margo said.

He glanced up from the paper and saw her give him a direct look that stripped away his stupidly bland attempts at conversation, saw right into his soul.

'It was because of our kiss.'

Our kiss. Memories raced across his brain, jumpstarted his libido.

He took a sip of coffee and answered evenly. 'Yet you were the one who stopped it.'

'Actually, *you* were,' she answered.

'Semantics,' he returned. 'You were the one who stopped responding, Margo.'

'I know.' She looked down at her plate, her long, slender fingers toying with her fork, her face hidden.

'Why did you, as a matter of interest?' Leo asked, half amazed that he was asking the question. Did he really want to know the answer? 'It wasn't because you weren't interested. I could feel your desire, Margo. You wanted me.'

'I know,' she said softly. 'Whatever you think…whatever you believe…I've never stopped wanting you, Leo.'

'Ah, yes, of course,' he drawled sardonically. 'It's *loving* me you have a problem with.' *Damn it*. He had *not* meant to say that.

She looked up, her gaze swift and searching. 'But you don't love me, either.'

'No.' So why did he feel so exposed, so *hurt*? He let out a short, impatient huff of breath. 'I'm not sure why we're even having this conversation.'

'Because I think we're both trying to navigate this relationship,' Margo answered quietly. 'This marriage. And I'm not sure I know how to be businesslike with my husband.'

'You seem to be managing fine.'

'Maybe, but when you came into my room last night... when you felt the baby kick...it made me realise that we're actually going to be parents.' She let out a self-conscious laugh and continued, 'I knew it before, of course, but for a moment I had this image of us together with a child— giving it a bath, teaching it to ride a bike. Boy or girl, this baby is ours and we'll both love him or her. I know that. And I don't know where being businesslike fits in with that. With a family. The kind of family I want...that I've always wanted—' She broke off, averting her face.

Leo stared at her. 'Yet you're the one who has said you don't wish to be married, who viewed this marriage as a sacrifice,' he reminded her. Reminded *himself*. As much as he wanted to, he couldn't get past that. The real feelings, or lack of them, that she'd shown when he had proposed.

'I said that because I thought you'd hate me after what I said before,' Margo said. 'About there being someone else.'

'And why *did* you say that?' Leo challenged in a hard voice. 'Why did you choose to lie in such an abominable way?'

'I told you before. Because it was the only way I could think of to—to make you leave me.'

Everything in him had crystallised, gone brittle. 'Yes,

I remember. And why did you want me to leave you so much, Margo?'

She was silent—so terribly, damnably silent.

Leo reached for his fork and knife. 'I see,' he said quietly, and he was afraid he saw all too well. The brutal rejection of it, of *him*, was inescapable.

Margo had come to breakfast after a restless, sleepless night, determined to talk to Leo and, more than that, to come to an agreement. An arrangement. Even though the details remained vague in her head. She didn't want to be businesslike any more—didn't want this polite stepping around each other.

Yet what was the alternative? How did you engage your heart and mind and maybe even your soul without risking everything?

And she knew she wasn't ready to do that. She hadn't even been able to tell Leo that the real reason why she'd refused his marriage proposal was that she'd been so very afraid. Annelise... Her mother... The foster parents who had decided she wasn't what they wanted... So many had turned away, and she knew she couldn't take it if Leo did. Not if she'd given him her heart—fragile, trampled on thing that it was.

But her silence had led to this terrible strain, with Leo having turned back to his newspaper, his expression remote and shuttered.

'What are you doing today?' she blurted, and he looked up from the paper, not even a flicker of interest or emotion on those perfectly chiselled features.

'Working in the office, as usual.'

'I should probably arrange to go to Paris soon. I still need to finish things at Achat.'

'If you feel well enough,' he said, sounding uninterested. 'I don't see a problem with that.'

Margo stared at him, her heart sinking right down to her toes. She didn't want this. She'd come down this morning wanting to try to make things better, and she'd only made them worse.

'Leo, you gave me a tour of the villa, but I haven't seen the rest of the estate or the olive groves. Do you think you'd have time today to show me?'

There. That was her peace offering—her attempt at building some kind of bridge. She just hoped Leo would take the first step onto its flimsy surface.

He gazed at her, his eyes narrowed, and then gave a brief nod and folded up his newspaper. 'I suppose… I'll come back to the villa after lunch.'

Margo spent as much time getting ready for her tour of the olive groves as if it were a first date. Not that she'd had many of those. Both her short-lived and frankly disappointing relationships prior to Leo had made her wonder if she was even capable of a real, loving relationship. She certainly didn't have a lot of experience of them.

It was cold out, at just a little less than two weeks before Christmas, and Margo struggled to fit into her jeans. She couldn't zip them all the way up, and the button was a lost cause. She wore a tunic top of aquamarine cashmere that fell nearly to her knees and fitted snugly round her bump while hiding the undone zip and buttons.

She left her hair loose, which she rarely did, and put on a bit of eyeliner and lipstick. She didn't necessarily want to look as if she was trying too hard, but she definitely wanted Leo to notice.

Unfortunately he didn't say a word when she met him in the foyer, and Margo suppressed the flicker of disappointment she felt at his silence. Had she really expected him to compliment her? She was wearing *jeans*, for heaven's sake. Still, she noticed that Leo seemed terser than usual as they headed out into the bright, frosty afternoon.

'There isn't actually all that much to see in the olive groves at this time of year,' he remarked as they walked along the gravel road that went past his office and led to a pair of wrought-iron gates. 'The trees are bare, and they won't begin to bud until March.'

'I still want to see,' Margo said, trying to keep her tone upbeat. 'This is my home now, after all. I don't know the first thing about olive trees or oil or *any* of it.'

'You don't need to learn.'

So he really was rebuffing her.

'I *want* to learn, Leo. You told me you wanted me to be a part of things. That's what I'm trying to do.'

He stared at her, as inscrutable as ever, and she decided to try a different tack.

'Tell me about your childhood. Did you grow up playing hide-and-seek in these groves?'

They'd stepped through the gates and were now walking among the trees, the trunks twisted and gnarled, the branches stark and bare.

'A bit,' Leo answered. 'I grew up here, certainly.'

'Did you like it?' she asked, for she sensed more than reticence in Leo's reply, and wondered at his memories.

'I loved the olive trees,' he said after a moment. 'The white waxy blossoms, the dusty scent in summer, the nuttiness of the oil...' He shook his head. 'I probably sound ridiculous, but I love it all. I always have.'

So why, Margo wondered, did he sound so regretful? So *bitter*?

'It's a good thing you're in the olive oil business,' she said, and Leo gave her a rather tight smile.

'Yes.'

'Why,' Margo asked after a moment, as they walked between the bare trees, 'do I feel as if you're not telling me everything?'

'What do you mean?'

She shrugged, half afraid to press, yet wanting to know more about him. Wanting to keep building this bridge, flimsy as it seemed. 'When you talk about the trees, the business, you sound…tense.' She hesitated and then added, 'Almost angry.'

Leo was silent for a long moment, and the only sound was the wind soughing through the trees and making the branches rattle. 'I suppose,' he said finally, 'that's because I am. Or was, at least. I think I'm getting over it. I hope so, anyway.'

Leo's face gave nothing away, and yet Margo knew instinctively this was a big admission for him to make. 'Why, Leo?' she asked quietly. 'What happened?'

He sighed, shrugging and shaking his head at the same time. 'Just complicated family politics.'

'Tell me.'

He hesitated, then said, 'My grandfather started the business from scratch. He was a dustman before he scraped together enough drachmas to buy a bit of property, and he built it from there. We've always been so proud of how we came from nothing. How we built this empire with our own hands. First my grandfather, and then my father…'

He trailed off, frowning, and Margo dared to fill in, 'And now you?'

'Yes. But it didn't happen as seamlessly as that.'

'Your brother…?'

'Yes, my brother.' His face tightened. 'Antonios was my father's favourite. The oldest child and his heir…I suppose it was understandable.'

'It's *never* understandable,' Margo countered. 'If we have more children I won't favour one more than the other.'

He gave her a swift, blazing look. 'Do you *want* more children, Margo?'

'I...' She swallowed hard. More children to love. *More children to lose.* And yet a proper family—the kind of family she'd always longed for but had been afraid to have. Was afraid she didn't deserve. 'I don't know.'

He kept staring at her, his gaze searching and yet not seeming to find any answers, for eventually he looked away and resumed his story.

'Well, understandable or not, Antonios was the favourite. I didn't accept that, though. I tried—*Theos*—how I tried to make my father love me. Trust me—'

He broke off then, and Margo ached to comfort him. But she didn't, because everything about Leo was brittle and tense, and she had a terrible feeling—a fear—that he would shake her off if she tried to hug him as she wanted to.

'To make a long story short,' he continued finally, his voice brusque, 'he never did. He had a heart attack and he sent for Antonios—told him the truth about the business. He'd been involved in dodgy dealings for years, trying to make back the money he'd lost on bad investments. He was a hair's breadth away from losing everything. He made Antonios swear not to tell anyone...not even me.'

'And *did* he tell you?' Margo asked.

Leo shook his head. 'Not for ten years. Ten years of my not understanding, feeling cut off and kept in the dark. Well...' he shrugged and then dug his hands into his pockets '...I don't suppose I should have been very surprised. My father never trusted me with anything—why would he with the truth?'

'But your brother...?'

'Antonios didn't either. Not until I pushed and pushed

for him to say something—and then I think he only did because of Lindsay, his wife. She wanted an end to all the secrets, all the acrimony.'

'And *has* there been an end to it?' Margo asked.

'I…I don't know. We get along—more or less. Antonios resigned as CEO, as you know, and is happier working in investment management.'

'Are *you* happy?' Margo asked, and the question hung there, suspended, encompassing so much more than just the business.

'I don't know,' Leo said again, and he turned to look at her, his face more open and honest and vulnerable than she'd ever seen it before—even when he'd asked her to marry him. 'I don't know,' he said again, and it seemed like more than an admission. It seemed like a revelation… to both of them.

They started walking again, back towards the gates, neither of them speaking. This time, however, the silence didn't feel strained, Margo thought, more expectant. Although what she—or Leo—was waiting for, she had no idea.

The gates loomed ahead of them and Margo had the strange sensation that once they passed through them things would change. The spell of intimacy and honesty that had been cast over them amidst the trees would be broken.

She turned to tell Leo something of this—something of herself—but before she could say anything her foot caught on a twisted root and she pitched forward. The moment felt as if it lasted for ever, and yet no time at all, no time to try to right herself, or even to break her fall with her hands.

She fell hard onto her front, her belly slamming into the ground, her face and hands and knees scraped and stinging.

'*Margo*—' Leo's voice was sharp with alarm and even fear as he knelt at her side.

She got onto her hands and her knees, her heart thudding from the fall.

Leo put a hand on her shoulder. 'Are you all right? Let me look at you.'

Slowly, wincing from the bruises and scrapes, she eased back into a sitting position, the ground hard and cold beneath her.

'I think I'm okay,' she said, and pressed one hand to her belly, her fingers curving around her bump, willing the baby to give a little comforting kick in response to the silent question her hand was asking.

Then she caught Leo staring at her; his face was pale, his eyes wide, and he leaned forward, grabbing her arm.

'What—?' she began, but Leo was already sliding his phone out of his pocket and dialling 112, which she knew was the number in Greece for the emergency medical services. 'Leo, I'm okay,' she said.

And that was when she felt a sticky wetness between her thighs, and when she looked down she saw blood spreading across the hard earth.

CHAPTER ELEVEN

'No!' MARGO'S VOICE was hoarse as she stared at the blood on the ground, and then she let out a harsh, keening cry that tore at Leo's heart. '*No.* Leo—no, no, *no*—' Her voice caught and she struggled for a moment, every breath an effort as panic swamped her.

'I have an emergency medical situation,' he snapped into the phone. 'I need an ambulance at the Marakaios estate immediately.'

He tossed the phone aside and reached for Margo. She was rocking back and forth, her arms wrapped around her middle, her whole body trembling.

'Margo, breathe,' he commanded. 'Nice and even. It's going to be okay.'

She took a few hitched breaths, her shoulders shaking, and then finally managed to speak. 'Don't lie to me, Leo,' she said raggedly. 'Don't ever lie to me. It's *not* going to be okay. You can't know that.'

'You're bleeding,' he acknowledged steadily, 'but that doesn't mean anything is wrong with the baby.'

But Margo seemed barely to hear him. She shook her head, tears streaking down her face. 'This can't happen,' she whispered to herself. 'This *can't* happen. I won't let this happen again.'

Again? Leo's mind snagged on the word, but now was hardly the time to ask her what she meant.

'An ambulance will be here in a few minutes. I'm going to move you so it can reach you more easily.'

Gently he scooped her up into his arms and carried her out of the olive grove. He could see the blood staining her jeans and coat and his stomach roiled with fear. Margo had been right. He couldn't know if it was going to be okay.

Soon an ambulance came screeching and wailing up the drive. Leo saw his sisters and Maria crowd onto the villa's portico as he carried Margo towards the vehicle. A paramedic came out to help her onto a stretcher.

'Leo!' Xanthe cried, and he shook his head.

'I'll call you,' he promised, and then climbed into the ambulance with Margo.

She looked so vulnerable, lying there on the stretcher, her eyes huge and dark in her pale face, and she scrabbled for his hand, her fingers fragile and icy in his as the paramedic took her vitals and then asked Leo what had happened.

Leo gave the details as clearly and evenly as he could; he could feel Margo clinging to his hand, her breath coming in little pants as she tried to control her panic.

Dear God, he prayed, *let nothing have happened to the baby.*

The next half-hour was a blur as the ambulance took them to the hospital in Amfissa, and then to an examination room in the A&E. A doctor, brisk and purposeful, came in with an ultrasound machine while Margo lay on the examination couch.

'The first thing to do,' the doctor said in Greek, 'is a scan, so I can see what's going on.'

Leo translated for Margo and she nodded frantically, still clutching his hand.

The next few minutes, as the doctor set up the machine, seemed to last for ever. Leo watched as she spread cold, clear gel on Margo's belly and then pressed the wand against her bump. The silence that stretched on for several seconds was the worst thing he'd ever heard, and Margo gave a soft, broken little cry before turning her head away from the ultrasound screen. Tears snaked silently down her cheeks, and Leo felt the sting of tears in his own eyes.

This couldn't be happening.

'There it is,' the doctor said in Greek, and Leo stared in stunned disbelief as she pointed to the screen and the tiny heartbeat, still going strong.

'*Margo—*'

'She has a partial placenta praevia,' the doctor said, and Leo tried to listen as she explained how the placenta was covering the cervix and the fall had aggravated it, which had caused the bleeding.

He could barely take it in, however—all he could do was stare at that wonderful little pulsing assurance of life.

'Margo…' he said again and, touching her cheek, he turned her face to the screen.

She blinked, tears still slipping down her face, as she stared in confusion at the screen.

'It's okay,' he said softly. 'It really is okay.'

Smiling, the doctor turned up the volume, and that wonderful, whooshing, galloping sound of the baby's heartbeat filled the room. Leo thought Margo would be relieved, that she might even smile or laugh, but as she heard the sound of the heartbeat her face crumpled and she collapsed into sobs, her shoulders shaking with their force.

Leo didn't think past his overwhelming need to comfort her. He leaned over and put his arms around and she buried her face in his shoulder as her whole body shook and trembled.

Quietly the doctor turned the machine off and wiped the gel from Margo's bump. 'She should stay overnight—just for observation,' she told Leo. 'Tomorrow we can do another scan to see how the bleeding looks and if the placenta has moved any more.'

Leo nodded wordlessly. He'd have to process all that later; the only thing he could think about now was Margo.

Eventually she eased back from him and wiped the tears from her face, managing the wobbliest of smiles. A nurse came to transfer her to a room, and Leo called his sisters while Margo showered and changed into a hospital gown. When he came back into the room she was lying in bed, her hair brushed and her face washed, but her eyes still looked puffy and red from crying.

He sat on the edge of her bed and took her hand. 'The doctor said you have a partial placenta praevia,' he said. 'To be honest, I can't remember what that means, exactly, but I'll arrange for a doctor who speaks English to talk to you about it.'

'I know what it means,' Margo said.

She sounded exhausted, emotionally spent, and Leo squeezed her fingers. 'The important thing is the baby is okay.'

'Yes. For now.'

She bit her lip, and Leo saw her eyes glisten with the sheen of new tears.

'There's no reason to be afraid, Margo—'

'Oh, Leo, there's every reason.' She leaned her head back against the starchy white pillow and closed her eyes. '*Every* reason.'

'I don't understand…'

He thought once more of how she'd said she didn't want this to happen *again*. He wanted to ask her what she'd meant, but he knew Margo was feeling too fragile now for such an emotional conversation.

'Is there something you're not telling me?' he asked instead, needing to know that much.

She opened her eyes and shook her head. 'Nothing that really matters.'

'Then why—?'

'I'm just so afraid.' She bit her lip. 'I'm *always* so afraid. That's why I didn't want to have children.'

He stared at her in confusion, trying to understand what she meant. He thought of when he'd met her in that hotel bar, looking sassy and smart in a black wrap cocktail dress, her long legs encased in sheer tights, a stiletto dangling from one slim foot. She'd looked like the most fearless person he'd ever met, and she'd always seemed that way to him: breezing into hotel rooms, giving him a naughty smile, shrugging out of her dress with confidence and ease.

He'd liked that about her, had enjoyed her sense of confidence. But now he wondered. Since Margo had come back into his life he'd wondered what she'd been hiding, what secrets she had. Had that breezy confidence all been an *act?*

'You don't need to be afraid,' he said, squeezing her fingers.

But, withdrawing her hand from his, Margo just turned away and said nothing.

Frustration bit hard but he forced himself not to demand answers or explanations. Once again he was being kept in the dark about something. It felt like another kind of rejection, because Margo obviously didn't trust him with whatever truth she was keeping from him. But he wouldn't press. He wouldn't beg.

Reluctantly he eased himself off the bed. 'Is there anything I can get you?' he asked. 'Something to drink or eat? Or something from the villa? Your own pyjamas or clothes?'

She was still looking away from him, her hair brushing her cheek. 'No, thank you.'

He hated how formal she was being, even though that morning he'd decided that was just how he wanted it. Things had changed. Both their conversation in the olive grove and the terrifying events afterwards had changed him. And they'd changed Margo too—but not in a way he liked or wanted.

Everything about her, from her brittle voice to the way she wouldn't look at him, made him think she wanted him to go. But he wasn't going to leave her here alone, whatever she wanted, so he settled himself into a chair opposite the bed and waited.

Neither of them spoke for a very long time, and eventually Margo drifted off to sleep.

When Margo awoke the room was dark, and panic doused her in an icy wave. She struggled upright, one hand going to her middle, curving over the reassuring bump even as the remnants of the nightmare she'd been having clung to her consciousness.

'Leo—'

'I'm here.'

In the darkness she couldn't see him, but she felt his hand come and close over hers. Even so she couldn't stop shivering.

'I had the most awful dream.' Her voice choked and her throat closed. She'd dreamed about Annelise—something she hadn't done in a very long time. 'It was so terrible—'

'It was just a dream, Margo,' Leo said, his voice soft and steady. 'It wasn't real. Everything's all right. The baby's all right.'

She nodded and gulped, wanting, *needing* to believe him and yet not quite able to do so. The dream had been real once upon a time. She'd relived the worst memory she had in her nightmare, and she was so afraid of it happening again. But Leo couldn't understand that because she hadn't told him.

'Don't leave me,' she whispered, and he squeezed her hand.

'I won't.'

But she needed more than just his reassurance; she craved the comfort of his touch. 'Leo…' she began, and then, thrusting any awkwardness aside, she blurted, 'Would you hold me?'

Leo didn't answer, and Margo braced herself for his refusal—because they didn't have that kind of relationship. That kind of marriage.

Then wordlessly he rose from the chair and peeled back the covers on her bed. He kicked off his shoes and slid into the narrow bed next to her, pulled her carefully into his arms.

Margo wrapped herself around him, burying her face in his neck, breathing in the clean, comforting scent of him. She'd needed this—needed him—more than she could ever have put into words.

He didn't say anything, just held her, one hand stroking her hair, until she felt the icy panic that had frozen her insides start to recede, the nightmare begin to fade. Her breathing evened out and her body relaxed into his embrace.

Lying there, safe in his arms, she felt a creeping sense of guilt for how much she'd kept from him. He'd been her rock since she'd fallen in the olive grove—he'd never left her, never wavered for an instant, offering her unconditional encouragement and support.

The realisation brought a lump to Margo's throat and she pressed her face more snugly against the hollow of his neck, breathing him in more deeply...

She must have fallen asleep again, for when she woke up the pale grey light of early dawn was filtering through the curtains and Leo was still in her bed.

Margo eased back to look at him. His eyes were closed, his thick, dark lashes fanned out on his cheeks. His jaw was rough with morning stubble, which made his lips look all the more lush and mobile and eminently kissable.

He was still in his clothes from yesterday, his shirt unbuttoned at the throat, his tie tossed on a chair. Margo felt as if a fist had wrapped around her heart and squeezed.

Then the door to the room opened and a nurse wheeled a machine in. 'Time to take your vitals,' she said cheerfully, and Margo blinked in surprise.

'You speak English?'

'Yes, Kyrie Marakaios requested that someone who could speak English attend to you. Or French, he said. But no one spoke good enough French.' She gave a little smile and a shrug, and then took out a blood pressure cuff and wrapped it around Margo's arm.

Leo had woken up and was now easing himself to a sitting position, wincing slightly at the stiffness in his body from spending a night fully clothed on a hospital bed. His hair was rumpled and he blinked sleep out of his eyes before turning to Margo.

'Are you all right?' he asked quietly.

She nodded. The fear that had gripped her so tightly yesterday had now eased a little, thanks to Leo.

He rose from the bed and while the nurse took Margo's blood pressure and temperature he left the room in search of coffee and a shave.

'The doctor will visit in a little while, for another ultrasound,' the nurse told her. 'And in the meantime you can have breakfast.'

Margo nodded, and a few minutes later Leo returned with two cups—one of coffee and another of ginger tea.

'Where on earth did you get *that*?' Margo asked as he handed her the cup.

'I make sure to always have some on me. Just in case.'

'You're so thoughtful,' she said, almost wonderingly.

Leo laughed ruefully. 'Don't sound so surprised!'

'I *am* surprised,' she admitted. 'There haven't…there haven't been that many people in my life who have been thoughtful.'

Leo frowned and Margo looked away. She wasn't ready to tell him any more than that, but she could tell he had questions. Questions he wanted answers to.

Before he could ask anything the door opened again, and a smiling woman brought in a breakfast tray.

After breakfast the doctor came with the ultrasound machine, and they both silently held their breath as she set it up—until the image of their baby came onto the screen, still kicking up a storm.

'Oh, I can feel that!' Margo exclaimed, one hand pressed to her bump. 'I hadn't felt anything since I fell, but I felt that.'

'This little one doesn't like being poked,' said the doctor, who also spoke English, with a smile. 'Everything looks fine. You'll have your twenty-week scan in a few days, and we'll check on the placenta praevia then.' Smiling, the woman put the machine away and Margo pulled down her shirt. 'You're free to go.'

It wasn't until she was dressed and they were back in the car, heading towards the estate, that Leo turned to her, his expression serious.

'Margo, we need to talk…'

Her body went tense and she turned to stare blindly out of the window.

'What are you not telling me?' Leo asked, his voice quiet but insistent. 'Because there's something.'

'It doesn't matter.'

'It *does* matter. It matters because in the hospital you were terrified—'

'Of course I was!' She turned to look at him. 'Leo, I was afraid I was losing my baby.'

'*Our* baby,' he corrected quietly, and Margo bit her lip. 'Don't shut me out, Margo.'

She turned back to the window without replying, and they drove in silence all the way back to the Marakaios estate.

CHAPTER TWELVE

WHEN THEY ARRIVED at the villa Leo helped Margo out of the car, one hand on her elbow as he guided her inside.

Xanthe, Ava and Maria all met them in the foyer.

'You're all right?' Ava asked, her face pinched with anxiety.

'Yes—and, more importantly, the baby is all right,' Margo said, and smiled when Maria muttered a prayer of thanksgiving and crossed herself.

'I'm going to get Margo upstairs,' Leo cut across his sisters' anxious chatter. 'It's been an incredibly long twenty-four hours, and I don't think either of us slept well last night.'

Actually, Margo had slept better than she had in months, wrapped in Leo's arms. But she could imagine Leo had spent a considerably less comfortable night, cramming his large body onto the narrow bed, still in his suit.

They went upstairs, and as Margo came into her bedroom she breathed a sigh of relief. She wanted to crawl into the big, soft bed and stay there for about a million hours—good night's sleep or not.

Behind her, she heard Leo close the door. 'I need to shower and change,' he said, 'and I imagine you'd like to freshen up. And then we'll talk.'

His tone was implacable, leaving no room for arguments. Still, Margo tried. 'I'm very tired, Leo—'

'There will be plenty of time for you to rest today. But I won't let you put me off, Margo.' He hesitated, seeming to want to say more, but then simply turned and left the room.

Margo went into the bathroom, stepping into the huge two-person shower with its marble sides and gold fixtures. As the water streamed over her body she had a sudden image of Leo joining her there. They'd showered together a few times during their stolen weekends away, but that felt like a lifetime ago. She felt like a different person from the insouciant, carefree career woman she'd been back then, embarking on a no-strings affair.

But then she *was* a different person—because that carefree woman had been nothing more than a part she'd played, a mask she'd worn. She hadn't dared try to be anything else. Anything deeper or more lasting.

In just a few minutes Leo was going to demand answers, and if she was brave enough she would drop that mask for ever and tell him everything. She knew he deserved to know.

She rested her head against the cool marble, willing herself to be strong enough for that kind of hard honesty.

A few minutes later she was dressed in a pair of loose yoga pants and a soft hoodie, curled up on the window seat that overlooked the villa's gardens, the grass now coated with a thick rime of frost.

Leo tapped once on the door that joined their bedrooms before poking his head in and then coming through completely. His hair was damp from his shower, and he wore a soft grey tee shirt and faded jeans that were moulded perfectly to his muscular legs. Wordlessly he walked over and joined Margo on the window seat.

Neither of them spoke for a long moment; the only

sound was the wind rattling the bare branches of the trees outside.

Finally Margo spoke, and each word felt laborious, even painful. 'I'm not who you think I am.'

'Who do you *think* I think you are?' Leo asked quietly.

'The woman you met in that bar. That glamorous, confident, sexy woman.' She let out a shaky laugh. 'Not that I'm trying to be arrogant, but that's how I wanted to be... to seem.'

Leo was silent for a moment, then finally he asked, 'Who are you, then?'

'A street rat from Marseilles.' She glanced at him, expecting to see if not disgust then at least surprise. But Leo looked completely unfazed.

'How did a "street rat from Marseilles" end up as a confident career woman in Paris?' he asked after a moment.

'Luck and hard work, I suppose.' She tucked her hair behind her ears and gazed out at the wintry afternoon. 'But I've always felt like a street rat inside.'

'That doesn't mean you *are*, Margo. I don't think anyone feels like the person they present to the world all the time.'

She pretended to look shocked. 'You mean you *don't* feel like an arrogant, all-powerful CEO all the time?'

He smiled and gave a little shrug. 'Well, obviously I'm the exception.'

She laughed at that, and then shook her head. 'Oh, Leo.' She let out a weary sigh, a sound of sadness. 'If you knew about my childhood...'

'Then tell me,' he said.

And although his voice was soft she knew it was a command. A command she should obey, because she'd already come to the decision that she needed to tell him the truth. But truth was a hard, hard thing.

'I grew up one step away from the street,' she began

slowly. 'And sometimes not even that. My mother was a drug addict. Crystal meth—although I didn't realise that until later. But it…the drug…controlled her life.'

Now, surely, he would look shocked. But when Margo looked at him his expression was still calm, although his mouth had pulled down at the corners with sympathy.

'I'm sorry.'

'So am I.' She let out a wobbly laugh that trembled into a half-sob. 'Oh, God, so am I.'

'Was she able to care for you?'

'No, not really, and sometimes not at all. At the beginning, yes. Before she became an addict. At least I think she did. I survived, anyway. But my father left when I was four—I only have a few fuzzy memories of him.'

'That must have been hard.'

'Yes.'

The few fuzzy memories she had were precious—of a man who'd pulled her into a bear hug and swung her in the air. *Why* had he left? It was a question that had tormented her for years. How could a man walk away from his family? Had she not been lovable enough?

'After he left my mother went very much downhill.'

She lapsed into silence then, because she did not want to tell him how grim it had been. The sheltered housing, the stints in various homeless shelters, the weeks when she'd been taken away from her mother and sent from one foster home to another. Some of them had been good, some of them mediocre, and some of them had been very bad. But always, in the end, she'd been brought back for her mother to try again, having promised she'd stay clean, and for a few days, sometimes a few weeks, she had.

Life during those periods had been normal, if fragile, and sometimes Margo would begin to believe it was going to be okay this time. Then she'd come home from school to find her mother strung out, or manically high, the promises all broken, and the whole cycle would start once more.

Until Annelise. But she really didn't want to talk about Annelise.

'Margo?' Leo prompted softly. 'Tell me more. If she couldn't care for you, how did you survive?'

She shrugged. 'Sometimes not very well. I was in and out of foster homes my whole childhood. When I was old enough I learned to take care of myself.'

'And how old was that?' Leo asked in a low voice.

'Seven…eight? I could use the gas ring in our bedsit and I could make basic meals. I got myself to school most days. I managed.'

'Oh, Margo.' He shook his head, reached for her hand. 'Why didn't you tell me this before?'

'I don't talk about my childhood to anyone,' she said, her voice thickening. 'Ever. It's too awful. And in any case, Leo, we didn't have that kind of relationship.'

His fingers tightened on hers. 'Do we now?'

Her heart lurched at the thought. 'I…I don't know.'

Which was what he had said to her yesterday morning. So much uncertainty, for both of them, and yet here she was confessing. Trying.

'Tell me more about your childhood,' Leo said after a moment.

She closed her eyes briefly. 'I could go into details, but I'm sure you can guess. It…it wasn't pretty, Leo.'

'I know that.' He was silent for a moment, his fingers still entwined with hers. 'But there's something more, isn't there? Something you're not telling me?'

'Yes.' She took a deep breath. 'When I was eleven, my mother had a baby. My half-sister. There was no father ever in the picture.' Another breath to keep herself going. 'Her name was Annelise.'

'Was?' Leo said softly, his fingers tightening on hers. 'What happened to her?'

'She...she died.'

She closed her eyes against the memories, but they came anyway. Annelise cuddled up to her in her bed, one chubby hand resting on her chest. Annelise toddling towards her with a big toothy grin, hands outstretched as she called Margo 'Go-Go'. Annelise with her arms wrapped around her neck, her cheek pressed to Go-Go's.

'I'm so sorry, Margo.'

'My mother was lucky not to have Annelise taken away from her right at the beginning,' she said, the words just barely squeezed out. 'With her history. But we'd flown under the radar for a couple of years by then. I was managing to get myself to school, and my mother seemed like she could control her addiction.'

She held up a hand to stop Leo saying anything, although he hadn't even opened his mouth.

'Which is ridiculous, I know, because of course an addiction can't be controlled. But she...she functioned, at least, and then when she found out she was pregnant she cleaned herself up for a while—enough for Annelise to be born and brought home.'

'And then?'

'As soon as Annelise was home she lost interest. I didn't mind, because I took care of her. I *loved* taking care of her.'

'But you had school—'

'I stopped going to school. I had to, for Annelise's sake. I told them we were moving, and nobody bothered to check. It was easy. Honestly, if you don't want to be noticed by the authorities it can be remarkably easy.'

'And so you stayed home and took care of Annelise?' Leo was silent for a moment. 'What did you do for money?'

'We got a little bit from the government. And my mother

would sometimes…' She hesitated, not wanting to admit just what her mother had done to score her drugs, but Leo must have guessed because his mouth tightened.

'She found a way to get money?' he surmised.

She nodded. 'Yes.' And then, because now that she'd started the truth-telling she felt she needed to say it all, she blurted, 'She sold herself. To men. For money.'

Leo nodded, his jaw tense, and Margo wondered what he thought of her now. In and out of foster homes, her mother a prostitute… She hated him knowing it.

'So what happened to you and Annelise?'

'I was her mother,' she whispered. 'I did everything for her. *Everything*.' She blinked rapidly and managed, 'She called me Go-Go.'

She stared down at her lap, at their entwined hands. And she thought of Annelise—her soft baby's hair, her gurgle of laughter.

How, after seventeen years, could it still hurt so much?

'How did she die?' Leo asked quietly.

'The flu. *The flu*.' Her voice choked and a tear slipped down her cheek. 'She just had a fever at first. I was taking care of her. I gave her some medicine and had her sleep in my bed, but…' She drew in a gasping breath. 'The fever spiked, and I was so scared, but I knew if I took her to hospital the authorities would get involved and they might take her away. I couldn't bear that, so I just bathed her in cool water and gave her more medicine.'

'And then…?' Leo asked softly.

'And then she started having convulsions. I begged my mother to take her to hospital then, but she…she wasn't herself.' She'd been high on drugs, barely aware of her children. 'So I took her myself. I carried her to the hospital in my arms. When I got there a nurse took her from me. She…she was already dead.'

She bowed her head, the memory and the pain and the guilt rushing through her.

'It was my fault, Leo. My fault she died.'

She'd never said those words aloud—never even admitted her guilt to herself. And saying it now made her feel both empty and unbearably full at the same time. She bowed her head and tried to will back the tears.

'Oh, Margo.' Leo's arms came around her and he pulled her towards him, her cheek against his chest. 'I'm so, so sorry.'

He didn't speak for a moment and she simply rested there, listening to the steady thud of his heart, letting the grief subside.

'It *wasn't* your fault, you know. You were twelve. You never should have had to bear that kind of responsibility.'

'I wasn't a child. And it *was* my fault. If I'd gone to the hospital earlier they could have given her antibiotics. Brought her fever down. Maybe she'd have been taken away, but she'd still be alive.' She spoke flatly, dully, knowing it was the truth and that nothing Leo could say would change it.

'What happened after that?' he asked after a moment. His arms were still around her, her cheek still against his chest.

'I was put into foster care—a few different families.'

She spoke diffidently, not wanting to admit all the terrible details. The foster mother who had dragged her by the hair into the bathroom because she'd said Margo was dirty. The family who had left her, at fourteen years old, in front of the council offices with nothing but a cardboard suitcase because they hadn't wanted her any more.

'It was tough for a few years,' she allowed. 'I missed Annelise so much... I acted out. I was hard to deal with.' And so people had chosen *not* to deal with her.

'When I was sixteen,' she continued after a moment, 'I finally calmed down. I stayed with a family for a year. They were good to me. They helped me find a job, saw me settled.'

'Are you still in touch with them?'

'No. It wasn't that kind of a relationship. They had a lot of different foster kids. I was just one of many. We wrote letters for a while, but...' She gave a little shrug. 'I am grateful to them. And really,' she continued quickly, 'I don't blame anyone except myself. The people who fostered me all tried their hardest. They didn't *have* to take children in. They were doing their best. And I really was difficult. I can't blame anyone but myself for that.'

'But you were a *child*,' Leo protested, 'in an incredibly difficult situation.'

'Yes, but I was mature for my age. I'd had to be. I could have...controlled myself.' Except she hadn't wanted to. She'd been wild with grief, wanting and needing to strike out. To hurt someone as she'd been hurting.

'And this is why you're so afraid now of something happening to the baby?' Leo said slowly. 'Because of what happened to Annelise?'

She nodded. 'I know it's not rational, but everyone I know has left me at one time or another. And Annelise... losing Annelise was by far the worst. I don't think I could survive something like that again, Leo. I really don't think I could.'

'You won't have to.'

'But you can't know—'

'I don't have a crystal ball to predict the future, no.' Leo took her chin his hand, turning her face so he could look her in the eye. 'But do you believe me, Margo, when I tell you I will do everything in my power—absolutely everything—to keep you and our child safe and healthy? I won't let you down, I swear to you. You can trust me.'

'Thank you,' she whispered, and although she didn't know if she had the strength to believe him she was still glad he'd said it.

Then, simply because it felt right, she leaned forward, closing the small space between them, and brushed her lips with his. It was barely more than a peck—a kiss that wasn't sexual or even romantic, but something else entirely. Something deeper and more tender.

Leo stilled under her touch, and then he eased back, his expression serious. 'Thank you for telling me. For trusting me that much.'

'I'm sorry I didn't before.'

'Like you said, we didn't have that kind of relationship.'

And did they now? Margo still didn't know. She didn't know what she was capable of, or what Leo wanted.

'You should rest,' Leo said as he stood up from the window seat. 'It's been a very long couple of days.'

'Yes...'

But she didn't feel tired, and after he'd left she paced the room restlessly, her mind starting to seethe with doubt and worry. She'd just unloaded a huge amount of emotional baggage onto Leo. When they'd struck their business deal he hadn't expected to have to cope with all that. What if he decided she was too much work? Or if he withdrew emotionally rather than deal with all the neurotic fears Margo had just confessed? Going back to being business-like would be even harder and more painful now she'd confessed so much.

Tired with the circling questions she knew she couldn't answer, she decided to keep busy instead of simply pacing and worrying. She went to the adjoining bedroom that was meant to be a nursery and started sketching ideas to transform it into a space for a baby.

It had been weeks since she'd exercised her mind or her creativity, and it felt good to think about something other than the current anxieties that revolved around Leo and the baby. To remember that she'd had a career, one she'd enjoyed, and could still put to use, if only in this small way.

And as she sketched and planned she felt her uncertainties fall away, as if she were shedding an old skin, and she knew that she wanted to move forward from the past, from the pain. She wanted to move forward with Leo and have a real marriage. A loving one.

If she dared.

CHAPTER THIRTEEN

IN THE DAYS after Margo told him about her childhood Leo found himself going over what she'd said and connecting the dots that before had seemed no more than a scattered, random design of inexplicable behaviour.

Now he was starting to understand why Margo had decided to marry for the sake of their child.

After a childhood like hers, he could see how the stability of a family life was something she would want to provide for her child…even if they didn't love each other.

Except that basis was one Leo realised he could no longer assume. *Did* he love Margo? *Could* he love her? He certainly admired her resilience and her strength of spirit, her devotion to their unborn child. He was still deeply attracted to her, God knew. And if he let himself…if he stopped guarding his heart the way he suspected Margo was guarding hers…

Could this businesslike marriage become something more? Did he even want that? Margo had rejected him once. He understood why now, but it didn't mean she wouldn't do it again.

Things at least had become easier between them, and more relaxed: they shared most meals and chatted about ordinary things, and Margo had shown him her preliminary designs for the nursery, which he'd admired.

They were rebuilding the friendship they'd had before his marriage proposal, and this time it was so much deeper, so much more real.

One morning at breakfast Leo told her that Antonios and his wife Lindsay would be coming after Christmas for a short visit.

'Are you looking forward to that?' she asked, her dark, knowing gaze sweeping over him.

'Yes, I think I am,' Leo answered slowly.

He hadn't seen his brother since right after his mother's funeral, when Antonios and Lindsay had moved to New York and Leo had taken the reins of Marakaios Enterprises. He and Antonios had made peace with each other, but it was an uneasy one, and although they'd emailed and talked on the telephone since then Leo didn't know how it would feel to be in the same room, to rake over the same memories.

'It will be nice to meet some more of your family,' Margo said, breaking into his thoughts. 'Sorry I can't return the favour.'

She spoke lightly, but he saw the darkness in her eyes, knew she was testing him, trying to see how he felt about what she'd told him now that he'd had time to process it. Accept it.

And what he felt, Leo knew, was sadness for Margo. Regret that he hadn't known sooner. And a deep desire to make it better for her.

'We have all the family we need right here,' he said, and she blinked several times before smiling rather shyly.

'What a lovely thing to say, Leo.'

'It's true.'

'It's still lovely.'

That afternoon they headed into Amfissa for Margo's twenty-week scan. The last time they'd come to the hospital they'd been in an ambulance, filled with panic and fear. Leo saw the vestiges of both on Margo's face as he drove into the hospital car park and knew she was remembering. Hell, he was too.

The panic didn't leave Margo's face or Leo's gut until they were in the examination room and they could see their baby kicking on the screen.

The technician spent a long time taking measurements, checking the heart and lungs, fingers and toes. Leo held Margo's hand the whole time.

'Everything looks fine,' she said, and they both sagged a bit with relief. 'The placenta is starting to move, so hopefully the praevia will clear up before delivery. But we'll keep an eye on it. If it doesn't move completely by thirty weeks we'll have to talk about a scheduled Caesarean section.'

Margo nodded, her face pale. Leo knew she would do whatever it took to keep their baby safe and healthy, although such an operation was hardly ideal.

'Do you want to know the sex?' the technician asked. 'Because I can tell you. But only if you want to know.'

Leo and Margo looked at each other, apprehensive and excited.

'Could you write it down?' Leo asked. 'And put it in an envelope? Then we can open it together.'

'On Christmas Day,' Margo agreed, clearly getting into the spirit of the thing. 'A Christmas present to both of us.'

He smiled at her, and she smiled back, and Leo felt a kind of giddy excitement at the thought of knowing—and of knowing together.

Margo was determined to have a wonderful Christmas. The Christmases of her childhood had been unmarked, simply another day to survive. As an adult she'd decorated her apartment, and she and Sophie had exchanged presents, but that was as far as the celebrations had gone. Now, with a home and family of her own, she wanted to go all-out.

Leo told her that they'd never made much of Christmas either, when he was a child. In the Greek Orthodox church Easter was by far the greater holiday. Besides eating a grand meal on Christmas Day, and exchanging presents on January the sixth, Christmas passed by most Greek households virtually unnoticed.

'But I think we have much to celebrate this year,' he said, 'so I wouldn't mind changing things.'

So Margo did.

She wanted to keep the Greek spirit of things, and tried her hand at different Christmassy Greek treats: *melomakarona*, honey-dipped cookies stuffed with nuts, and *kourambiedes*, cookies dusted with powdered sugar. She and Maria made loaves of *christopsomo*—a round loaf decorated on the top with a cross, one of which adorned just about every Christmas table in Greece.

She gathered evergreen and pine boughs from around the estate and decorated the mantels and banisters; soon the whole villa smelled like a forest.

Leo brought in a Christmas tree and Margo made dough ornaments with Timon when Parthenope came to visit, enjoying the time with her husband's nephew and imagining how one day it would be her own child at her side.

It still seemed too good to be true, too wonderful to trust that it would actually happen. But with each day that passed she felt her faith in the future grow stronger...even as she wondered about herself and Leo.

Things were better, certainly, and far from businesslike. But they hadn't actually talked about the future, or what they felt for each other, and Margo wasn't brave enough to be the first one to confess that her feelings were growing and turning to love. She hardly wanted to admit it to herself, afraid that the fragile happiness they'd found would shatter into a million pieces…just as it had before.

In any case, there was still much to enjoy.

They all went into Amfissa on Christmas Eve for a midnight service. The Byzantine *kalandas* were different from the traditional songs and hymns Margo knew, but she liked them all the same.

Afterwards Ava and Xanthe retired to their rooms, and once she and Leo were alone in the sitting room, a fire crackling in the hearth and the Christmas tree glowing with fairy lights, Leo took an envelope out of his pocket.

'Shall we?'

'It's not Christmas yet,' Margo protested, even as she felt a tremulous thrill of excitement.

'It's after midnight.' Leo sat cross-legged on the thick rug in front of the fire and patted the space next to him. 'We'll open it together, so we can see at the same time.'

'All right,' Margo said, and a little bit awkwardly, because of her growing bump, sat next to him on the rug.

Wordlessly they opened the envelope, their fingers brushing as they withdrew the single slip of paper and read the single sentence in English the technician had written there.

It's a…boy!

'A boy…' Margo repeated wonderingly.

She felt jolted, almost unsettled. She'd been excited to find out the sex of their baby, but now that she knew it, it made things more real and less real at the same time.

She put both hands to her bump. 'A son. We're going

to have *a son*.' She glanced at Leo, who looked as gob-smacked as she felt. 'Are you happy?'

'I'm…overjoyed.' He put one hand over hers, on top of her bump. 'What about you?'

'Yes. It's strange, but it seems so hard to believe.'

'I know what you mean. But you're not…you're not disappointed?'

'Disappointed? Why would I be?'

'Because…because of Annelise.'

Just the name caused a little ripple of pain to go through her, but no more than that. Her hands curved more possessively around her bump. 'A baby girl wouldn't have replaced Annelise, Leo.'

'I know. Nothing can replace her. But it might have eased things, a bit.'

'No, it's better this way. A whole new start, for all of us.'

She caught her breath, her heart starting to thud as she realised just how much she meant that. How much she wanted it.

And Leo must have understood that, because Margo saw his eyes darken and his gaze move to her mouth.

'Margo…' he said, and then he kissed her. Softly, one hand cradling her face, the other still resting on her bump.

It was the most perfect moment, the most intimate and tender thing she'd ever experienced.

Then Leo broke away. 'I want you,' he said bluntly, and the simply stated fact caused a tremor to run through her. 'I want you very badly. But only…only if you want me.'

The vulnerability on his face made her ache. Those awful words she'd flung at him so many months ago still had the power to hurt.

She raised her hand to his cheek, cradling his face just as he'd cradled hers. 'I want you, Leo. I want you very much.'

'And it's safe…?'

'The doctor said it was.' She gave a small smile. 'And we don't need to worry about birth control.'

He laughed softly and kissed her again, this time holding nothing back, his tongue and lips causing a symphony of sensation inside her as beautiful and wondrous as any *kalanda* they'd sung that night.

'We could go upstairs,' Leo whispered, and he moved from her lips to her shoulder, kissing the curve of her neck as his hand found the warm swell of her breast, one thumb running over its already taut and aching peak.

Letting out a shudder of longing, Margo glanced at the crackling fire, the Christmas tree sparkling with lights. The house stretched all around them, quiet and dark.

'No, let's stay here,' she whispered, and began to unbutton Leo's shirt.

It felt like a wedding night, with the lights and the fire and the quiet sacredness of what they were doing.

Leo stilled under her touch as she finished unbuttoning his shirt and then slid the crisp cotton from his shoulders, revelling in the feel of his skin, so hot and satiny, under her fingers. She pressed a kiss to his collarbone, needing to feel that hot, smooth skin under her lips. Leo let out a groan as she touched her tongue to his skin, tasted salt.

'You will undo me before we've even begun...'

She looked up, mischief in her eyes. 'Would that be a bad thing?'

'A very bad thing—because I want to savour every moment.'

Smiling, he undid the tie on her jersey wrap dress and it fell open. Margo felt only a little self-conscious in her bra and pants, with the swell of her bump visible and making her shape so different from the last time they'd been together like this.

Yet they'd *never*, she realised, been together like this. So intimate. So tender. So honest.

Leo slid the dress off her shoulders and then rested one hand on her bump, his skin warm on hers. 'You are so very beautiful.'

'Even pregnant?'

'Especially pregnant. Knowing you are carrying my child makes you impossible to resist.'

He bent down and pressed a kiss to her bump, and then gently he laid her back on the rug, its soft bristles tickling her bare back as he stretched out beside her.

Margo gazed up at him, everything about her open and trusting as Leo pressed a kiss to her mouth and then worked his way lower, kissing her breasts and her bump, and then all the way down to her thighs. Margo gasped as he kissed her *there*, spreading her legs wide so he could have greater access, making her feel even more vulnerable…

And yet she didn't mind. She felt treasured rather than exposed, and she wanted Leo to feel the same way.

'My turn now,' she said with a little grin, and Leo arched an eyebrow as she pushed him onto his back.

'If you insist,' he said—and then let out a groan as Margo began to kiss him, taking her time, savouring the salty tang of his skin.

She kissed her way down his chest and Leo's hands tangled in her hair as she moved lower, his breath coming out in a hiss as she freed his arousal from his boxer shorts, sliding one hand up its smooth, hot length before taking it into her mouth.

'*Margo*…' His breath ended on a cry as his hips arched upwards.

Margo watched him with hot eyes, his own desire making hers ratchet higher.

Then Leo reached for her, pulling her up towards him

so she was straddling his hips. She sank onto his shaft with a sigh of relief that turned into a moan of pleasure as he began to move, his hands tightly gripping her hips so she moved with him in an exquisite rhythm.

The firelight cast shadows over their bodies as they moved together, climbing higher and higher towards that barely attainable peak. Logs shifted and cracked, sparks scattered, and Margo cried out as she finally reached the apex, drawing Leo even more tightly into her body as she threw her head back and her climax shuddered through her.

Afterwards they lay tangled together on the rug, warm and sated, their breathing only just starting to slow.

'Thank goodness Maria didn't come down for a glass of warm milk…' Leo said.

Margo stiffened. 'She wouldn't—?'

'She is known to on occasion. It helps her sleep.' He kissed the top of her head. 'But don't worry. No one came. Except you, that is.'

She laughed softly and snuggled up against him. 'And you.'

'Most certainly. And *that*, I have to say, was a long time to wait.'

'There wasn't…?' She hesitated, not wanting to spoil the mood but needing to know. 'There wasn't anyone else? Since…?'

'No one,' Leo told her firmly. 'No one but you for over two years now, Margo.'

'And there was no one but you for me, Leo. You *do* believe me?'

'Yes.'

He spoke with such certainty that she relaxed once more into his embrace. Just asking the question had made her tense.

They lay there in a comfortable silence, as the sweat cooled on their bodies and the fire cast its shadows, and Margo felt completely, wonderfully content. This, she thought, was what a true, loving marriage could and should be. If only it could last…

CHAPTER FOURTEEN

A FEW DAYS after Christmas Antonios and Lindsay came to the villa, all the way from New York. Margo had spent hours getting ready: supervising the preparations for meals, tweaking the decorations, and finally seeing to her outfit. She was nervous about meeting Leo's brother and his wife—both for her sake and his.

Their relationship had been growing stronger in the last few days, but it still felt fragile. They hadn't said those three important words, and Margo quaked inwardly to think of actually committing herself in that way to Leo, of making her frail hopes real and spoken. Of losing it all.

She'd known the worst to happen so many times; she couldn't help but expect it now.

With Antonios's upcoming arrival, Leo had withdrawn a bit, spending more time in the office, coming to bed late at night. At least they now shared a bed. They hadn't discussed it; Leo had simply joined Margo there on Christmas Eve, after they'd made love. And he'd continued to join her every night, much to her relief and joy.

The night before she'd turned to him, smoothed a thumb over the furrow in his forehead. 'Tell me what's going on,' she'd said quietly.

Leo had twitched under her caress. 'Nothing's going on.'

'Are you worried about seeing Antonios again?'

'I'm not worried.'

'But there's something. You haven't been yourself, Leo—'

'I'm fine.'

He'd rolled onto his side, away from her, and Margo had sunk back against the pillows, more hurt than she'd wanted to admit even to herself.

'Leave it alone,' he'd muttered, and they'd gone to sleep in silence.

Now she stood on the portico, shivering slightly in the wintry breeze, as Antonios and Lindsay's hired car came up the estate's sweeping drive. Leo joined her on the step, his expression inscrutable as the car came to a stop in front of them.

Margo had felt a distance between them this morning; apparently their new relationship didn't extend to the kind of honesty and intimacy she'd been looking for last night. Lesson learned.

Lindsay got out first, waving her welcome. She was beautiful in a pale, almost ethereal way, and she smiled at Margo. Leo had told her a few days ago that Lindsay suffered from social anxiety, but with Antonios's help was able to manage it. Margo wanted to make things as easy for her new sister-in-law as possible and she started forward, smiling her own welcome.

'I'm so very glad to meet you.'

'And I you. Although I haven't heard that much about you.' Lindsay gave Leo a teasing look, and he smiled back tightly.

Margo knew Lindsay had no idea about their complicated history; she certainly wasn't going to mention it now—not when she was wondering yet again just what *was* between her and Leo.

'Come inside,' she said, drawing Lindsay up the steps towards the villa. 'It's freezing out.'

Although Antonios was only just getting out of the car Margo could still feel the tension emanating from both of the brothers. Better, she decided, for them to have their reunion in private. Leo had already shown her he didn't want her involved.

Lindsay came behind her into the villa, stopping to admire the garlands of greenery looped over the banisters and along the doorways. 'Oh, but it's beautiful! Did *you* do this?'

'Yes, I wanted a proper Christmas,' Margo said, feeling rather shy.

Lindsay beamed at her. 'I love it. I wish I could make our apartment back in New York look half as nice. I'm hopeless with decorating and things like that. Hopeless with almost everything except for numbers.'

'I doubt that.'

Leo had told her that Lindsay was a brilliant mathematician, and was currently teaching at a university in New York City. Looking at her sister-in-law, Margo couldn't help but feel a bit intimidated. Lindsay might have social anxiety, but she hid it remarkably well. Margo was the one who felt and no doubt *looked* anxious…about so many things.

Xanthe, Ava and Parthenope came into the room, greeting Lindsay with warm hugs, reminding Margo that she was still on a somewhat fragile footing with Leo's sisters. It would come right in time, she told herself, and sat down on a settee while Maria came in with coffee for everyone. Just as things would with Leo. She had to trust that—had to believe that things would work out this time.

But that was easier said than done.

Eventually the three women finished their greetings and catch-up and turned to Margo.

'Leo is a dark horse,' Lindsay said teasingly. 'I didn't even know he was seeing someone.'

Margo's insides tensed. 'He likes to keep things quiet, I suppose,' she said.

'You're one to talk, Lindsay,' Xanthe said, grinning. 'Antonios showed up with *you* with no warning whatsoever!'

'That's true,' Lindsay agreed with a laugh.

Desperate to direct the spotlight away from herself, Margo said, 'That sounds like there's a story to be told.'

Lindsay agreed, and then told Margo how she and Antonios had met and married in New York City all within a week.

'When you know, you know, right?' she said, with a smile that Margo suspected was meant to create solidarity but only made everything inside her shrink with apprehension.

Lindsay made it sound as if everything was obvious and easy when you were in love, but Margo still felt so much uncertainty, so much fear. She wanted to embrace this new life, and yet still she was holding back, and Leo was too. Perhaps they always would.

It was certainly hard for *her*. Everyone had let her down at one point or another. No one had been there for her when she'd needed it. It was so difficult to let go of that history—not to make it affect her choices even now. Difficult not to brace herself for when Leo would fail her, or say he'd had enough, or just walk away. Everyone else had—why wouldn't he?

Antonios and Leo finally came into the sitting room. Margo shot Leo a swift, searching look, but she couldn't tell anything from his face and she wondered what had passed between the two brothers.

The conversation moved on to Parthenope's family, and little Timon's antics. Margo sat back and let it all wash over her; it felt good to be part of a family—even if she was just sitting and listening to everyone else. She caught Leo's eye and he smiled at her, and the uncertainty that had been knotting her stomach eased a little.

It was going to be okay. She would believe that. At least she would try.

Leo sat on the settee across from Margo, barely listening to everyone's chatter. The stilted conversation he'd had with Antonios out on the steps replayed in his mind.

It had been strange and unsettling to see his brother again, standing there in front of their childhood home, remembering the death of both of their parents, a decade of hostility and suspicion between them... Leo had felt himself tense, his hands ball into instinctive fists. He'd seen from the set of Antonios's jaw and his narrowed eyes that he felt the same.

They could clear the air, they could forgive the past, they could say they were moving on, but the reality was that memories still clung. They still held power. And if he couldn't move past things with Antonios, how could he with Margo?

He wanted to tell her he loved her, wanted to trust that what they had was real and lasting. But the memory of her last rejection still had the power to hurt. To make him stay silent. They'd had just over a month together...a few intense moments. Nothing, he acknowledged, that actually constituted a real, loving, trusting relationship.

'How's marriage?' Antonios had asked as they'd stood outside in wintry silence.

'Fine.'

'I didn't know you were seeing anyone.'

'It's not as if we keep each other up to date on our personal lives,' Leo had answered. He'd meant to sound light, but it had come out terse and dismissive instead. 'You're one to talk, anyway,' he'd added, trying for a joke, but it had fallen flat.

Antonios had just nodded, his jaw bunched, and they hadn't spoken again until they were settled in the sitting room with everyone else—and then only about innocuous matters.

Leo's gaze kept straying to Margo. She was listening to everyone, but he thought she looked tense, maybe even unhappy, and he wished they could be alone. Wished he could be sure of her feelings...and of his own.

'Is everything all right between you and Antonios?' Margo asked as they got ready for bed that evening.

They hadn't spoken much during the day, busy as they'd both been with their guests. Margo, Leo noticed now, looked pale and tired, with lines of strain around her eyes.

'As well as they can be, I suppose,' he said as he stretched out on the bed.

Leo still kept his clothes in the adjoining room, but he'd brought a few things into Margo's bedroom: his books, his reading glasses, his pyjamas. Small yet intimate things that spoke of building a life together. But lying there he felt as if his presence in Margo's life, in her bed, was transient.

Margo took down her hair, and Leo felt a frisson of sensual pleasure as he watched her raise her slender arms, anticipating the sudden tumble of dark, wavy hair down to her waist.

'What does that mean?' she asked as she reached for the satin nightdress she wore to bed and quickly undressed.

Leo had tantalising glimpses of her breasts and thighs, milky-pale and soft-looking, before she shrugged the nightdress on and slid under the covers, pillows propped behind her as she looked at him and waited for his answer.

'We have ten years of hard history,' Leo said slowly. 'Even though we've talked about it and tried to put it behind us, I don't think it's that easy or simple.'

'No,' Margo agreed quietly. 'It isn't.'

He knew she was thinking of her own past hurts. As much as she might want to, could she move on from her appalling childhood and the many wrongs that had been done to her? Could *they* move on from the hurt they'd caused each other?

He wasn't about to ask those questions. They spoke of his own past, his own uncertainty and fear. He'd spent his childhood trying to prove himself to his father—wanting Evangelos to love him,and receiving only rejection.

And it was those experiences that kept him silent now.

'Do you think things will get better in time?' Margo asked, her gaze serious and intent on him.

For a second Leo thought she was asking about things with them. Then he realised she meant Antonios.

'Maybe,' he said with a shrug.

He didn't sound hopeful.

Wanting to end the discussion, he reached for her, wrapping a thick tendril of hair around his wrist as he pulled her gently towards him. She came with a smile, her features softened and suffused with desire, their bodies bumping up against one another as Leo brushed a kiss across her mouth.

They'd made love many times in the days since Christmas Eve. Their chemistry had always been explosive, right from the beginning, but in the last week it had become even more intimate and arousing.

Margo let out a soft little sigh as she brought her arms up around his neck, her body yielding to his in a way that made Leo's head spin and desire spiral dizzily inside him. He slid his hand from her shoulder to her waist to her hip, loving the silky feel of her skin, the ripe fullness of her breasts and hips.

She twitched slightly beneath his caress and he stilled his hand. 'What is it?'

'Just the normal fears of a pregnant woman,' she said with an uncertain little laugh. 'I feel fat.'

'Fat? *Fat?* Margo, you are not remotely fat. You are fecund and beautiful and glowing. I like your body more, I think, than before you were carrying our baby.'

'You do *not*!'

'You doubt me?' he said in a mock growl, and she let out another laugh, this one breathless with anticipation.

'I do.'

'Then perhaps I should prove to you just how beautiful you are,' Leo said, and bent his head to her breasts, taking his time to give each one his full, lascivious attention.

Margo let out a sigh of pleasure, her hands tangling in his hair, and Leo lifted his head.

'Does that satisfy you?' he demanded, and she gazed at him with a mischievous smile.

'Not…quite.'

'I see I'll have to prove it to you some more.'

'You just might.'

Laughing softly, he slid a hand between her thighs. 'I can do a lot of proving,' he murmured, 'if that's your wish.'

'It is,' Margo whispered back, her hips arching upwards. And then they lost themselves to their shared pleasure.

The next day Leo and Antonios repaired to the office, to discuss matters relating to Marakaios Enterprises, and Lindsay sought out Margo up in the soon-to-be nursery, where she was comparing fabric swatches.

'Hello,' she said, poking her head around the door, and Margo gave a self-conscious smile before welcoming her in.

'Sorry, I'm not trying to hide away.' She rubbed her lower back while motioning to the swatches. 'Just trying to make a decision about fabric. It can take ages for it to come in once you place an order.'

'I wouldn't know,' Lindsay answered with a laugh. 'But Leo mentioned you worked in decorating before…?'

'I was a buyer for a department store in Paris. Home furnishings.' It occurred to her this must seem like a rather useless job to a brilliant mathematician, but Lindsay appeared genuinely interested.

'Do you miss it? When Antonios and I lived here I missed my old life a lot more than I thought I would. My old job…'

Margo was intrigued to think that Lindsay and Antonios's marriage hadn't always been as perfect as it now seemed.

'I don't *miss* it exactly,' she answered slowly. 'But I miss feeling productive and useful sometimes.'

Lindsay nodded in sympathy before saying in a rush, 'Look, I think I may have put my foot in it yesterday, which isn't all that surprising, considering how bad I am at social situations. But when I mentioned not knowing that you and Leo were dating…' She swallowed, a blush staining her pale cheeks. 'Well, it's none of my business whether you were dating or not. I didn't mean to make you feel awkward.'

'But you noticed that you *did*?' Margo answered with an uncertain laugh.

'I'm sorry.'

'No, don't be. It was a perfectly innocent question. And the truth is my relationship with Leo is…complicated.'

'I can relate to that.'

'Can you?' Margo glanced at her sister-in-law with open curiosity. 'Because from where I'm standing you and Antonios seem to have the fairytale.'

'Oh, don't say that!' Lindsay cried, and Margo raised her eyebrows. 'It used to seem like a fairytale,' she explained. 'Meeting the way we did in New York. Antonios sweeping me straight off my feet.' Lindsay sighed and shook her head. 'But life isn't a fairytale, you know? Reality sets in. And when it did for Antonios and me, it was hard.'

'How so?'

'Did Leo tell you about my social anxiety?'

'A bit...'

'As soon as we were married Antonios whisked me off here and put me in charge of the household. He thought he was honouring me, but in truth it just terrified me. I've had social anxiety since I was a child—talking in front of crowds, being the centre of attention...it all makes me start to panic. And when I landed here...with all of Antonios's sisters as well as his mother looking at me, measuring me...it was hard.'

'But his sisters love you now,' Margo remarked.

Lindsay smiled wryly. 'That doesn't mean they weren't taken aback when Antonios showed up with me out of the blue.'

'The same way Leo showed up with me,' Margo admitted with a laugh. 'Poor girls. They've had an awful lot of shocks.'

'So why *did* you and Leo marry, if you don't mind me asking? *Were* you dating...?' Lindsay's blush deepened. 'Sorry, I'm being inexcusably nosy. But, if you don't mind me saying so, you remind me a little bit of me when I came here. A little overwhelmed...a little lost.'

'Do I?' Margo could hear how stiff and stilted her voice

sounded and busied herself organising the swatches of fabric, just to give herself a little time to order her thoughts.

'Am I wrong?' Lindsay asked quietly.

'Not exactly. Coming here as Leo's wife was overwhelming—especially considering the circumstances.' She glanced down at her bump and Lindsay nodded her understanding. 'I don't have a lot of experience with big families or houses. I've pretty much been on my own my whole life.'

'As have I,' Lindsay said quietly.

Margo looked at her in surprise. 'We seem to have quite a bit in common.'

'Not least being married to difficult Marakaios men.'

They both laughed at that, and then Margo said seriously, 'But Antonios seems to dote on you.'

'Antonios can be stubborn and set in his ways. He tends not to see another person's perspective unless it's pointed out to him. *Repeatedly.*' Lindsay softened this observation with a smile and added, 'But I'm utterly in love with him, and he with me, and that makes all the difference.'

'Yes, I'm sure it does,' Margo murmured.

She thought of how she and Leo had made love last night, spending the whole night sleeping in each other's arms. Was that love? It seemed like it, on the surface, but the fact remained that she still felt wary and guarded, and she thought Leo did too. They were both still holding back, both afraid to commit fully to their marriage... Or maybe Leo just didn't want to. Maybe what they had was enough—was all he wanted.

And yet she knew she wanted more. She wanted the fairytale.

CHAPTER FIFTEEN

A MONTH PASSED in wintry days spent with Margo decorating the nursery and managing the household, getting to know Leo's sisters—and getting to know Leo.

They spent far more time together now than they ever had in their two years of dirty weekends and meals out. They chatted about everything—from politics to music and books, to places they'd like to visit. He was becoming as good a friend as he was a lover.

And yet she still felt that reticence in him, and in herself. They still hadn't said *I love you*, hadn't discussed anything about the future. Leo still hadn't moved his things into her bedroom.

As the weeks passed Margo wondered if this wasn't actually a *good* thing. If Leo kept a little distance, then she could too. Maybe they could enjoy each other's company and bodies and still stay safe. Still not risk getting hurt.

Yet she knew that for a lie when she thought about the possibility of losing Leo. She would be utterly devastated.

At the end of January Leo came into the house, where she'd been browsing through a catalogue of baby toys, and asked if she'd come to the office with him.

'The office? Why?'

'I need your opinion on something.'

Surprised and a bit bemused, she walked with him across the estate to the long, low-lying building that overlooked the olive groves.

'What do you think of these?' he asked, and gestured to a box of olive-based bath supplies.

Frowning a little, Margo examined the items, noting the pleasingly thick glass bottles, the nutty smell of the olives.

'They feel expensive,' she offered. 'Although they smell a bit more like cooking oil than something you'd want to put in your bath.'

He nodded. 'I was afraid of that. I want to develop a new range of bath products to supply the Adair chain of hotels, but I don't think these are up to scratch.'

'A little olive oil goes a long way, I suppose,' Margo answered with a smile.

'I could use your expertise here,' Leo said. 'If you're willing to give it. Someone with a good eye for design and good taste to offer an opinion about our merchandise.'

Margo just stared.

'Not a full-time job, necessarily,' he continued. 'I know with the baby coming you wouldn't want that. But you have a lot of talent and expertise to offer, Margo, and I don't want to squander it.'

And so she started going into the office two days a week—to review the different products Marakaios Enterprises was offering and strategise the best way to market them. She enjoyed the work—and even more so because it meant she and Leo were working together…a true partnership.

Leo glanced across the breakfast table and smiled to see Margo balancing her teacup on top of her bump. Her hair was loose and dark about her face, her expression thoughtful as she read a journal about decorative art. They'd been married for only two months but they were already acting like an old married couple, reading their separate periodicals over breakfast.

Not that Leo minded. He loved these mornings with Margo, even when they weren't talking to each other. Just being in her presence, seeing her smile or watching the way her eyes darkened intently as she listened to him, made him happy.

Several weeks ago Margo had asked him if he was happy and Leo hadn't been able to answer. Now he knew he could. Yes, he was happy with Margo. He was happy—and in love—with his wife.

Just acknowledging that fact to himself gave him a little fizz of anticipation, as well as a twist of apprehension. He wanted to tell her how he felt, *all* he felt, and yet he held back. No time felt right. What if she told him she didn't love him back? What if she wasn't capable of it? He understood why she'd kept herself from love and life before, but it wouldn't make it any easier to accept now.

Rejection, Leo thought bleakly, was still rejection.

'How would you like to go to Paris?' he asked now, and she looked up from her journal, her eyes widening in surprise.

'Paris? Why?'

'I have a little business there. We could make it pleasure too, though. We could check on your apartment and see the city together. Visit some of our old haunts.'

'That sounds good,' Margo said slowly, almost as if she didn't trust that he'd want to go to Paris with her. 'It would be great to check in with Achat too. I gave my notice, obviously, but it would be good to have a proper goodbye. I worked there a long time.'

'Very well. Shall I make the arrangements? We could leave tomorrow.'

Margo nodded, her gaze still moving over him, and Leo looked away. He didn't want anything in his face to reveal the surprise he was planning for her.

They left early the next morning, driving to Athens and then flying on to Paris; they were in Margo's apartment on the Île de la Cité by mid-afternoon.

Leo stood on the threshold of the living room and gazed at the picture window overlooking Paris, the twin towers of Notre-Dame visible in the distance.

He'd asked Margo to marry him here. He'd felt the painful sting of rejection, the bitter and furious hurt that had led to the baby boy now nestled inside her waiting to be born. So much had changed, and yet for a moment he felt mired by the past.

He didn't actually know what Margo wanted. Once, six months ago, he'd thought he did. He'd asked her to marry him, feeling confident of her answer.

Looking back, he knew that his confidence had in fact been arrogance. Margo had given him no hint that she'd wanted a ring on her finger. Everything about her—her bold, sassy, sensual confidence, her easy acceptance of their arrangement—had indicated otherwise. And yet she'd admitted that the persona she'd adopted was nothing more than a mask.

So did the *real* Margo, the lovely, thoughtful, interesting woman he'd come to know beneath that mask, want what he wanted now?

'Leo…' She came up behind him and rested her hands lightly on his shoulders.

Leo blinked back the memories before turning around to face her and slip his arms around her waist.

'We'll always have Paris,' he quipped, and though she smiled he saw her eyes were troubled.

'Will we?' she asked softly, sadly, and too late Leo re-alised how that had sounded.

They would always have Paris and the memories they'd made here…whether they wanted them or not.

Margo tried to banish the disquiet that fluttered through as she saw Leo's eyebrows draw together in a faint frown. She'd been nervous about coming back to Paris, to the city where they'd met so often during their affair, and the very room where Margo had rejected him. She didn't think she'd imagined the suddenly shuttered look on Leo's face as he'd come into her apartment, and she had a terrible feeling he was remembering how he'd proposed to her here and what her answer had been.

Now, however, he smiled, his face clearing, and looked around her sitting room. 'Do you know, before I came here I would have thought you'd have some modern, sleek pent-house? All chrome and leather and modern art.'

'You mean like your bachelor pad in Athens? I prefer a homier place to live.'

'Which is why you were a buyer of home furnishings, I suppose?'

She nodded and he strolled around the apartment, not-ing the squashy velveteen sofa, the Impressionist prints, the porcelain ornaments and figurines. She'd had a lot of her things sent to Greece, but there were certainly enough left for Leo to examine and make her feel oddly exposed.

'How did you get into the buying business, anyway?' he asked as he picked up a carved wooden figurine of a mother holding her infant.

It had been whittled from one piece of wood and the result was a sinuous, fluid sculpture in which it was im-possible to tell where the mother finished and the child began. Margo had always loved it, but never had it seemed so revealing of her life, her secret desires and heartache.

'I got a job with Achat, working on a sales counter, when I was sixteen. From there I moved up through the ranks,' she said. 'I've never actually worked anywhere else.'

'And you wanted to go into the buying side of things? Home furnishings in particular?'

'Yes, that was what I always liked.'

The bedsits and sheltered housing, the homeless shelters and foster placements that had comprised her childhood homes had never felt like proper places to grow up. Safe or loving places. And she had, Margo knew, been trying to create that for herself—through her job and in her own apartment.

Somehow she had a feeling Leo knew that too.

He put the figurine down and turned to her. 'You have a beautiful home here,' he said. 'You have a real talent for making a space feel cosy and welcoming.'

'Thank you.'

'If there are any more things you'd like to take to Greece I can arrange for them to be shipped.'

'I'll look around tomorrow and box things up.'

He smiled and reached for her again. Margo snuggled into him, grateful for the feel of his arms around her, making her feel safe. *For now.*

While Margo went to Achat to say her goodbyes Leo attended to his business in the city. He'd been acting a bit mysteriously, which had made Margo wonder what he was doing or planning, but she told herself not to be nervous and just to wait and see.

In any case, her arrival at Achat put Leo out of her mind for a little while, as she was caught up in reunions with different acquaintances, a bittersweet meeting with her boss, who wished she could stay, and then a catch-up with Sophie.

They left the office for a café with deep velvet chairs and spindly little tables a few blocks from Achat. Sophie ordered them both bowl-sized cups of hot chocolate with lashings of whipped cream.

'A celebration,' she proclaimed, 'since things seem to have turned out all right for you.'

'How do you know they have?' Margo challenged as she took a sip of the deliciously rich hot chocolate.

'You haven't sent me any panicked texts,' Sophie answered, 'and, more importantly, you look *happy*, Margo. Happier than I think I've ever seen you.'

'I *am* happy...' Margo said quietly.

Sophie arched an eyebrow. 'Why do you sound so uncertain, then?'

'Because happiness can be so fleeting.' She took a deep breath. 'And Leo hasn't actually told me he loves me.'

'Have you told *him*?'

'No...'

'Well, then.'

When Margo had first been pregnant Sophie had heard the full story of Leo's proposal and Margo's rejection.

'Can you really blame him for not going first?' she asked, and Margo sighed.

'Not really.'

'So why *haven't* you told him you love him?'

'Because I'm afraid that's not what he wants to hear. Because we're both holding back.'

'Then stop,' Sophie suggested with a smile.

'It's not that simple,' Margo said. 'It's...' She hesitated, thoughts and fears swirling around in her mind. 'I feel like if I try for too much—if I do anything to jeopardise what we have—it will all topple like a child's tower of bricks because it's not strong enough to stand...'

'Stand what?' Sophie asked gently.

'*Anything*. Anything bad.' Margo swallowed. 'I know I'm afraid, and that I'm letting my fear control my actions. I understand that, Sophie, trust me.'

'But it's keeping you from doing something about it.'

'I think I'd rather just hold on to what we have and be happy with it than try for more and lose,' Margo confessed quietly. 'If that makes me a coward, so be it.'

Sophie eyed her sceptically. 'As long as you *are* happy,' she said after a moment.

Margo didn't answer.

Sophie's words still pinged around in her head as she headed back to her apartment. *Was* she happy? *Could* this be enough?

Maybe Sophie was right, and Leo was holding back simply because *she* was. Maybe if she made the first move and told him she loved him he would tell her back.

They were going out to dinner tonight. Leo had made the arrangements, although he hadn't told Margo where. But they'd be alone, and it might even be romantic, and it would be a perfect opportunity for Margo to tell Leo the truth.

To tell him she loved him.

She spent a long time getting ready that evening. First she had a long soak in the tub, and then she did her nails, hair and make-up before donning a new maternity dress of soft black jersey.

It had a daring V-neck that made the most of her pregnancy-enhanced assets and draped lovingly over her bump before swirling about her knees. She'd put her hair up for the simple pleasure of being able to take it down again in

Leo's presence later that night, and had slipped her feet into her favourite pair of black suede stiletto heels.

And now she waited—because Leo still wasn't home.

He'd been due back at seven to collect Margo for their date, but as the minutes ticked by Margo's unease grew. It figured that the one night she'd decided to tell Leo how she felt he'd be AWOL. It almost seemed like a sign, a portent of things to come. Or rather not to come.

At seven forty-five she texted Leo. At eight she took off her heels and her earrings—both had been starting to hurt—and curled up on her bed.

Her phone rang at eight-fifteen.

'Margo, I'm so sorry—'

'What happened?' Her voice was quiet and yet filled with hurt.

'I had a meeting with Adair Hotels. It's an important deal and the meeting ran long. I didn't even realise the time...'

'It's okay,' she said. And it *was* okay. At least it should have been okay. It would have been okay if she hadn't built this evening up in her own mind.

Maybe she'd built *everything* up in her own mind.

In that moment she felt as if she couldn't trust anything or anyone, least of all herself. It was nothing more than a missed dinner, and yet it was so much more. It was everything.

'When will you be back?' she asked, and Leo sighed.

'I don't know. Late. Talks are still ongoing, and we'll most likely go out for drinks afterwards.' He hesitated and then said, 'Don't wait up.'

And somehow that stung too.

She was being ridiculous, over-emotional, overreacting. She knew that. And yet she still hung up on Leo without replying.

* * *

Leo stared at the phone, the beep of Margo disconnecting the call still echoing through his ear. Had she actually just hung up on him? Simply because he'd missed dinner?

He let out a long sigh and tossed his phone on the desk. He felt as if something big had happened, something momentous, and damned if he knew what it was.

But then he hadn't known what was going on for a while. For the last month he and Margo had been existing in an emotional stasis which he suspected suited them both fine. Neither of them had been ready to take their relationship up to that next level. To say they loved each other… to bare the truth of their hearts.

At least *he* hadn't. Maybe Margo had nothing to say… nothing to bare.

'Leo?' One of his staff poked his head through the doorway, eyebrows raised. 'Are you ready?'

Leo nodded. This deal was too important for him to become distracted about Margo.

And yet as he went back into the conference room he couldn't stop thinking about her. About the hurt he'd heard in her voice and the way she'd hung up on him. About all the painful truths she'd shared about her childhood and all the things he hadn't said.

He lasted an hour before he called the meeting to a halt.

'I'm sorry, gentlemen, but we can resume tomorrow. I need to get home to my wife.'

After she'd hung up on Leo, Margo peeled off her dress and ran a bath. Perhaps a nice long soak in the tub would help alleviate her misery—or at least give her a little perspective. It was one missed dinner…one little argument. It didn't have to mean anything.

Sighing, Margo slipped into the water and closed her

eyes. She felt as if she couldn't shift the misery that had taken up residence in her chest, as if a stone were pressing down on her.

At first Margo thought the pain in her belly was simply the weight of that disappointment and heartache, but then the twinges intensified and she realised she was feeling actual physical pain. Something was wrong.

She pressed her hands to her bump, realising she hadn't felt a kick in a while—a few hours at least. She'd become used to feeling those lovely flutters. Now she felt another knifing pain through her stomach, and then a sudden gush of fluid, and she watched in dawning shock and horror as the water around her bloomed red.

CHAPTER SIXTEEN

THE APARTMENT WAS quiet and empty when Leo came into the foyer just after nine o'clock.

'Margo?'

He tossed his keys on the table, a sudden panic icing inside him. Had she left? Left *him*? He realised in that moment that he'd been bracing himself for such a thing, perhaps from the moment they'd married. Waiting for another rejection.

'Margo?' he called again, but the only answer was the ringing silence that seemed to reverberate through the empty rooms of the apartment.

He poked his head through the doorway of her bedroom, and saw how the lamplight cast a golden pool onto the empty bed. Her dress and shoes were discarded and crumpled on the floor and the bathroom door was ajar, light spilling from within. All was silent.

He was about to turn back when he heard a sound from the bathroom—the slosh of water. He froze for a millisecond, and then in three strides crossed to the bathroom, threw open the door, and saw Margo lying in a tub full of rose-tinted water, her head lolling back, her face drained of colour.

'Margo—' Her name was a cry, a plea, a prayer. Leo

fumbled for his phone even as he reached for her, drew her out of the tub. 'Margo…' he whispered.

She glanced up at him, her face with a waxy sheen, her eyes luminous.

'I've lost the baby, haven't I?'

'I don't know—' He stopped, for she'd slumped in his arms, unconscious.

Margo came to, lying on a stretcher. Two paramedics were wheeling her to an ambulance, and panic clutched at her so hard she could barely speak.

'My baby—'

One of them reassured her that they were taking her to a hospital, and Leo reached for her hand. His hand felt cold, as cold as hers. He was scared, she realised. He knew the worst was happening.

The worst *always* happened.

Just hours ago she'd been buoying up her courage to tell Leo she loved him. Now everything had fallen apart. Nothing could be the same. Her relationship with Leo had been expedient at its core; without this child kicking in her womb there was no need for a marriage.

And yet she couldn't think about losing Leo on top of losing the baby; it was too much to bear. So she forced her mind to go blank, and after a few seconds her panic was replaced by a numb, frozen feeling—a feeling she'd thought she'd never have to experience again.

It was the way she'd felt when she'd realised Annelise was gone. It was the only way she'd known how to cope. And yet she hadn't coped at all. And she didn't think she could cope now—except by remaining frozen. Numb.

She felt distant from the whole scene—as if she were floating above the ambulance, watching as the paramedics sat next to her, taking her vitals.

'Blood pressure is dropping steadily.'

She barely felt a flicker of anything as they searched for the baby's heartbeat. They found it, but from the paramedics' mutterings it was clearly weak.

'Baby appears to be in distress.'

In distress. It seemed such a little term for so terrible a moment.

'Margo…Margo.' Leo was holding her hand, his face close to hers. 'It's going to be okay. *Agapi mou*, I promise—'

My love. The words didn't move her now, didn't matter at all. 'You can't promise anything,' she said, and turned her face away.

The next few minutes passed in a blur as the ambulance arrived, siren wailing, at a hospital on the other side of the Île de la Cité—one of Paris's oldest hospitals, a beautiful building Margo had walked by many times but never been inside.

Now she was rushed into a room on the emergency ward, and doctors surrounded her as they took her vitals yet again. She could see Leo standing outside, demanding to be allowed in. A doctor was arguing with him.

Margo felt herself sliding into unconsciousness, one hand cradling her bump—the only connection she had to the baby she was afraid she'd never meet.

'Madame Marakaios?'

A doctor touched her arm, bringing her back to wakefulness.

'You have had a placental abruption. Do you know what that is?'

'Is my baby dying?' Margo asked. Her voice sounded slurred.

'We need to perform an emergency Caesarean section as your baby is in distress. Do you give your consent?'

'But I'm only twenty-seven weeks…'

'It is your child's only chance, *madame*,' the doctor said, and wordlessly Margo nodded.

What else could she do?

They began to prep her for surgery and Margo lay there, tears silently snaking down her face; it appeared she wasn't that frozen after all.

And yet neither was she surprised. Wasn't this what happened? You let people in, you loved them, and they left you. Her baby. *Leo.*

The last thought Margo had as she was put under anaesthetic was that maybe it would have been better not to have trusted or loved at all.

CHAPTER SEVENTEEN

LEO PACED THE waiting room restlessly, his hands bunched into fists. He hadn't been allowed inside the operating room and he felt furious and helpless and desperately afraid. He couldn't lose their son. He couldn't lose Margo.

He wished more than ever that he'd had the courage to tell her he loved her. Three little words and yet he'd held back. He'd held back in so many ways, not wanting to risk rejection or hurt, and all he could do now was call himself a fool. A frightened fool for not speaking the truth of his heart to his wife.

If Margo made it through this, he vowed he would tell her. He would tell her everything he felt.

'Monsieur Marakaios?' A doctor still in his surgical scrubs came through the steel double doors.

Leo's jaw bunched and he sprang forward. 'You have news? Is my wife—?'

'Your wife and son are all right,' the man said quietly, 'although weak.'

'Weak—?'

'Your wife lost a great deal of blood. She is stable, but she will have a few weeks of recovery ahead of her.'

'And the baby? My son?' A lump formed in his throat as he waited for the doctor to respond.

'He's in the Neonatal Intensive Care Unit,' the doctor

answered. 'He's very small, and his lungs aren't mature. He'll need to stay in hospital for some weeks at least.'

Leo nodded jerkily; he didn't trust himself to speak for a moment. When he had his emotions under control, he managed, 'Please—I'd like to see my wife.'

Margo had been moved to a private room on the ward, and was lying in bed, her eyes closed.

'Margo?' he said softly, and touched her hand.

She opened her eyes and stared at him for a long moment, and then she turned her head away from him.

Leo felt tears sting his eyes. 'Margo, it's okay. You're all right and our son is all right.'

'He's alive, you mean,' she said flatly.

Leo blinked. 'Yes, alive. Small, and his lungs aren't mature, but he's stable—'

'You can't know that.'

'The doctor just said—'

She shook her head.

Leo frowned and touched her hand. 'Margo, it's going to be okay.'

She withdrew her hand from his. 'Stop making promises you can't keep, Leo.'

Helplessly Leo stared at her, not knowing what to say or do. 'I know it's been frightening—'

'You don't know *anything*!' She cut across him, her voice choking on a sob. 'You don't know what it's like to lose everything again.'

'But you didn't—we didn't—'

'I want you to go.' She closed her eyes, tears leaking from under her lids and making silvery tracks down her cheeks. 'Please—please go.'

It went against every instinct he had to leave Margo alone in this moment. He wanted to tell her how he loved her, and yet she couldn't even bear to look at him. How had this happened?

'Margo—' he began, only to realise from the way her breathing had evened out that she was asleep. He touched her cheek, wanting her to know even in sleep how he felt, and then quietly left the room.

'It's difficult to say what's going to happen,' the doctor told Leo when he went to ask for more details about his son's condition. 'Of course there have been terrific strides made in the care of premature babies. But I don't like to give any promises at this stage, because premature infants' immune systems aren't fully developed and neither are their lungs. It's very easy for them to catch an infection and have it become serious.'

Leo nodded, his throat tight. He'd just tried to promise Margo it was going to be okay. But she was right: he couldn't promise anything. And he didn't know if their marriage, fragile as it was, would survive this.

He stood outside the neonatal ICU and watched his impossibly small son flail tiny red fists. He was covered in tubes to help him breathe, eat, live. It made Leo ache with a fierce love—and a desperate fear.

Eventually he went back to see Margo. She was awake and sitting up in bed, and while the sight of her lifted his spirits, the expression on her face did not.

'The doctor says the next few weeks will be crucial,' Leo said.

Margo nodded; she looked almost indifferent to this news.

'He'll have to stay in hospital for a while—at least a month.'

Another nod.

'He can't be taken out of the ICU,' Leo ventured, 'and

we can't hold him yet, but I could wheel you up there so you can at least see him?'

Margo stared at him for a moment before she answered quietly, 'I don't think so.'

Leo stared at her in shock. 'Margo—'

'I told you before, I'd like to be alone.'

She turned away from him and he stared at her helplessly.

'Margo, please. Tell me what's going on.'

'Nothing is going on. I've just realised.' She drew a quick, sharp breath. 'I can't do this. I thought I could—I wanted to—but I can't.'

'Can't do what?'

'This.' She gestured with one limp hand to the space between them. 'Marriage. Motherhood. Any of it. I can't let myself love someone and have them taken away again. I just...*can't.*'

'Margo, I won't leave you—'

'Maybe not physically,' she allowed. 'You have too much honour for that. But you told me yourself you didn't love me—'

'That was months ago—'

'And nothing's changed, has it?' She lifted her resolute gaze to his in weary challenge. 'Nothing's changed,' she repeated.

Leo wondered if she was saying that nothing had changed for *her*. She didn't love *him*.

For a second he remained silent, and a second was all Margo needed for affirmation.

She nodded. 'I thought so. We only had a couple of months together, Leo. They were lovely, I suppose, but that's all they were.'

'No.' Finally he found his voice, along with his resolve.

'*No*, Margo. I don't accept that. I won't let you torpedo our marriage simply because you're afraid.'

'Of *course* I'm afraid,' she snapped, her voice rising in anger. 'Do you even know what it's like to lose some-one—?'

'I lost both my parents,' Leo answered. 'So, yes, I do.'

'Yes, of course you do,' she acknowledged. 'But a *child*. A child *I* was responsible for—a child who looked to *me* for love and care and food and everything—' Her voice broke and her shoulders began to shake with sobs.

'Margo…Margo…' Leo crooned softly and, sitting on the edge of the bed, gently put his arms around her.

She stilled, unable to move away from him but still try-ing to keep herself distant. Safe. But safety, Leo realised, was Margo knowing how he truly felt.

'I love you,' he said, and then, in case she still doubted him, he said it again. 'I love you. And that will never change. No matter what happens. *No matter what.*'

To his surprise and dismay her shoulders shook harder.

She pulled away from him, wiping the tears from her face. 'Oh, Leo. I don't deserve you.'

'*Deserve?* What does this have to do with deserving?'

'It's *my* fault Annelise died. Maybe it's my fault our son is in such danger. I might have done something… I don't deserve…'

'Margo, hush.' Tenderly he wiped the tears from her cheeks. 'You must stop blaming yourself for what hap-pened.'

She'd been tortured by both guilt and grief for years, and he longed to release her.

'What happened to Annelise could have happened to any child, any mother. And you were only a child yourself. As for our son…you've been so careful during this preg-nancy. I've seen you. Nothing is your fault.'

She shook her head but he continued.

'You must let the past go and forgive yourself. You must look to your future—*our* future—and our son's future. Because I love you, and I wish I'd told you before. I wish you'd known how much I loved you when you went into surgery. I wish you'd had that to hold on to.'

She blinked up at him, searching his face. 'Do you mean it, Leo?' she asked quietly. 'Do you really mean it?'

'With all my heart.'

'I haven't even said how I feel.'

'If you don't love me,' he answered steadily, 'it's all right. I can wait—'

'But I *do* love you.' She cut him off. 'I was going to tell you tonight, when we had dinner—'

'Nothing turned out quite as we expected, did it?' he said, and pressed a kiss to her palm. 'But now we've told each other, and we have our son, and I will do everything in my power to keep you safe and secure and—'

'I believe you!' With a trembling laugh she pressed the palm he'd just kissed against his lips. 'You don't have to convince me.'

'I want to spend a lifetime convincing you.'

Tears sparkled on her lashes. 'And our little boy…?'

'Why don't you come and see him?'

Margo's heart was beating with thuds so hard they made her feel sick as Leo wheeled her up to the ICU. He parked the wheelchair in front of the glass and Margo stared at the row of plastic cradles, the tubes and the wires, the tiny beings fighting so hard for life.

And then she saw the words *'Enfant Marakaios'* and everything in her clenched hard. Her son. Hers and Leo's.

'Oh, Leo,' she whispered, and reached for his hand.

They stared silently at the baby they'd made, now waving his fists angrily.

'He's got a lot of spirit—or so the doctor says,' Leo said shakily. 'He'll fight hard.'

Margo felt a hot rush of shame that she'd considered, even for a moment, protecting herself against the pain of loving this little boy. Of loving Leo. She'd spent a lifetime apart, atoning for her sins, trying to keep her shattered heart safe. But Leo, with his kindness and understanding and love, had put her back together again. Had made her want to try. To fight, and fight hard—just as their son was.

'I'm sorry—' she began, but Leo shook his head.

'No, don't be sorry. Just enjoy this moment. Enjoy our family.'

'Our little man,' Margo whispered, and then looked up at Leo.

He smiled down at her, his eyes bright with tears. Her family, Margo thought, right here.

There were no certainties—not for anyone. No guarantees of a happily-ever-after, no promises that life would flow smoothly. Life was a rough river, full of choppy currents, and the only thing she could do was grab on to those she loved and hold on. Hold on for ever.

And, clinging to Leo's hand, that was just what she was going to do.

EPILOGUE

'WHERE ARE WE GOING?' Margo asked as they stepped out onto the pavement in front of her apartment.

It was three months since their son had been born, and he was coming home from the hospital tomorrow. To celebrate, Leo was taking her out to dinner.

It had been a long, harrowing three months.

Annas—the name meant 'a gift given by God'—had had several lung infections that had terrified both Leo and Margo at the time, and twice it had been touch and go. Margo had felt more fear then than she ever had before, and yet with Leo's support and strength she'd met every challenge head-on, determined to believe in her son, to imbue him with all the strength and love she felt.

And he was healthy now—weighing just over five pounds, and more precious to Leo and Margo than they ever could have known.

Leo hailed a cab, and as the car pulled to the kerb he leaned over the window to give directions. He'd been making a big secret of their destination, which made Margo smile.

When the cab pulled up to the Eiffel Tower she looked at him in surprise. 'Sightseeing…?'

'In a way,' he answered, and drew her by the hand from

the cab to the base of the tower, where a man stood by the elevator that surged up its centre, waiting for them.

'*Bon soir*, Monsieur Marakios,' he said as he ushered them into the lift.

Margo looked at Leo with narrowed eyes. 'What is going on?'

'You'll see.'

They stepped out onto the first floor of the tower, saw the city stretched all around them. The platform was completely empty, as was the upscale café.

'What…?' Margo began, and Leo explained.

'I reserved it for us.'

'The whole tower?'

'The whole tower.'

'You can't do that—'

'I can,' he answered, and Margo let out an incredulous laugh.

'No wonder you've been looking so pleased with yourself.' She moved into the café, where the elegant space was strung with fairy lights, and a table for two flickered with candlelight in the centre of the restaurant. 'Oh, Leo, it's amazing.'

'I'm glad you think so.' He pulled her to him to kiss her lightly on the lips. 'Truth be told, I was afraid you might think it all a bit much.'

'No, it's wonderful. It's perfect.'

The sheer romance of it left her breathless, overwhelmed, and very near tears. They'd come through so much together, and she loved him more than ever. More than she'd ever thought possible.

'I can't believe you hired the whole of the Eiffel Tower,' she said with a shaky laugh as Leo guided her to a chair and spread a napkin in her lap.

A waiter came unobtrusively to pour wine and serve a

first course of oysters on crushed ice before quietly disappearing.

'Some might say that it is a *bit* over the top,' she teased, and Leo grinned.

'Well, I wanted to do it right this time.'

'This time?'

He took a sip of wine, his expression turning serious and making everything in Margo clench hard in anticipation.

'When I proposed again.'

'Proposed? Leo, we're already married.'

'We had a civil service, yes.'

'You want to have another marriage ceremony?'

'No, I don't want to have another ceremony. The one we had was real and binding. But I want to do it right this time—to make a proposal we can both remember.'

'You don't—'

'I know. But I want to. Because I love you that much.'

'I love you, too. So much.'

'So…' With a self-conscious smile Leo rose from his chair and then dropped to one knee. Margo let out another shaky laugh as he took her hand in his. 'Margo Marakaios—I love you more than life itself. I love the woman you are, the wife you are, the mother you are. Every part of you leaves me awash in amazement and admiration.'

'Oh, Leo—' Margo began, but he silenced her with a swift shake of his head.

'I mean it—every word. You are strong and brave and—'

'But I've been so afraid for so much of my life!'

'And you've overcome it. Overcome so much tragedy and pain. That's strength, Margo. That's courage.'

She pressed a hand to his cheek. 'You're strong too, Leo. You're my rock.'

'And yet I lived in fear too. Fear of rejection. Whether

it was by my father or brother or you. You've helped me to move past that, Margo. Helped me to realise just how important love is. Loving *you* is.'

'I'm glad,' she whispered.

He withdrew a black velvet box. 'Then will you accept my ring?'

'Yes!' She glanced down at the sapphire flanked by two diamonds. 'It's beautiful...'

'Each stone symbolises a person in our family. Annas, you and me.' He slid it onto her finger. 'So, Margo Marakaios, will you marry me?'

She laughed—a sound of pure joy. 'I already have.'

'Phew!' Leaning forward, Leo brushed her lips with his as the city twinkled and sparkled all around them. 'Thank goodness for that...'

* * * * *

LET'S TALK
Romance

For exclusive extracts, competitions
and special offers, find us online:

- f facebook.com/millsandboon
- 🐦 @MillsandBoon
- 📷 @MillsandBoonUK

Get in touch on 01413 063232

For all the latest titles coming soon, visit
millsandboon.co.uk/nextmonth

Want even more
ROMANCE?

Join our bookclub today!

'Mills & Boon books, the perfect way to escape for an hour or so.'

Miss W. Dyer

'Excellent service, promptly delivered and very good subscription choices.'

Miss A. Pearson

'You get fantastic special offers and the chance to get books before they hit the shops'

Mrs V. Hall

Visit millsandbook.co.uk/Bookclub
and save on brand new books.

MILLS & BOON